INTRIGUE

Seek thrills. Solve crimes. Justice served.

Wyoming Mountain Investigation
Juno Rushdan

Campus Killer
R. Barri Flowers

MILLS & BOON

WYOMING MOUNTAIN INVESTIGATION
© 2024 by Juno Rushdan
Philippine Copyright 2024
Australian Copyright 2024
New Zealand Copyright 2024

First Published 2024
First Australian Paperback Edition 2024
ISBN 978 1 867 91743 0

CAMPUS KILLER
© 2024 by R. Barri Flowers
Philippine Copyright 2024
Australian Copyright 2024
New Zealand Copyright 2024

First Published 2024
First Australian Paperback Edition 2024
ISBN 978 1 867 91743 0

MIX
Paper | Supporting
responsible forestry
FSC® C001695

Published by
Harlequin Mills & Boon
An imprint of Harlequin Enterprises (Australia) Pty Limited
(ABN 47 001 180 918), a subsidiary of HarperCollins
Publishers Australia Pty Limited
(ABN 36 009 913 517)
Level 19, 201 Elizabeth Street
SYDNEY NSW 2000 AUSTRALIA

Cover art used by arrangement with Harlequin Books S.A.. All rights reserved.

Printed and bound in Australia by McPherson's Printing Group

Wyoming Mountain Investigation

Juno Rushdan

MILLS & BOON

Juno Rushdan is a veteran US Air Force intelligence officer and award-winning author. Her books are action-packed and fast-paced. Critics from *Kirkus Reviews* and *Library Journal* have called her work "heart-pounding James Bond-ian adventure" that "will captivate lovers of romantic thrillers." For a free book, visit her website: www.junorushdan.com.

Visit the Author Profile page
at millsandboon.com.au for more titles.

DEDICATION

For all the survivors of tragedy who never lost faith or hope.

CAST OF CHARACTERS

Liz Kelley—Once the victim of a tragic fire, she rebuilt her life despite the scars she still carries. As an FBI agent, specializing in arson and bombings, her priority is seeing justice served. Her worst nightmare is going back home, but she has no choice in order to stop a killer.

Sawyer Powell—Arson investigator. He's haunted by the fire that changed both his and Liz's lives forever, destroying the future they had dreamed of together. Fifteen years later, he can't forget Liz or let go of the love he has for her.

Ted Rapke—Laramie Fire Department chief.

Erica Egan—This journalist will cross any line for a scoop and to see her name in the byline.

Holden Powell—Chief deputy sheriff and Sawyer's supportive brother.

Ashley Russo—A dedicated deputy in the sheriff's department.

Prologue

Wild Horse Ranch
Located between Laramie and Bison Ridge,
Wyoming
July 3
Fifteen years earlier

Sprinting as fast as possible, lungs burning, he ran full-out from the clearing into the dark forest to be sure no one saw him. Once well in the woods, he stopped and leaned against a tree. Heart pounding, he caught his breath.

Beneath black clothes, he sweated from exertion. From the sweltering July night despite the strong breeze. From anticipation pumping in his veins. From fear that his plan might not work.

Come on. It should be an inferno by now. What was taking so long?

Another full minute ticked by. The big house should've gone up like dry kindling.

What had he done wrong? Did he need more accelerant? Should he go back to check?

Patience. Just wait.

Looking past the horse stable and two cabins of sleeping teens, he stared at the main house on the hill where Dave and Mabel Durbin lived. He'd made sure no one could help the unsuspecting Durbins. First, he'd locked the doors of the summer camp cabins and then the bunkhouse that was located far behind the stable. The barracks-like building was full of men who worked on the ranch.

Sweat dripped down his face and body, collecting everywhere on his skin. He clenched his jaw, his breath still coming hard from his chest, his nerves strung tight.

A gust of wind whipped through the dry leaves, rattling the brittle branches of the trees overhead. On the hill, smoke rose in the air, the smell filling his nose. Finally, the fire was taking hold. Flames burst to life on the house with a crackle that swelled to a roar. Like a supernatural monster, crimson and gold, it clawed and crawled its way up the sides of the house.

More perspiration rolled down his face, stinging his eyes. He lifted his mask and wiped his face with a gloved hand, but caution had him pull it back down *just in case*.

The fire blazed bright now, pulsing with hunger, growing bigger and hotter, spreading across the roof. He stared with grim satisfaction.

So beautiful. Powerful. Hypnotic against the pitch-black sky.

His creation. He'd been the one to give it life and set it loose.

A sudden gust of dry wind, bearing hard from the north, swept over the house, fanning the flames. Carrying sparks on the breeze to nearby trees. Glowing embers rained from the branches, falling on the two cabins. It wasn't long until the timbers of both roofs caught fire. The flames swirled and swelled, slithering down the walls, burning faster than he imagined possible. Much faster than the main house.

This wasn't part of his plan. A few of those sleeping teens trapped inside were innocent. The rest he blamed even more than the Durbins. He'd intended to make them suffer, too, once they were older and had more to lose than just their lives.

Fate was intervening, making it happen sooner rather than later. In a way they were all to blame. Guilt by association. The fire would make them pay. Without remorse. Without mercy. It would punish those responsible. This was sweet vengeance.

After tonight, the summer camp on the ranch would close forever.

He smiled, excitement bubbling in his chest. Watching the flames do what was necessary, he was enthralled. No. He was in love. This was the best high of his life. Better than playing football and scoring touchdowns. Better than sex.

If only he'd known what a thrill this would be,

he would've done it sooner. For Timothy…and for Birdie.

There weren't any screams yet. The cabins weren't up to code and didn't have smoke detectors. No alarms to wake them. Maybe the smoke would kill them in their sleep before the flames. Not quite the punishment or death he'd wanted for them. They deserved much worse.

Twigs snapped, hurried footsteps trampling the earth. He spun in the direction of movement—to his left in the woods. Two figures raced toward the clearing.

No!

A teenage girl darted from the tree line first, her long hair flowing in waves under the moonlight. Lean, pale limbs pumped hard in panic.

Liz. She worked at the camp and was on his little hit list. Why wasn't she locked in the girls' cabin with the others?

The answer burst from the woods, not far behind her. Sawyer Powell. Her stinking boyfriend. He wasn't a camper or a worker and had no business being there.

Sawyer was like his self-righteous brother, Holden. The former was the star of the basketball team, the latter was the quarterback. Golden boys who thought they walked on water at high school. Did whatever they wanted. Of course, he'd break the rules by being here.

"I'm calling 911." Liz was dialing as she ran.

No, no. Liz and Sawyer, a pair of meddlers, getting in the way. The dude ranch was smack-dab between both towns. One of the fire departments might get there in time.

Liz bolted to the double doors at the front of the girls' cabin and yanked on them. "I can't get it open! They've been tied shut!"

Although he'd made knots that would be hard to undo, in hindsight, chains and padlocks would've been smarter than using ropes.

"Break a window!" Sawyer grabbed a rock and shattered a windowpane, smashing around the frame. The lanky guy hopped up, disappearing inside the boys' cabin.

Liz did the same, scrambling into the other cabin. Those two were ruining everything.

Fists clenched, every sense alive, he gritted his teeth. This was not how it was supposed to end, with Liz Kelley and Sawyer Powell being heroes.

Teens dressed in pajamas funneled out through the broken windows, jumping onto the grass. Coughing and gagging, they backed away from the cabins. Some of them hurried up the hill toward the main house, shouting for the Durbins and yelling for help.

Liz and Sawyer might have stopped his plan, but they wouldn't stop him.

Everyone involved with what happened to Timothy would either burn or wished they had after he was finished with them. All the people who'd remained silent. Those who had looked the other way. Those dirty souls who benefited.

He saw their faces. Knew their names. Not only the ones on the ranch tonight. There were others and there would be justice. He would light their world on fire and burn it to the ground. One day. No matter how long he had to wait.

Liz emerged from the fiery cabin with the last girl. They backed away from the flames as Sawyer climbed out the boys' cabin window. Dropping to the ground, he gulped in air. Liz turned away from the cabins. Her jaw dropped and she took off.

He pivoted to see where she was going. The horse stable was burning, too! The wind was spreading the fire with blistering speed, feeding it fast, making the thinner structure of the barn go up like tinder. Horror whooshed through him. Helpless animals weren't supposed to get hurt.

Liz threw open the doors and rushed into the stable. A moment later, horses darted from the barn, one at a time. Could she get the stalls open and save them all in time?

For a painful second, his heart squeezing in his chest, he contemplated helping the horses. But he'd be seen for certain. He would be caught.

Hacking on the ground, Sawyer glanced around. He stumbled to his feet. "Liz!"

"She's inside the stable!" a girl screamed, pointing at the building engulfed in flames, and Sawyer made a beeline for it.

Men busted through the door of the bunkhouse, storming outside and sprinting into action. Some ran toward the main house while the rest headed for the stable.

Horses were still being set free. Sawyer was almost there. Another horse charged out of the burning barn, but no sign of Liz. Fire shot out through the roof. Sawyer hesitated. Afraid.

With a thunderous crunch, the roof of the stable collapsed, sending sparks shooting into the air like a million mini flares.

Two men wrapped themselves in blankets. Others threw buckets of water on them. Then the men rushed into the stable.

Why bother? Could she have survived?

Doubtful. Even if she had, the chances were slim they'd get her out alive. The only thing that could save Liz now was luck.

Chapter One

Fifteen years later
Present day

Special Agent Liz Kelley made her way through the Denver International Airport, eager to get back to work at Quantico.

Her cell phone buzzed. She fished it out of her oversize laptop bag. Glancing at the caller ID, she groaned. "Hi, Mom," she said, forcing herself to sound upbeat.

"How was the law enforcement symposium, sweetheart?"

"Fine, I suppose, all things considered."

"I'm sure it was better than fine," her mom said, ever the optimist. "I bet you did fantastic."

Only if *fantastic* meant "regrettably stilted and anxious." Since she survived a tragic fire as a teenager, she preferred to stay in the shadows. She still carried scars from that night on the inside and out. Being in the spotlight, the sole focus of more than a hundred people for an hour, had been brutal. She'd choose taking down a serial bomber any day instead.

Reaching her gate, Liz took a seat far from the desk and most of the other passengers, sitting with her back to a wall. Scanning the area, always assessing whether any potential threats lurked, she parked her rolling carry-on beside her.

"Not really, Mom." She adjusted her scarf that covered the puckers on her neck. In her profession, it was easy to hide the telltale signs of the numerous skin grafts and most of the remaining scars that ointments didn't smooth out with long sleeves, her shoulder-length hair and trademark neckerchiefs. "The only reason my boss chose me is because the book has gotten so much attention. Public speaking and teaching really aren't my forte."

"You have to stop downplaying your achievements, Liz. You wrote an insightful book, and you're one the FBI's top profilers working for a special task force."

"It's called the BAU," Liz said, referring to the Behavioral Analysis Unit, where she'd worked at Quantico for the past eighteen months. A series of tough cases and a track record of impressing her supervisors had earned her a coveted spot. "It's a specialist department, not a task force." They coordinated investigative and operational support functions, as well as criminological research to assist federal, state, local and foreign law enforcement agencies investigating unusual or repetitive violent crime.

"Anyway, my point is that you're exceptional, and the FBI recognizes it."

Shaking her head, Liz smiled at how her mother looked at her through rose-colored glasses. "It does take a certain type of person who thrives at getting into the minds of the sickest, darkest criminals out there. An achievement that I'm sure is hard for you to brag about during your quilt guild meetings or bridge club."

"They're not the right audience, but it's their loss. Your dad's hunting buddies think it's cool." Her mom's voice brightened with enthusiasm. "Sweetheart, I hope you appreciate how lucky you are."

Lucky Liz. That's what everyone in her hometown had called her after she had survived the fire on the dude ranch. The one that had killed Dave and Mabel Durbin. Yet they'd always said it with a wince or such unbearable pity in their eyes that her parents decided to move from Bison Ridge, Wyoming, to Missoula, Montana, to give her a fresh start, where she could heal. Homeschooled for the remainder of high school. Gone were the days of wearing shorts and tank tops and running on the cross-country team. An end to nosy townsfolk and concerned friends dropping in uninvited, forcing a smile at the sight of her, with stares that lingered too long. No more whispers when they thought she couldn't hear them. *At least her face wasn't ruined. That's still pretty.*

Her parents had sold most of the land on their property to the Shooting Star Ranch next to them, owned by the Powells, but had kept the house, which had been in the family for generations. They hoped she, their only child, would want it someday.

As far as Liz was concerned, she never again wanted to set foot within a hundred miles of where she'd suffered and had lost so much. Too many painful reminders.

Even being in Denver was cutting it a bit close for her liking.

"Yeah, Mom, I know I'm fortunate." And she was. To be alive. To have a successful career where she got to make a difference and save people.

But the blazing inferno that summer had robbed her of beauty and the chance for a normal life at only seventeen years old. In its place, she had been given a need—an obsession—to understand the mind of someone like the arsonist responsible for changing her world forever.

None of it felt like the kind of luck that was good.

Her phone beeped. She glanced at the screen. It was Ross Cho, the special agent in charge of her subsection, BAU 1. "Mom, I've got to go. It's work on the other line. My boss probably wants to hear all about the symposium as well."

"Okay. Love you."

"Love you, too. Give Dad a hug from me." Liz disconnected and answered the other call. "Kelley."

"Where are you?" SAC Cho asked, his tone curt.

Liz stiffened. "At the airport, sir. I managed to get a standby seat on an earlier flight back to Virginia." There was no need to stay for the entire symposium once she'd done her part.

"Glad I caught you before you boarded. There's a change of plan. We received an urgent request for assistance from a fire investigation office that find themselves under an accelerated timeline. There appears to be an arsonist who is rapidly escalating. He's struck four times in the past twelve days. Five dead so far, another hospitalized in critical condition and not likely to make it. The most recent fire was earlier today, around eight this morning. Based on how things have been spiraling, we extrapolated that it's likely there could be another incident within the next day or two."

This was perfect for her instead of being a show pony at a conference. She lived for this kind of case.

Standing, she hoisted the strap of her laptop bag on her shoulder and pulled up the handle of her rolling carry-on. She had everything she needed, including her field jacket—windbreaker with FBI identifier—and agency-issued Glock. "I'll change my flight. Where am I headed and who is my point of contact?"

"We've booked a rental car for you. Check your email for the reservation. Looks as though driving is faster. Should take you roughly two and a half hours to reach Laramie."

A chill ran through her veins as the breath stalled in her lungs.

Laramie.

Time froze, as if her brain had shut down.

"The deputy state fire marshal there made the request and will be your POC," SAC Cho said. "He'll meet you at the site of the latest incident. I forwarded the address to you along with his information. The name is Powell. Sawyer Powell."

Sawyer, her ex-boyfriend? He's a fire marshal?

She hadn't seen or spoken to him since she'd moved away. Not that he hadn't tried to stay in contact after she left, but it had been too hard for her. The sight of him over video chat, the sound of his voice on the phone, even his bittersweet emails—all cruel reminders of another thing that she had lost.

Her first love.

Quickly, she banished the resurrected demons from her mind and gathered her thoughts. "Why me, sir? Surely there's someone in the Denver field office who could take this."

"You're the best I have on arson and bombings. There's no one in the Denver office more qualified to handle this than you. Besides, you're from Laramie. Don't you want an all-expense-paid trip back home?"

It was the last thing she wanted, considering the emotional havoc it might wreak for her.

"I'm from the neighboring town, Bison Ridge," she said, needing to make the distinction for some odd reason.

"Regardless, you know the lay of the land and you're in the area, more or less. What are the odds, huh? I guess the stars have aligned in your favor, as luck would have it."

Yeah, just her brand of luck. *Bad.*

Her voice, when she spoke again, was a rasp. "I guess so."

"I thought you'd sound more enthusiastic about being assigned this case," SAC Cho said. "It's the type you'd beg me to give you, but I'm sensing otherwise right now. What am I missing here? Is this going to be a problem?"

Squeezing her eyes closed, she reminded herself of what was most important, why she did this job. Her tragedy had led her to the FBI, to become a criminal profiler with this specialization. What most civilians didn't understand, the part that wasn't shown on TV or covered in the newspaper was the long-term impact of arson. What it did not only to property but also to people, to families, to neighborhoods, to businesses. How it could destroy a small town.

If she could prevent another fire and the loss of more lives, then she had to do everything in her power to try. No matter the personal cost.

Liz opened her eyes and headed toward the rental cars. "No, sir," she said, stripping any weakness or doubt from her voice. "This won't be a problem. Thank you for the opportunity."

"That's more like it." Papers shuffled across the line. "There's one more thing before you go," Cho said, no doubt saving the best part for last. "This is about to get national coverage. Powell can't dissuade the mayor any longer from talking about it live on a major network."

Her stomach cramped. "Does the mayor have any idea how dangerous it is to give that kind of media attention to the UNSUB?" she asked, referring to the unidentified suspect. It would most likely make matters worse, only encouraging further incidents.

"Powell also thinks it's unwise, but the mayor isn't listening to him. It's an election year, citizens are dying, and businesses are being burned to the ground. Doesn't look good. The politician wants to control the narrative." He sighed as though there were more. "Listen, you've closed every case you've been assigned. Your record is flawless. I need you at your best on this one. Do you understand what I'm saying?"

Failure wasn't an option and she wouldn't have it any other way. Even though she was going back home, where the worst thing in her life had happened, all she had to do was keep the past in the past. There was never any room for feelings on an assignment. This time, it was especially true.

"Yes, sir. I understand." Absolutely nothing would get in the way of doing her job.

ARSON. AGAIN.

In his gut, Sawyer Powell was certain of it. Soon enough he'd have the evidence to support his hunch. Wearing his full PPE—personal protection equipment—kit, he followed protocol, starting with the least burned areas and moved toward the most damaged ones. Firefighters worked around him, making the scene more chaotic than he would've preferred. The fire had been extinguished, but now they were conducting overhaul. The process of searching for and putting out any pockets of fire that remained hidden under the floor, the ceiling or in the walls was laborious, but a single cluster of embers could cause a rekindling.

Ideally, he'd examine the area before overhaul began to ensure important evidence wasn't lost or destroyed. The station didn't enjoy having him underfoot, either. Yet they were working in tandem since time was something neither he nor the fire department had.

Sawyer was under mounting pressure from the mayor while the station was operating with only a small crew. They barely had enough for their three shifts that worked forty-eight hours on duty and ninety-six hours off duty. In their small town, where most of the action came from wildfires, that wasn't a problem. Until now.

He slowly walked the perimeter of the charity thrift store, jotting down notes for his report and taking photographs like an archaeologist mapping out a ruin. The air smelled of burned rubber and melted wires. Damp ash covered the floor, sticking to his boots.

Fire was a predictable beast. It breathed. It consumed. More importantly, it also spoke, telling a story. Sawyer only had to interpret. One thing he loved about his job was that fire didn't lie. Whatever it showed him would be the truth.

He picked up a large piece of glass from one of the broken windows. On it was a revealing spiderweb-like design. *Crazed glass.* A key indicator that a fire had burned fast and hot, fueled by a liquid accelerant, causing the glass to fracture.

He pushed deeper into the two-thousand-square-foot building. Ducking under insulation and wiring that hung down from the exposed ceiling, he came to the front of the office, where the victim who was now in the ICU fighting for her life had been discovered. Two firefighters inside had already opened up the walls and were getting ready to pull the lathe in the ceiling.

"Hey, guys, stop!" Sawyer called out, and the

two looked over at him. They weren't from the station, but he recognized them from the volunteer crew that were sometimes called in. Many of them he knew by name. Not these two. "What are you doing? I need to examine this area before you destroy any potential evidence."

"Oh, okay," one said. "The chief told us to clean out the whole room. Nobody wants the dreaded and embarrassing call back to the scene because of a rekindle."

Sawyer tamped down his rising anger. "Slow everything down and think about what you're doing. In fact, why don't you take a break until I'm done?"

"But we were called in to give some of the station guys a break," the other one said. "We're fresh and ready to help. What do you want us to work on?"

Sawyer didn't care as long as they got out of his way. "Go ask the chief."

The pair shrugged and vacated the area.

Exhaling a perturbed breath, Sawyer looked around. He cleared some of the torn-down gypsum board and noticed deep charring along the base of the walls. Gases became buoyant when heated. Flames naturally burned upward. But this fire had burned extremely low down.

Near the door inside the office, he moved the remnants of a chair out of the way. Peculiar char patterns shaped like puddles were on the floor underneath. The type produced by a flammable or combustible liquid that caused a fire to concentrate in those kinds of pockets, creating *pour patterns*. What made the char strange was the intensity of the fire.

The same markings had been at the other two crime scenes along with something else. He removed more debris, sifting through ashes until he found it. Remnants of a mechanical device. He collected it, along with some of the surrounding rubble.

He snapped pictures and took samples to send to the crime lab. The bad news was it'd take several weeks to get the results. He glanced up at the ceiling and smiled. The good news was the clues the substance left behind pointed to gasoline as the accelerant. It burned downward, producing a hole exactly like the one at the center of the pour pattern on the floor. Then there was the highly volatile air and vapor mixture that always formed above burning gasoline, rising to the ceiling where it would ignite. He took photos of the severe ceiling damage over the spot.

Searching for any other similar burn patterns throughout the building, Sawyer identified a total of three points of origin. A fire had been set not only in the office but also by the rear and front doors. No doubt the fire had been intentionally set, creating a barrier to prevent the victim from escaping and from help easily reaching her.

The sadistic perpetrator had set a death trap. Disgust welled in Sawyer.

Stepping outside the building with the samples and his camera in the toolbox, he winced at the size of the crowd that had gathered nearby, a combination of civilians and reporters. It had doubled since he'd arrived.

Sawyer spotted Fire Chief Ted Rapke speaking to the two volunteers who had almost messed up the scene. He braced himself in expectation of the conversation that was to come.

They never got along when they worked side by side as firefighters, and after Ted was promoted to chief while Sawyer became the new fire marshal, instead of Ted's close friend, Gareth, things only got worse.

Ted raised a hand in Sawyer's direction and headed over to him. "There must have been some miscommunication, but there was no need for you to snap at those guys. Unlike us, they don't get paid to be out here. They freely volunteer their efforts as a way of serving and giving back to the community. I can't afford to lose them while some firebug is torching the city, killing people."

Sawyer pulled off his helmet and tucked it under his arm, aching to remove the rest of his gear in the sweltering ninety-degree August heat. "And I can't afford to have them tearing up valuable evidence if we're going to have any chance of catching whoever is doing this. Look, I get that your people are getting hammered."

"Try completely overwhelmed. I won't have you scaring off essential volunteers."

"That wasn't my intent." Sawyer took a breath, not wanting to utter the words on the tip of his tongue, but it couldn't be avoided any longer. "Overhaul is strenuous. The firefighters involved in suppression may be so fatigued afterward that they overlook hazards, along with evidence. As for the volunteers, they're not focused on preserving the scene so I can do my job. Their only concern is to help put out a fire and prevent a rekindling. Perhaps you should consider sticking to thermal imaging until after I've investigated and you can get a fresh crew for overhaul."

Ted folded his arms across his chest and narrowed his eyes. "Did you have the audacity to try and tell me how to do my job?"

"It was only a suggestion." One given to help them both be more effective.

"That takes some nerve, buddy," Ted said, "after Mayor Schroeder just got on national television and basically called you incompetent."

Clenching his jaw, Sawyer didn't even want to get started about the *mayor*.

Someone cleared a throat behind him. "Excuse me, gentlemen," a woman said, the voice familiar.

Sawyer pivoted, facing Liz Kelley, and the world dropped out from under him. Special Agent

Cho had told him she was coming. Part of him refused to believe it until he saw her himself. The mention of her name alone had sent his pulse racing with anticipation.

Now, here she was standing in front of him. Her pale green eyes met his and he took in the sight of her. Same long wavy light brown hair. Same rose-colored lips. Trim figure albeit less gangly and curvier. A decade and a half older, and she still took his breath away.

"Oh yeah," Ted said. "Forgot to mention an FBI agent is out here waiting to do *your job* since you're having so much trouble on your own." The chief stalked off.

Ignoring Ted and their typical friction, Sawyer didn't take his gaze off her. "Liz." He stepped in to hug her as she extended a hand to shake his instead. In the awkwardness, they both backed away, not touching each other at all. "Have you been here long?"

"Only a few minutes. The chief told me you were inside."

"It's good to see you. I only wish it was under better circumstances." Unease—the same he'd carried since Liz ended any contact—churned through him. All he wanted was to close the distance between them and be free of it. They'd once been inseparable, sharing everything, including a vision of the future. He missed that. Missed her.

She adjusted the scarf around her neck, pulling it up a bit over her scars. "Me too."

"FBI. How do you like working for the bureau?"

"It's fine. Good to have a purpose." She walked around him and faced the ruined building. "Are you sure this one is also arson?" she asked, cutting straight to business.

He removed his gloves. "With the classic V, multiple points of origin, crazed glass and puddle configurations caused by an ignitable liquid hydrocarbon accelerant that has a high boiling point, my guess is gasoline. I'm one hundred percent positive," he said, confident she understood all the jargon after having read her impressive book on behavioral analysis of serial arsonists and bombers.

She studied him a moment. Did she doubt him?

"I can get you some gear and we can take a look inside together," he offered, and it occurred to him she might not be comfortable going into a building that had been on fire only hours ago. How foolish to even suggest it. Then again, he wasn't sure how to manage this situation. Walking through the aftermath of a fire was probably regular protocol for her, but still he said, "Sorry if you'd rather not go inside."

Taking another step back, she shook her head. "It won't be necessary. You're the expert in determining the cause. I'm here to help you figure out who's behind this."

It was the reason she was finally back in Laramie. To see justice served. To stop a sadistic killer.

He understood the drive and respected her for it. If only he knew how to handle working this case with her and the total gut punch he felt every time he thought about her.

"Do you mind?" he asked, opening his coat, not wanting to endure the heat any longer.

"Go right ahead." She took his toolbox and helmet, giving him a hand.

He stripped off the heavy turnout gear, leaving his pants and boots and his navy blue T-shirt that read Wyoming State Fire Marshal on the back.

"What can you tell me about the latest victim?" she asked.

"Ermenegilda Martinez. Thirty-one years old. Married. No kids. She runs the Compassionate Hearts charity and is currently in the ICU. It doesn't look good."

"This place doesn't open until nine. Any idea why she was here so early in the morning?"

He shook his head. "I'm hoping her husband will be able to shed some light on that."

"Have you been able to find a link between the victims?"

"Nothing so far." A failure that ate away at him, keeping him up at night.

"I haven't had a chance to review the case file since I drove straight here. I'd like to walk through all the details with you."

The back of his neck tingled, and he got the sense someone was watching him. He scanned the crowd of gawking spectators.

Of course, he was being watched. Right along with everyone else working. Many of the people in town were friends and associates. Most he knew by sight if not by name. Only one high school served both Laramie and Bison Ridge. He'd gone to school with almost everyone around his age, who'd grown up here, and had played sports with at least half of those working in the department. Scanning the faces of those who'd gathered, no one stuck out as a stranger.

Still, he couldn't shake the prickle of warning, which was worrisome. "Let's go to my office," he suggested, "away from prying eyes. And we can go over everything there."

"All right."

"Where's your car?"

"About three blocks away," she said. "There was no place to park around here."

"My truck is closer. I'm over there." He gestured in a direction less than a block away. "I'll take you to your car and you can follow me."

They walked past the fire station ambulance parked off to the side and around the crowd-control barricade, avoiding the mass of spectators. Serial fires and murders were unusual in the small, quiet town, where neighbors looked out for one

another, and were bound to draw a ton of macabre interest.

A woman darted from the cluster of onlookers,
rushing straight for them. He gritted his teeth at
the sight of her, wishing they had been able to
sneak by.

"Excuse me, Fire Marshal Powell!" She held out
a recorder as she caught up to them. "I'm Erica
Egan from the *Laramie Gazette*."

"I know who you are." *A menace.* Sawyer
picked up his step and Liz kept pace with him.

Egan drew closer, her arm brushing his. "I've
been trying to pin you down about the fires."

"I'm aware." He'd been warned about her. She
had a reputation for pinning down and cozying
up to guys for an exclusive. Didn't even matter
if they were married. Sawyer wasn't one to buy
into distasteful gossip that could ruin someone's
career, but he didn't care for Egan's brand of reporting. Pure sensationalism.

"Would you care to comment on the things
Mayor Schroeder had to say about you and the
fires on the *Morning Buzz*? Is it the reason the
FBI is here?"

He glanced over at Liz's jacket, which conspicu-
ously announced the presence of a special agent.
"I didn't watch or read about the mayor's appearance because I've been too busy working." It made
him wonder how Ted had so many colorful details.

His truck wasn't much farther ahead. In a minute, he could hop inside and dodge answering any more questions.

"I'll recap for you." Egan shoved the recorder closer to his face. "The mayor said, and I quote, 'Arson Investigator Sawyer Powell'—"

"Hang on. Can you be quiet a moment," Liz said, putting a hand on his forearm, forcing him to slow down. "Do you hear that?"

He was about to ask, *What?* but in the quiet, it became obvious. There was a faint clicking sound. Was it coming from his vehicle?

"Bomb!" Liz yelled.

In the next heartbeat, his silver truck exploded in a fiery burst of heat and searing light, the violent boom rattling him to his core.

Chapter Two

Liz threw up an arm to shield her face. The ear-shattering blast rocked the ground, propelling the rear of the truck into the air and slamming it back down. The punch of the explosion knocked them off their feet as Sawyer wrapped his arms around her and the reporter.

Breath left Liz in a whoosh, pain shooting through her back when they landed hard on the pavement. Sawyer's sharp exhale rushed across her cheek. Her heart jumped into her throat.

A firestorm of blazing metal rained onto the street and over other vehicles. Liz was stunned, shaken but needed to get her bearings. Needed to move.

Get up. Get up!

She rolled Sawyer off her and started to sit up. A second explosion sent one of the truck doors whizzing through the air, flames erupting out the windows. Sawyer was back on top of her, protecting her with his body as fragments of glass and shrapnel sliced into the storefront sign beside them.

The smell of melting rubber and burning gasoline filled her nose. Her ears rang. Her eyes stung.

Liz pulled in deep breaths, trying to shake off her daze. Sawyer rolled onto his back with a groan.

She glanced to the right. "Are you okay?" she asked the reporter, who was lying face down with her hands covering her head. "Are you burned?"

"No. I don't think so." The woman whimpered. "Is it safe to move?"

"Yeah. I think so." Liz turned, checking on Sawyer.

Sitting up, he hissed in pain. She looked him over for injuries. There was a gash on his thigh and along the side of his torso where pieces of hot metal had scorched across his skin. His arm was pink, slightly singed.

"You're hurt." If only he had left his gear on or hadn't tried to shield her and the reporter from the eruption of fire and killing debris. She caressed his cheek, thankful it hadn't been worse.

"Oh my God." The reporter sat upright. "I—I can't believe what just happened."

Neither could Liz. Someone had tried to kill Sawyer and had nearly succeeded.

He fingered the rip in his trousers. "It's a clean cut." His gaze drifted to the pile of burning metal that used to be his truck.

"Can't say the same for your abdomen," Liz said, taking a closer look. A shard of metal was embedded in his flesh. "I'll get an EMT."

"No, I'll go." The reporter brushed off her clothes and slowly climbed to her feet. "It's the least I can do." A slight tremor rang in her voice. "You two saved my life."

Sawyer remained riveted on the wreckage. A bit of color had drained from his handsome face. Flames danced in his eyes. "A few feet closer, seconds really, and we would've been toast." He shook his head at the inferno that had been his truck.

Liz gingerly peeled up his shirt and looked at the wound. "It's bleeding pretty bad." But she didn't dare put any pressure on it with the piece of metal lodged in his side.

"I'll hurry." The reporter took off.

"Any chance you've upset someone that you know of?" Liz hiked her chin at the fireball.

"Enough to kill me?" He shook his head.

"Then whoever our suspect is did this."

"But why?" His voice dropped into a graveled tone.

Possibilities ran through her head. "They don't like the investigation. Maybe you're closer than you think to figuring this out. But the more important question is, why aren't we dead?"

Sawyer pulled his gaze from the flames and looked at her. "Come again."

"That bomb was planted with the intent to kill you."

"Maybe it was an aggressive tactic to scare me off."

She gave Sawyer a slow, noncommittal gesture with her head as she considered it. "Maybe." Although she doubted that was the case. "The bomb was big enough to set off a secondary blast," she said, thinking aloud. "That kind of explosion was meant to kill, not scare."

"Then why didn't he wait until we were in the vehicle to let it explode."

More possibilities rushed through her mind. "I can't say for sure, but I do know that it's one thing to kill a fire marshal and quite another if it's a federal agent," she said, and he grimaced. "No offense, but it's the difference between a state level and federal crime. Not to mention drawing the ire of the entire bureau by blowing up one of their own. The BAU would descend upon Laramie like the four horsemen of the apocalypse determined to bring the end of days to the perpetrator. Anyone smart would avoid that."

Smart enough not to let their agenda override common sense. She hoped her presence was the reason they hadn't been in the truck when it exploded. If it was something else, then this was bigger than she feared.

The ambulance pulled up. Sawyer tried to take the toolbox full of evidence with him, but Liz took it from his hands. She'd ensure it stayed in her possession or locked safely in her trunk.

Once the paramedics got him on a gurney and loaded into the back, she ran to her rental car and raced over to the emergency room at Laramie Hospital. After she flashed her badge, a nurse didn't hesitate to show her to the bay where they had put him.

Sawyer was lying on a bed propped up with pillows. She'd kept pictures of him, but all the photos were of him as a teen. Today was the first time she'd seen him as a man, and seeing his face after all this time was just short of ecstasy. His intense baby blue eyes met hers, a grin tugging the corner of his mouth, and her stomach fluttered. She drank in the sight of him. His sunny blond hair was too long in the front, still curly at the top in a way that had always made her want to run her fingers through it, and messier than before the explosion, but the rough-and-tumble look on him was appealing. His jaw squarer than she remembered and covered in stubble.

Pulling her gaze from him, she stepped inside the bay.

"A doctor will be in to see him shortly," the nurse said.

Liz gave her an appreciative smile. "Thank you."

The nurse left, drawing the curtain behind her, giving them some privacy.

"My personal hero returns," he said.

Liz shook her head. "I'm no such thing."

"All evidence to the contrary. You've been here less than an hour and already saved my life."

"I can't take credit for being a default deterrent." Possible deterrent anyway. The culprit deliberately triggered the bomb early, which had caused the clicking sound—something they wouldn't have heard until they were inside the truck if the intent had been to kill them. Clearly the person didn't mind taking lives, enjoyed it even, but was fear of committing a federal offense really the reason they were alive right now? Maybe if they were able to figure out the answer, it would help them find the killer. "How are you holding up?" Liz asked, going to his side.

"I'm alive, so I can't complain."

Well, he could, and she wouldn't blame him if he did. But the old Sawyer she knew never was one to complain or criticize and always the first to give a compliment. The best type of friend, who'd never let anyone down, especially not someone in trouble. Kind. Confident. Strong. In high school, he loved basketball, her, and numbers. He had talked about having a double major in college, business and finance. The perfect combination to become a quantitative analyst. A far cry from what he did today.

"How did you end up a fire marshal?" she wondered. "I thought you wanted to be a *quant*."

"I guess the same way you ended up an FBI agent." The humor bled from his tone as the light in his eyes dimmed.

Her dream of wanting to be a museum curator felt like something from a past life. In fact, it was distant enough to have been someone else's desire.

The tragedy that summer had altered the courses of their lives forever.

"I was a firefighter for a long time," he said, "until I realized I was better suited for going into the building after, piecing it together and figuring out the why."

Sawyer had always been a handsome hunk with picture-perfect looks, but she'd found his analytical mind even more attractive. It was good he was using it to help stop criminals instead of finding ways to make companies more profitable.

"Is there anyone I can call for you to let them know you're in the ER? Your wife? Girlfriend?"

Part of her hoped he had found happiness with another woman. A larger part wished he was unattached, which didn't add up in her head since she had been the one to cut him off. What he did with his life, the job he chose, who he loved, shouldn't matter, but in her heart, she'd clung to him. Out on a run, making dinner for one, in bed alone, in the stillness of the dark, he'd emerge like a phantom, haunting her.

"Nope. Not even a lover to complain when I work overtime," he said, and relief trickled through her. "I never got into anything serious, and anything fun tends to fade fast. More often than not, being with the wrong person is lonelier than being without them."

Something in his voice saddened her, too, making her regret her selfishness. He deserved to have the full life that she never would. "I'm surprised. You wanted to be married by twenty-five and have a couple of kids by now."

"After all this time, you still don't get it." His gaze narrowed on her as he cocked his head to the side. "That was *our* plan. The life I wanted with you."

His words sliced at her heart with the precision of a scalpel, but she didn't dare allow long-buried feelings to bleed through.

The bay curtain opened with a whoosh, thankfully diverting their attention.

"Hello," said a woman, entering as she stared at a medical tablet. "I'm Dr. Moreno." Her head popped up and she flashed a smile. "I hear you're not having a good day."

"You have no idea," Sawyer said.

Dr. Moreno set the tablet down and pulled on latex gloves. "Let's take a look."

"I'll step out," Liz said.

Sawyer put a hand on her forearm. "I'd prefer it if you stayed."

Dr. Moreno grabbed a pair of scissors and set

it down on a tray. "He'll need a distraction in a moment."

"Then there's no one better than you, Liz," he said.

The doctor treated his leg first, cleaning the wound and applying a bandage. She slathered ointment on the pink area of his arm. Then she moved on to his abdomen and cut his T-shirt off, revealing his bare torso.

Warmth shot up Liz's neck, heating her face. He'd aged but hadn't changed for the worse in the past fifteen years. Somehow, he'd only gotten better looking. A few small lines etched the outer corners of his stunning eyes. He had quite a bit more bulk. The body of a teenage basketball player had been replaced with ridges and valleys of lean, sculpted muscle on a firefighter turned investigator.

He'd developed this body not only in the gym but the hard way. Hauling eighty pounds of gear and equipment up flights of stairs and into dangerous situations.

At least he no longer battled fires, but unless they found whoever planted a bomb in his truck, he'd be in danger.

"Okay, this next part is going to hurt." The doctor traded the scissors for forceps. She pressed down lightly around the wound and then gripped hold of the piece of shrapnel. As Dr. Moreno began extracting it, Sawyer grimaced. "Talk to him."

Liz took his hand in hers and squeezed. Thinking of something to say, anything to take his mind off the pain, she blurted the first thing to pop in her mind. "Hey, do you remember that time we went swimming, and afterward you surprised me with a picnic?" The lunch he'd packed had contained all her favorites.

He laughed. "Yep. I was the genius who laid out the blanket right under a hive of angry, territorial hornets. How could I forget?" He hissed when the doctor started the sutures.

Liz pressed her palm to his cheek, caressing his flawless skin with a thumb and drawing his full attention. "Right up until we got stung, the day had been perfect. Eighty degrees. Sunny. Warm breeze. Blue skies. Cool water. We swam and played around in the lake for goodness knows how long." He'd even brought an MP3 player. They'd danced and made out, and it had seemed like they'd have forever together. Kissing. Hugging. Dancing. Laughing. Holding each other close. "Another surprise—the tickets to the ballet in Cheyenne. *Swan Lake*." He'd been an A-student and star athlete who also knew classical music and appreciated art—interests they'd shared. Everything she'd wanted in a life partner. "Nothing could've made the day better. Other than not getting stung."

There were no more perfect days. She hadn't even put on a bathing suit since...

"None of that is what made the day special." He tightened his fingers around hers. "It was perfect simply because we were together." The sincerity in his voice caused a pang in her chest.

"All done." The doctor removed her gloves with a snap of latex.

Liz slipped her hand from his. In her effort to distract him, she'd only sabotaged herself, rehashing beautiful memories she couldn't afford to dwell on. Every time she thought about Sawyer, what it was like to be with him, she softened.

It made her weak.

"The wound should heal in two to four weeks," Dr. Moreno said. "No arteries were cut, but I'm glad you didn't take the chance of removing the piece of metal. The stitches will dissolve on their own over time. I'll prescribe an antibiotic to prevent an infection and get you discharged. Take an over-the-counter analgesic for pain. Do you have any questions?"

"You have anything I could put on?" He gestured at his bare chest. "Other than a hospital gown."

"Sure. Plenty of scrubs around. I think we can rustle up a top for you."

"Thanks."

With a nod, she whipped back the curtain and disappeared.

"Liz." Sawyer reached for her.

But she stepped away from the bed. They needed to focus on finding a killer, not ancient history. "While we're here at the hospital, we should go up to the ICU. See Mrs. Martinez. Speak with her husband. We can go over everything else pertinent to the case afterward."

"Of course. Back to business. But we should also make time to talk. Clear the air. About us."

"There is no *us*," she said, almost as a reflex.

"You made sure of that by not returning any of my emails or phone calls. I get why you left Wyoming, but I never imagined you'd leave me, too."

They had been connected. The strongest bond she'd ever had, other than the one with her parents, but she'd acted in both their best interests.

"I went to Montana to see you once," he said, and her heart sank, not wanting old wounds to reopen. "Drove all night without sleeping. I need to know. Were you home that day when I knocked on the door?"

Of course she was there. After the move, it took her a year to leave the house. Her father had gotten rid of him without even asking her, which had been just as well since she'd hidden in the closet.

Like a coward.

"I would've sworn you were there," he said, "so I stood outside, calling for you."

The sound of him—screaming her name at the top of his lungs, pain racking his voice—had gutted her. The memory had tears stinging the back of her eyes.

"I was out there trying to remind you what you meant to me until I was hoarse and your dad called the cops."

No reminder was necessary. They'd practically grown up together, with their properties adjacent. Hers on the side of the Bison Ridge town line and his in Laramie. Since they were thirteen and first kissed, they'd been making plans.

Listening to him outside, she hid in the closet, grief-stricken over the end of her world as she'd known it, over the loss of the life they'd never have together. She forced herself to accept the reality that nothing would ever be the same again.

He'd needed to move on without guilt or any obligation to stay with her, the scarred girl who survived. And she had needed something he couldn't give her. To heal on her own. To build a new life. To do what felt impossible—reimagine her future without him.

It was the toughest decision she'd ever made, but she'd thought a clean break was best.

"Were you home?" he asked. "Just answer that much."

She had never lied to Sawyer. Not once. And she wouldn't start now.

Liz swallowed around the tight knot of guilt rising in her throat. "I'm not back in Wyoming for personal reasons," she said, telling him the one truth they needed to discuss at the moment. Emotions blurred lines, leading to mistakes, which endangered lives. After the bomb in his truck, one thing was certain. Failure could get them killed. She stiffened her spine along with her resolve. "I'm only here because of the case. It's all that matters right now."

SAWYER RODE IN the hospital elevator beside Liz, his chest aching. How could she think he'd be engaged, much less married with kids when he was stuck? His heart was trapped in limbo.

Not that she would know. She'd washed her hands of him without looking back and considering the impact of her choices on him.

He'd wished for a chance to talk to her face-to-face so many times, memorized the questions he'd ask, how she'd respond, wondering whether he'd finally get a sense of closure. None of his hopes included the two of them working a case together or her using it as an excuse to avoid having a long overdue conversation. Still, he clung to two little words: *Right now.*

He took that to mean eventually she would be willing to discuss what happened between them. Just not right now.

The pain he'd kept bottled up for a decade and a half—holding him prisoner to the past, unable to move on—would have to fester a while longer.

The doors opened to the ICU floor. He stepped off the elevator with his sole focus on the job.

They headed to the reception desk. "Hello. I'm Fire Marshal Powell," he said, pulling his badge from his pocket and flashing it at the nurse when she eyed his medical scrub top, "and this is Agent Kelley. We'd like to get an update on Mrs. Martinez."

"Her condition hasn't changed." The nurse's face tightened into a grave look. "She's on life support, but the extent of her injuries makes survival highly unlikely. The doctor thinks she has seventy-two hours at the most."

"Can you notify us if there's any change?" Liz asked, handing her a business card, and the nurse nodded. "What room is she in?"

"Three." She pointed to it. "Her husband is there with her. Only one person at a time is allowed inside."

"Thank you." This was the part of the job that sucked the most. Fire marshals had to pay these kinds of visits, too. Tell someone a loved one had died in a fire so severe their body was unrecognizable. Or ask them questions, probing into their life when they needed space to deal with their emotions. It was always hard on him.

They crossed the open space and stopped at the large window that provided the nurses with a view of the patient. Mr. Martinez sat in a chair beside the bed, his head bent, his hand resting near his wife's, wrapped in bandages, like her face, arms, and most of her body.

Her injuries were severe and extensive. Far worse than the condition Liz had been in. Sawyer had been by her side, too, giving her parents breaks, staying during the wee hours so they could go home, rest, shower and eat.

As close as he had been with Liz, their love strong and real, even for teenagers, he didn't presume to understand the magnitude of what Mr. Martinez must have been experiencing.

A thread of anger wove through Sawyer. They had to stop whoever was responsible before more lives were destroyed.

He glanced at Liz and saw the dark shadows swimming in her eyes. A slight shudder ran through her but only lasted a second. Anyone not carefully watching would've missed it. The sight of the latest victim fighting for her life in the ICU had to be hard on Liz, bringing awful memories to the forefront.

Once, when Sawyer was little, he was playing with one of his brothers, racing through the kitchen, and collided with his mom, who had been holding a pot of boiling water. The burn on his arm that formed had blistered and stung for a week. But his pain had been nothing in comparison to the agony Liz had endured.

Running into a burning building to save kids and horses took a singular kind of selflessness and courage. Her reward had been getting trapped under a burning beam that had fallen in the stables, flames melting her flesh and months of slow healing.

After suffering the unimaginable, she chose a career focused on arson and bombings. Faced what she must fear on a regular basis. She was remarkable.

Always had been.

"Are you all right?" he asked.

Her face was calm but her spine rigid. "I'm fine." The tight, clipped tone of her voice confirmed what he suspected despite her words.

She wasn't okay, but she was too strong to say otherwise.

Mr. Martinez looked up, catching sight of them. A burly man, he wiped tears from his eyes, stood in a weary way as though he might fall back into his chair and approached them.

They met him at the threshold.

"I'm Special Agent Kelley and this is Fire Marshal Powell. Can we speak with you for a moment regarding your wife?"

He nodded and she gestured for them to move over to a corner.

"Do you know who did this?" the husband asked.

"That's what we're trying to find out," Sawyer said.

Liz pulled a small notepad from her pocket.

"What time does the Compassionate Hearts store open?"

"At ten. Every day."

"Any idea why she was there two hours early?" Liz asked.

Mr. Martinez sniffled. "To catch up on paperwork. She used to do it late at night, but I used to worry about her. Bad things can happen late. I thought earlier in the day was safer." A tear leaked from his eye.

"Generally speaking, it is," Liz said, taking notes. "Did anyone know she made a habit of coming in early?"

The husband shrugged. "Maybe some of the staff."

Sawyer thought back on how the fire had three points of origin and a theory he had. "When your wife went in early before the store opened, did she lock the door behind her or leave it open?"

"I can't say for sure, but I believe she locked it. Doris Neff worked mornings. She'd know."

"Do you have any idea why someone would have a reason to burn down the charity or harm your wife?" Liz asked. "Please try to think carefully about the smallest thing."

Mr. Martinez shook his head. "The thrift store gives all its revenue to help disabled veterans and impoverished children. Most of the people who work there are volunteers. As for my wife, she's the sweetest soul. No one would have any reason to hurt Aleida."

Sawyer exchanged a look with Liz before turning back to Mr. Martinez. "We thought her name was Ermenegilda."

"It is, an old family name but a mouthful. No one ever calls her that. Her grandmother went by Gilda. So, my wife uses her middle name. Aleida."

Liz tensed. "Neither are very common names. Thirty-one would put her at the right age. By any chance, is your wife Aleida Flores?"

"Yes, that's her maiden name. Do you know her?"

A strange look crossed Liz's face for a moment, and then it was gone, replaced by a stony expression. "I'm from around here. Bison Ridge, actually. I know a lot of people from there as well as Laramie. Thank you for your time. If you think of anything else, give me," she said, handing him a business card from her pocket, "or Fire Marshal Powell a call."

"The fire station can reach me if you dial their main office. We'll let you get back to your wife." They left the ICU. In the elevator, Sawyer waited until others got off and they were alone. "How do you know Aleida Flores?"

It was probably nothing, like she'd said. She knew lots of people, as did he, but something about her expression worried him.

"From the camp on the dude ranch," she said, her voice a whisper. "Aleida was there that night."

Everything inside him stilled. Silence fell like a curtain, the space around him becoming deafeningly quiet.

"One of the girls you rescued?" he finally clarified.

Staring straight ahead, her body stiff, Liz gave one slow nod. The strange expression came over her face again. She was probably thinking the same unsettling thing running through his head. Aleida had been saved from a deliberately set fire fifteen years ago only to be in critical condition with an unlikely chance of survival because of another one.

Coincidences happened every day, but this one he didn't like.

Chapter Three

Emotions seesawed through Liz. Seeing Mrs. Martinez had been harder than she had expected. While staring at the poor woman, for a heartbeat, Liz was trapped back in the burning stable, panic flooding her veins, frenzied horses, the crackling terror of the fire, the beam falling—pinning her, flames lashing her body, smoke clogging her lungs, searing pain.

Liz flinched. She often had terrible nightmares about that night, but this was the first time in over a decade that she had experienced a fresh wave of sheer fear while awake.

She couldn't help thinking back to her own time in the ICU, the mind-vibrating cacophony of the machines, the tubes, being in and out of consciousness while others whispered, thinking she couldn't hear. The shuddery breaths of her mother crying to her father. *Oh, honey, our little girl was perfect. Now I can barely look at her.*

Liz clenched her hands at her sides. Her internal wounds remained raw despite the time that had passed.

The elevator chimed and the doors opened. She shoved the horror of her personal tragedy into a far corner of her mind as they stepped out onto the first floor.

Another shiver ran through Liz. The shock from learning Aleida, the last girl she'd gotten out of a burning cabin and to safety, was Mrs. Martinez hadn't dissipated.

How could the universe be so twisted and cruel?

Or was there something else at play?

There was a saying that if you saved a life, you became responsible for it. Whether or not it was true, Liz didn't know, but she was more committed than ever to finding the monster who was setting the fires.

They had almost reached the doors to the parking lot when Erica Egan hopped up from a chair and made a beeline for them. The woman did not give up.

Liz hated the journalist's persistence as much as she admired it.

"You again?" Sawyer asked with a disgusted shake of his head.

The double doors opened with a whoosh.

Egan followed them outside. "I have a job to do, the same as you."

"Not quite the same," Sawyer said. "The more

you stalk me, the more time you take away from me investigating."

The determined reporter hurried around to the front of them and raised her recorder. "Give me a quote. On the record," she said, but when Sawyer glared at her, she continued. "I just need something to work with. Anything. Come on."

"I've got a quote for you." Liz stepped close to the recorder. "Fire Marshal Sawyer Powell is doing an incredible job, getting closer to the truth each day. That's why he or she—but I'll stick with *he* since ninety percent of arsonists are white males from midteens to midthirties— targeted Powell today by planting a bomb in his truck that nearly took his life, as well as yours and mine."

Sawyer glanced at her with a quirked brow but didn't say a word.

"If that's true and he's doing such a good job, why is the FBI taking over the case?" Egan asked.

Liz folded her arms. "I'm not here to take over. I'm only here to assist. For a complex case such as this, usually an entire Behavioral Analysis Unit is required. Not one fire marshal working alone. Rather than being criticized, Sawyer Powell should be commended for having the foresight to reach out to the FBI."

The journalist cracked a smile.

"That's all for now," Sawyer said. "Egan, if you want to be part of the solution and not the problem, stop glorifying this pyromaniac who's murdering people. Less sensationalized prose about the fires in your articles that will only embolden him. Focus more on the innocent victims and the destruction of property, like a charity. This guy is a monster. Brand him as one and you'll get more quotes."

"Call me Erica." Shutting off the recorder, the pert reporter stepped closer to him, tilting her head as her features softened. Egan's face was classically beautiful. Platinum blond hair. Deep blue eyes. A svelte figure only a dead man wouldn't find attractive. "My writing style has boosted readership, which is what I was hired to do. I'm willing to consider what you've said, but not simply for more quotes. I want an exclusive. From you. We could discuss further over drinks. I'm buying."

Liz suddenly felt like she was intruding on something by simply standing there. Who was she to stand in the way of him having fun if that's what he wanted? "Sawyer, I'll wait for you over—"

"No need, Liz. Ms. Egan is the one leaving." He glanced back at the other woman. "I have no interest in having a drink with you, but if you reconsider your angle in future articles like I've asked, *we'll* give you an interview together when it's all over."

Egan's eyes went sly. "That could take weeks. How about a chat over coffee every morning?"

Liz swallowed a sigh, listening to this negotiation.

Sawyer glanced at her from the corner of his eyes, probably picking up on her irritation. "Once a week?" he countered.

"You don't expect to catch this guy soon, then." Egan flashed a slithery smile. "Every other day, locations to be determined by me."

A muscle ticked in Sawyer's jaw. "Fine," he said, wearily.

Triumph gleamed in the woman's eyes. "By the way," she said, turning to Liz, "what's your name? For my article."

"Special Agent Liz Kelley."

"The one who wrote the book?" Egan asked.

Liz was taken aback. "I'm surprised you've heard of it."

"You're famous around here. Sorry I didn't recognize you."

Was this town and Bison Ridge still talking about that tragic summer? About the *lucky* girl who survived?

Sawyer clasped her shoulder and squeezed. "It's not what you think," he said, his voice soothing. Their eyes met and recognition was written on his face about what was going through her head. "The Sage Bookshop had it in stock. Signed copies. Your mom even had a huge poster made with your picture on it. They hung it in the front window for months."

She remembered her mom had asked her to sign a bunch of copies, so she'd always have an autographed one on hand. Liz hadn't believed the far-fetched story, but she hadn't pushed for the truth, either. When it came to her mom, sometimes it was better not to ask.

The reporter's gaze landed on the spot where Sawyer touched Liz. "What's the history between you two?" Egan switched the recorder back on and held it up.

Sawyer dropped his hand as Liz backed away from him.

If only they could stop touching. "We're old friends. We used to be neighbors. Our properties are adjacent, but there are plenty of acres between us," Liz said, completely caught off guard, hearing herself babble. Not her style. Ever. She simply didn't want the past dredged up and rehashed on the pages of the *Gazette*.

She bit the inside of her lip to stop the verbal diarrhea.

"We're done here. Now, if you'll excuse us, we have work to do." Sawyer took Liz by the arm, cupping her elbow, and walked off.

Liz glanced over her shoulder. Egan watched them for a moment before she strutted off across the parking lot.

"At least you're going in the right direction,"

Liz said. "I don't recognize Egan. Is she from around here?"

"Moved here a couple of years ago."

Relieved the reporter was gone and hopeful Egan hadn't caught the whiff of a scoop, Liz took a deep breath. "There's my rental." She pointed out the sedan.

"Thanks for the quote." He let go of her arm. "You didn't have to say all that stuff about me."

"Yes, I did. Because it's true." Although she should've given her words deeper consideration rather than spouting off a knee-jerk quote. On the bright side, it was only a few lines in a local paper. Not a ten-minute tirade on a major national news network. "I heard what the mayor had to say about you on satellite radio during the drive. I don't know why Bill Schroeder is trying to hang you out to dry, but I won't stand for it."

She was acquainted with Bill well enough and had never cared for him. They were around the same age, with him being two years older, but Bill's entitled attitude rubbed her the wrong way. He was a bully back then and still was. Only this time he was using his position as mayor to pick on a civil servant who was trying to do his job.

"Voters are going to want to blame someone if I don't catch this guy."

"If we don't. You're not in this alone. Not anymore. We're going to nail this person. Together."

Thinking back on Aleida in the ICU, Liz intended to see justice served.

"The one thing I miss about being a firefighter is working on a team. Being a fire marshal gets a little lonely." The corner of his mouth hiked up in a grin, his blues twinkling, making her stomach dip like she was seventeen years old again.

Shake it off, Liz.

She hit the key fob, unlocking the doors.

"Want to grab dinner over at Delgado's and go over the case?" he asked.

Eating at Delgado's with him, the way they used to, was an easy *no*. Too familiar. More nostalgia was the last thing she needed.

"I'm starving, but let's get it delivered to your office," she said. "There we can talk privately and openly, combing through the details while we wait for the food." She pulled on the handle, opening the door.

He put his hand on the top of the frame, blocking her from getting inside the car. "Did you mean what you said about us being a team?"

"Of course."

"Good, but it's going to require trust. The kind of trust where my life could be in your hands and vice versa. Until we get this guy, we're going to be joined at the hip. Can you handle all that?"

She wasn't the same petrified seventeen-year-old girl who hid in a closet because she didn't know how to stand on her own two feet after losing so much. "I can handle anything."

"Even if it's with me?" His gaze held hers, a clear challenge gleaming in his eyes.

He had no intention of putting the past behind them. He would keep pushing for answers, for the discussion that didn't take place in Montana all those years ago. The one she owed him.

She'd thought reliving the trauma of the fire would be the hardest part of coming back. Instead, the most difficult thing was blond, blue-eyed, six-three and two hundred pounds of pure stubbornness.

Time for her to go into damage control mode before he went on the offensive.

She drew closer, bringing them toe to toe. No more backing away from him, averting her gaze or acting like an awkward teenager scared of the slightest touch, giving him reason to doubt she could handle this—being "joined at the hip." Their familiarity could be a strength. They'd once been so in tune that they finished each other's sentences. They only had to find a new rhythm without letting the tempo get out of control.

"Even with you," she said. "I'll make you a deal. After we catch this guy, we'll sit down and talk." As much as she disliked scrapping her plan to hightail it out of town once the job was finished, it might be the only thing to appease him. "Really talk until you're satisfied. Okay?"

Leaning in, Sawyer brought his face dangerously close to hers, eliciting a different kind of shudder from her, but instead of retreating, she steeled her spine.

"Satisfying me won't be easy." A slow, knee-weakening smile curved his lips.

There went those stupid butterflies in her belly again. She knew from delicious experience what a passionate, generous, tireless lover he was as a teenager. She could only imagine how experience and patience had improved him. They'd fit perfectly together, their limbs tangled, melting from pleasure.

Not that she'd had other lovers to compare. She didn't even wear a T-shirt on a run, opting instead for a long sleeve, lightweight UV top. The idea of taking off all her clothes in front of a guy, the sight of her probably making his skin crawl, was unthinkable.

But Sawyer was the only man to ever give her butterflies. Let alone with just a smile.

With their lips a hairbreadth apart, she couldn't help but wonder if he tasted the same.

She tried to prevent any emotion showing on her face, not letting him see how much his proximity or his words or smile affected her. "Like I said, I can handle anything."

"We'll see." He stepped aside. "Let's go catch a killer."

Chapter Four

Closing the door to his office inside the fire station, Sawyer gestured for Liz to make herself at home.

"Have you been able to find any connection between the victims?" she asked, sitting on the sofa in the back of the room.

"None so far." Something he'd lost sleep over, wondering, why them?

"It would be good to have someone photograph the crowds at any other fires during the remainder of this investigation." Settling in, she removed her jacket but kept on the scarf, which, he now noticed, matched the color of her slacks.

Gunmetal blue. Custom-made.

Did she always wear a neckerchief around others? Or was she ever at ease in her own skin with someone else?

If so, he wanted nothing more than to be that someone. Still. Always.

"Do you think our suspect will be out there, again?" Sawyer sat behind his desk.

"It's highly likely. From the looks of what was left of the Compassionate Hearts building, he loves destructive fire. Roughly one-third of arsonists return to the scene. The primary attraction can be a desire for control and power. Not just watching the firefighters battle the blaze, but it's the thrill of seeing how much damage they've caused."

He hadn't considered someone would risk raising suspicion by hanging out for hours in this small town, but it was probable, considering the bomb in his truck and the aggressive nature of the fire that had been set. "The office where Aleida Martinez was found went up fast and hot with no windows for her to escape. There was no need to start two additional fires unless the goal was to ensure the whole building burned to the ground."

"If you've got a local law enforcement contact who could handle taking the photos, it would be helpful."

"As a matter of fact, I do. My brother Holden is the chief deputy in the sheriff's office." His cell phone buzzed. He pulled it from his pocket. "Speak of the devil. Give me a minute."

Liz nodded.

Sawyer answered. "I was just talking about you."

"And I was just looking at your truck," Holden said. "Or should I say what's left of it. Please tell me you're in one piece. I don't want to be the one to have to give Mom bad news."

"No worries on that front." Sawyer spun around in his chair, facing the wall and lowered his voice. "Guess who's in my office?"

"I hate suspense."

"Liz."

A long beat of silence. "Your Liz?" his brother finally asked.

It had been a long time since he'd heard anyone refer to her as his. Didn't change how he'd never stop thinking of her that way.

"I can hear you," she said in a singsong voice.

Sawyer winced. "Yep. Listen, I need a favor." He explained to Holden about the need to have a deputy take discreet photos of any crowd that gathered at future fires.

"I'll get on it as soon as we're done collecting what little forensic evidence is left out here."

"Once you get it, hang on to it. Liz has a contact at Quantico who will fast-track lab results. We're sending him everything."

"Roger that. I'm relieved you're okay. Truly. I'll see you tonight. Heads up, Grace might want to look you over."

No might about it. With Grace, Holden's wife, it was a guarantee. She was a nurse, drop-dead gorgeous and the sweetest soul, who his brother was madly in love with. There would be no hiding his injuries from her.

"I've got stitches in my side, a minor burn on my arm and a cut on my thigh," Sawyer said, coming clean.

"Smart man to fess up. It'll make her examination faster. Later."

"Thanks." They hung up and he spun back around, facing Liz.

She gave a wry grin. "You a fire marshal *and* Holden a deputy? Unreal," she said with a shake of her head.

"Actually, all of my brothers ended up in law enforcement."

Liz shot him an incredulous look. "All of you? Wow. What about Matt?"

Matt Granger was his first cousin on his mother's side. After Sawyer's aunt bankrupted her family with gambling debts and ran off with another man, Matt, who was only seven at the time, and his father came to live at the Powell ranch. Matt was raised almost like a brother rather than a cousin and his father became head manager, overseeing the cattle.

"As soon as Matt turned eighteen, he joined the army. Did black ops. Then he came back and believe it or not became a cop. He was recently promoted to chief of campus police at the local university."

"Your maternal grandfather was a cop, right?"

"A sheriff. Like his father before him. My mom planned to join the FBI after she finished her degree. Dad was going to leave Wyoming and follow her wherever she went, but my granddad got sick. My dad had to take over the Shooting Star. Then Mom got pregnant with Monty and all their plans changed."

"I didn't know. I guess law enforcement runs in your blood, but I thought for sure you boys would've taken over the family ranch. At least one of you. My money was on Monty," she said, and Sawyer would've made the same bet. "That was always your father's dream. He must be proud of you guys, but I'm sure he's also kind of disappointed."

The words tugged at his heart. His father had four sons who loved the ranch and enjoyed working on it, but they'd all been called to do something else. "Long story. The short version is my dad isn't thrilled about it but he claims to understand. I think he's secretly holding on to hope that one of us will give up the badge and take over the ranch someday."

Sawyer opened his bottom drawer and grabbed a fresh work T-shirt. As he pulled off the scrubs top, Liz's gaze slid over his body, a blush rising on her cheeks, before she looked away.

He had to check his grin, but it was nice to know he could still catch her eye. That would have to be good enough for right now.

"Walk me through the other two fires," she said.

Although Liz had a digital copy of everything

on the case, he pulled out the physical file, crossed the room and sat beside her on the sofa. He set the folder on the coffee table in front of her and opened it. "The first was a restaurant. No casualties. The owner is devastated. He recently spent a boatload renovating the place. The loss financially ruined him since insurance won't cover arson. The perpetrator started a leak from a gas line, let it build and left a device to get the fire started. Caused an explosion. There wasn't much left, but when I inspected, I found remnants of a timer."

"A timer?" She looked over the file.

"Found the same at the Compassionate Hearts and the fires before that. A cabin over in Bison Ridge. I cover that town, too. Four guys hunting over the weekend. And then a nail salon. Happened after-hours when the head nail tech was doing inventory in the basement."

"Our guy loves fire but likes to set it at a safe distance. Doesn't want to risk getting burned himself. The timer also shows control. Patience. Same accelerant?"

"I believe so. Gasoline."

"What was used to ignite it?" She looked up at him.

"My guess, based on the intensity of the burn pattern at the point of origin, something really hot. I'm thinking a flare."

"Like the kind used on the road for an emergency?"

"It's possible. Easy enough to get. Certainly burns hot enough at 1,500 degrees Fahrenheit. I believe the timer was rigged to set it off. I won't know for certain about the flare or get confirmation on gasoline as the accelerant until I get the results from the lab. They're backed up as usual. Could take six to eight weeks."

She raised her eyebrows in surprise. "Long time to wait."

"Welcome to my world." He had to rely on the crime laboratory that processed forensics for the entire state. Waiting two months was standard procedure.

"Actually, let me introduce you to mine." She took out her cell and dialed a number. "Hey Ernie, this is Kelley. SAC Cho sent me to Laramie, Wyoming, to cover the—" She paused as she listened to the guy on the other end. "You saw it on the news earlier. That's the case. Yeah, lucky me," she said with a bit of a grimace. "Listen, we need assistance processing the evidence from the fires ASAP. The faster, the better on this one." Her gaze bounced up to Sawyer's. She nodded and smiled. "Thanks. I owe you one for this." She disconnected. "Once he gets it over at Quantico, he'll do his best to get us answers in less than forty-eight hours."

"Wow." He was impressed. "Must be nice having friends in high places."

"We'll need to drive over to Cheyenne and pick

up what you've already submitted to DCI," she said, referring to the Division of Criminal Investigation, where the lab was located.

"No need. I can have Logan send it to your contact. He's a DCI agent. Still lives on the ranch, like me. Only he has a longer commute."

"Holden is chief deputy. Logan is with DCI. What about Monty?"

"State trooper."

"Do you all live on the ranch?" she asked with a teasing smile.

"Afraid so," he said.

Her smile spread wider. "But why? You're all rich."

Sawyer huffed a tired chuckle. "Correction, Holly and Buck Powell are rich," he said, talking about his parents. "My brothers and Matt and I are living off civil servant salaries." It wasn't as bad as it sounded. Their parents had built Monty his own house on the property after everyone thought he was going to get hitched. The engagement fell through, but the place was still there and his. Last year, Holden and his wife moved from the apartment above the garage to their own home a few acres away from Monty once construction was completed. Sawyer took the garage apartment while Logan stayed in a large room in a separate wing of the house from their parents. Matt built his own place, not wanting to stay in the main house or wait to have his aunt and uncle pay for it provided he ever got married. "Besides, Mom and Dad like having us close." It also made it easy for them to pitch in to help on the ranch when needed. "Speaking of living arrangements, where are you planning to stay while you're here?"

"Home. My mom has an old friend who looks after the place. I called her on the drive up. There'll be a key waiting for me under the front mat."

He turned toward her, and his knee brushed against hers, causing an electric spark where they touched. Holding off on a conversation about the past was one thing, but he found it impossible to ignore feelings that welled inside him every time he looked into her eyes. Feelings that reminded him of what they once had. How only physical contact with her would ease the dull ache in his heart.

Their great chemistry hadn't dissipated, but what he wanted from her wasn't sexual, or rather not only sexual. He longed for the intimacy he hadn't known since her, to hold her while she fell asleep. To listen to her breathing. To feel her heart beating against his chest.

If only she needed the same, but at least she didn't pull away this time. A good sign.

"If you get lonely out there all by yourself," he said, reaching over and putting his hand on her knee, "remember, I'm just a few acres away." On horseback, he could reach her in minutes, but that was still too far for his liking. "You could stay on the ranch if you'd prefer. Plenty of guest rooms, and I can guarantee three things—a comfy bed, hot breakfast and strong coffee. In full disclosure, I make no promises that my mom won't cater to your every whim."

A demure smile pulled at her mouth, holding back a laugh.

What he wouldn't give to hear her laugh again.

"I'll be fine," she said. "I'm used to solitude."

"Just because you're used to something doesn't mean you like it. Or have to endure it. Especially not while I'm around. If you were at the ranch, it'd be easier to talk. About work. Only the case," he said, clarifying. He didn't want her to bring the wall back up between them when he'd just gotten her to lower it. "I won't push on the rest." *Only a nudge here and there.*

She hesitated, her expression tightening.

"It'd be safer for you, too," he added. "You're assuming the bomb went off early because you were there and this guy didn't want to kill a federal agent. But what if you're wrong? What if the detonator malfunctioned? What if he didn't want to kill the reporter? Egan has been giving him a lot of coverage that I'm sure he's lapping up. There are a lot of what-ifs." He'd been calculating them. Each one made her theory less likely. "If he planted a bomb in my truck because of my investigation, then you're going to be a target right along with me going forward."

"I can handle myself."

So could he, with an assailant he could see and fight. He hadn't stood a chance against a car bomb.

"You've never been targeted by someone like this," he said.

"Before I was assigned to BAU in Quantico, I worked a case undercover. I had to infiltrate an extremist group. Find their bomb maker. Some people who make explosives bear the marks of their handiwork. The bureau thought I was a perfect fit. They were right. I was able to lure him in. He was attracted to my scars. A sick, twisted guy, but when I caught him, made the bust, it hit the news. My name, my face were out there. The only good thing to come from having my identity exposed was I could publish the book I had been working on. What most people don't know, the part that didn't make it in the news, was I barely got through that alive. In the end, it came down to him and me, but I didn't let him win."

Sawyer wasn't most people. Although he lacked the resources of the FBI, he stayed abreast of what was happening in her life. He was aware of what she'd been through.

"This is different," he said. "You don't have other agents for backup, surveilling your every move."

What if this guy found out where she was staying and lit the house on fire while she was asleep? Or planted a bomb in her rental?

The horrific idea made his blood boil. Made him want to find the culprit and put an end to him before he had another chance to hurt her. He'd taken a piece of shrapnel in his side, but the door that blew off his truck had nearly taken off her head. They were both fortunate to be alive and he intended to keep it that way.

He realized the nature of her job meant sometimes she would face danger, but if it was in his power to protect her, to keep her from suffering, then he would.

"There are no houses near yours." His place was the closest, but it wasn't as if he could stick his head out the window and see her. Bison Ridge was a small mountain-town with a fairly large surrounding landscape, along with a sheriff, a general store and only a few other ranches. "Anything could happen to you out there. My family's ranch is better. Safer." No one was getting in uninvited. If by chance they did, everyone in his family was an excellent shot, thanks to his father making certain of it. Plus, they had twenty armed cowboys in the bunkhouse and a security system.

Liz stared down at his hand on her knee before putting hers atop his and giving it a small squeeze. Her mouth opened. He knew she'd protest because she was a fighter, but he had a sound rebuttal. A knock on the door stopped her from speaking.

They shifted apart.

"Come in," he said.

The door opened. Gareth McCreary poked his head in. He was the assistant chief, managing day-to-day operations, filling in for the chief or one of the battalion commanders as needed. Catching sight of Liz, he hesitated. "I don't mean to interrupt. Do you have a minute?"

Unlike Ted, Gareth was levelheaded. A relatively nice guy. Sawyer never had a problem with him, even when they were going after the same job as fire marshal. "Sure."

"Glad to see you're all right after the bomb tore your truck to pieces." Gareth stepped inside, holding an armful of turnout gear. "We gathered your stuff for you," he said, setting it down in a chair.

"Thanks. I appreciate it." His gear had been the last thing on his mind once the ambulance had arrived and Liz had the foresight to transport the evidence. "Were you on the team today?" The assistants usually worked different shifts from the chief.

"No. When I heard about the fire, I went to check out the scene. Ted is taking off early. Engagement party planning. I'm filling in for him."

"Great." Since Gareth hovered, Sawyer asked, "Anything else I can do for you?"

"It's what I can do for you. I heard things got heated between you and Ted earlier."

Sawyer shook his head. "Not on my end."

Raising his hands in mock surrender, Gareth kept his expression neutral. "With this recent string of fires and murders, we need to remember we're on the same team. Ted agrees. As a gesture of goodwill," he said, tossing him something from his pocket.

Sawyer caught the keys to one of the station's command SUVs. "I was told there wasn't funding in the budget for me to use a department vehicle."

"You need wheels to do your job," Gareth said. "Until you wrap this case, we'll treat any fire like it might be arson. You go in before overhaul. Also—" he beckoned someone else inside "—I think you know this guy."

Joshua Burfield entered and waved hello.

"I do." Stepping over, Sawyer shook the volunteer's hand.

"I asked Josh to brief the others in the VFD," Gareth said, "to ensure we don't have any further miscommunication. The sooner you catch the sick guy doing this, the better for everyone. Including us."

"Please let the volunteers know I appreciate their efforts." Sawyer wanted to make that clear. Their assistance was essential during a crisis such as this. "I hope there are no hard feelings."

Josh shrugged. "If there are, I'm sure it'll blow

over. We're here to make things easier. Not harder for anyone in the department."

"One more thing, and we'll let you two get back to it," Gareth said. "Dinner is ready in the kitchen. I volunteered to cook and picked up groceries on my way in. Spaghetti and meatballs. My mother's recipe. You two feel free to help yourself."

"Thank you," Liz said. "Very kind of you."

"Unfortunately, we've already ordered from Delgado's." Sawyer sat back on the sofa.

"If you change your mind, you know where the kitchen is," Gareth said before leaving with Josh and shutting the door behind them.

"That's a first. Make that two," Sawyer said. "I was one of them for more than ten years, I work in the same building, and I haven't been made to feel welcome to join any meals since I started this job. Now I get a dinner invitation and keys to a department vehicle in one day."

Another knock on the door. This time it was their dinner delivery. Sawyer tipped the driver and they dug into the food.

Liz moaned. "I didn't realize how hungry I was," she said around a mouthful of food.

"Ditto." He bit into his burger.

"Or how much I missed Delgado's beef French dip sandwiches with au jus."

He hoped she'd realize there were other things and people she missed, too.

"Hey, what does Ted have against you?" Liz asked before stuffing some fries in her mouth.

How nice to see she had a healthy appetite and didn't only stick to bird food. "He thinks—well, they all think I got the job over Gareth because my last name is Powell." It was a fact and no secret that his parents had friends in high places and enough influence to give him the advantage if he and Gareth were equally qualified. It was also a fact, but a lesser-known truth, that they never would. They came from the school of hard work and had ingrained in their sons the importance of earning their achievements. The only handouts were free room and board, only to keep their kids close, but Sawyer and his brothers even paid for that by working on the ranch. He had the calluses and occasional sleep deprivation to prove it.

"If only they knew you better." Liz patted his leg. "You'd never accept a job you hadn't earned on your own merit," she said with such confidence it filled him with warmth.

She had been more than his girlfriend. More than his lover. She was his best friend. The one person outside his family who knew him, had his back and believed in him without question. Something he hadn't been able to find with anyone else. To be so completely loved. To be the center of another's life.

"Take the invitation and the vehicle as an olive

branch." She set down the sandwich, wiped her hands and picked up the file.

"Lizzie, staying at your house alone—"

"If he used a timer and a flare, how did he hide it?" she asked, cutting him off.

"I believe he planted some kind of canister filled with gasoline, the timer or detonator and flare attached, all concealed in something nondescript. Like a box. At Compassionate Hearts, I found the remnants under a chair in the office and two other spots. He probably planted it the night before around the closing of the restaurant, the nail salon and the thrift store when workers were tired, eager to leave and wouldn't have noticed a small box. It would've been easier to do at the cabin in the woods."

She riffled through the pages. "Where was the device left at the salon?"

"In the basement. Near the stairwell. The fire would've blocked the only way to escape."

"Located in the back of the building?"

Sawyer nodded. "Both of them."

"Then he would've wanted to make sure the nail tech and Aleida were in the right spot when it went off. If this guy was watching, he couldn't have seen them from the street, known for certain they were where he wanted them."

Sawyer connected the dots. "Unless he'd called them. There was a phone line in the basement of the salon and office. They answer, he gets them talking, keeping them on the line until the timer goes off."

"I'll get the phone records. Maybe this guy was stupid enough not to use a burner." She flipped through a couple of pages and stiffened.

"What is it?" he asked.

The color drained from her face. "Can't be," she said, her voice barely a whisper as she stared at the page. "Look." She pointed to the four victims of the cabin fire. "Do you recognize the names? Those three?"

Sawyer glanced at the pictures and the names that went along with them, but nothing rang a bell. He was acquainted with most of the victims. More than a handful of times, he'd been in Compassionate Hearts, had spoken with Martinez in passing. He'd eaten at the restaurant before it had been renovated and burned to the ground. His mother had gotten her nails done at the salon often, and everyone there was pleasant enough. All of them, including the hunters he'd gone to high school with, though he hadn't known them. But that didn't give him the answer as to why they had been attacked.

They didn't go to the same church, belong to the same clubs or even use the same banks. Four lived in Laramie, the other two in Bison Ridge.

"What am I missing?" he asked.

"The hunters, Flynn Hartley, Scott Unger, Randy Tillman, the nail salon technician, Courtney O'Hare, and Aleida Martinez. They were all there at the summer camp the night of the fire."

Sawyer took the file from her and looked it over. He hadn't attended the camp and wasn't familiar with those who had. Though the fire had left indelible scars on the inside for him, he hadn't memorized the list of teens who had escaped. "What about the fourth hunter, Al Goldberg, and the restaurateur, Chuck Parrot? Were they there, too?"

Liz thought for a moment, squeezed her eyes shut and shook her head. "No. They weren't."

He took the file and turned to the incident where the nail tech had been killed. "What about the owner of the salon? Do you recognize the name?"

She glanced at the page. "No."

"What if the murderer had mistaken the tech for the owner and killed O'Hare by accident. This might not be what you're thinking." He hoped like hell that it wasn't.

She sucked in a deep, slow breath, and then her gaze lifted to his. "Five out of the seven people targeted were there that night. You're the math guy. Statistically, is that a coincidence? Or are we dealing with something else? Could the connection be the fire?"

"It's possible Goldberg is an outlier. A result of human error. The murderer didn't care if Goldberg was in the wrong place at the wrong time and was acceptable collateral damage in order to kill the other men. But why Parrot's restaurant?"

"Maybe our guy torched the restaurant to hide his real motive. Arsonists do it all the time. With Goldberg, perhaps it's like you said, he's an outlier. Wrong place. Wrong time."

They needed to be careful not to skew the data to fit an emotional model. The fire fifteen years ago changed the trajectory of their lives, upended their worlds. The cloud of it, hanging over their heads to this day, could be overshadowing the way she looked at the facts. "We can't jump to conclusions and see threads where there aren't any. There has to be another link we're missing between them."

Liz nodded but with a doubtful expression.

Whatever the connection, they had to find it and be certain. Fast.

Chapter Five

He checked his watch. 10:35 p.m.

Time to shake things up.

He whipped out his burner cell phone and made the call.

On the third ring, the line was answered. "Hello," Neil Steward said.

"You deserve what's about to happen."

Neil didn't respond right away. "Oh yeah, and what's that?"

"Fireworks."

"Bob, is this you messing around?"

"This isn't Bob. The fireworks and much more you deserve. Your son is a different story." The authorities would find his twenty-three-year-old son's body inside the Cowboy Way Tattoo Parlor, where he worked at his father's shop. He'd killed Mike a little earlier. Slit his throat. Then set the devices to start the fire. "But sins of the father..."

"Who is this?"

He triggered the timer and counted down in his head. "My name is Vengeance. You're guilty for what happened to Timothy. You stood by and did nothing to stop it. You stayed silent. Sold your soul. That's why I've taken your boy and your shop." To teach Neil about true loss.

"I—I—I don't know what you're talking about or what you want, but if anything happens to my son, the police are going to get involved. You hear me?"

If only he'd told the police the truth years ago, Mikey would be alive now. But then Neil wouldn't have been paid for silence or had the money to start his own tattoo shop. Neil was a liar and a coward who valued money more than doing the right thing, and when the authorities questioned him tonight, the odds were he'd even lie about this phone call.

"Listen to me, Neil. You're going to burn in hell." *Three*. "No need to call the cops." *Two*. "Your son's body will be found before long." *One*. "They'll be in touch shortly."

The fire had started. Too bad he couldn't be there to see it just yet. Soon. Patience.

Right on cue, Neil yelled colorful expletives over the line, but that wouldn't bring his son back.

He disconnected.

Neil would try to call his son first, then go looking for him at the shop.

Any minute now, a passerby on the street would smell smoke, notice the flames and dial 911. The fire department would be on the scene in less than ten minutes, and a large crowd would gather once more.

Then he could see the Cowboy Way burn.

But how long until you arrive, Liz?

LIZ PULLED UP to her family house and parked the car. *Home.* She'd always think of it as such even if she didn't want to stay.

Sawyer was right behind her in the department vehicle.

She'd declined his offer, again, to stay at the Shooting Star Ranch, but he insisted on making sure she got to her place safely.

Popping the trunk, she hopped out of the car. "See. Nothing to worry about."

"Let's check the place out, sweep for any planted devices before we issue an all clear. Okay?"

Wise words. She wouldn't protest since it had been her plan to search the house.

He reached for her bags, but she grabbed them.

"You're injured." She frowned at him. "And I'm more than capable of carrying my things. I do it all the time."

He took the bags from her hand and closed the trunk. "First, I'm fine. Second, you've been gone so long you've forgotten how a cowboy operates."

Chivalry was not dead in the Mountain West. Another thing she missed.

She led the way up the porch. Under the mat, she found the key and unlocked the door.

Sawyer's phone rang. As they stepped inside, he answered, "Hello." He got quiet as he listened, his features tightening with worry. "You've got to be kidding me." More silence. "We'll be there as soon as we can." He hung up. "There's another fire."

"Already? We extrapolated that there wouldn't be another for a day or two. Not in less than twenty-fours. It's too soon."

"I don't care about FBI projections. I care about the firefighters. The team is exhausted from putting out and overhauling the one at Compassionate Hearts. Not only are innocent civilians being killed, but with this grueling pace of these attacks, the lives of firefighters are being jeopardized."

After they stepped outside, she locked the front door. "Where is it?"

"Back in Laramie. Town center."

Thirty minutes away.

"I'll drive," he said, heading for the SUV.

BITING BACK A SMILE, he watched Liz Kelley climb out of the red LFD SUV and fall into step beside Sawyer, her gaze glued to the fiery beast devouring the Cowboy Way Tattoo Parlor.

Magnificent.

As much as he wanted to stare at the flames and savor the devastation on Neil Steward's face, he kept Liz in sight.

FBI was printed in bright yellow letters on the jacket she wore like armor. The same way she wore the scarf that hid her puckered skin. Relying on her attractive face to appear normal when she was anything but. Covering up her scars when she should've exposed them with pride. The marks of a survivor.

All proof she was still clinging to who she had once been—a pretty, vapid doll, good for nothing besides spreading her legs for Sawyer—instead of embracing what the fire made her, forged into someone new.

A wasted gift. One he'd take back.

It was no coincidence Liz was in town.

Providence brought her to Laramie. Vulcan, the god of fire, summoned her...just for him.

At first, when he spotted her in front of the smoking heap of what was left of Compassionate Hearts, it had been a shock. Then his surprise slowly twisted to anticipation.

Years ago, he thought Liz would be the one to get away. The fire had taken everything from her. Left her scarred and scared. On the run from life itself, which had been sweeter than killing her. But here she was, bigwig FBI agent, risen like a phoenix from the ashes, returned right on time.

Back on his list with the others who would pay.

Earlier, he had salivated at the idea of taking her out along with Sawyer Powell in one fell swoop with the truck bomb, the remote detonator itching in his hand.

But the reporter, covering his handiwork with

such flourish, had been with them. Gave him reason to reconsider. So he'd set it off early and got to witness how the air shook with the explosion, glass bursting from the windows, flames lapping at the metal. The second concussive blast was better than the first, with the truck door nearly decapitating Liz and shrapnel wounding Sawyer.

Good thing they hadn't died quickly and painlessly.

The explosion gave him insight. In the aftermath, watching them—how Sawyer tried to shield Liz, the way she caressed his face, the worry in her eyes before she ran to her car, no doubt to race to the hospital—was like old times. Something still burned between them.

Sawyer was a nuisance that he simply wanted out of the way, but with Liz, he could do something special. Toy with her. Break her. Take away someone she loved to show her how it felt before he killed her.

Even if she was FBI.

He wasn't a fool and didn't need the Feds breathing down his neck. So he'd wait until she left Wyoming to end her. After all, he was a patient man. Better to torch her in Virginia anyway. Then her death wouldn't appear related.

Finishing the list and keeping his promise would be worth it in the end. It was the only way to get what he wanted. Needed more than anything else in the world.

Staring at Liz, he knew exactly how to have fun with her while he bided his time to kill her.

He wondered if she could feel the heat of his flame standing so close or sensed what was to come.

Chapter Six

"Is it our guy?" Liz approached Sawyer, who had snagged Gareth's attention as the assistant chief came out of the tattoo shop. "Did he do it again?"

Gareth moved them farther away from the building. "It appears so."

"What happened?" Sawyer asked.

"The owner of the shop next door smelled smoke, went outside to check it out and reported the fire at about 10:40 p.m. Our company and the VFD responded at 10:47 p.m. and 10:55 p.m., respectively. Once we got inside, I immediately saw the similarity to the other fires. That's when I came back out and called you. After I hung up, I heard Neil Steward, the owner, screaming that his kid, Mike, was inside." Gareth gestured to the poor man. "His wife, Evelyn."

Horror and sad resignation welled in Steward's glassy eyes as he held his wife, who was sobbing.

Liz swore under her breath. Her heart ached with pity for the couple.

"Two went in to look for him," Gareth said.

"The pair checked the first floor where they do the tattoos, but he wasn't there."

"Did they search the basement or office?" Sawyer asked.

"The office is on the second floor. Can't get close enough yet. Two more devices went off near a pile of flammable materials that were in the shop."

Dread slithered up Liz's spine. "Has that happened before, devices going off while you were inside?"

Gareth shook his head. "No. First time."

"Were the devices exposed or were they hidden inside anything?" Sawyer asked.

"Concealed in cardboard boxes."

Sawyer sighed. "This guy is escalating things. Deliberately endangering firefighters."

"Well," Gareth said, tipping his hat back, "he's definitely slowing us down."

"Strange," Sawyer muttered, staring at the blaze.

She studied his face. "What is it?"

"Our guy wanted the other places to burn to the ground. Hot and fast. Why not this one?" Sawyer mused. "With the other devices going off later, he wanted to take his time for some reason."

Turning, Liz stared at the tormented looks on the faces of Mr. and Mrs. Steward, their gazes fixed on the inferno that had once been their business. "Maybe it's not about the firefighters. I can't imagine anything worse for a parent than this. Having to watch the fire that has taken away their livelihood while waiting to find out if their child is alive or dead."

She scanned the crowd. This guy was out there, taking it all in, relishing the pain and devastation he caused. No way he'd miss it.

Liz spotted someone on the periphery of the crowd discreetly taking pictures. A woman with an athletic build and long hair in a ponytail. "Hey, is that a deputy in plain clothes?" she asked Sawyer.

He followed her gaze. "Deputy Ashley Russo."

"Good." Liz nodded once, briskly. "We'll have a picture of him. He's here. I'm sure of it."

Sawyer leaned in, putting his mouth close to her ear. "The Stewards, were any of them in the fire at the camp—Neil, Evelyn or Mike?"

"They weren't there." She knew the names of every camper that had been locked in the cabins and all the men from the bunkhouse who had worked to save her life and rescue the Durbins that night.

How were the Stewards connected to the other recent victims?

Two firefighters emerged from the tattoo parlor.

"We want to talk to them," Sawyer said to Gareth.

"Come on. It's Anderson and the probie Johnson. Hey!" Gareth started toward the fire engine where the two were headed. "Anderson, Johnson, over here!"

The two turned and trudged toward them in full turnout gear with their breathing apparatuses hanging around their necks. One was a woman, which surprised Liz. She wasn't sure why. In her job, she'd met more than a few female firefighters. Maybe she hadn't expected to find one here in Laramie.

Both had looks of weary devastation.

"Anderson, Johnson," Sawyer said, "this is Agent Liz Kelley. Well? Did you find Mike Steward?"

"We thought we had a chance of saving him," Anderson said, her voice rough from the smoke. "The fire didn't reach the second floor. We managed to put it out, but he was already dead."

"Smoke inhalation?" Sawyer asked.

Johnson shook his head. "His throat had been cut. I thought I was going to retch right there. Never seen anything like it."

"Me either. My God." Anderson's voice was heavy, horrified. "Do you think the fire was set to cover it up?" she asked.

"He wanted us to find the body like that." Liz crossed her arms. "Otherwise, he would've set a device upstairs. Probably would have doused it in gasoline, too, to hide the wound until the ME examined the body."

"Tell me what you saw when you first went in," Sawyer said.

"Not much at first." Anderson opened the top part of her coat. "Smoke was too thick. Black."

"The spray turned to vapor straight away," Johnson added.

"You should know the fire was up high, Sawyer," Anderson said. "In certain areas, the ceiling looked the same as the recent fires."

"He used gasoline again."

"Same accelerant," Anderson said with a nod. "The others got a handle on the secondary fires." She tugged off her gloves. "We kept moving. Checked the basement first since we found the nail tech down there. But nothing. We finally got up to the second floor."

Johnson closed his eyes. "I almost—" he paused and swallowed convulsively "—slipped in the blood. There was so much."

"It's not an easy sight," Liz said, trying to console him. "Even if you've seen it before, you never really get used to it."

Anderson looked at Sawyer. "Got a second?" She hiked her chin to the side, and they took a couple of steps away.

"You all right, Tessa?" He pushed her hat back and put a comforting hand on her shoulder, and unwelcome annoyance prickled Liz.

"I've been better." Even dirty with a soot-smudged face, she was girl-next-door cute. "When my shift from hell ends, I really need to blow off some steam. Decompress. You interested in having some fun tomorrow night?"

One side of Sawyer's mouth hiked up in a wry grin.

The idea of him having fun with the pretty, probably flawless, firefighter sent a wave of jealousy through Liz so hard and fast it astonished her.

Get a grip. Although she had been living like a nun, there was zero reason for a handsome hottie like Sawyer Powell to be celibate. Girls had been throwing themselves at him since high school. He'd had his pick, could've chosen anyone, but he'd fallen for her. She'd been truly lucky then, before the fire.

Sawyer probably had a lot of *fun* on a regular basis, and it was none of her business. Only this case was.

Giving herself a stern mental shake, she looked away as Sawyer replied to Tessa too low for Liz to hear and turned to Gareth. "Has anybody talked to the crowd?"

"Yeah, Sawyer's brother Holden." Gareth looked around. "He's out there somewhere."

"I'll find him."

"Hey." Gareth stopped her from walking away. "We didn't really know each other well back in the day."

She tensed, bracing herself for it. She'd run

into more people from high school than she cared to remember since she'd been back. Gareth was going to be the first to bring up the fire. "We didn't hang out in the same circles. But I hear you and Ted are still best friends."

Whenever you saw one, you saw the other. Frick and Frack was what everyone called them in school.

Odd how things and people she hadn't thought of in ages were coming back to her now.

Gareth's smile was tight and didn't reach his eyes. "Ted can come across a bit abrasive." He lifted a brow. "But he's a good guy."

"If you say so."

He met her gaze squarely. "Anyway, what happened to you back then was awful. It's good to see you again, doing so well."

"Yeah." She never knew how to respond when all she wanted was to walk away. "Thanks."

"Hotshot FBI. I bought a copy of your book. Most of us at the station did. It's signed, but before you leave town, would you mind personalizing it for me?"

Inwardly, she cringed but kept her discomfort from surfacing on her face.

Sawyer left Tessa Anderson's side.

"Sure, I'll sign it if you want. Excuse me." Liz stepped away from Gareth. "Sounds like you've got a hot date tomorrow night." As soon as the words left her mouth, she regretted saying them. *Why did you go there?*

He stopped and stared at her. "Do you care?" he shot back, his gaze boring into hers.

She shouldn't, but she did. "You're free to do what you want when you're not working. Everyone needs downtime to blow off steam. You deserve it."

"That includes you, too, right?"

Nice going. "I'll go for a run. It's how I unwind. I'll be fine."

"You're fine a lot. Fine working for the FBI. Fine out in Virginia. Fine with your solitude. Fine staying at that old house in Bison Ridge alone regardless of the risks. Fine going for a run instead of getting sweaty with someone. But are you ever happy, Lizzie?"

She rocked back on her heels. Why was she suddenly under attack? And how dare he analyze her and try to dissect her life. "I shouldn't have made the comment about the hot date. It's not my business. I wasn't judging."

Sighing, he lowered his head. "I'm glad you said something. It's the only way I'd know if you cared." His gaze flickered back up to hers. "And, no, I don't have a date. Tessa claims she wants fun, but I know better. What she really wants is a husband."

"You'd make a great one. You're the settling-down type. Clearly you two have chemistry."

A muscle ticked in his jaw. "Chemistry isn't the same as compatibility. No marriage should be based on sex. Even if it is mind-blowing."

Not only did he have fun with Tessa, but it was *mind-blowing*. A detail she did not need or want to know.

"Bottom line," he continued, "I'm not the guy for her and she's not the woman for me. Not that you care though, right?"

Movement from the corner of her eye told her this conversation wasn't private.

She pivoted and faced Holden Powell.

"Sorry to intrude. I didn't realize," Holden said to Sawyer. "Hey, you." He wrapped her in a big hug, lifting her from her feet.

It was unexpected and warm and lasted way too long.

Finally, he put her down, leaving her breathless. She wasn't used to affection anymore, much less the big, cowboy kind.

"It's been ages since I've seen you," Holden said.

She pulled up her scarf that had slipped down her neck. "Yeah." She glanced at Sawyer, but he didn't meet her eyes, wouldn't even look at her. Did she want him to?

Staring at him, she no longer knew *what* she wanted besides solving this case.

"I need to go inside the shop." Sawyer turned for the department SUV, with Liz and Holden following behind him. He grabbed his boots from the trunk and sat on the tailgate.

Liz watched him slip them on, his jaw clenched, his fingers clumsy on the clamps of the boots. This type of emotional distraction, worrying about him and herself, rather than concentrating on the job, was precisely what she wanted to avoid. It was bad enough that doubt always found a way to slide in regardless of how many cases she closed. For her, there were always waves of self-confidence with an undercurrent of insecurity. She didn't need complicated emotions thrown into the mix. "This is why I wanted to keep things professional. Not make it personal. Can you let this go?"

Giving a chuckle full of ire, he grabbed his kit. "*You* brought up *me* having a hot date," he snapped. "You got personal. But sure, I can let it go. I'll store it in my locked box where I keep everything else bottled up until I have your permission to unpack it."

Holden whistled softly.

She opened her mouth to set him straight, and her mind went blank. Except for one thing. He was right. About all of it. Her focus had slipped. She'd gotten jealous when she had no right and then opened a giant can of worms by discussing it.

Liz let out a long breath.

Holden put a hand on his brother's shoulder.

"Are you okay to go in there injured? You've got stitches."

"I'm medically cleared to do my job, Mom." Shoving past them, Sawyer flipped on a flashlight and stalked off into what remained of the tattoo shop, carrying his kit.

"Man, you got him riled up." Holden elbowed her. "Deep down, he's just happy to have you back in town."

"I can tell." She looked up at him. He was a little shorter than Sawyer and no longer broader. When Holden played football, he was beefy. Since then, he'd gotten leaner, which suited him. He was clean-shaven. None of the scruffy rough-and-tumble two-day stubble Sawyer had down so well, making him look edgy.

Holden stared at her with those kind eyes of his and flashed a sympathetic smile. "You've been gone too long."

"Or not long enough."

"He always swore you'd come back. And here you are. Getting a wish fulfilled after fifteen years is a lot to process when you're simultaneously investigating the toughest case of your career alongside the woman who was the love of his life."

But she didn't come back for him. A pang of guilt lanced her chest.

Get to work. She bit down on the inside of her lip and refocused on the task at hand. "What did you learn from the crowd?"

"Not too much. The hours at the shop varied. According to the owner of the store next door, Mike didn't take many walk-ins. Mostly appointments. Whoever did this might have made one to get him here when he wanted. No one saw or heard anything suspicious other than the smoke. You'll want to speak to Neil Steward. He claims he received a strange phone call. Someone threatened to hurt Mike. Hard to get more out of him right now. Might be best to speak to him tomorrow."

Gareth was giving the Stewards the news about their son. The wife wailed and Neil broke down in tears. The couple needed a chance to grieve.

"Yeah. Can you ask them to come in?" she asked.

"Sure. Is the sheriff's office okay?"

She nodded. "Could you also go through the pictures Deputy Russo is taking? See if anyone stands out for any reason?"

"We'll take care of it."

"Chief Deputy! Miss FBI!" A man pushed through the crowd and slipped under the police barricade. He was holding an open bottle of whiskey. "It's high time you put a stop to this!" He took a long swig from the bottle.

Liz couldn't put a name on the face, but she recognized him.

"Chuck." Holden approached him. "I can't have

you drunk and disorderly on the streets with an open container."

"I've lost everything. The restaurant. My house that I put up for collateral on the loans. Penny is gone, too. Packed a bag. Went to her mother's in Nebraska. And you want to give me a citation for trying to drown my troubles when you all should be putting a stop to this."

"Mr. Parrot, I'm Agent Liz Kelley."

"Everybody knows who you are. The girl who survived." He put the bottle up to his mouth and guzzled more liquor until Holden snatched it from his hands. Chuck lifted his chin, his eyes narrowed. Cold. Furious. Drunk. "When are you going to arrest Kade Carver?"

Holden put a fist on his hip. "What does he have to do with this?"

"Everything." Parrot threw his arms out wide and teetered. "He's the reason this is happening."

"Who is Kade Carver?" she asked, whispering to Holden.

"A wealthy developer."

"More like business wrecker," Parrot said, his words slurred. "He wants to buy out the entire block. Build a fancy townhouse community. Right here. In the center of it all. My restaurant. The nail salon. Now Neil's tattoo parlor. On the same damn block. Come on. Wake up and smell the conspiracy. With these fires, he'll get everything on this block dirt cheap now. I'm talking pennies on the dollar."

Liz looked at Holden. "Another name to add to the list for tomorrow." She glanced at Parrot. "We'll look into it."

"About time that you do." Parrot spun around, stumbled, swayed and lumbered away.

"Be prepared," Holden said. "Carver will lawyer up. It's going to be an exhausting day. Double shift for me since I'm in charge of the office while my brother-in-law is on vacation with his fiancée."

Liz patted his shoulder. "Congratulations on getting hitched. I'm glad you finally found someone willing to put up with you," she said, and he laughed. Then she pieced together what he'd said. "Wait a minute, your brother-in-law is the sheriff?"

He nodded. "My relationship with Grace happened fast and unexpectedly. It made things awkward at work for a while, but her brother has come around since the wedding. Now he's at the ranch all the time for family dinners. Anyway, where are you staying? B&B in town? The Shooting Star?"

"Bison Ridge."

Holden frowned at her. "After the car bomb, is it wise to stay out there alone?"

Ugh. "Not you, too. If I were a man, would you ask me that?"

He shrugged. "Maybe. I've always thought of you as a sister, and considering what nearly happened to Sawyer, I don't want any member of my family who is investigating this case staying somewhere isolated."

"I appreciate the concern, but I'll be fine." After all, she was a trained agent and armed.

Smiling, Holden shook his head. "You're just as stubborn as ever. Nice to see some things never change. You should get some rest."

If only. She'd been up since three that morning with nerves over her presentation at the symposium. "I've got to wait on Sawyer since we came together." *Joined at the hip.*

Holden raised his eyebrows. "Going to be a long ride to Bison Ridge with Mr. Grumpy Pants."

"Yeah. It is." But there were more important things to think about. "Come on. I'll help you finish canvassing the crowd."

Chapter Seven

A shotgun racking nearby made Sawyer jackknife upright from his sleeping bag. The sharp signature ratcheting sound, which couldn't be mistaken for anything else, had him wide awake. In the morning light filtering into his tent, he grabbed the pistol at his side.

"Whoever is in there," Liz said from outside, "come out slowly with your hands up, or I'll shoot first and ask questions later, provided you're still alive to answer."

Hearing her voice calmed his racing pulse. Exchanging his gun for his Stetson, he put his black cowboy hat on and climbed out of the tent, wearing nothing else but his boxer briefs and a smile. "Good morning to you, too."

Eyes flaring wide, Liz lowered the shotgun. Irritation etched across her face. She wore jeans, a tank top and an open button-down shirt that she had probably thrown on in haste. Her gaze dipped, traveling over his body, and a blush rose on his cheeks.

"When you dropped me off last night," she said, meeting his eyes, "and didn't hassle me again about staying out here alone, I thought you had dropped the issue."

His temper had simmered on the ride back, and he'd thought it best to be quiet. No point arguing. Nothing would've been achieved. She'd made up her mind to be stubborn, and he had made up his to be equally obstinate. "Guess you don't know me so well anymore. I told you, now that you're a part of the investigation, you could become a target as well. It's not safe for you to be out here by yourself."

"So you decided to pitch a tent in the thicket a couple hundred feet from my house and spy on me. I'm FBI. You didn't think I'd notice?"

He chuckled. "You say 'spy,' I say 'protect.' And you didn't notice my camouflaged tent until the sun came up and you were staring out the window while making coffee."

She narrowed her eyes. "How do you know that?"

Educated supposition. She was dressed and he could see the steam rising from a mug she'd left on the porch railing. "Guess I still know you pretty well."

Yawning, he stretched, and her gaze raked over him once more, making him smile.

She put a fist on her lean hip. "I'm tempted to knock that grin off your face."

"Feel free to indulge." Tipping his hat at her, he stepped within striking distance. All she had to do was reach out and touch him. "When it comes to physical contact, I'll take what I can get with you."

She leveled a look at him, hard ice in her eyes, her expression beyond chilling, but he still felt the heat from being near her. "You're incorrigible," she said, "and you're trespassing."

"Correction. You're trespassing. Ten feet before you reach the thicket is where your property line ends and mine begins." He pointed it out. "You're standing on Powell land."

Shaking her head, she sighed. "I forgot how much of it my parents sold. On the bright side, the parcel is probably small enough to put up a high fence to keep prowlers from spying."

No fence would keep him out where Liz was concerned. "I'd strongly encourage it. The investment would mean you intend to stick around." He would love nothing more than to have her stay.

Her gaze fell, the humor draining from her face. She spun around, heading back to the house, carrying the shotgun on her shoulder.

"Can I get a cup of coffee? And take a shower?" he called out after her.

Stopping, she looked back at him. "Are you kidding me?"

He shrugged. "It'll save me from driving all the way back to the ranch." His vehicle was parked down the road, but a ten-minute ride one way. "More efficient to get ready here."

She had always been a stickler about efficiency. He hoped he'd pushed the right button.

Liz considered it a moment before waving to him to follow her.

Bingo. Smiling, he ducked back into his tent. He put on his boots, grabbed his weapon and a small duffel bag with essentials and then hurried to catch up.

In the kitchen, she set the gun on a large wooden farmhouse-style table. The place brought back memories. Most of them fond. Laughter around the table at dinner with her parents. Some of them steamy. Sneaking upstairs and making out in her room. The last few memories had been heart-wrenching.

"Did your parents leave it here?" He gestured to the shotgun.

"No, the caretaker left it for me, along with a stocked fridge." She took a mug from the cabinet and filled it with steaming black coffee. "You still take two sugars and cream?"

"I wish." He patted his stomach. "Not any-more." He was trying to keep the love handles away. "I usually just add a little protein powder to it these days, but black is fine."

She picked up a resealable bag filled with a cream-colored powder from the side of the sink. "I carry some with me whenever I travel. Better than relying on burgers every time I need a quick meal." She set it on the table. "Whatever you're doing, it's clearly working," she said, eyeing his torso and handing him the mug.

As he took it from her, their fingers brushed, and he let the contact linger. "Why did your parents keep this place?" he asked, already knowing the answer. "They never come here."

She dropped her hand. "It's been in the family forever. They want me to move back here someday. Pass the place down to my children. I keep telling them I'm never getting married or having kids, but hope springs eternal with them."

His gaze fell to her exposed throat. The side was a shade lighter than the rest with discernible scars that disappeared beneath her shirt. He took in the rest of her, silky hair reflecting the sunlight, tempting cleavage, trim waist, long legs that had once curled around his hips, holding him close.

She reached for the scarf on the table.

Setting down his coffee with one hand, he caught her wrist in his other before she could take the neckerchief. "You don't need to hide from me."

She tensed. "Habit. I hate when people stare."

"I wasn't staring," he said, honestly. "I was admiring all of you." Also the truth.

A soft laugh of disbelief came from her as she rolled her eyes. "You don't have to say things like that."

She tried to pull away, but he tightened his grip.

Nothing forceful. She could release the hold if she wanted. No doubt she could knock him on his butt, too, in the process.

"Why won't you ever get married or have kids?" He stepped toward her, erasing the space between them. "You're also the settling-down type." He kept his tone gentle. "You'd make a great wife. An amazing mother. You always wanted your own family."

She reeled back with a grimace, but not hard enough or far enough to break the contact. "Stop it. You know why I can't."

He drew closer, putting her arm against his chest and flattening her palm over his heart. "I don't."

"We agreed not to talk about this." Her voice was firm, but she trembled. "About us."

"I'm not talking about us. I'm asking about you," he said, his voice low and soft. "When was the last time you let someone hug you, hold you?"

His confidential source had told him Liz didn't date. Ever. Didn't hang out with friends after work. No bestie to turn to for comfort. Only traveled for business. Didn't visit her parents. A workaholic who chose to be alone.

She hesitated, and he saw in the startled depths of her pale green eyes that it had been far too long. Years.

His heart ached for her. He at least eased his pain, the loneliness, by seeking temporary comfort with others. A warm body here and there. A distraction, a reminder of what he truly missed. It always brought him full circle in the end. Right back to wanting the one person who no longer wanted him. Liz.

"A few hours ago," she stammered.

He chuckled when he really wanted to grit his teeth at how his brother had gotten his arms around her first. Born eleven months apart, with Holden being older, they'd competed most of their lives. His brother usually came out on top. But the win of hugging *his* Liz first irked him to the bone. "Holden doesn't count."

"I say he does." Her eyes hardened. "Don't you need to get ready so we can get going? We have work to do."

This case was important. No doubt about that. Lives were at risk. Another fire could be set, another murder committed at any moment. But now he realized that she didn't simply bury herself in work, she used it as a deflection, as the greatest excuse. She'd survived the fire, but she wasn't truly living.

Deep down, if he was honest, neither was he. Like recognized like.

"I think we both need something else first." He wrapped his arms around her, bringing her into his body for a hug.

She stilled, and he thought she might pull away, but she didn't. At first, she was so stiff he could have been hugging a statue. Slowly, her body relaxed against him. He tucked her head under his chin, where she fit perfectly. Resting her cheek on his shoulder, she kept one palm on his chest, spread her fingers wide and brought her other hand to his lower back, not quite returning the hug, but he'd take it.

The searing heat from having skin on skin, hers on his, sent sensation coursing through him, warming his heart, releasing the tension he carried in his chest. He wanted to tear down the protective wall she'd built around herself. The one that kept her isolated. Surround her with light and love and affection. All the things she denied herself and deserved.

Tightening the embrace, not wanting to ever let her go, he pressed his mouth to the top of her head. Inhaled the scent of her hair, breathing her in. She smelled like spring flowers after a storm. Heady. Sultry.

Sweet.

Her spine of steel softened, her body melting into his, triggering every cell in his brain to remember the passion and pleasure they'd known in each other's arms. As well as the peace. With his thumb, he made soothing circles on her back over her shirt, dipping lower. His other hand drifted to her waist and then slid to her hip. Tenderness turned to desire in a flash. No holding back. No hiding his arousal. He soaked in the heat from her body, the softness of her curves, the smell of her.

"Liz." Only a rasp of her name filled with the longing that was growing inside him.

She sighed against his chest.

The sound slight, hinting at the vulnerability she dared show, only stoked the wild need firing in his blood. She was everything he remembered. Everything he never stopped wanting. No matter how hard he had tried to get her out of his head, each time he'd failed.

She lifted her chin, their gazes locking, and she shuddered against him.

"You smell good," he whispered. *Feel good, too. Oh, so good.*

They were different people. Things had changed between them. They'd attempted to move on. But there was no denying they had grown in the same direction. Fighting for justice. Sacrificing everything to see it served. Through it all, this remained—heat and longing—the memories that wouldn't let either of them go. The feel of her against him, beneath him, when he was inside her. The taste of her in his mouth. The scent of her. The thousand little things about *her* he simply couldn't forget.

"You smell like you need a shower," she replied.

Chuckling, he cupped the side of her face, his palm cradling her cheek. "It was hot in the tent."

Sweltering. Between making sure Liz was safe and the warm night air, he'd barely rested.

"You've gotten soft if you missed the AC."

They had slept under the stars more than once, enjoying not only the summer heat but also what they generated together. Sweat coating their skin, dripping from their bodies as they cuddled close. He'd taken it for granted that he'd have endless moments of holding her.

If only he'd known...

He ran his thumb over her mouth. Her lips parted with a tremble, her green eyes burning with unsure desire. Gravity pulled his head to hers, and he did what he'd longed to since he'd seen her at Compassionate Hearts. He kissed her, soft and subtle. She froze, making his heart pound with fear. Then her arms were around his neck as she rose on the balls of her feet and kissed him back, her tongue seeking his. Everything quickly became insistent, far more demanding. She arched against him, moaning, and he forgot how she'd walked away, turned her back on him, abandoned their plans for the future, forsaking him to uncertainty and a new kind of devastation. The heartache that had only deepened over time. Left him hollow. Uneasy. Aching.

Until this moment.

Her hands tangled in his hair, her body rubbing against his. He gloried in the surrender of her response. Oh, he'd miss this...missed her so much.

Need rocked through him. He slid his hand from her jaw, cupping the side of her neck, wanting her even closer.

She stiffened and shoved him away. "I can't."

His heart squeezed at those two words. "Liz." Desperation was a cold hard fist in the pit of his stomach. "Please. I'm—"

"I can't," she repeated in a harsh whisper, tears glistening in her eyes, but her hands were curled into fists at her sides.

She was ready to charge into battle—against him.

But he didn't have a clue how to fight whatever this was. For so long, he thought she needed time. Needed to heal. Needed to regain her confidence. Needed to remember how strong she was. All of which she'd done.

"Can't what?" he demanded. Bear to be touched? Bear to be seen? Bear to love him anymore?

Pressure swelled in his chest like a balloon inflating.

"Do *this*." Pulling her shoulders back, she wiped any emotion from her face, her expression turning guarded. "There's no room for distraction."

His stomach dropped. That's what she thought of him, of fate bringing them back together? "This here, you and me, was once everything. Never a distraction."

"That was then. We can't repeat the past. Not everything we want deep inside works out."

Her words landed on his heart like hailstones.

Proof of what she'd said stood right in front of him. Rejecting him. Using work as an excuse.

She grabbed her holstered sidearm, sheathed knife, field jacket and scarf. "I'll meet you at the sheriff's office. I don't want to be late for any interviews." She stormed outside, letting the screen door slam shut.

Once more leaving him alone, sucking all the air out of the room. He couldn't breathe.

For years, he'd pushed forward, battling his own demons by becoming a firefighter and then fire marshal. As if putting out enough fires, saving enough people, stopping enough arsonists, would make up for his failure at keeping her safe. Change the fact that he hadn't gone into the stables after her, and if he had, the beam wouldn't have fallen on her and she wouldn't have been burned. That the universe would bring her back to him.

All the while, he refused to get attached to anyone else because no other woman was Liz. *His* Liz.

He'd waited for this chance to show her how much he still cared. That the accident didn't matter. And he blew it.

Thinking it would be simple. Easy. As if a hug and a kiss would change anything. He didn't know what in the world had come over him besides pure instinct. Standing in that kitchen like they'd done many times before, unable to keep his distance from her, he hadn't thought. The need to touch her had been all-consuming.

Nothing else had mattered. Not even the consequences.

Regret pooled in his gut, making him sick. He'd pushed too hard, too far, too fast and she ran away from him. Again.

Only this time, she was more out of reach than ever, and he had no idea what to do other than get back to work.

Chapter Eight

In the car, Liz couldn't stop shaking as she drove. She'd made a deal with him, had drawn a line in the sand, and he'd crossed it. No, he'd completely erased it. Even worse, she'd let him. Sure, he weaponized his good looks, standing in her kitchen only wearing his underwear, cowboy hat and boots. Oozing charm. Flexing his muscles. The sight of him, showing all that skin, was more temptation than any woman could resist. Even a hardened agent like her.

Crossing the line with him had been impulsive and wrong, despite feeling so right. He'd stopped her from grabbing her scarf and looked at her with those baby blues, turning her stomach fluttery, the same way he used to, the tingle spreading to her thighs. One touch, one look, and he slipped past the defenses she'd painstakingly built. She was at a loss as he wrapped her in his strong arms, the warmth of him seeping beneath her skin, the smell of him—pine and sweat, all man—enveloping her senses, completely overwhelming her, the sensations stripping her bare.

In that moment, it was impossible to make herself numb. To pretend she was fine being alone. To ignore the throbbing ache in her soul, a wound of her own making when she ended things with him.

Then he kissed her, melting her like warm butter, awakening something deep inside her that had been dormant for so long. His mouth familiar, like coming home, and at the same time new—an adventure she yearned for without realizing.

She couldn't breathe, couldn't think. Everything faded besides him and the burning need to be held by him, caressed and cherished, and to forget about the scars.

No matter how far she ran, how busy she stayed, the one truth she couldn't escape in his arms was how much she still loved him. How she wanted him more than her next breath.

But when his hand slid to her neck, she remembered why she'd left Wyoming. Why she'd left him.

Sawyer was deadly handsome. He deserved a partner who was equal in every way.

He had no idea what she looked like without clothes. Touching her, he remembered the girl she'd once been. Never quite as picture-perfect as him but overall attractive. Appealing.

Now, her body looked like a patchwork quilt from the grafts. Some areas smooth, some goose-fleshy, others mottled. Almost Frankensteinesque. The sight of her nude nothing less than tragic.

She could track terrorists, infiltrate an extremist group undercover, subdue a suspect twice her size. What she could not do was risk baring herself to him, seeing pity or revulsion in his eyes, feeling hesitation in his touch.

That would break her into a million pieces with no way for her to recover.

She parked at the Sheriff's Department and took time collecting herself. *Only the case matters. Treat him like a colleague. Not a former lover who you miss more than anything in the world.* She needed another minute. Or two. Closing her eyes, she fell back on her training and shut down her emotions.

After tying the scarf around her neck and buttoning up her shirt, she headed inside. She approached a deputy sitting at the front counter and flashed her badge. "Agent Kelley here to see Chief Deputy Powell."

"He's not in yet, but Deputy Russo is waiting for you in the sheriff's office. We were given instructions to let you and the fire marshal set up in there. Come on through."

With a nod, she said, "Thanks."

The deputy hit a buzzer, and she entered through a half door at the end of the counter. She made her way through the bullpen to the sheriff's office and knocked on the door.

Deputy Russo, in uniform, hopped up from behind the desk and greeted her at the threshold. "Pleasure to meet you. I'm Ashley Russo." She extended her hand.

The shake was firm. "Agent Kelley."

"We left a message for Mr. Carver late last night. He called bright and early this morning to say he would swing by on his way to a worksite with his attorney. Sometime this afternoon."

He was lawyering up, but at least he wasn't stalling. Her gut told her he'd have a solid alibi. His type always did. "What about Mr. and Mrs. Steward?"

"They said they'd come in but didn't commit to a specific time."

Completely understandable. The horror of what they'd been through was unimaginable, something no parent should have to suffer. "You were the one taking photographs of the crowd last night. Have you had a chance to look through them?" Liz asked.

"Yes, I have. I came in at seven to get started on it. I pulled them up on the computer. Also, I enlarged them, focusing on individual faces and printed those for you. I started putting names to a couple. There's still a lot to go through."

Overachiever. Liz liked that. "By any chance, would you be able to continue helping this morning?"

"As a matter of fact, I can. Those were my

marching orders from Deputy Powell." She glanced at the clock. "He should be in soon." Russo went around the desk and pulled the chair out for her.

Liz sat and clicked through all the photos, getting oriented. Russo showed her the ones of individuals that had been enlarged and enhanced. Some had a strip of general-purpose masking tape on them with names written in Sharpie. She took in the various expressions, searching for any that stood out. Unemotional. Excited. Aroused. Happy.

"What are we working on?" a familiar voice asked from the doorway, stirring more than the physical in her.

She looked up to see Sawyer Powell waltz into the office sporting his cowboy hat, fire marshal T-shirt and jeans that highlighted his sculpted physique. Her blood pressure spiked at how good he looked. His holstered sidearm and badge hooked to his belt reminded her that not only was he a fire marshal but also a law enforcement officer.

His gaze met hers, and instead of fight in his eyes, she only saw sadness, a haunted and desolate expression hanging on his face that stunned her.

"Putting names to the faces in the crowd last night in front of the Cowboy Way," she said.

"Find anything interesting yet?" Holden asked, coming in behind his brother.

Liz glanced back at the photos. "Not yet. Russo

and I could use help identifying people. I'd say the more, the merrier, but really, it'd only be faster."

"I can help for a bit." A cell phone buzzed. "I got a text from Logan," Holden said, glancing at his phone. "He is about to board a plane to drop off the evidence at Quantico. His boss insisted on preserving the chain of custody. Nobody wants any issues if we're able to take this to trial."

"Great." The news was the best she could've hoped for, but she couldn't muster more than a humdrum response while looking at Sawyer. "Ernie will get started on it today."

As Sawyer approached the desk, she noticed he was carrying a take-out tray with two cups and a bag from Delgado's. He set one of the to-go cups down in front of her. "This is better than the sludge they perk here."

"Hey." Holden elbowed Sawyer's good side. "It's not that bad."

"Yes, it is." Sawyer opened the bag and set two wrapped sandwiches on the desk. "Breakfast. Egg whites and cheese. One has turkey bacon. The other turkey sausage."

Why did he have to be so sweet? His charm was hard to resist.

The smell of the sandwiches made her stomach growl. Apparently, he really did watch what he ate. Even last night, he'd had a side salad with his grilled chicken, making her feel naughty by inhaling the beef sub.

"No breakfast sandwich for me?" Holden asked with a teasing grin. "I am letting you guys use the sheriff's office."

Neither she nor Sawyer smiled in response or looked away from one another.

"You always eat at home since you and Grace got married." Sawyer sipped his coffee, not taking his sad eyes off her, doing his best to make her squirm.

But it didn't work. She never let a colleague get under her skin.

Holden shrugged. "The gesture would've been nice."

"I'm not hungry. You can have mine," she said flatly, holding Sawyer's gaze, no matter how uncomfortable it made her with the air backing up in her lungs. "Thanks for the coffee."

Sawyer grabbed both sandwiches and tossed them, one at a time, sinking each into the trash bin without even looking. "You want to let your blood sugar drop. Fine. Neither of us will eat."

"Hey. Why are you wasting perfectly good food? Do you know what Mom would say?" Holden went to the bin and fished them out. "Ashley, are you hungry?"

"Actually, since I came in so early, I skipped breakfast. I'd like one," the deputy said, and Liz regretted not offering it to her.

"Bacon or sausage?" Holden asked.

"Sausage please."

He handed it to her. "I'll have the other for a midmorning snack." His gaze bounced from Liz to his brother. "This energy is different from last night. What is going on between you two this morning?" he asked, picking up on the tension that thickened the air.

"Nothing," she said, not letting any emotion leak into her voice or show on her face.

"On that we can agree," Sawyer grumbled.

She was thankful he didn't elaborate. There was a time when the two brothers spilled their guts to each other. No topic or detail off limits. Maybe Russo's presence stopped him.

Liz couldn't get over the injured expression on Sawyer, and warning clanged in her head, reminding her that wild animals were more aggressive, more dangerous when wounded.

Not that he should be the one upset. She'd only asked to wait to hash everything out until after they finished the case. Not for a reckless one-off kiss in her kitchen that dredged up in excruciating clarity everything she'd missed the past fifteen years. Aroused by pressing against that solid wall of muscle he called a chest. Teased by tasting him. Tormented by wanting to do it again. *Thank you very much.*

"Why don't we each take a stack of photos," Holden suggested. "If you can't ID the person, set it in the middle of the desk, and someone else will take a crack at it."

Everyone grabbed a chair. Russo dug into the sandwich with gusto, and before she finished, Holden had started on his second breakfast. The yummy aroma had Liz wondering if she'd made the right choice.

Deputy Russo needed it more than me.

They worked for a couple of hours, getting most of the names, discussing any contentious history between individuals that might be relevant when she came across a picture that gave her chills. White male. Late twenties. Brown eyes. Dark hair. Grinning like it was Christmas morning. The smile on his lips was subtle, but the gleam in his big bright eyes gave her pause.

Putting her coffee cup down, she held up the picture. "Who is this?"

Holden stared at the photo. "I know this guy. His name is on the tip of my tongue." He snapped his fingers, trying to think. "Released three or four months ago."

Tapping the photo, Liz said, "I bet he's a fire-bug."

Russo slipped in behind the computer. "I'm on it." She clacked away, typing for a few minutes. "Found him. Isaac Quincy. Convicted arsonist. Released three months ago."

"Can I take a look at the file?" Liz asked, and Russo moved aside. She skimmed through it. "According to his record, he has been in and out of jail since he was sixteen. Every arrest was for arson. Accelerants used were gasoline, kerosene and lighter fluid." She reviewed each incident. "Hmm. The fires escalated in aggression. His last two stints in jail were for burning down his childhood home while his parents were on vacation. He had been house-sitting. In the parents' statement, they said he was a 'good boy' who simply couldn't control himself. Mom didn't want to press charges. Dad did for his son's own good. The last one was for torching a dumpster while a homeless person was inside of it. Quincy claimed he didn't know the man was asleep inside. The victim suffered second-degree burns. No fatalities."

"Do you think he could be our guy?" Sawyer asked.

"It's possible." She looked around the room at the others. "He fits the profile, but these recent fires feel—"

"Personal," Sawyer said, finishing her sentence. "He didn't just set fires. He blew up the restaurant and turned the Compassionate Hearts into an inferno."

She nodded. "Not the work of a random firebug. But his recent release from prison coinciding with serial arson can't be dismissed, either."

"Maybe he was hired," Holden suggested, "by Kade Carver. I can't see him getting his hands dirty. I spoke to a couple of owners of other shops in those two blocks. They were reluctant to sell before, but after the fires, they've decided to accept Carver's offer."

"Deputy Russo, could you dig into it?" Liz asked. "See if there's any possible connection between Quincy and Carver. Find a thread, no matter how thin, we'll pull it and see where it leads."

"Sure." Russo left the office.

"I've been thinking we should set up a hotline for any tips," Liz said.

Holden frowned, not liking the idea. "Requires manpower to sort through all the crank calls we'll get."

That was a definite con. She was more concerned with the pros. "Can you spare it?"

"Will it be worth it?" he countered.

Sawyer sat back in his chair. "Do you really think we'll get a viable lead from a hotline?"

"No, I don't. I'm not going to hold my breath waiting to hear from a witness."

Holden sighed. "Then why bother?"

"Serial arsonists enjoy manipulating authorities. They like to communicate, explain themselves."

"You're hoping he'll call," Sawyer said.

She nodded. "We should check in with the medical examiner. See if we can get a time of death for Mike Steward."

"Easier to squeeze details out of Roger Norris in person. He doesn't like to talk over the phone." Sawyer stood. "It's a ten-minute walk."

Fresh air would be good. She needed to stretch her legs. "Let's go."

Neither of them initiated conversation along the way, which was for the best. He appeared resigned and she appreciated it. Maybe he'd gotten the message and would simply focus on the job. Something in her gut, though, told her not to cling to false hope since the air of misery hanging around him troubled her.

In the medical examiner's office, Roger Norris wore narrow rectangular glasses and his white lab coat over a gray AC/DC T-shirt with orange lettering. His thin dishwater blond hair was slicked back. His attention was focused on one of his many screens while he noshed on a banana.

Her stomach rumbled, and she wished she had eaten the breakfast sandwich instead of refusing out of anger. Or principle. If she had accepted the coffee, why not the food, too?

It made no sense, but Sawyer had her spinning in circles.

Roger nodded when they came in. "Sawyer Powell walks into my joint yet again. Can't stay away from me these days, can you?"

"Unfortunately not. This is—"

"Liz Kelley. I read your flattering quotes about the fire marshal in the *Gazette* today."

It was good of Egan to print it. She hoped her comments would change public opinion about

Sawyer. "What can you tell us about Mike Steward?" Liz asked.

"Oh, plenty. Found something quite interesting." He scooted on his stool over to another screen. "His last meal was a burger, fries and a Coke. Based on his fractured skull, he was knocked out before his throat was cut. I got a lockdown on the estimated time of death. It was between four thirty and five thirty."

Nice and tight. That would be helpful.

"Was that the interesting part?" Sawyer asked.

"No, not at all. I'm getting to that. Saved the best part for last." Norris brought up something on his screen. A picture of a small typed note. "Found that stuffed in the victim's mouth toward the back of the throat."

It read, *SINS OF THE FATHER*.

"Any prints?" Sawyer asked.

Norris shook his head. "The perp was careful."

"Our guy wants to talk to us," Liz said. Just like she thought. "We've got to persuade Holden to dedicate manpower for a hotline."

"Consider it done." Sawyer glanced at her. "The only question is what sins did Neil Steward commit?"

Chapter Nine

The awkward silence between Sawyer and Liz, when they weren't discussing something pertinent to the case, unsettled him. She made it look easy, shutting off her emotions, staying laser-focused on work while he was struggling.

Back in the sheriff's office, Holden agreed to the hotline without protest after learning about the note the killer had left inside Mike Steward's mouth. By the time they'd eaten lunch, not a word exchanged between them, it was up and running.

"The *Gazette* and local news station will spread the word about the hotline. Everyone will know about it. We'll weed through the garbage," Holden said. "I'll only bother you with any tips that might be legit or if the perp calls in."

"Thanks," Sawyer said to his brother while keeping his gaze on Liz. Not that it seemed to faze her at all.

"I think Carver is here." She hiked her chin toward the hall.

Two men in business suits had entered the Sheriff's department.

Holden glanced over his shoulder. "Yep. That's him and his lawyer."

She shoved back from the desk and got up. "I can do the interview alone if you'd rather not do it together," she said, her voice flat.

"This is my case." He wiped his hands and crumpled up the wrapper from lunch, throwing it away. "You're welcome to join in the interrogation room. If you can handle it."

"I don't see why I wouldn't be able to. There's nothing personal about this for me."

Her rejection earlier was like a knife in the gut, and here she was twisting it. "You've made that clear. We can talk to them in interrogation room one."

She pulled on a phony professional smile. "I'd like to question him here in the office instead."

"Why?" Sawyer asked.

"It'll make him less defensive. He might let something slip since he'll be less guarded."

Sawyer nodded. "Fine with me."

"I'll show him in," Holden offered.

"If you don't mind, I'll do it." She headed for the door. "Believe it or not, I'm good at putting suspects at ease."

Watching Liz walk away down the hall, Sawyer wanted this *wound*, deep in his heart, to scab over, to scar and fade. Instead, it festered and hurt. Infected by the past.

Holden turned to Sawyer. "Why is Liz acting like a robot? Her voice is all monotone and her eyes are blank. And you threw away food earlier. Fess up. What happened?"

Sawyer watched her greet Carver and his lawyer with a plastic grin. "I happened. I kissed her this morning."

"Well, that's a good thing, right?"

He glanced at his brother out of the corner of his eye. "Based on what you've observed thus far, does it look like it was a good thing?"

"Sorry." Holden folded his arms across his chest. "You've waited fifteen years for this. What's the plan?"

Liz said something that made Carver grin and look down at his suit with pride before he ran a hand through his white hair.

"There is no plan. All she wants to do is give me the Heisman or run away from me." Each time it was like being kicked in the teeth. "She doesn't want me."

What if their time together had been lightning in a bottle? Not meant to last or not meant for them to have a second chance.

Then he thought of her pressed against him. The way she'd tightened her arms around him in the hug, sighed like she wanted more. Kissed him back. No restraint. Full of desire like she *did* want him.

"Maybe it's not you she doesn't want," Holden said. "Maybe she just doesn't want to get hurt."

"But I'd never hurt her."

"She might not be so sure of that."

Sawyer glanced back down the hall. He noticed Liz tugging up her neckerchief as she had a deputy get two cups of coffee for Carver and his lawyer.

What she'd said to him in the kitchen came back to him. How she'd never get married and have kids and that he knew why.

His heart sank at the thought of her denying herself the kind of life she wanted because of the scars. The accident had never mattered to him, but it still mattered to her. Perhaps in a way he couldn't fully understand.

Holden put a hand on Sawyer's shoulder. "Remember that basketball game you finished with a broken foot sophomore year?" his brother asked.

It had hurt like hell. "Yeah, of course." He'd never forget it.

"Any other player would've stayed off that foot. Avoided putting any pressure on it. Human nature to protect yourself from what's going to hurt. But not you, because you don't quit," Holden said. "No matter how painful, no matter the consequences, you don't give up when you're going after something you want. Your Liz is back in town. You can't quit now. Stop moping like a puppy that lost its home. Remember what you are."

Liz started escorting them over.

"And what's that?"

"A coyote," Holden said, referring to their high school mascot. His brother howled low enough for only them to hear and then crossed the hall to his office and closed the door.

The pep talk lifted his spirits. Holden was good at that. In fifteen years, Sawyer hadn't given up hope. Today, he had not only held Liz, but he got to kiss her, and for a moment it was everything.

Progress.

Only a coward or a fool would quit now. Sawyer was neither.

He grabbed an extra chair and brought it around behind the desk. Liz ushered them into the office. The two older men sat across from the desk.

Sawyer took the seat near the computer.

"Once again," Liz said, sitting beside him, "we appreciate you taking the time out of your busy schedule to come down here."

"Of course. I'm happy to help." The fifty-five-year-old man took a sip of his coffee, gagged and set the mug on the desk. "I just don't know how I can."

"We understand you're interested in purchasing all the businesses between Second and Third Street from Kern Avenue to Sycamore Road," Sawyer said.

"I am. It's to build a townhome community in the town center." Carver folded his hands in his lap. "Part of a housing growth plan I've coordinated with the mayor."

"Would you say you're hands-on with your businesses?" Sawyer asked. "That you're aware of details."

With a nod, Kade Carver grinned. "Certainly. It's how I became so successful. I even know the name of every tenant. The devil is in the details."

"Have you had any holdouts who have refused to sell?" Sawyer asked.

"A few."

"Chuck Parrot recently invested a lot to renovate his restaurant." Liz's tone was soft, casual. "Was he interested in selling?"

Clearing his throat, Kade Carver narrowed his eyes. "He overextended himself with the loans he took out for the renovation. He was having trouble making the payments, so he was considering my offer."

"What about the nail salon?" Sawyer sipped his coffee that had been delivered with lunch.

Carver's mouth twitched. "We were in negotiations for a price we both felt was fair until the fire."

"Did Mr. Steward, the owner of the tattoo parlor, indicate he was interested in selling?" Liz asked.

Carver's gaze slid over her. "I'm not exactly

sure where this line of questioning is leading. Are you accusing me of something?"

Smiling, Liz shook her head. "Sir, you are not being charged with a crime. Can you answer the question?"

His lawyer leaned over and whispered in his ear.

"No, the Stewards didn't want to sell," Carver said. "At first. But like any good businessman, I got to the root of their hesitation and came up with a viable solution. I assured them I would find them a suitable replacement location, which was the sticking point. Neil agreed to sell his place if he liked the alternate site. Otherwise, no deal. Seemed fair to me. I wasn't worried about it. They have a cult following and a reputation that'd ensure the business would thrive regardless of where it was moved. Or at least it did."

"The recent fires have lowered the property value of the businesses located on the two blocks you're interested in purchasing." Sawyer let that hang in the air for a moment. "Isn't that correct?"

The man shifted in his seat, looking a tad uncomfortable, but his lawyer saved him from responding. "My client hasn't had a chance to thoroughly review how the fires have affected the value."

"I hope you don't think I'm running around town torching these places," Carver said. "I may be a cutthroat businessman, but I am no killer.

And why would I burn down a cabin? Or Compassionate Hearts? Huh?"

"To throw off the investigation," Sawyer said pointedly. "To keep the trail from leading to you. It's called misdirection."

Carver puffed up his chest, his cheeks growing pink. "I was at home last night. With my wife."

Liz nodded. "Of course you were. I'm certain she'll verify."

"She will indeed. And when the cabin was burned down and those hunters were murdered," Carver continued, "I wasn't even in the state. I was in Florida. With my wife."

"Mr. Carver," Liz said, holding up a gentle hand, "we don't think you doused any of these places in an accelerant and lit the match."

The man gave a smug grin. "I should hope not."

Leaning forward, Sawyer rested his forearms on the desk. "But it is entirely possible that you paid someone to do the dirty work for you," he said, and Kade's jaw dropped. "You're the only person who would financially benefit from any of these fires. Mr. Parrot swears you're behind it."

"Chuck Parrot is a drunk and a liar." Carver's tone turned vicious. "Only a fool would listen to him."

"This interview is over." The lawyer set his coffee mug down and stood, prompting Carver to do the same. "We've cooperated and graciously answered your questions. Unless you charge my client with a crime, he has nothing else to say. Good day."

"Mayor Schroeder is going to hear about this." Carver wagged a finger at them. "Trying to pin this on an innocent businessman because you can't do your job."

The lawyer beckoned his client to hurry along. As they stalked out of the office, they ran into Neil Steward, who was coming into the department.

Mr. Steward marched up to them, shaking a fist in Carver's direction. "If you're behind this, like Chuck is saying, if you're the reason my boy is dead, I'll kill you." The deputy at the front desk jumped up and got between them. "Hear me? I'll kill you!"

"Thank you for threatening my client, not only in a room full of witnesses, Mr. Steward, but also law enforcement. Should any harm come to him, they know who to arrest." The lawyer steered Kade Carver out of the department.

"What do you think?" Sawyer asked Liz.

She glanced at him, and he could see the wheels turning in her head. "I hate it when loved ones are used as alibis because it can be hard to get to the truth, but it's a lot of people to kill just for profit."

"More have been killed over less."

She nodded. "Unfortunately, that's true. The restaurant was the first fire set. Then the nail salon. The cabin and the thrift store could be about misdirection."

Neil Steward was headed their way.

"I hate the type of conversation we're about to have with a grieving parent," she said.

"Me too." It was the hardest part of the job.

"I'd never given it much thought before, how fire marshals also have to do this." The first glimmer of emotion flickered in her green eyes.

They stood as Neil Steward walked into the office. In his midforties, he was a burly guy, full mountain man beard, tattoos covering his exposed arms.

"I'm Agent Kelley and this is Fire Marshal Powell. We're sorry for your loss. You have our deepest sympathies." Liz shook his hand. "Please have a seat. Is your wife joining us?"

With bloodshot eyes, he dropped down into a chair. "She's too distraught to get out of the bed."

Understandable. They had just lost their only child.

"Can we get you a coffee?" she asked, and he shook his head. "We understand you received a threatening phone call right before the fire started."

"Sure did. Some weird guy. Said I deserved what was about to happen. 'Fireworks.' That was the word he used. I thought it was a buddy of mine messing around, but then he said he was going to take my boy and my shop."

Sawyer exchanged a look with Liz. "Did he

say why he believed you deserved it? Have you crossed anyone that you can think of?"

Scratching his beard, Neil thought about it. "No, no, he didn't give me a reason. I just assumed the guy was a whacko. He was talking bananas. My wild days are long behind me. I don't make trouble with anybody. You can ask my wife. She'll tell you."

"May we see your phone?" Liz held out her hand. After he unlocked it and placed it in her palm, she looked through his calls. "Is this it? At ten thirty-five?"

The grieving father nodded. "Yeah. That's the one."

"From the exchange, it looks like it's from a disposable phone. A burner." Liz wrote the number down along with how long the call lasted. "Did you recognize the voice?"

Another shake of his head.

"Are you sure the guy didn't say anything else? I only ask because one minute and forty-five seconds is a long time." More had been said, Sawyer was certain of it.

Neil glanced around the room, once again thinking. "No. He, um, repeated it a few times. Yeah." He scratched his beard. "Wanted to make sure I got the message."

"Fireworks, he was going to take your son and your shop because you deserved it, but no reason was given. That's all?" Sawyer asked, wanting to be clear, and Neil nodded. "Do the words *Sins of the father* mean anything to you?"

Neil swallowed convulsively, his Adam's apple bobbing in his thick neck as his eyes turned glassy. "No," he said in a pained whisper. "Should it?"

It was plain to see that it did. Why not share everything he knew to help them catch this killer? What was he hiding?

"When was the last time you spoke with your son?" Liz asked.

"Sometime earlier. Before dinner. It's in there." He pointed to his phone.

Mike's name came up a little after four.

That confirmed the estimated time of death the ME had given them, between 4:30 p.m. and 5:30 p.m. "What did you two discuss?"

"Not much." Neil shrugged. "Someone had called him earlier and made a same-day appointment for that night. Mike planned to be in the shop for five to six hours."

Liz made a note. "Did he say who the appointment was with?"

"A guy who requested Mike. Insisted on having privacy and didn't want a bunch of other tattoo artists gawking at him. He wanted a really intricate tattoo on his chest of Vulcan, the god of..." His voice trailed off.

"Fire." Sawyer got up and came around the desk, sitting beside him. When Neil raised his head, with tears brimming in his eyes, Sawyer put a comforting hand on his forearm.

"The sicko who killed my boy and burned the place to the ground made an appointment?" Horror filled his face.

"It's our understanding the shop's hours varied." Liz's tone softened. "The only way to ensure Mike was the tattoo artist available at a specific time was to make an appointment."

Neil dropped his head into his hands and sobbed. "Do you think the murderer made Mike give him the tattoo before he killed him? If so, that's how you could find him. Right? Look for the tattoo."

"No. I don't believe he actually got a tattoo from Mike." Liz clasped her hands on the desk. "The killer wouldn't want to linger any longer than absolutely necessary."

There were no CCTV cameras near the front of tattoo parlor to capture the person going in around the time in question. "Did you have security cameras inside the shop?" Sawyer wondered. "With a backup downloaded to an online server?"

"No need. We don't keep cash in the shop. Debit or credit card only. Nothing inside a meth head would break in to steal. We've never had a problem. Until now."

"Did Mike live with you?" she asked, and Neil shook his head, tears leaking from the corners of his eyes. "Did he usually call when he was done for the night? Maybe after he locked up?"

"No, we didn't keep tabs on him like that. He was twenty-three. Did his own thing. We spoke to him once a day. Sometimes every other day."

"Mr. Steward, did you agree to sell your tattoo parlor to Kade Carver under the right terms?" Sawyer asked.

"I was willing to consider it." Neil sniffled. "If he found a new location that I liked. The offer, the money was pretty good. Evelyn, my wife, wanted me to take it. Mike didn't care either way."

Sawyer glanced at her to see if she had any more questions.

She shook her head. "Mr. Steward, if you can think of anything else, perhaps, if more details about the phone call come back to you, please don't hesitate to contact us." She handed him her card.

"You have to catch whoever did this." Neil stood and trudged out of the office.

Watching him pass the front desk, Sawyer turned to her. "You think he's holding back about the phone call, too?"

"A hundred percent. Whatever was said might be the key to helping us find the killer, but for some reason he's not sharing."

Deputy Russo made a beeline to the office. "There's a connection between Kade Carver and Isaac Quincy. Kade owns an apartment complex. Four buildings. One hundred units in total. Quincy is one of his tenants."

"Good work." Liz flashed a genuine smile.

"Carver is into details. Claims to know the names of all his tenants. He'd also know that Quincy has a record, and it would be easy enough to find out he's got a penchant for playing with fire," Sawyer said. "It can be hard for a convicted felon to reintegrate in society. Get a job. Maybe Carver offered him money or free rent to start the fires."

"Only one way to find out." Liz stood. "You got an address?"

Russo held up a piece of paper.

"Thanks." Sawyer took it from her, and the deputy left. "Are we riding separately or together?" he asked Liz.

"I didn't realize you were going to give me a choice."

He grabbed his cowboy hat from the side table and put it on. "That's the thing, Liz. You decide for both of us. It's always been about your choices." He could've kicked himself for going there. He hadn't meant to; the words had just slipped out and there was no taking them back.

A blank expression fell over her face like a mask, and the distance between them grew without either of them moving.

After holding his gaze, without responding for so long, tempting him to speak first, she finally breezed past him and out into the hall. The clipped pace of her steps all business. No seductive sway of her hips, no grace. A formidable stride that he loved.

He hurried to catch up.

"One car," she said flatly over her shoulder, not looking at him. "It's more efficient."

She was something else, and man, did he love her.

Chapter Ten

After the quiet car ride, where they each stayed in their respective corners, Liz let Sawyer take the lead at Quincy's third-floor apartment.

He approached the front door and knocked. Hard. "Isaac Quincy. LFD and FBI. Open up."

Movement came from inside, a shuffling sound and then hurried footsteps, but not toward the door. Metal creaked. "Fire escape?"

"He's running." Sawyer drew his weapon and kicked in the door, busting the frame. Glock at the ready, he swept inside.

Pulling her sidearm, Liz followed behind him.

The window at the back of the living room was wide open. She caught a glimpse of the top of Quincy's head as he pounded down the steps.

Sawyer darted through the living room and ducked out the window. Liz was right behind him.

Lifting his head, Quincy glanced at them with a panicked look and clattered down the first flight. The fire escape led to the roof of a smaller adjacent building. Quincy leaped over the metal railing, landed on the smooth blacktop, slipped once and took off.

Liz swore under her breath. "Quincy, stop!"

Sawyer hopped the railing with the skill of a gymnast over a pommel horse, but when his feet touched down, he clutched his injured side with a groan.

With little effort, she made it over the railing and kicked it into high gear. Sawyer chased him. Liz followed.

They ran across the rooftop. At the edge, Quincy jumped to the next building, making the six-foot leap, but dropped to his knees.

"Sawyer! Stitches!" she called out, not wanting him to aggravate or reopen his wound from absorbing the shock of the landing.

He halted at the ledge, either listening to her or using caution, and raised his weapon, taking aim. "Freeze, Quincy. Or I'll shoot."

The man dared to get up and take off running again.

Holstering her sidearm, Liz lengthened her stride, jumped to the next rooftop and landed in a tuck and roll. Then she popped up to her feet. "Stop!" she yelled.

But he didn't.

And neither did she.

Liz dashed after him and lunged, tackling Quincy, forcing him to his belly. She wrangled his arms behind his back and slipped on handcuffs. "Now we're going to chat down at the station instead of your apartment."

STARING THROUGH THE one-way glass of the observation room in the sheriff's department, Liz studied Isaac Quincy and considered how to play the interrogation.

Sawyer was standing in the back of the room, silently plotting how to throw her off guard, no doubt. She could feel his gaze on her, burning a hole in her backside.

"You were impressive back there." Sawyer came up beside her. "You jump from rooftops a lot?"

"Not every day." She glanced at him. "How is your side?"

"Sore, but I'm good." One corner of his mouth hitched up in a half smile.

Maybe it was the irresistible look he gave her or the adrenaline still pumping in her system that made her want to caress his cheek. Whatever the reason, she put it in check. "Are there any smokers out there?" She gestured to the bullpen.

"I think there are a couple. Why?"

Without answering, she headed out to the main area of the station. "Who has a lighter I can borrow?"

The deputy manning the front desk stood. He dug into his pocket, pulled out a Zippo and tossed it to her.

Catching it, she said, "Thanks." She dropped it in the pocket of her FBI jacket that she was still wearing and turned to Sawyer. "Let's go question him."

They headed down the hall. He opened the door for her.

She went in first, taking a seat at the metal table across from Quincy. The young man was pale and lean. A bit sweaty, which was to be expected after he ran. Wary brown eyes. Dark hair.

Sawyer pulled out the chair next to hers, making it scrape across the floor.

Straightening, Quincy began to fidget.

Liz met his nervous gaze. "We want to talk to you about the recent string of fires."

"I didn't start any of those fires." He spoke, using his hands in an animated way. His tone was immediately defensive. "I swear, I'm innocent."

"Of course you are." Sawyer leaned back in his chair. "That's why you were doing wind sprints across the roof, forcing us to chase you."

Perspiration beaded Quincy's forehead. He was anxious, but his eyes were angry. "I'm just tired of being harassed every time someone lights a match in this town."

"You're a convicted arsonist." Liz eyed him. "It's routine for us to question you when something like this happens."

"I did my time." Quincy put his elbows on the table, his expression turning indignant. "I got treatment inside. I'm rehabilitated. Ask my parole officer. Better yet, ask my court-appointed therapist."

"Oh yeah?" Liz wished she had a dollar for every time she heard that one. "So you don't get off on fires at all anymore?"

"That's right." He gave her a smug smile.

She reached into her pocket and slowly pulled out the Zippo. Watched Quincy's gaze drop to it. She fiddled with the metal lighter, turning it in her hand while he stayed transfixed. Flipping it open, she made him wait a few seconds before letting him see the flame.

Wrapping his arms around his stomach, he tried to look away, once, twice, and failed.

Liz snapped the lid of the lighter closed and watched the disappointment cross his face. "Want another?" She already knew the answer.

He nodded like a junkie in need of a fix.

She gave it to him. Holding the Zippo at eye level, even closer to Quincy's face, she struck the flint wheel, producing a flame. "Tell me about the Cowboy Way shop fire."

Licking his lips, Quincy smiled. "Perfection. It was a thing of flipping beauty." His eyes glazed over with that same Christmas-morning look. "In full swing by the time the fire department showed up."

Sawyer crossed his arms. "You admit to being there?"

"Well, I was at the grocery store two blocks away. Smelled the smoke. Had to follow it, and I found that glorious sight. So, yeah, I watched it. Along with half the town. No crime in that, or are you going to lock up everyone who was there?"

"Not everyone." Sawyer shook his head. "Only the firebug with a record."

"What did you think of the other fires?" Liz waved the flame. "Were those beautiful, too?"

Quincy shrugged with his gaze on the lighter. "I didn't see them. I was working the night the restaurant and the nail salon burned down. No reason for me to go to Bison Ridge."

"What about the inferno at Compassionate Hearts?" Warily, Sawyer studied him. "I'm sure you didn't miss that one."

"Wish I'd seen it, from what I heard on the news, but when I got off work, I went straight to bed. The fire happened sometime later while I was asleep."

Not unusual for him to keep track of the fires. "Where do you work?" She closed the lighter.

"Night shift. Road work. We're repaving Route 130." Quincy rattled off the name and number of his supervisor.

"Has Kade Carver ever asked you to work for him?" Sawyer asked. "In exchange for money or free rent?"

Confusion furrowed Quincy's brow. "Mr. Carver? No."

"What about any of Mr. Carver's employees?" Sawyer followed up.

The young man shook his head.

"Have you ever set a fire for someone else?" She put the lighter in her pocket. "For money?"

Quincy snickered. "That's not why I do it."

No, it wasn't. "Please answer."

"Never."

"Hard to believe," Sawyer said, "considering the way you looked at that lighter. Like a man willing to set a fire for any reason at all."

"You don't know me. You cops are all the same. I want a lawyer. Or I want out of here right now."

"You're free to go." Liz gestured to the door, and Sawyer gave her a side-eyed glance.

Isaac Quincy didn't waste a second scurrying out of the room.

"What are you doing?" Sawyer sighed. "We didn't even verify his alibi."

"He admitted to being at the Cowboy Way fire without him knowing we already had proof he was there. Quincy talked about it like he was admiring someone else's work. Not his own." She shifted in the chair, facing him. "It's natural for him to follow the other fires in the news, to remember when they happened. His alibi will check out."

"Don't tell me you believe he's rehabilitated."

Standing, she headed for the door. "Not at all. It's only a matter of time before he sets another fire. When he does, it won't be for someone else and certainly not for money."

They walked together down the hall.

"Some arsonists are paid," he said.

"True." She stopped in the doorway of the sheriff's office and leaned against the jamb. "But not Isaac Quincy. He's a pyromaniac."

He rested his shoulder on the other side of the door across from her, standing close. Intimately close. "That's exactly my point."

She could feel the heat radiating from his body. "I came here after giving a presentation at a symposium. During my seminar, I asked the participants—fire agency personnel, law enforcement, even a few insurance investigators—what was the definition of pyromania? Not a single one got it entirely right. Pyros deliberately set fires more than once. Showing tension or oftentimes arousal before the act. They are fascinated and attracted not only to fire but also to its paraphernalia. They feel pleasure, a sense of relief when setting them. But above all, they must also set fires for fire's sake. Not for money or revenge or attracting attention."

He hooked his thumb in his belt and leaned in. "Well, I guess I'll have to reread that chapter in your book." His minty breath brushed her face. "But if you're so sure Quincy is a pyro and not our guy, why did we haul him in for questioning?"

"I suspected earlier, but I wasn't sure until we

had him in the interrogation room. Running didn't help him, either. The more I think about this, whoever is behind the fires isn't a professional arsonist providing a service or doing it for profit. This is way too personal. Especially with Mike Steward's throat being cut. Then calling Neil, luring him to the fire, making him watch."

"Revenge. For the sins of the father."

"Most adult arsonists who aren't for profit are almost always seeking revenge."

"If only we knew why Neil Steward 'deserved it,'" he said, using air quotes.

"Makes me wonder if the others 'deserved it,' too, in the mind of our perpetrator. Did Chuck Parrot say whether he got a call before the fire?"

"When I talked to him, his entire focus was on the substantial amount of money he'd just lost and the fact he was financially ruined. He didn't mention it, and I didn't know to ask at the time."

Someone came into the station, drawing her gaze. "Don't turn around."

Sawyer did exactly what she told him not to do. A string of curses flew from his lips. "Bill Schroeder."

The mayor beckoned to someone with a stiff hand, and Deputy Russo hurried over to talk to him.

Liz grabbed Sawyer's arm and tugged him into the office. "Do yourself a favor and let me do the talking."

He glanced down at where she was touching him. "You expect me to stay tight-lipped and simply accept whatever horse manure he decides to dump on me?"

She let him go. "You're angry with me, I know—"

"I'm not angry." He stepped toward her. "I'm hurt. Confused. Because you won't talk to me. Fifteen years of no returned calls or emails. Here we are standing in the same room together, and I still can't get any answers."

Something in his eyes squeezed at Liz's heart, and she had to batten down her emotions. If she could have the toughest conversation of her life while working on this case with him and not lose focus, she would, but even she had her limits. "After things settle down." She looked back at the bullpen, where Russo and Schroeder were still talking.

"We could've been killed by that car bomb yesterday," he said, drawing her attention squarely back to him. "Things never settle down. There's always something."

Looking irate, Bill Schroeder headed for the office.

"Right now, that something is the mayor." She took a deep breath, wishing he'd stop pushing, even though he made a valid point. "But there is one thing I can do for you."

"What?"

"Protect you." When this case was done, he had to live in this town. Mouthing off to the mayor would not make his life easier. "Let me."

With a reluctant nod, Sawyer went around the desk, sank into a chair and propped his boots on the corner as Bill Schroeder charged inside the office and slammed the door shut.

"Why on earth would you accuse an upstanding citizen from a good family such as Kade Carver of arson and murder?" he asked, staring at Sawyer like Liz didn't exist.

"Bill." Removing her FBI jacket, she took a tentative step toward him. "Liz Kelley. I don't know if you remember me."

He'd been ahead of them in school by a couple of years and had also been a teen camper at the Wild Horse Ranch, but his last summer had been the one prior to the fire.

Finally, he met her eyes. His scowl softened. "I remember you. I also know about your little book. You're supposed to be an expert. I shouldn't have to tell you that the guy doing this is probably some lowlife who comes from a broken, abusive home with a history of violence and couldn't possibly be Kade Carver."

"Mr. Carver wasn't accused or charged," she said. "Simply questioned as part of this investigation."

"When I was informed the FBI would be assisting with this case, I was relieved at first. But now I see why nothing is getting done," Bill said, with a sneer. "Are you here to work or to canoodle with your old boyfriend?"

Sawyer let out a withering breath, but without uttering a word, he took out his phone and lowered his head.

Clasping her hands in front of her, Liz held tightly to her composure. "I'm here in a strictly professional capacity. My colleague, who, even after an attempt was made on his life to impede this case and was injured, has been working tirelessly to see justice served."

Bill rolled his eyes. "Spare me the song and dance. Save it for the press. Apparently, Erica Egan is lapping it up. Great article in the *Gazette*, by the way. Really pulled at the heartstrings," he said sarcastically. "What I want to know is if you're both incompetent? I demanded an update from Deputy Russo. She informed me that you had a convicted arsonist in your custody as a suspect and released him."

"Because he didn't set these fires." She strained for calm. "Would you like us to arrest anyone who fits the profile regardless of innocence or guilt?"

"How about you arrest someone? That'd be nice. The longer this goes on, the worse it looks for me." Bill smoothed down the lapels of his suit. "My opponent is running a tough-on-crime campaign. I need to be tougher. Do you understand?"

She swallowed a sigh. The man only cared

about himself and getting reelected. Some people never changed.

He and Sawyer were both from old money, the kind that came with influence and power. Bill's family made it from the Schroeder Farm and Ranch Enterprises, part of the largest distribution network of major suppliers of agricultural inputs. Sawyer's family made it from the Shooting Star Ranch, one of the biggest in the Mountain West region. That's where the similarities between the two of them stopped.

"I can assure you, Bill, that what will not help us resolve this case any faster is you getting on television talking about the arsonist, giving him all the attention he craves. Less than twelve hours after your reckless appearance on a major news network, which only served to embolden the perpetrator, he burned down the Cowboy Way and killed Mike Steward."

"How dare you accuse me of making this situation worse," Bill said, fury giving his voice a razor-sharp edge. "As though exercising my first amendment right somehow encouraged him to strike again."

"If the cowboy boot fits," she said.

"I could have your badge. Do you know that?" Bill crossed the room, coming up to her. "One call to my daddy." He held up a single finger, his tone setting her teeth on edge. "He plays golf with the governor, who knows the attorney general. Your boss's boss," he said, now pointing in her face, and she was half tempted to break the digit that was an inch from her nose to teach Bill the consequences of bad manners.

Sawyer barked out a laugh. "Did you really pull the Daddy card?"

He had been doing so well being quiet. Of course, it couldn't last.

Bill's gaze snapped to Sawyer, fixing on him.

But she stepped in front of the mayor, redirecting his anger. "I suggest the only comments you have to the press about this case are 'No comment.' Let the professionals working on this speak to the media about the facts. My boss is SAC Ross Cho." She scrawled his number, including extension, on the back of one of her cards. "Give him a call, he'll tell you the same, and by all means, take your chances trying to get me fired." Her record spoke for itself. No one at the bureau was going to cave because an entitled man-child was having a tantrum.

"We'll see if you're untouchable, *Lucky Liz,*" Bill said, and hearing the nickname sent a chill through her. "As for lover boy, if he doesn't solve this soon by putting someone behind bars or in a grave, I'll call a city council meeting and have his badge. You can bet your bottom dollar it won't be a game of chance then. That's a promise."

Bill waltzed out, leaving the door open and her exasperated.

"How did he get elected?" Spinning around, she waited for an answer from Sawyer.

"His daddy's money. Also, he puts on a good show at town hall meetings. Packs away his real personality and pretends to be someone pleasant."

"I forgot what he was like." She ran a finger under her scarf, longing to take it off. "How awful he could be."

Sawyer put his feet on the floor and sauntered over to her. "I didn't." He held up his phone, showing her what he'd been doing.

"You recorded the conversation?"

"Bet your bottom dollar I did," he said, imitating Bill.

She laughed, as he'd meant for her to.

"Let that schmuck call his council meeting." He smiled, his eyes glittering. "You did a great job drawing his fire away from me. Once again, impressive."

Fighting for him, having his back was nothing. She'd do anything for him. Sacrifice everything if it meant he'd be happy.

Snapshots of their teenage days together flickered through her head. Then she remembered something Bill had said. "Have you seen the *Gazette* today?"

Sawyer walked over to the side table, picked up a copy and quickly scanned it. When she tried to look, he pulled it away from her line of sight. "You don't want to see it."

Dread slithered down her spine. "Give me the gist."

"Egan dug." He grimaced. "She brought up the past. The fire. Us. All of it."

She cringed. This town was already overflowing with busybodies who delved into everyone's business for sport. Now her painful past had been rehashed as entertainment. It wasn't news.

Sawyer put a hand on her back and rubbed. She was tempted to accept the comfort, almost did, but she noticed everyone in the bullpen watching them.

Adjusting her scarf, she moved away, turning her back to the gawking deputies.

"Let's get back to work." He tossed the paper in the trash. "Instead of focusing on garbage."

He was right. She should've said it first.

"We need a lead. We're missing something with this case." But what?

Sitting behind the desk, she brought up on the computer screen the original pictures Russo had taken, not the zoomed in versions that focused on individuals, and looked them over, one after another. A sinking sensation formed in the pit of her stomach. Staring at the photos, she should've seen it sooner.

"What is it?" he asked. "You're thinking something dark."

"There's a possibility that we have to consider,"

she said, reluctantly. "Investigate to rule it out if nothing else."

His brow furrowed. "I'm not going to like this, judging by your tone, am I?"

She shook her head. He was going to hate it. "Some arsonists are firefighters."

"No," he snapped.

"Hear me out. It's a persistent phenomenon and a long-standing problem. Sometimes they suffer from hero syndrome, but I don't think that's the case here. It's clear this is about revenge."

"Not in my station," he said with a definitive shake of his head. "I know those people. Trained with them. Battled fires with them. No."

"Arsonists start early. Usually in their teens. If he was never caught and convicted, he could be flying under the radar. He's skilled. Knows how much accelerant to use, where to place it, the timer, the car bomb. It would be easy for him to hide in the department," she said, and he scrubbed a hand over his face. "We'd be looking for someone with a decreased ability to self-regulate. Might drink a little too much. Unlikely to succeed in relationships. Divorced. Never married. White male. Sixteen to thirty-five."

"That's half the station. Most are divorced or unmarried. Hell, I fit that profile."

"If there's a firefighter with a vendetta, who is using arson to kill his victims—"

"You're reaching. Yesterday, you thought this

string of fires and murders might be related to what happened at the summer camp."

She took a deep breath, hating the unease worming through her over having been mistaken about the link to the summer camp. "We have a time of death. Let's question them to see where they were." Since all the fires had started using a timer, they had no way to pinpoint when the devices had been planted. Mike Steward's death, as horrific and senseless as it was, might be the only way to find the killer. "Verify alibis. Investigate those who don't have one. Rule them out as suspects, if nothing else, and move on." *Hopefully.*

His frown deepened as he raked his hands through his hair, considering it.

"Do you have a better idea?" she asked.

"We talk to Chuck Parrot again to see if anyone called him before the fire."

"That will take five minutes. Questioning all the firefighters in your station as well as the volunteers will take hours. Possibly days. And that's with help from the deputies that Holden can spare. We need to get the ball rolling tonight. We can do it at the fire station to minimize the inconvenience and impact. Chuck Parrot can swing by there. What do you say?"

He groaned. "The olive branch they extended to me, consider it kindling."

Chapter Eleven

In his office at the fire department, Sawyer sat on the sofa trying to prepare himself to do this. Question his own as though they might be guilty. It left a bad taste in his mouth.

Gareth took a seat in the chair opposite him and Liz. From his expression, he wasn't too happy about this either but had agreed to let them interview everyone currently on shift and had someone calling those who were off to see if they didn't mind swinging in tonight. Otherwise, they'd be expected to come in tomorrow.

"Thank you for letting us get started with this as soon as possible," Sawyer said.

Resting an ankle on his knee, Gareth settled back in the chair. "Don't thank me until after you've spoken with Ted," he said, his lips giving a wry twist.

Sawyer wasn't looking forward to it.

Liz picked up her pen and notebook, about to get started, when the alarm in the building clanged. "Just when I thought we'd get through the day without a fire."

Gareth was up on his feet, rushing for the door. "Let me find out what it is." In less than a minute, he was back, already pulling on his gear. "Not a fire. Bad accident on I-80. A fuel truck and three cars. Interviewing the team will have to wait until tomorrow. But one off-duty person showed up. Tonight isn't a complete bust for you." Ducking out of the office, he waved at someone to go in and then was gone.

Tessa strutted inside, flashing a tentative smile. She was a slender woman with tempting curves on display in a formfitting sundress pulled off the shoulders. The hem was only a few inches lower than her backside. She wore matching cowboy boots and makeup, lips a bold, daring shade of red. Her dark blond hair was all glossy curls, skimming her bare shoulders. And she smelled good, too.

There was no denying she was a beautiful woman or that his hormones recognized it, but his heart only beat for Liz.

"Gareth told me you had some questions for everyone," Tessa said, her gaze fixed on his, and flipped her hair over her shoulder, kicking up the scent of her sweet perfume.

Clearing her throat, Liz tensed. "We do. Please have a seat. We'll try to make it quick."

Tessa slipped into the chair and crossed her legs, flaunting a dangerous amount of skin.

"You were on duty yesterday?" Sawyer asked.

"Yep." Smiling, she swung her leg and drummed her red-painted fingernails on the arms of the chair.

He kept his gaze up above her neck. "Did you leave the station at any time while on duty?"

"Twice. To respond to the fire in the morning at Compassionate Hearts and later that night to respond to the fire at the Cowboy Way."

"You were here in the station between four thirty and five thirty, and someone can verify it?" Liz asked, staring down at her notepad, even though she wasn't taking any notes. She was clutching the pen so tight her knuckles whitened.

"I was. We had gotten up from a nap around three. Then a group of us played cards until dinner."

Liz jotted it down. "Who did you play cards with?" she asked, and Tessa provided the names. "Then I think that's all we need from you."

"When I got here," Tessa said, "I was told I'm the only one coming in tonight," she said, and Sawyer wondered if her buddy Bridget was the one making the calls and had ensured no other off-duty personnel would show up.

He glanced at his watch and then at Liz. It was almost nine. "I guess we'll call it a night. It's late anyway." They could start fresh in the morning.

The three of them stood.

Tessa slinked up beside him and slid a hand up his arm, curling her fingers around his biceps. "Sawyer, can I speak to you privately?"

He turned to Liz, her face inscrutable, and then caught a flash of jealousy in her eyes. Or was it his imagination and he was seeing what he wanted?

"Take your time." Liz's voice was encouraging, even enthusiastic. She grabbed her things and headed for the door without looking back at him. "I'm going home. See you tomorrow," she said in a rush, disappearing out the door and shutting it behind her.

He gritted his teeth that they'd driven to the fire station separately to avoid the hassle of doubling back to pick her vehicle up later. He knew how this must appear to her and didn't want her leaving with the wrong idea. More importantly, he didn't want her at the house alone.

"Can we sit for a minute?" Tessa glanced at the sofa.

Sitting was how it would start. Then she'd climb onto his lap and lower his zipper. "I'll stay standing. What'd you need?"

"I know your heart and head is in the right place, but I don't think questioning everyone is going to go over well with the others," she said cautiously.

"There might be some tension for a few days, but once we catch this guy, it will all be worth it."

She moved closer, brushing her curves, the ones that could make a monk ache to touch her, against his body. "I know you said not tonight, but I'm free and you're free, and I could use the pleasure of your company." Running her hands up his chest, she wrapped her arms around his neck. "Let's go to my place and get dirty together." She moistened her lips. "Or we could lock the door and do it right here while everyone's out."

Many men would've loved to take what she was offering. He wasn't one of them.

Sawyer pulled her arms from around his neck and put lots of space between them. "Tessa, we won't be hooking up anymore." They hadn't for a while, not since she asked him if he ever wanted to get married and have kids and when would they start going out to dinner on a proper date? Alarm bells went off in his head, and that had been that for him. He had hoped they could've avoided the dreaded conversation. "It's not you. It's me."

"I scared you off, didn't I? I figured if I gave you a little time, a lot of space, you'd come back because you missed me."

He only thought of her when he saw her in passing and hadn't missed her, which was telling. But he didn't want to hurt her, either.

"I don't need things to get serious right now. I'm good just having fun. No strings attached," Tessa said, lying to him, possibly even lying to herself.

Putting his hands in his pockets, he edged farther back. "This isn't what I want."

"Tell me the truth. I know you've got needs, and one day you'll settle down."

"The truth is I want to get serious."

Her gaze flickered over his face as understanding dawned in her hurt eyes. "Just not with me."

He picked up his hat and put it on. "The right woman is back in my life. I can't lose her again."

"Liz."

Sawyer gave one firm nod.

"I got that feeling last night. When I pulled you to the side, you kept glancing over at her while we spoke. I had to give it one more shot."

"Did Bridget make sure no one else was coming in tonight?"

Biting her lower lip, she gave him a guilty smile.

"You're going to find the right guy," he said. "When you do, he's going to be lucky to have you."

Tessa sighed. "I got all dolled up for nothing. At least tell me I look nice."

"You look really nice."

"Thanks for being honest with me. I know plenty of guys who would've taken me up on my offer for a good time on that sofa and, once finished, would've chased after the woman he really wanted."

"I'm not that kind of guy." And Tessa deserved better.

She pressed a palm to his cheek. "Which makes this even harder. Because you're one of the good ones."

"I have to go."

"To chase after her?"

In a manner of speaking. "Yeah."

Confronting Liz about the past and getting answers he deserved was one thing. Knowing for certain whether she was still attracted to him, wanted him or cared for him was another story. The idea of her being afraid of getting hurt— by him—made something inside his chest crack open and bleed. And if that was the case, then he needed a different approach.

LIZ FINISHED BRUSHING her teeth and slipped on her cotton pajama bottoms and tank top. Turning off the light, she couldn't stop thinking about Tessa, her svelte figure or the dress she wore, which left very, very little to the imagination.

Not that Sawyer needed to imagine. He'd already enjoyed Tessa Anderson's entire package.

He was probably doing it again right now.

Good for him.

Acid burned through her veins. She needed to finish this case and get back to Virginia.

A car pulled into the drive.

Grabbing her weapon, she jumped from the bed and crept to the window. She shifted the edge of the curtain to the side and peeked out.

It was a red Fire Department SUV. Liz checked the time. She'd only been home for thirty minutes. He must have turned Tessa down. Surely, no easy feat, considering the dress, the hair, the cowboy boots.

Relief and regret battled inside her. He deserved to act like it was business, or rather fun as usual, not restricting himself simply because she was in town. Soon enough, she'd be gone.

Sawyer climbed out of the vehicle and shut the door, but instead of traipsing off toward the trees, he was making a beeline for her front door.

Her pulse spiked.

As if he sensed her watching him, he looked right up at her window, straight at her through the silver of darkness where she hid. Then he disappeared under the porch.

The doorbell rang. Her chest tightened. It rang again. And again.

What did he want? It was late, she was exhausted, the lights were out, and the house was quiet. Obvious "do not disturb" signs.

He knocked at the door.

Maybe there was another fire or murder and rather than call, he wanted to tell her in person. She put her weapon on the nightstand beside the knife she wore strapped to her ankle, grabbed her long-sleeve pajama top, buttoned it and headed downstairs. As she made it to the first floor, the knocking turned into a fist pounding.

She opened the door and yawned like he had roused her from sleep. "What is it that couldn't wait until morning?"

"I had a question." He stepped across the threshold and stalked toward her.

Liz shuffled away, but he kept coming. She backed up until she had no place left to go. He didn't say a word as he placed his palms on the wall behind her, on either side of her head. He leaned in, and his mouth crushed hard on hers, making her breath catch and her legs turn to jelly. She didn't fight. Didn't pull away. The wind had been knocked out of her by the suddenness, the urgency under it, and the scorching need that slammed into her like a force of nature.

He was kissing her with a hot, focused intensity. She couldn't stop herself from kissing him back, drinking in the taste of him, slipping her fingers into his hair, bringing him even closer. A moan slid up her throat, and the next thing she knew, her mouth was free.

He'd taken a step back and stared down at her, studying her, assessing something.

"What are you looking at?" she asked, her voice shaky, fragile. She hated the sound.

"I've got my answer." Sawyer winked, spun on his heel and headed for the door. "Good night." He slammed the door closed.

Had he asked a question?

THE NEXT MORNING, Liz rolled over in bed and hit Snooze on her beeping alarm clock for the fourth time, which was unlike her. She usually forced herself to get up, threw on her clothes and went for a run. Today, she was physically, mentally and emotionally exhausted. Between the arsonist-murderer on the loose and Sawyer wearing her down, she'd earned the extra rest.

Last night, after he kissed her, leaving her lips swollen and awareness coursing through her body, she couldn't sleep for hours. She'd ached.

Ached to be touched.

Ached to be with him.

Still did.

Looking down at her bare arm on the side that was worse, she ran her fingers over the variation in shades and texture.

As a rookie, she'd tried to get intimate with a guy, a fellow agent. They'd met during the academy, became friends, flirted. She told him about the accident. Downplayed the scars. Why go into graphic detail? After graduation, he asked her out. Back at her apartment, she'd swallowed her fear and thrown caution to the wind following a couple of shots of whiskey. Once her shirt came off, their make-out session changed, the gleam in his eyes slid from desire to distaste.

The awkwardness lasted for a moment and an eternity. She fumbled to shut off the light, as if that'd make a difference. The sun eventually had to rise—no hiding forever. He uttered an excuse about forgetting something work-related and having to get up early. That was that.

Even though she had built a life, stitched herself up with so many missing pieces, to this day, she wondered if some holes could never be filled, some wounds never healed.

Staring at her arm, she was painfully aware of the stark difference between knowing a thing and seeing it. Touching it.

The ache inside swelled. Tears gathered in the corners of her eyes. She clenched her jaw against the loneliness closing in around her.

I'm fine. I'm fine.

A buzzing pulled her from her thoughts. She glanced at her phone and cringed. Was there another fire? Another victim?

This case was a mess of cruel death and fiery destruction.

Shaking off her self-pity, she answered the phone. "Agent Kelley."

"Hello, this is Nurse Tipton calling from Laramie Hospital. Mrs. Martinez didn't make it through the night. She's passed."

Sitting up, Liz shoved back the covers and put her bare feet on the worn wooden floor. "Thank you for letting me know." She clicked off.

The weight of another senseless death was heavy not only on her shoulders but also in her heart. They had to find this guy before he did more harm.

She rushed through a shower. Not bothering to blow-dry her hair, she brushed it thoroughly. She decided on slacks, a gray scarf with delicate blue polka dots, and light blue button-down.

In the kitchen, she made coffee as she stared out the window at the tent Sawyer had slept in again. She fired off a text to him about Aleida and got to work on whipping up a quick breakfast. She was at the stove scrambling egg whites and chopped up veggies with her back to the door when she heard him come in. The screen door snapped closed behind him.

"I'm sorry," he said. "About Aleida."

She didn't turn to look at him. Simply nodded.

He stood still a minute and then headed upstairs, and the shower started. She made a couple of breakfast burritos and, after leaving one for him on the table, took hers and coffee in a travel mug outside onto the porch.

She sat in one of the old rocking chairs and, though her appetite hadn't kicked in yet, munched on the food.

Her father had been a fourth-generation farmer. Their property—before they'd sold most of it to the Powells—reached up from the break land plateau to Big Horn Ridge. She loved the snowcapped rolling mountains, the brown and green hills, wide open space, clean air, the lack of congestion. The view helped put things in perspective, making it hard to deny the sense of loss inside, the gnawing emptiness that hollowed her out that had nothing to do with the case.

Not once in her career had she allowed her personal business to interfere with her job. Somehow, she had convinced herself it was due to the fact she was a good agent. Every time she looked at Sawyer, she questioned that conviction. Not her being a good agent part. Maybe it had been so easy for her to separate the personal from the professional because she'd never had anything else in her life before that she cared about.

And she did care for him. Deeply.

The screen door creaked as he stepped outside, shutting the front door. "I'm ready if you are."

Getting into his vehicle was her response. Sawyer drove while he ate. With her fingers laced together, hard, she stared out the window until they pulled up to the fire station on the side of the building where his office was located.

There was a long moment of silence, the only sound the running engine and AC blowing. Sawyer reached over and covered her hands with one of his palms. She hadn't realized how cold she was until his warmth penetrated.

A knock on the driver's side window drew their attention, and he moved his hand. Erica Egan stood on the other side wearing a skintight tank top, bent over, with an enviable amount of cleavage on display. She held up a tray with three coffees and flashed a pearly white smile. "Time to chat."

As Sawyer groaned, they both got out of the car.

He slammed the door shut. "After the last article, no more quotes." He headed for the door to the building.

Wearing khaki shorts and heels that showed off her long, taut legs, she click-clacked ahead of them and threw herself in front of the door. "We had a deal."

Liz's gaze swept over Erica, her bare arms, smooth legs—her effortless sex appeal. It made Liz wonder why she hadn't ever appreciated the curve of her neck when she was younger, the smoothness of its skin. How she had even taken for granted her pale freckles.

She tugged on the neckerchief.

"You brought up painful things that should've been left in the past and out of the *Gazette*." Sawyer crossed his arms. "Things that have no bearing on this case."

"I beg to differ," Erica said. "You two have history, and I picked up on a certain vibe between you, which might affect how you handle the investigation."

"What you picked up on was that I'm not interested in letting you sidle up to me for information." He reached for the door handle.

The journalist blocked him. "I framed both of

you in a positive light and used the entirety of Agent Kelley's glowing quote about you."

Erica offered Liz a coffee cup. She accepted it, though she wouldn't drink it. Paranoia prevented her from consuming food and beverages from strangers. Not that she thought the reporter was going to poison her. She simply couldn't do it, but accepting the coffee was a gesture of good will.

"I also did as you asked," Erica continued. "No vivid descriptions of the fire. I painted the perpetrator as a monster and highlighted not only the loss of two parents but also the awful impact on the entire community."

"You read the article, Sawyer." Liz glanced at him. "Did she?"

By the tightening of his jaw, Erica had. "Nothing else about the fire fifteen years ago or describing Liz as the girl who survived. Agreed?"

Grinning, Erica handed him a cup.

He took the peace offering.

"A source told me you are changing the focus of your investigation to the firefighters, as you may suspect one of them is the culprit. Can you confirm or deny?"

How did she find out so quickly? Sawyer had to call Gareth, who in turn called Ted, last night to set up the interviews for all personnel today, but word had traveled much faster than either of them had expected.

"Who told you?" Sawyer asked. "And don't give me any hogwash about confidential sources."

"I overheard a couple of firefighters griping about it at the bar last night. Beyond that I can't reveal my sources. Is it true?"

"We have to examine every possibility," Liz said. "Today we're only conducting routine interviews. We thank the fine men and women of the LFD and VFD for their cooperation and appreciate their invaluable service to the community."

"Have a good day, Ms. Egan." Sawyer grabbed the handle and opened the door, letting Liz inside first. Once the door closed on the reporter, he said, "Holden and his deputies will be here soon to help out."

"It's going to be a long day." Probably grueling. "Are you ready for this? For their skepticism. For the hostility." She'd been in this situation before—questioning firefighters—and what she'd faced was nothing short of vitriol.

"Does it matter if I'm ready? We have a job to do."

Chapter Twelve

"This is unbelievable," Ted Rapke said, sitting in a chair in Sawyer's office, his face rigid with tension. "You actually think it's one of us?"

"I don't." Sawyer's head was throbbing after going through this for hours. The same questions, similar responses, different firefighters. "But it's necessary."

Scooting to the edge of the sofa beside him, Liz rested her forearms on her thighs. "Please answer the question. Where were you between four thirty and five thirty last night?"

Ted sighed. "I left my shift early. Around three. Three-thirty. I met my fiancée, Cathy, and was with her the rest of the night."

"I'm sure she'll verify." Liz gave a tight smile. "Why did you leave early?"

"We recently got engaged. I haven't given her much input on the engagement party. Telling her whatever she wanted was fine with me apparently wasn't good enough. Her mom was coming into town this morning, and she wanted to go over things the night before. Put on a good show. You know? Gareth agreed to cover for me."

"Has your relationship been rocky?" she asked.

Ted's gaze swung to Sawyer and then back to Liz. "What has that got to do with anything?"

Sawyer gritted his teeth, hating to subject the guys to this. "She needs to form a complete profile of everyone."

"Not per se." Ted rubbed his hands up and down his thighs. "I've been married twice before. I want to make this one work."

"What time did you meet her and where?" Liz opened a bottle of water and took a sip.

Ted shrugged. "Maybe four. At her place."

"Do we have enough?" Irritation ticked through Sawyer.

Liz sat back and crossed her legs. "Sure. We'll need to contact your fiancée, but that's all for now."

"You know we've all been through a background check. We risk our lives every day to save people. It's one thing to question us, dragging us in on our day off, or asking us to lose sleep, but you shouldn't put the volunteers through the wringer." He pushed to his feet, with disgust stamped on his face. "Their numbers dwindle every year."

"One more question," Liz said. "You know everyone in the department and the volunteers very well."

Ted narrowed his eyes at her. "That's a statement, not a question, but yeah, I do."

"Do you have any rock stars? Someone who can't get enough of the job, works extra shifts, a volunteer who joined young and is at every single call, at the front of every work detail."

Ted's face hardened. "You should be ashamed of yourself, Liz. Now you want to go after someone who's dedicated and earnest. Is this a joke? What kind of investigation are you running?"

"Sadly, this is no joke." Liz stood. "At least one hundred arsonists who are also firefighters are convicted every year. In North America alone. That's only the ones who've been caught. If this arsonist is a firefighter, then 'earnest' is precisely who we are looking for, because beneath that layer of dedication is a need for self-importance. It's the type we go after when a serial arsonist is running around, and frequently enough, there's good reason."

Waving a dismissive hand at her, Ted walked out of the office.

Sawyer jumped to his feet and went after him. "Hold up," he said, and Ted stopped but didn't turn around. He hurried around to face him. "I don't like this any more than you do. The goal is to eliminate everyone in the LFD and VFD as suspects. But if this guy is hiding somewhere in our ranks, it's unacceptable. One thing we take pride in is our integrity and the trust that the community has in us. If one of our own is an arsonist and a murderer, he's everything we detest."

The words gave Ted pause, deflating the anger in his face. Slowly, he nodded. "You're right, but that's still a mighty big *if*."

A door across the hall from them opened. Holden and Joshua Burfield stepped out and shook hands.

Ted walked away, heading over to Josh. "Want to get out of here and grab a quick drink before I have to explain to my future mother-in-law why we're being questioned?"

"Sure, let's get Gareth," Josh said. "Hey, have you set a date for the engagement party?"

After this, Sawyer doubted an invitation was in the cards for him.

"Not yet." Ted gave a weary shake of his head. "Can't agree on a venue. I don't want to spend as much money on this party as we will on a wedding."

Holden followed Sawyer back into his office and closed the door.

"How's it going?" Liz asked.

"So far, most everyone we've questioned have had alibis."

"Let me guess." Liz sighed. "Thirty percent were here on duty. The rest were with loved ones."

Holden put his finger on his nose. "Bingo. Girlfriend, fiancée, brother, mother. I'll have a deputy verify them all."

"We have a list, too," Liz said. "At the top of ours is Ted Rapke. We need solid times from the fiancée."

Sawyer bristled. Ted could be aggravating and hold a grudge. That didn't make him a murderer and an arsonist.

"I've also got two we have to look into deeper," Holden said. "Alibis are weak."

"Who?" Sawyer sat down.

"Gareth McCreary. He wasn't on duty at the time in question because he was getting ready to fill in for Ted. States he went to the grocery store on Third to pick up stuff to cook dinner for the company, paid cash and can't find the receipt. Arrived at the station at five. Someone else said he didn't arrive until five thirty. We'll check the surveillance cameras at the grocery store to see when he was there."

"The store is only two blocks from the Cowboy Way." It had been a quick walk for Isaac Quincy.

"The other person?" Liz asked.

"Johnson, the probie."

Sawyer recalled seeing him at the fire. "But he was on duty."

"He was, but he left the station earlier that day to run an errand. Picked up a prescription and pastries from Divine Treats."

Not good. Wincing, Sawyer scratched the stubble on his jaw. He needed to shave. "The pastry shop is around the corner from the tattoo parlor."

Liz stretched her neck and adjusted her scarf. "What time?"

"He was gone from five to six. It'll be easy to establish exactly when he picked up the prescription. Divine Treats is a different story. There are no cameras inside or at the traffic lights on the block. We'll check with the stores across the street. I think there's even an ATM, too."

"Sounds good." Liz finished her water. "If we can't clear McCreary and the probie, let's see if they'll agree to take a polygraph test."

"All right. One more thing. Josh Burfield couldn't convince all the volunteers to come in for questioning. Two took it as an offense. One quit. I'll talk to them personally tomorrow." Holden yawned, and exhaustion was starting to set in for Sawyer, too. "It's getting late. I'm cutting my deputies loose, but I'll stick around a few more hours to help you question the next team on the way in. Best to push through what we can tonight." His cell phone buzzed. He answered it. "Chief Deputy Powell." While he listened, his gaze slid to him and then Liz. "Okay. Wait a sec. I'm going to put you on speaker." As he did so, he said to them, "We got something on the hotline Russo thinks you need to hear." He moved closer. "Go ahead and play it, Ashley."

"This came in a few hours ago, but we just now got to it because we've been inundated with worthless calls and phony tips. Here you go."

The message played. "You think I'm a monster. I'm anything but." The voice was deep and sinister. Electronically modified. "I am vengeance, making them reap what they have sown. Ask them how they built their businesses, where they got the seed money. And they will lie. Ask what they're hiding. And they will lie. I took a son for the sins of the father. Did he tell you about our chat? Did he tell you why he has been punished? Or did he lie? I have taken everything from two, leaving them their lives and their lies as their cross to bear. Fire was my weapon. My anger, my hatred, was best turned into a flammable fuel. Because it's effective and nothing burns as clean."

"That's the end of it," Russo said. "We're trying to trace where the call came from."

Sawyer swallowed around the thick knot in his throat. "I thought I'd be relieved if he left a message," he said, feeling the complete opposite. "Like we'd get a clue, or he'd tip his hand, and we'd see some way to stop him."

"Can you play it again?" Liz asked. The second time they listened to it, she took notes. "Russo, we're going to speak to Parrot today. Can you contact Neil Steward and ask where he got the money to open the tattoo parlor? The same with Aleida Martinez's husband. He might be able to fill in some blanks for us."

"I'm on it."

Holden disconnected.

"He may not have left us a clue," Liz said, "but he gave us a way to find one. It's getting Steward to tell us what he's hiding."

"Maybe Parrot will be more forthcoming," Sawyer said, hoping for the best but expecting more lies. Neil had lost his son and his shop, and still he was determined to protect his secret.

A deputy poked his head into the office. "I've got another firefighter for you to question."

"I'll take him," Holden said, moving to the door.

Sawyer glanced at his watch. It was only five, but it felt much later. "Thanks, Holden."

"No problem." His brother gave a two-finger salute. "Here to serve." He left the office.

"It almost sounded like our guy was finished." Sawyer grabbed a bottle of water. "The way he used the past tense."

"Possibly. It's been two days with no fires. No car bombs. No murders." She stared at her notes. "But part of it was also in present tense. I *am* vengeance. *Making* them reap what they have sown. He was careful with the way he worded it for a reason. His type gets a thrill out of manipulating law enforcement."

"I hope he's done and that there are no others he intends to punish. But he does want us to find out what Steward and Parrot are lying about. Perhaps that's part of his plan. How he gets to us. If it's illegal, then we'll finish the punishment."

"That's what they do. Manipulate while reminding us that he's in charge. Even if he is finished with his vendetta, we're not going to let him get away with murder and arson." Resting her head on the back of the sofa, she pinched the bridge of her nose and closed her eyes. "We need a break in this case. What if you're right and we're wasting time conducting these interviews?" She heaved a shuddery breath. "What am I missing?"

"I never said it was a waste of time. I don't want to believe someone I know, I trust and I've worked with is capable of something like this. Have your instincts been wrong before on other cases?"

Her lashes lifted. "No, but—" she tilted her head toward him "—being back here is messing with my head."

She neglected to mention whether he was having any effect on her heart. He didn't want to be a distraction. Something to avoid. He wanted to be a safe place for her to fall when she needed it. He wanted to be there for her in every way.

Sawyer took her hand in his and the minute their skin touched sparks fired through his whole body. He rubbed the tendons along her inner wrist, a careless caress. Or maybe a careful one. He wasn't sure, but when she didn't pull away, he was starting to think that if he wore her down bit by bit, she'd eventually stop running. Talk to him.

"What's your plan tonight?" she asked.

"What do you mean?"

"Where do you intend to sleep? I hope it's at

home in your bed and not in the tent again. You need a good night's rest."

Still rubbing her wrist, he stretched his torso until a twinge in his side made him stop. "I'm touched you care, even though you keep denying it."

"If you're tired, you're not going to be at your best during this investigation."

Leaning back, he angled toward her so that their thighs touched. "I see. You're only concerned about my job performance."

"That's not what I meant." Her voice softened.

Sawyer brushed hair away from her face, trailing his fingertips along her cheek to her chin and let it linger there. That was the thing about Liz. She always made him want to get closer. Always pulled him in, without even trying. "Care to clarify?"

A charged silence bloomed between them. She stared at him, her eyes pale green pools of warmth and uncertainty. All he wanted was to erase her doubt. About herself and him.

"I don't want to repeat the past," he admitted. "I know you've said you can't, but you need to know that I can't stop trying because I've never stopped loving you."

Her lips parted, her eyes going wide.

A sharp rap on the open door had them pulling apart. Chuck Parrot entered. "I guess the *Gazette* got it right about you two."

The last thing Sawyer wanted was for anyone to mention the article again.

Liz's shoulders tensed. "What do you mean?" she asked, and Sawyer was grateful she didn't know all the details in the article.

Parrot schlepped in—his thinning red hair wild and wiry as though he hadn't combed it—and plopped down in a chair like he'd been drinking or hadn't stopped in days. "Erica Egan wrote that you two had been lovers years ago until tragedy separated you and that this case has rekindled your connection."

The reporter had swapped one sensational focus for another. "Egan only cares about seeing her by-line beneath the front-page headline."

"Doesn't mean she's wrong." Chuck pulled a flask from his back pocket.

"You'll have to wait," Sawyer said, "until we're done here to resume drinking."

Flattening his mouth in a thin line, Chuck sagged in his seat but kept hold of the flask, resting it on his round belly. "Well, hurry up so I can get back to drowning my sorrows." He shook the metal container.

Sawyer glanced at Liz to see how she wanted to handle it. She intensely eyed Parrot like a puzzle she wanted to piece together. So he got to the point. "Did you receive a threatening phone call shortly before your restaurant was burned down?"

The question sobered him quickly. He straightened, his eyes turning alert. "Excuse me?"

Sawyer waited for a beat, studying him. "Did someone call you minutes before the fire and threaten you?"

Chuck hesitated, and Sawyer could see the deliberation on his face. "No. No one called me. Why do you ask?"

"Because someone called Neil Steward right before the Cowboy Way was torched," Sawyer said. "Threatened to take away his son and his shop."

His gaze bounced around as Chuck lowered his head. "Did the man say why he was going to do that to Neil?"

"I never said it was a man who called Neil."

Chuck opened the flask and took a sip. "Merely assumed."

"I know you from somewhere," Liz said. "Don't I? Your face, your voice, very familiar."

"I don't think so. Maybe I have one of those faces. People seem to think they know me for some reason."

The round shape. Freckles. Pale complexion. Orange-red hair. His face was distinctive. Chuck was forty-two, ten years their senior, though he looked older, so Liz didn't know him from school.

"It'll come to me. In the meantime, may we see your cell phone?" she asked.

His brows drew together, and he moved his

hand, covering his pocket that had the bulge of his phone. "No, you may not."

"Withholding information or evidence in a criminal investigation is obstruction of justice." Her tone was soft.

"I'm the victim here. You might want to remember that."

"Don't you want to help us catch this guy?" Sawyer asked.

"Yeah," Chuck spat out, nodding, "of course."

Sawyer cocked his head to the side. "Then tell us about the phone call."

"I would." Chuck stood. "But I didn't get one." He headed for the door.

"CP," Liz called out, and Parrot spun around. "That's what everyone called you on the Wild Horse Ranch."

He didn't say anything, his face turning ghostly white.

"It took me some time to recognize you. Easier here in the light of the office. You've put on weight. Your hair has thinned. Aged quite a bit. But you worked there my first year." She rose and edged toward him. "As a ranch hand, but you weren't there the next summer when the fire that killed the Durbins happened, right?"

Chuck shrugged. "Sure. So what?"

"Why did you say I didn't know you?"

Another shrug from him. "Guess I didn't make the connection. I don't recall every stinking kid that passed through there. Why? Is that a crime, too?"

He was a bad liar. Chuck Parrot had already admitted to reading the article in the *Gazette*. The Wild Horse Ranch fire had been mentioned. Even if he didn't remember Liz, he was aware of the connection.

Liz smiled in that practiced saccharine way Sawyer recognized. "Did Neil work there around the same time as you?"

Chuck turned the flask up to his mouth, taking another hit. Probably stalling. "You'll have to ask him about his previous work history."

"Where did you get the seed money to open your restaurant?" she asked.

Chuck's brow furrowed, and he rocked back on his heels like the question had been a physical blow. "Wh-what difference does it make?"

Maybe all the difference in the world.

"Where?" she pressed.

He rubbed his hand over the back of his neck. "Loan from the bank."

Ask and they'll lie.

Why?

"Which bank gave a ranch hand a five-figure loan to open a restaurant with nothing for collateral?"

Sawyer loved watching Liz work. She was sexy as she closed in, throwing razor-sharp questions to get at the truth. Not to mention seeing her chase down a suspect had been oddly thrilling.

"You don't know me or what I had to use as collateral," Chuck said defensively. "Frankly, it's none of your business. What should be is finding the sick SOB who took everything away from me. Is there anything else?"

She shook her head and followed him to the doorway, where she watched him leave. "How much do you want to bet Neil worked there, too?"

"It was a popular place. The Durbins hired many ranch hands over the years, and they were the only camp within a hundred miles that catered to older teens."

She cast a glance at Sawyer over her shoulder. "You still don't think there's something there, at the very least, something about the Wild Horse Ranch, rather than the fire, is the connection?"

"I'm not saying that." He was playing Devil's advocate. Statistically, this was more than coincidence. "We've got to look at it from all angles. Test the theory."

"I wonder if any records from the ranch still exist."

"The fire wiped out the main house and the cabins. The property was sold. Everything leveled. The Durbins didn't have any kids who we could speak with. But I do think there's something there." He came up alongside her. "Chuck knows you, but he lied about it because he didn't want us to associate him with the ranch. He also lied about not getting a threatening phone call and where he got his seed money for the restaurant. For whatever reason, Chuck and Neil are hiding the same thing. If we can figure out what it is, the connection will be solid."

"It'll have to wait." She gestured down the hall. The next team of firefighters had arrived to be questioned.

Chapter Thirteen

He had enjoyed calling into the hotline, airing his grievance, giving his retribution a voice. Now others would wonder about the dirty deeds of those on his list. What he didn't enjoy was Liz's meddling. Yet again. He thought he'd be able to savor making her suffer, taking Sawyer away while she was forced to watch and dealing with her later in Virginia.

Turns out, she was a sharper agent than he'd assumed and should have given her more credit. She and Sawyer were asking all the right questions to all the right people, circling like sharks, getting closer than he could allow, smelling blood in the water.

Somehow, they had even corrupted the lovely Erica Egan. In the *Gazette*, she lauded Kelley and Powell for their efforts in the investigation. Baited readers to root for the star-crossed lovers on their journey to prevail as they rekindled a connection. It made him want to gag. All the while, Egan failed to describe the glory of his handiwork. Instead, she labeled those who had sold their souls to the devil as innocent victims. Called him a monster!

When he was only seeking justice.

Removing Liz Kelley and Sawyer Powell from the playing field was the safest answer to his growing problem. Then the reporter would revert to her old style—he was helping sell more papers—and he didn't need those two meddlers to ruin his game. After all, he had a spectacular finale planned. Something no one expected. Something no one could stop once it started. Something the likes of which no one in the Mountain West had ever seen. He was going to finish with a big *boom*.

More pain and suffering and fire was necessary. The greater the effort, the grander the gesture, the sweeter the reward. In the end, he'd get what he wanted, what he needed, and all the patience he'd shown, the risks he had taken, all the blood he had shed, would be worth it.

But first, he needed Liz and Sawyer out of the way. No more underestimating them.

He watched the cursed lovebirds slide into the red SUV that was parked right in view of the surveillance camera. He hadn't been able to get anywhere close to it. The inconvenience only forced him to improvise.

Regrettably, he wouldn't be able to take care of those two himself tonight. In case something went wrong, he needed an airtight alibi that was above reproach. For this one, he needed assistance. Someone he trusted.

Liz's luck was finally about to run out. She and Sawyer were completely unaware of what lay ahead and how their night would end.

SAWYER HAD TOLD her that he still loved her. Liz didn't know if that was possible. Or healthy. Or best for him.

That was all she could think about on the nerve-wracking drive back to Bison Ridge. Maybe he wouldn't bring it up tonight. Let them get some sleep and tackle it tomorrow.

She glanced at her cell. It was on ten percent power. She needed to grab her phone charger from the rental.

Sawyer pulled up behind her vehicle, which was in front of the house, and put the SUV in Park.

"I don't know about you, but I'm exhausted." She hopped out. "Good night," she said, closing the door.

He was right behind her. "Are we going to talk about it?" His voice was dark and deep and rumbly.

No. "Tomorrow. Okay?" She headed for the rental. "I'm beat."

She wasn't up to handling Sawyer. Not tonight. He'd always been able to see right through the mask she tried to wear to hide her emotions.

Training had made her better, but still, he had that way about him. Like he could see her soul. The last thing she wanted was for him to glimpse her weakness.

"I told you I love you."

She faltered to a stop, her stomach tightening in a knot. "I know."

He put a hand on her shoulder and turned her around to face him. "I deserve a response," he said, gentling his tone, making it soft as cotton. Then he waited and waited. "Give me something, Lizzie," he said, the only one she ever allowed to use the nickname.

"Thank you." The two clumsy words tumbled from her mouth.

Sawyer shook his head as if he hadn't heard her correctly. "Thank you?" He reared back, pulling his hands from her shoulders. "Thank you," he snapped. "Tell me you don't love me. Tell me what you felt died a long time ago. Tell me that you don't want me the way I want you. Or tell me that you *do* love me. But don't say 'thank you.'"

Steeling herself, she looked at him, meeting his darkening stare, concealing the agony roiling inside her. "I don't want you to sleep in the tent tonight. Call Tessa. Give her a real chance. You might be more compatible than you realize."

He nudged the tip of his black cowboy hat up with his knuckle. "You're still trying to decide for both of us. As though what I want isn't a factor in this equation. You've gotten too accustomed to acting stoic, running away from anything that makes you feel something. No boyfriend. No husband. No friends. No pet. What about your family? All you've got is that badge and a gun when you deserve a hell of a lot more to fill the empty spaces in your life."

"You're one to talk. Where's your girlfriend or wife or pet?" she asked, skipping over the friends and family part since he had her there. "Who are you to judge me?"

"I noticed you neglected to address how you keep making unilateral decisions that affect both our lives. I'm done letting you kick me to the side with no explanation. You want to know why?" he asked, but he didn't wait for her to answer. "I am not a puppy, who'll slink away and lick his wounds. I'm a coyote." He started howling.

At her.

What in the world? Had he lost his mind?

COLOR ROSE IN her cheeks. The only proof he was getting to her, making her feel something.

"Please," she said, "stop howling like some wild thing."

He howled again, this time even louder, letting out his frustration and his misery.

She heaved out a breath. "You have no right to make unfounded assumptions about my life," she said, raising her voice over his howls. "I have a great job. I'm proud to be an agent. To have a purpose." She glowered at him.

There she went, bringing up work as a deflection, so he kept on howling.

"I've built a good life and I'm perfectly f..." Her voice trailed off as she caught herself, something dawning in her eyes.

"What? You're perfectly *fine*?"

He must have struck a chord. She narrowed her eyes, lips thinning, spun around and opened the door to her rental car.

"I appreciate your concern, but go home." Her tone was weary. She reached inside the car and grabbed something. "This day has pushed us to our breaking point. You need to get some sleep. We both do."

Go home. He should do as she asked and let her be, but something inside him demanded he stay. This was where they needed to be, at their breaking point, so they could have a breakthrough.

She slammed the car door, holding a phone charger, and turned toward the house.

But he was right on her, closing the distance. He gripped her arms, making her face him. "Every good memory I have is tied up with you." His heart thudded in his chest.

Tears glistened in her eyes. "Then it's time to make good memories with someone new."

"Do you ever think about us?"

Her bottom lip trembled. "I try not to," she said, her voice breaking right along with his heart.

"I think about you every single day." Though his nights were the hardest. Yes, he'd had other lovers, but being with them only made him miss her more. When he was alone in his bed with only his memories for comfort, his regrets tortured him. "I've loved you for so long that I don't remember what it's like not to."

He'd let her run away before, but this time, things would be different. This time, he would fight for her and not give up.

A vehicle approaching, the engine a loud growl, had him pivoting toward the sound. A black motorcycle came down the road way too fast for the speed limit. Alarm pulsed through him. The person was wearing all black, a helmet covering his face. Sawyer had a split second of recognition as the motorcycle slowed, moonlight bouncing off steel. A gun.

An icy wave of fear rushed over him.

"Sawyer!"

Liz's voice barely registered as instinct kicked in. He whirled her away from the line of fire, and then they were both on the ground with his body covering hers, pain flaring in his side as a shot cracked the air.

The window where they had been standing shattered. Glass rained down on them. Thunder from more gunshots breaking windows in the house. He pressed her flat to the ground as another shot punctured a tire. He drew his weapon. A third bullet pinged off the frame only centimeters from his head, close enough to feel biting heat. He shifted even lower.

The motorcycle sped away, gunning the engine, tires screeching, leaving the odor of burnt rubber in the air.

Sawyer lay there, his body fully covering hers, one arm curled around her head, his face buried in her hair. He waited for a fourth shot that never came. They were gone. For now. He strained to hear if the vehicle had turned around and was coming back. Or perhaps stopped down the road and the gunman was on foot.

It would have been reckless, not to mention foolish, for the person to get off the motorcycle or give them a chance to catch the license plate. Then again, their assailant shot at an FBI agent in front of her house, so how wise could he be?

Sawyer's shoulder had taken the brunt of the fall when they'd landed. Her right arm was beneath him, her Glock looking heavy in her small hand. She'd drawn her weapon as he'd pulled her down, and he'd done likewise. "Are you hit? Injured?"

"No, but you're smothering me. Does that count?" She pushed his chest and he moved.

"I'm going to go after him." Anger burned along his nerves. This had gone too far. Liz could've been hurt. Or worse killed. Before he could get up from the ground, she caught his arm.

"You were shot. You're bleeding." She touched his forehead.

It stung. "Just a scratch. The bullet grazed me." He hadn't even realized how close he'd come to getting shot in the head. "He's getting away."

Still, she held on to him, worry heavy in her eyes. "He's already gone. Made it to the fork in the road by now. We can't be sure which way he went, and the motorcycle gives him off-road options. We are not splitting up."

Was that all it took, nearly taking a bullet for her to see reason?

"We'll call it in, and I'll get you cleaned up." She holstered her weapon and found her phone.

"You're not staying here."

"This is my house. I won't be run off."

"It isn't safe. First the car bomb. Now this. We're going to the ranch." His voice brooked no argument. He would do anything to keep her safe.

She squeezed her eyes shut. "I don't think I can face your family, handle the hugs and kisses and questions—"

"I live in the apartment above the garage. No one has to know you're there, if you stay with me instead of a guestroom in the main house." There was also the B&B in town, but it was much more exposed, leaving their vehicles vulnerable. "You can have the bed and I'll take the sofa. Okay?"

He waited for more arguments and was ready with alternative solutions. No matter her response, she wasn't staying. He was going to make sure she was protected.

Reluctantly, she nodded. Her gaze flew back to the cut on his head and she threw her arms around him in a tight hug. "I'm so glad you're alive."

So was he.

Glad they were both alive.

Chapter Fourteen

Liz was still shaken by the close call. Whoever had shot at them had gotten away without a trace. They didn't catch the license plate to have something substantial to go on.

The sheriffs in Laramie and Bison Ridge as well as the police in nearby Wayward Bluffs had patrols on the lookout for one man, wearing black, riding a black supersport bike. Neither she nor Sawyer had caught the make to narrow down the field of what they were looking for.

Sawyer pulled up to the wrought iron gates emblazoned with his family ranch's shooting star brand. He punched in the code and the massive gate swung open. They pulled through, taking the long, tree-lined driveway illuminated by LED lights, and a wave of memories assailed her. All good and warm but still hard to face.

The Powell ranch was something out of a fairy tale or a movie, and she had once thought this would be her home.

"Are you sure no one will know I'm here?"

"It'll be fine," he said. "With the hours I'm working on the case, no one is going to come out to the apartment. Trust me."

She did trust him. Always had.

They passed the enormous main house that even had wings. Ten bedrooms. Twelve bathrooms. Buck and Holly Powell loved their family and wanted to keep them close. They built the main house hoping to have weddings, host holiday celebrations and throw big birthdays there. Enough space for grandkids, extended family, in-laws and friends to stay. They were a loving, close-knit family. Buck and Holly wanted part of their legacy to be keeping it that way for generations.

Liz had not only appreciated their vision but had also shared it. Believing this was what her life with Sawyer would look like. That they would have been married here. Raised their kids on this ranch alongside their cousins.

He parked at the side of the garage near the outdoor staircase that led to the apartment. No one peeking out of a window in the house would be able to see her exit the vehicle.

She grabbed her laptop bag, he took her carry-on suitcase, they got out, and they hurried up the stairs. Quickly, he opened the unlocked door and ushered her inside.

After closing it, he flipped the lock and slipped on the chain. "Mom has a spare key. It's an extra precaution. She usually gives us plenty of space when we're in the grind. And Dad, well…" He shrugged.

Buck Powell preferred to have his children come to him, call him, let him know when he was needed. He was an anti-helicopter parent to the extreme, while Holly was a mama bear who wanted her children to be happy, healthy and safe.

"I'll put your bag in the bedroom." He started toward the room at the far end with the double French doors.

The garage apartment had been an idea for Monty, not yet realized the last time she was on the Shooting Star Ranch.

On the opposite end of the spacious apartment was a kitchen equipped with the essentials, including an island large enough to eat on. White cabinets and black quartz countertops. She took in the place. Hardwood floors and large area rug defined the living room with a cognac-colored leather sofa and large television. The place was cozy and warm and tidy.

Following him through the living room, she stopped in front of the framed picture hanging on the wall—an eighteen-by-twenty-four-inch poster of her posing with a copy of her book. It was surreal.

"I'm sure all the ladies you bring here love to see this." She gestured to it like she was Vanna White on *Wheel of Fortune*.

"As a matter of fact, they tell me it's what they like best about my place."

Surely, they loved the bed with Sawyer naked in it the best. "Did you get it from the bookstore?"

"Yeah. It's the one your mom custom-made. She paid a pretty penny for shipping." He stepped closer, eyeing it before looking at her. "Seriously, I don't bring anyone here."

"Why not?"

"Too personal. The ranch is about family." He went to the bedroom and set her bag down. "To bring them here would mean I'm interested in a future with them."

Questions rushed through her mind, but to ask them would only lead to trouble. "Mind if I shower?" She followed him into the room in the back.

The king-size bed was made, complete with accent pillows. The apartment looked like something out of a magazine, only lived in. His mother must have decorated.

"You let me use yours. Feel free to use mine." He flashed a weary smile, his eyes warm and sincere.

She looked at the bandage on his forehead, thought about the stitches in his side and ached to hold him close. Pulling her gaze away, she unzipped her suitcase. "Bathroom?"

He pushed open the door to the en suite. "Right here."

She fished out her toiletry bag and hurried into the bathroom before she acted on an impulse she'd regret. "Thanks." She closed the door and turned on the light.

The tile and stonework were dark and sophisticated. Masculine. Yet, there was still an airy spa-like feel. In the daytime, the skylights must have provided plenty of natural light. The large shower had smooth stone flooring and two showerheads. She started one of them.

She didn't take long getting cleaned up and brushing her teeth. Once finished, she looked around the bathroom and realized in her haste, she'd forgotten to bring her pajamas.

No way was she going out with only a towel wrapped around her. Sawyer was sitting on that bed waiting to talk to her. She just knew it.

She grabbed his navy robe from the hook on the back of the door, pulled it on and hung up the towel. Tying the belt, she rubbed her fingers over the ultrasoft cotton, nuzzled her nose in the collar and inhaled the scent of him. The loss hit her all over again. The stark reminder of what was waiting for her in Virginia. An empty condo and a cold bed.

Beyond the door waited a man who would push with questions that she owed answers to.

You can't hide in here forever, and there's nowhere to run.

She opened the door and stepped out of the

bathroom. Sitting on the bed, he lifted his head and his penetrating gaze locked on hers.

A breath shuddered out of her with a lump in her throat like a boulder. She shoved her hands in the pockets of the robe, faking casualness. "Hope you don't mind I put it on."

"Not at all." He pushed off the bed and came closer. "You look good wearing my things." He flashed a sinful grin that made her heart tumble over in her chest.

Averting her gaze, she caught sight of a copy of her book on the nightstand. She thought again about the poster hanging in the living room and something he'd said. Actually, a lot of things he'd said. "Tell me something."

He stopped less than a foot away, within arm's reach. "Anything."

"How did you know my mom spent a lot of money on shipping for the poster? How are you certain that I don't have a social life or get sweaty with someone sometimes or have a pet or anything besides work?" All true, but she hadn't shared those private, embarrassing details with him. The only thing he didn't seem to know was whether she'd been in the house the day he came to Montana. And the reason he didn't know was because her mother hadn't been home.

The grin slipped from his face. He scrubbed a hand through his hair. "Your mom and I have kept in touch."

Anger whispered through her. *My mother and Sawyer have been communicating behind my back*. "All these years? Keeping it a secret from me."

"When I was in Montana, your mom happened to be in town and saw the Missoula sheriff hauling me in to the station. She got me released, made sure no charges were pressed, took me to a diner and fed me. We talked for hours. She didn't want me to pull another stunt like that. I agreed on the condition that she'd tell me everything. Give me updates about you."

Although she didn't visit her parents and didn't encourage them to fly out to see her—far too busy with work—she confided in her mother, too much apparently, since the information was routinely shared with Sawyer. "How often?"

"We talk three or four times a week."

The frequency was staggering. More often than she talked to them. "About what? It can't just be about me." Not enough going on in her life.

"Quilting. Bridge. Hunting. My job. My parents. She knows everything going on with my brothers. Your parents even came to Holden's wedding."

Her parents were invited when she wasn't? Not that she would've gone. Still, the sting of betrayal cut deep. "You had no right."

He sighed. "Lizzie, just because you cut me off,

didn't mean I was ready to let go. You…you were my everything."

Her heart lurched. He had been her whole world, too. The first person she wanted to talk to about anything, good or bad. When they were together, everything felt possible because he was hers and she was his. Then the fire burned away the future they wanted, reducing it to ashes, but letting Sawyer go had been a different kind of devastation.

"I thought it would be easier if we didn't have any more contact." Her voice was a whisper.

"Easier for you maybe. But not for me. I loved you. With everything I am. I still wanted the future we had planned. Going to college together at SWU. Getting engaged after graduation. Married once we had settled into our careers. I didn't stop wanting a life with you because of the accident."

"We were silly kids. With preposterous plans. Your high school love isn't supposed to be your only one."

Yet he was hers. Not just her first but her only.

"Who says? Try telling that to my parents."

The ideal couple. High school sweethearts. Never had an off year to explore other romantic interests. Married for forty. Four kids. Unbearably affectionate. An impossible standard.

"I was there at your side every day as you recovered in the hospital. You lost twenty pounds in one week. I saw the pain. All your struggles.

Tried to help you through recovery, but you slowly started shutting me out until you moved away and cut off all contact."

A jolt of sorrow sliced through her. "I was doing you a favor. I thought that I'd be the only one who would suffer."

He shook his head. "You took away my choice. Made a unilateral decision for both of us." His voice was rough. Ragged.

"You were supposed to move on with some pretty girl and live the life you were always meant to have. Just with someone else."

Sawyer grimaced. "How could I move on when you haven't?" he asked, his tone intimate, bare. "How could I fall for someone else when all I do is compare them to you and hate how they don't measure up?" Lowering his head, he blew out a long breath. "Were you there that day in Montana? Were you home? Did you hear me, screaming for you until I was breathless?"

Her throat closed. A fresh wave of pain flooded her, but the ache was in her heart. "I was."

"Why didn't you come out and talk to me?"

Tears welled, threatening to fall. "Because I didn't want to be without you. I would've looked into your eyes, fell into your arms and never let go."

"That was all I ever wanted." He ventured even closer. "Why didn't you?"

She shut her eyes. Hot tears rolled down her

cheeks. "I was broken. I'd lost myself. Everything good and beautiful and strong was tied up in you." As though there was no Liz without Sawyer. Using him to fix what was fractured inside of her wouldn't have been right. Wouldn't have been healthy. "I had to let you go, so we could both be free. Even though it had killed me to do it." She looked up at him. "I had to heal, find a way out of the darkness and back into the light, alone. Eventually, I did, and it led me to the FBI." The bureau gave her a renewed sense of purpose.

"Then why are you still running from me?" he demanded, sounding bereft.

"You haven't seen it." A pang returned to her chest. "The scars. The skin grafts. What I look like."

Hurt flashed on his face. "Because you never gave me a chance."

"A chance? For what? To reject me?" Her back teeth clenched. "To stay with me out of obligation? Some twisted sense of loyalty. Or worse pity?" Burdening him with the expectation to love her after the fire had left her *damaged goods*. "Why drag out the inevitable part where you eventually wanted to move on and dumped me."

"Since you thought me leaving you was inevitable, you left me first. When all this time, you should've believed that *you* and *me* being together is what's inevitable."

"The fire *ruined* me." The only way he'd understand was to show him. Loosening the belt, she turned her back to him and shrugged off the top of the robe, letting it fall to her waist. Then she pulled her hair over one shoulder. "Nobody wants to look at this, much less touch it. Especially not..." A lover.

She trembled, baring herself to him, exposing the scars and grief she carried.

Her heart throbbed so hard it hurt until he wrapped his arms around her, bringing her against him, with his warm chest to her back. She nearly pulled away, the heat of his body was scorching, but she was tired of running from the one person she wanted to cling to.

"You are not ruined." He pressed his mouth to the nape of her neck, his breath sending a tingle down her spine.

Over the years, she'd imagined what it would be like to see him again, to hold him, to be held in return.

This was real. Not a memory. Not a fantasy she'd had a thousand times.

"You're a warrior who goes into battle against the worst of the worst." Kissing her softly, he trailed a path across her back. "You're brilliant and brave and beautiful. Even more so now. Not despite the scars. Simply beautiful, scars and all. And you're still the sexiest woman I've ever known."

Curling her hands around his forearms that

were banded tight around her, she closed her eyes and reveled in his touch, in the sincerity in his voice, in the way he smelled, in how he accepted all that she was.

He brushed her shoulder with his lips and slipped a hand inside the robe, palm pressed to her stomach.

His warmth penetrated past the scars and muscle, deep into her bones. With Sawyer, she was exposed. Vulnerable.

And it frightened her.

But then he did something even more terrifying.

He untied the belt, letting the robe fall to the floor and turned her around. His gaze swept over her body and there was only tenderness in his eyes. *Appreciation.*

Looking back up at her, he cupped her jaw, running his fingers into her hair. "I love you, honey. So much." He pressed the sweetest kiss to her lips. "Still. Always."

She was smiling and crying and shivering at the same time. "I love you, too."

A devastating smile broke over his face, and her thoughts scattered. He crushed his mouth to hers, his lips full of desperation and hunger. She kissed him back hard, longing sliding into every stroke of her tongue against his, concentrating on the taste of him.

He shuffled them backward, somehow caressing her as he pulled his shirt over his head. Their lips parted for a breath. Then his mouth claimed hers again, and they let out twin sighs of relief.

The years they'd been apart disappeared as if they'd always been and should always be together.

She unbuckled his belt, shoved down his pants and boxer briefs. A sigh escaped her. He was gorgeous. Everything about him sexy and strong.

"Do you want me to shower first?" He kicked off his boots, working his jeans off the rest of the way.

After fifteen years, she should be able to wait five more minutes. But she couldn't. "I need you right now. We'll shower after. Together. Put those two showerheads to good use."

"Then we can get dirty again."

She laughed as they tumbled onto the bed in a tangle. The delicious weight of him on top of her settled between her thighs, his hands exploring her body while she delighted in the feel of his skin and muscles and strength.

Her body relaxed and tensed with anticipation. "It's been a long time for me. I haven't done this since…you."

He stared down at her and smiled. "We can go slow. Start with me kissing every inch of you." He pressed his lips to the base of her throat, licked across her collarbone and nipped her shoulder, sending a shiver through her.

Although that sounded like a dream come true,

she didn't want to slow down. She wanted to rush forward. With him. "Let's save slow for tomorrow morning."

He kissed her again, his mouth warm and demanding as his hand slid down between her legs. The need unleashed within her was immediate— too powerful to deny. So much emotion in his touch. Love and joy and hunger. She felt the same. Fear wouldn't hold her back any longer.

Clinging to each other, tangled together. Connected. She thought needing him made her weak. Only now she saw their love made them stronger.

That need for him all-consuming. No restraint between them. Only intensity and heat and love.

This was everything.

She'd been running all this time from where she belonged. Where she was always meant to be.

They were inevitable.

Chapter Fifteen

Missed? How had his brother missed?

He never did like guns, in part because of the uncertainty. Is someone alive? Dead? Is the wound fatal?

And guns were too loud. Crude. Say nothing of the mess they caused. Unlike fire. That was a different beast. His animal of choice. Sophisticated when done right.

His brother thought Sawyer or Liz might have been injured, but he was certain they were alive. What if she called in more agents to assist with the case?

Even if she didn't, the sheriff's department was going to throw their full weight behind solving this case. Deputies were already conducting interviews to speed things along. This drive-by shooting was only going to fuel their efforts.

Then there was Sawyer. His protective instincts would put him in overdrive. That Powell would stop at nothing now.

At least his brother had removed the license

plates from the motorcycle and evaded the roadblocks authorities had set up. No danger of them
figuring out who they were.

Gritting his teeth, he groaned. He was under
pressure to see this through. Instead of being able
to draw this out, like he wanted, he needed to ac-
celerate his timeline.

Somehow, someway he would finish the list.
No better time than now to make it happen. Starting with Neil Steward and Chuck Parrot. No protective custody had been given to them. Neither
man had provided the authorities with enough to
warrant it, too busy hiding their precious secret.
Liars until the end.

*And I was smart enough to bait Liz and Sawyer
into thinking I was finished.*

Far from it.

In order for this to work, before the sun rose,
he needed to make sure Steward and Parrot were
dead.

SAWYER WOKE WITH light streaming in the windows and Liz nestled up against him. And it was
perfect.

She was perfect. For him. He only wished they
hadn't wasted so much time not being together,
but he finally understood why she'd needed to
recover and grow on her own without him. Saw
how she'd suffered. How she'd sacrificed for him.

Last night as he held her close, she'd told him

about the rookie agent who had made her question if any man would find her desirable. What a weak fool that guy was not to see she was gorgeous. His loss was Sawyer's gain.

Now Liz knew that he'd had other options and still only wanted her. There would be no fear of entrapment. Of obligation. Of resentment.

No doubt.

With open hearts, they were choosing this—to be together.

Liz snuggled closer, her leg between his thighs, nuzzling her mouth against the curve of his neck. "Good morning," she whispered, her voice throaty and sexy.

He tightened his arm around her. "How are you feeling?"

"A whole lot better than fine." She gave his shoulder a playful nip. "Amazing, actually." She ran her palm across his chest. "It was like riding a bike. You?"

Like he'd been living with one lung, barely able to breathe. Now? "Everything is right in the world with you back in my life." In his arms where she belonged. Sex had never been an issue for him. Intimacy had. She was the one woman he'd been truly intimate with, sharing his deepest secrets, his real self. "There's nothing like this." He caressed her face. "Like us."

"I'll never let go again," she promised.

"You better not." He wouldn't survive if she

did. "And last night." He gave a low whistle and kissed her. "I thought it was mind-blowing before, but that was next level."

"You're full of it." She leaned up on her forearm. "You said it was mind-blowing with Tessa."

"No, I didn't. I spoke in generalities that could be applied to any relationship." He brushed hair from her face and tucked it behind her ear. Caressed her cheek. Cupped the side of her neck. Felt incredible for her not to cringe. "Chemistry and compatibility aren't the same. We have both. Marriage shouldn't be based on sex, even if it's mind-blowing. That's what Dad told me after I informed him that I was going to marry you one day."

Her brows pinched together. "I don't know if I should be flattered that you were referring to us when you said 'mind-blowing' or creeped out that your dad knew so much about our sex life."

He chuckled. "Some private things had slipped out in an argument we had. I wanted to marry you right after high school. He thought we were too young and believed I was confusing great sex with love. That's when I came up with the plan to do it after college. But the takeaway is you should be flattered."

There was a loud knock on the door, and Liz tensed. His front doorknob rattled, someone trying to get in.

Good thing he'd locked it.

She yanked the sheet up, covering herself. "I thought you said no one would come here."

"Sawyer!" Holden's voice was urgent. "Open up."

"One minute," he called out and turned to Liz. "Sorry. I forgot Holden and Monty drive past the garage on their way out of the ranch." He jumped up and shoved his legs into his jeans. Leaning over the bed, he gave her a quick kiss.

After closing the French doors to the bedroom, he hustled to the front door, slipped off the chain, flipped the dead bolt and opened it, but stood holding on to the knob and frame so his brother wouldn't cross the threshold. "Hey, what's up?"

"I was heading out, about to call you and spotted your car. I thought you were camping out at Liz's. What happened? Did she run off the whipped puppy?" His brother tousled Sawyer's hair, and Holden's gaze flew to his forehead. "And what happened to your head?"

After Liz had called in the shooting, the Bison Ridge sheriff had responded, coming out to the house to take their statement. Sawyer had asked the deputies in Laramie not to notify his brother because Sawyer wanted to explain himself.

"Why were you going to call me?" Sawyer asked, redirecting him.

"Are you going to let me in?" He stepped forward, but when Sawyer didn't budge, Holden narrowed his eyes. "Is she inside?" he asked in a whisper.

Thankful his brother was discreet for once in their lives, Sawyer gave a casual nod.

Holden gave a loud howl that made Sawyer's gut tighten with embarrassment. "Way to go Coyote." He patted his brother's shoulder. "Morning, Liz!"

Sawyer groaned. He should've known better.

"Morning, Holden," she said from the back of the apartment.

"I'll give you both a minute to throw something on, and then I'm coming in. I need to speak with you two."

"Don't tell Mom she's here," Sawyer said.

"Why? She'd love to see her."

One step at a time. Sawyer let out a heavy breath. "Please. If not for me, then for Liz."

Holden gave a one-shoulder shrug, which was noncommittal at best. "Go get dressed, you filthy coyote."

Shaking his head, Sawyer closed the door and went back to the bedroom. Liz was already in the bathroom, brushing her teeth. After running a quick comb through her hair, she threw on clothes. While he waited for her, he got coffee started.

Coming into the living room, she was dressed in trousers and a button-down shirt—sans scarf. He didn't know if she'd leave the apartment without one but was happy to see she didn't feel the need to have it on when speaking with Holden.

Sawyer let his brother in, and he gave Liz a hug and a kiss on the cheek.

"We've got something to share, too." Sawyer grabbed three mugs and set them on the kitchen counter. "Who goes first?"

"Well, if your news has anything to do with that nasty cut on your head and the roadblocks that were set up last night around Bison Ridge, then you're up."

Sawyer poured the coffee and filled his brother in on what happened, as well as the necessity to keep Liz out of harm's way by bringing her to the ranch.

"Wow," Holden said with a grim look. "I'm glad you two are all right. You should've been out here at the ranch all along." He eyed Liz. "Am I supposed to keep this from Mom and Dad? The Liz secret is big enough. And don't expect me to keep it from Grace. My wife and I don't keep secrets from each other. Speaking of which, Grace is going to want to meet you, Liz. I promise you'll love her."

Liz drew in a deep breath. "I'll see everyone before I go back to Virginia." She patted his arm. "I promise."

Sawyer's chest tightened. He didn't know how things would work out yet, but he didn't intend to be separated from her, doing this long distance.

Holden glanced at him, most likely sensing what was on Sawyer's mind. "Well, I stopped by to let you know that Neil Steward and Chuck Parrot are dead."

"What?" Liz gasped. "How?"

"Car bomb with Neil. Same set up as yours, Sawyer. Parrot was different. His house burned down with him inside."

Another gruesome way to go. "Why wasn't I called?" Sawyer asked.

"It was clearly arson. Parrot must have fallen asleep drunk on his sofa. The window in his back door was broken. That's how our perp got in. He poured gasoline around the couch, and based on how severely Parrot's body was burned, we suspect he doused him, too, and then set it on fire."

"That's terrible." Horror soured his stomach. "Are they sure the accelerant was gasoline?"

Holden put a fist on his hip. "Here's the kicker, the guy left the five-gallon plastic gas can behind on the back porch steps. We dusted for fingerprints, but nothing."

Liz held her coffee cup in both hands. "Was Russo able to get anything out of Neil Steward before he was killed? Or Aleida's husband, Mr. Martinez?"

"Neil had nothing new to share. Claimed he got a business loan."

"Same as Parrot," Sawyer said.

"As for Martinez, Aleida told him it was family money that allowed her to invest in Compassionate Hearts franchise and open a store. He told Russo that Aleida was determined to give back to the community and to make a difference. Like a woman on a mission."

"Maybe one of redemption." Sawyer glanced at Liz. She had that faraway look in her eyes. Her wheels were turning. "What are you thinking about?"

"How Holden doesn't keep secrets from his wife," she said, glancing between them. "We need to talk to Evelyn Steward." Liz sipped her coffee. "She was married to Neil for twenty-four years. She must know something, and if she does, with Neil dead, there's no longer any reason for her to protect his secret."

THEY FOUND EVELYN STEWARD coming out of the funeral director's office.

She shook the man's hand. "Thank you for the support and the guidance. For taking care of everything."

"Certainly. That's why we're here."

Liz was never comfortable at funerals. The music, the flowers, the ceremony of endless words and weeping. She recognized it was necessary for closure and to celebrate a deceased person's life. An opportunity not to grieve alone. It simply made her uneasy.

Turning, Evelyn lumbered down the hall, her

clothes disheveled, her eyes red-rimmed. Liz and Sawyer approached her.

"Mrs. Steward, I'm Agent Kelley and this is Fire Marshal Powell. We're very sorry for your loss. We know this is a difficult time for you, but we need to speak with you for a moment."

Wringing her hands, the grieving woman nodded.

Sawyer showed her into an empty room where they could speak privately. "Mrs. Steward, we'd like to talk to you about Neil."

Evelyn sank down into a chair and burst into tears. Digging into her purse with a shaky hand, she pulled out a tissue. "First Mikey. Now Neil. I have to organize a double funeral." She sobbed uncontrollably.

Giving her a minute, Liz sat beside her and put a comforting hand on her shoulder. She had no idea what a mother must feel, or a wife, much less someone who had to bury a son and a husband at the same time.

Liz waited for Evelyn to regain her composure. "Did Neil tell you about the threatening phone call he received the night the Cowboy Way was burned down?"

"The night Mikey…" Dabbing at the tears in her puffy eyes, she nodded.

"What did the perpetrator say to Neil?" Sawyer asked.

"Um, the guy told him Neil deserved what was

about to happen." Evelyn wiped her nose. "Fireworks. That he was going to take the shop and our son." Her voice quivered.

Liz leaned forward, putting her forearms on her thighs. "Did he tell Neil why he was being punished?" she asked, and Evelyn hesitated. "If you keep Neil's secret and don't tell us what he was hiding, we won't be able to bring the man who did this to justice."

"I told Neil the same thing." More tears swam in her eyes. "That's why he wouldn't let me go with him to the sheriff's office. He thought I might let something slip. By accident or on purpose."

She exchanged a knowing glance with Sawyer. "Let what slip?"

"Neil was being punished for what happened to Timothy." Evelyn took a shuddering breath. "That's what the man said."

"Who's Timothy?" Sawyer asked.

Evelyn shrugged. "I don't know."

Impatience flashed through Liz, but she reminded herself of what this poor woman must be going through. "You know more than you realize. Your husband must've said something about it. I'm sure you questioned him."

"Questioned him?" She shook her head. "Not at first. We were too busy trying to find Mike, and by then, it was too late. But later, yeah. We got into a horrible fight. He said he couldn't talk about it. To protect me. From legal action. In case I went to the authorities."

"What kind of legal action?" Liz wondered. "Was he worried you would be implicated in a crime and that we might arrest you?"

"No." Tears spilled from her eyes. "He was worried about us getting sued."

Liz looked at Sawyer, and he shared in her confusion.

"We don't understand," he said.

"Neil signed an NDA."

"A nondisclosure agreement?" Liz asked for clarification because it came out of left field.

"Sixteen years ago, Neil up and quit his job at the Wild Horse Ranch. Out of the blue. Something happened. Something bad. He wouldn't talk about it. Because he'd signed an NDA." Her fingers clenched in her lap. "He was worried I might tell my mother. Or my sister. Or my best friend Kim. It's true, it's hard for me to keep secrets. My husband, knowing me so well, never shared the details. But he had a stack of money. Fifty thousand dollars. I'd never seen so much cash in my life. He decided to pursue what he loved. Drawing and ink. Eventually we saved enough and opened the Cowboy Way." Tears welled in her eyes. "We never talked about where the money came from or why it was given to him. Not until he got that phone call. He said he couldn't talk about Timothy because of the NDA. That's when I realized it was tied to whatever happened back then. I pushed him and I screamed at him, demanding to know if he had hurt or killed this Timothy. Needing to understand what was happening to us and why. He swore to me that he wasn't the one who had killed him."

Killed him? "It happened during the summer, sixteen years ago when Neil quit and came home with the money," Liz said.

"Yeah." Evelyn nodded. "Right around the Fourth of July. I remember sitting outside with him, drinking a beer, fanning myself with some of that money while we watched the fireworks."

Fireworks.

Liz combed through her memories, trying to remember any Timothy from the Durbin's. A camper or ranch hand.

Then it came to her. "Thank you, Mrs. Steward. You've been very helpful." She rose and started to move away when Evelyn caught her arm hard and it was all Liz could do not to flinch. She didn't, shaken when the woman's eyes filled with tears.

"Please find the wretched person who did this," Evelyn whispered, then let her go.

Liz straightened, her arm stinging like a live wire had zipped through it. "We will." She handed her one of her cards. "If you need me, call."

"Can you get their bodies released as fast as you can so I can—" her voice broke "—so I can bury them?"

"We'll do everything we can." Liz stalked out of the room with Sawyer beside her and they headed for the parking lot.

"I saw it in your eyes," Sawyer said. "What is it?"

"I remember a camper from that summer. New kid like me. Timothy. But he didn't die."

Chapter Sixteen

"I checked the records, sixteen years ago, around the Fourth of July," Holden said, setting down a folder on the desk. "There is an incident report. No 911 call, but Sheriff Jim Ames was called out. A kid died. Timothy Smith."

Shock washed over Liz's face.

Sawyer opened the folder, setting it where she could look along and read through it.

"I don't understand," Liz said. "A group of us were going out riding. Before we got too far out, I realized my horse had lost a shoe. One of the ranch hands, CP, told me to head back to get it fixed. When the others got back, the group was quiet, uneasy. Someone told me that Timothy had fallen. Broken his leg. But I remember the sheriff showed up and, a while later, an ambulance."

"Right here." Sawyer directed her where to look. "A fatal injury sustained from fireworks. The death was ruled accidental."

"If he died, wouldn't it have been in the news?" she asked.

Holden sighed. "I checked that, too. There was nothing in the paper."

"Whatever happened, they covered it up." Liz pressed a palm to her forehead. "The Durbins paid for silence."

Sawyer glanced at the list of kids and ranch hands who had been interviewed. Albert Goldberg, Chuck Parrot, Courtney O'Hare, Ermenegilda Martinez, Flynn Hartley, Neil Steward, Randy Tillman, Scott Unger. He got to the last name and clenched his jaw. "I don't think it was the Durbins who paid."

He pointed to the name William Schroeder. "I think Bill's daddy did."

"What I don't get is the sheriff came to the ranch." Liz pushed hair back behind her ear. "How was there a cover up, with people signing NDAs and getting paid off?"

A deep line creased Holden's brow. "You've missed a lot. Sheriff Ames ended up being dirty. You remember Dean and Lucas Delgado from school?"

She nodded. "Yeah, of course. It was because of Dean that Delgado's became the hangout spot."

"They killed Ames." At her surprised look, he continued. "Long story, but they're CIA now."

"Guess I have missed a lot."

"In the fallout of the scandal surrounding Ames, Holden went through a rough patch," Sawyer confided.

Holden shook his head. "Don't bring that up."

"Why was it rough?" she asked.

Holden sighed. "I'll tell her. I was deputy when everyone found out about the sheriff being dirty, and I didn't see the corruption right under my nose. Everybody thought I was either dirty, too, or an incompetent fool. That pretty much sums it up."

Liz reached out, took his hand, and gave it a squeeze. "I'm sorry."

"I got through it."

"My guess is that back then," Sawyer said, "with the Durbins and Schroeders being tight, Dave called Bill's dad and asked him how he wanted to handle the situation. From there, one of them contacted the sheriff, knowing he would go along with a cover-up for the right price."

Her shoulders stiffened. "If Bill's father orchestrated the payouts and the NDAs, then Bill must be responsible for Timothy's death. That would not only make him a target but the biggest one. Maybe our guy blames him the most and is saving him for last."

Holden headed for the door. "I'll get a deputy over to city hall to protect our esteemed mayor."

Picking up the file, Liz sat back in her chair as she looked it over. "Do you know if Roger Norris was the medical examiner at that time?" she asked Sawyer.

"I've been fire marshal longer than he's been ME. You want me to check with him, pull the case and give us his assessment of whether the death was accidental or not?"

"Exactly." She leaned over and gave him a quick kiss before turning her attention back to the file.

Although she had chosen to wear the scarf around her neck, she was lighter, looser, but not any less focused or dedicated. He liked it. A lot.

Sawyer made the call to Roger. Voicemail. Stifling a groan, he left a message and marked it Priority.

"Hey, I noticed something reading the sheriff's report. He wrote that he'd taken ten statements. But there are only nine. They're pretty much all verbatim. Like reading a script."

"Ames could've made a mistake." He got up and stretched his legs. "Or maybe he did take ten statements, but one person wasn't willing to accept the hush money, so they found a different way to silence them."

"Sloppy not to go over the report with a fine-toothed comb to ensure no errors in your counting," she said.

"Well, he was the sheriff, with powerful friends. His arrogance probably made him careless." He touched the cut on his forehead but didn't let Liz see him wince.

"If our guy is doing all of this because of something that happened sixteen years ago, why now?"

she asked. "Why not last year? Why not eleven years ago?"

Unease trickled down his spine as a thought occurred to him. "What if he did try before? Fifteen years ago."

She stiffened. "The fire at the camp that killed the Durbins. It would've been around the anniversary of Timothy's death." Her hand went to her throat. "It would make sense. They never found out who did it. No suspects. But why wait fifteen years to go after everyone else?"

At a loss, Sawyer shrugged. "They all have more to lose now than they did then."

Considering it, she nodded slowly. "We should talk to Timothy's mother. Louise Smith. The father died twenty years ago."

"Then let's."

She sighed. "I prefer to do it face-to-face, but Mrs. Smith lives in Big Piney."

That was a four-hour drive. He picked up the phone. "What's the cell number?" She read it off and he dialed. Once it started ringing, he put it on speaker.

"Hello," an older woman said.

"Hi, is this Mrs. Louise Smith?" he asked.

"Yes, yes, it is."

"My name is Sawyer Powell. I'm a fire marshal with the Laramie Fire Department and I'm here with Special Agent Liz Kelley."

"Are you calling about the recent fires? If so, I don't have any information that could help."

His gaze slid to Liz, and she sat forward with a shrug.

"Mrs. Smith, why would you think we're calling about the recent fires in Laramie?" Liz asked.

"Because that's all anyone in town can talk about."

Sawyer scratched his chin. "In Big Piney?"

Mrs. Smith chuckled. "Why heavens, no. Here in Laramie. I'm in town staying at my mother's place. Well, actually, it's my daughter's now. She got it in the will."

"May we stop by and talk to you in person?" Liz scooted to the edge of her seat. "We had some questions about your son, Timothy. About his death."

"Oh, um, well, I don't see why not." Louise gave them the address.

"Thank you. We're headed over now. See you shortly." Sawyer disconnected and grabbed his hat.

Liz took the glass of lemonade Mrs. Smith handed her from the tray. "Thank you."

"Certainly." A petite graying woman in her late fifties, Louise Smith handed one to Sawyer. "I whipped up some sandwiches for you. I didn't have time for anything else. They're made with Wyomatoes."

They looked lovely—little tea sandwiches with the crusts cut off. Liz salivated, thinking about eating one. She loved Wyomatoes. Another thing she missed living in Virginia. The organic tomatoes grown at a high elevation in Big Piney at the Wyomatoes Farm. They had a specific sweetness and juiciness to them unlike any others. But she found it difficult to stomach food when discussing death, and her paranoia didn't allow her to eat anything prepared by a stranger unless it was in a restaurant.

"Thank you." Sawyer grabbed one and took a bite without hesitation. He moaned with delight. "This is delicious."

"Dill is my secret ingredient."

Clearing her throat, Liz set the lemonade down without tasting it and opened her notepad. "As we said on the phone, we wanted to talk to you about Timothy's death. What were you told?"

Louise crossed her legs at the ankle. "The sheriff came by. Told us, me and my daughter Birdie, that there was an accident at the camp. Some kids were horsing around with fireworks. Timothy didn't know what he was doing and hurt himself. Didn't survive the injury."

"Did you have any reason not to believe the story?" Liz asked.

"Kids mess around. Sometimes they do silly, dangerous things. But Birdie didn't buy it for a second. She swore Timothy was being harassed at that camp and that he was killed."

"Did Birdie go to the camp with him?" Liz glanced at Sawyer, who had finished his lemonade and was taking a second sandwich.

Louise shook her head. "I'm afraid not. Wish she had. We were all living in Big Piney at the time. Every summer, the kids would stay here with my mother. One year, my mom thought it best to send him to the camp at the dude ranch. Timothy was a frail boy, sickly, the brainy kind who got along better with animals, horses you know, rather than people. Though, my mom said they had a couple of close friends in town that they met at the local rec center." Louise refilled Sawyer's glass from the pitcher on the table. "Birdie didn't want to go to camp, decided to hang out with her friends instead. My mom cajoled Timothy into going. Birdie said he called her almost every night complaining about the bullying. Mom thought he needed to toughen up. Stick it out. I was torn, thinking it was a good idea for him to be around some men, with his father gone." She sighed. "To this day, Birdie believes he was killed. She's never gotten over it. Blaming herself for not going with him."

Sawyer wiped his mouth with a napkin. "We'd like to speak with her. Is she here?"

"If she isn't working, she's working out. Today is her day off. I expect she's cycling, running, swimming." Louise laughed. "Anything to lose ten pounds before she gets married. I keep telling her that she's thin enough. It's the curves that she has that got her the man."

Liz gave a polite smile. "What does she do?"

"Health inspector. Good head on her shoulders. Actually uses her biology degree."

"I think that's all for now. Thank you for your time." Liz rose and shook her hand.

Sawyer did likewise before taking another sandwich to go.

"I'll see you to the door," Louise said, rising from her seat.

As they walked through the house, Liz wrote Sawyer's name and number on the back of her card and handed it to Louise. "When your daughter gets home, let her know that we'd like to speak with her. Preferably in person." She noticed Sawyer had stopped and was looking at a picture on the wall. "We're working from the sheriff's office. She can find us there or give us a call."

"Oh, I thought you would be over at the LFD. Aren't you questioning all the firefighters as suspects?"

For someone who lived out of town, Louise Smith was well informed on everything happening in town.

"Mrs. Smith, is this your daughter?" Sawyer pointed to the picture of a woman wearing a cap and gown. Something in his voice raised the hairs on the back of Liz's neck.

"Yes, it is. That's the day Catherine graduated from SWU. Proud day. Happy day."

"Ma'am, if you don't mind me asking, why do you call her Birdie?" Sawyer asked.

"I'm a bird-watcher. When the kids were little, my husband and I would take them all over to the best birding spots. Yellowstone, the Red Desert, Hutton, Seedskadee, Grand Teton, you name it. Back then, Catherine was this delicate, beautiful—she's still beautiful—perfect creature. Like a bird. Been calling her Birdie since she was three. Everyone does. Or used to. When she started college, she preferred it if folks called her Cathy, but I'm her mama, birthed her. I'll call her what I want."

"Please pass our message to your daughter," Sawyer said, his face set in stone. "We have to be going." He took Liz by the elbow and hurried her along to the car.

"What is it? You look like you've seen a ghost."

He rounded the car over to the driver's side and opened the door. "Birdie. Catherine Smith. Is Ted Rapke's fiancée."

Chapter Seventeen

As much as Sawyer disliked it, they had to question Ted in the interrogation room at the sheriff's office. His association with Catherine Smith was too damning.

"He brought a lawyer," Liz said, as though it were an admission of guilt.

Standing beside her in the observation room, he glanced at her. "Only a fool wouldn't have. Our second time speaking with him, he gets summoned to the sheriff's office on the heels of a string of fires and murders. He knows it's not a routine 'let's rule everyone out' chat this time."

She raised a brow. "Why are you so quick to defend him?"

"I'm just not ready to condemn him. He's only known her a short while. Ted didn't start that fire fifteen years ago."

Liz sighed. "Catherine has had friends here for years. It's possible she knew him back then and they've reconnected. The town is small. Catherine spent summers here. It's also possible that the same person who burned down the Wild Horse Ranch isn't the same person exacting revenge now. Catherine could be some siren luring men to do her bidding. All the possibilities need to be examined," she said, and Sawyer heaved out a frustrated breath. She put her hand on his chest. "We need to get to the truth, and you need to be prepared that you may not like it."

He nodded. Unclenched his fingers. "Only the truth and seeing justice served matters." Didn't mean he had to like it.

The door opened and Holden came in. They'd been waiting for him to start the interview since he wanted to observe.

"We can't find Mayor Schroeder," his brother said. "His staff haven't seen him since this morning when he left for a meeting. He was supposed to check out a potential site for an entertainment complex between here and Cheyenne with Kade Carver. They've tried to reach him on his cell." He shook his head. "I've had deputies looking everywhere. They found his vehicle about ten miles outside of town. His phone was in the floorboard of the driver's side."

This horrific nightmare kept escalating. The stakes mounting. What was next? When was it going to end?

Liz eyed Sawyer with a frown. "He was last seen at what time?" she asked Holden.

"Ten a.m. at city hall. He was supposed to meet Carver at ten thirty."

She put a hand on his arm. "Ready?"

With a nod, he said, "Yeah." He'd never had an investigation hit this close to home, pushing so many personal buttons. Something about this case had slithered under his skin, prickling him from the inside out. The sooner they found the perpetrator, regardless of who it was, the better.

They entered the interrogation room and sat across from Ted and his lawyer.

"Why am I here?" Ted asked. He was wearing jeans and a green T-shirt. His black hair looked shorter, as if he'd gotten it cut since they last spoke. "Was there another fire I haven't heard about?"

"Can you tell us where you were this morning between ten and ten-thirty?" Liz started.

"On a run," Ted readily answered, but then he swore. "Alone. I don't have anyone who can verify it. I slept in at my place, decided to go for a long run on one of the trails through the foothills of Elk Horn range."

"How long were you out there?" Liz asked.

Ted shrugged. "I did a six-miler. Maybe from nine thirtyish to ten thirty."

With no one to corroborate where he was this morning and his fiancée as his sole alibi for Mike Steward's murder, they needed to explore motive. "When did you meet Catherine Smith?"

His eyes narrowed, his brow creasing. "This again? Why do you keep circling around my relationship? How is it relevant to this case?"

Liz folded her hands on the table. "Please answer the question."

After his lawyer nodded, Ted said, "A year ago at Delgado's. She was inspecting the place and struck up a conversation, started flirting. One thing led to another."

"That's when you started dating," Liz clarified, "but was that your first time ever meeting her?"

Ted straightened. "Um, no, it wasn't. I'd seen her around over the years. During the summers at the rec center. We'd go there to shoot hoops. Play football on the field. Go swimming. Goof off. We knew each other in passing. Why?"

Liz slid a glance at Sawyer before turning her focus back to Ted. "The fires, the murders, are all about getting revenge. For the death of Timothy Smith. Catherine's brother."

His eyes flared wide. Ted looked between Liz and Sawyer in disbelief, which appeared genuine. "Are you sure? I mean, do you have concrete proof that's what all this killing has been about?"

Sawyer nodded. "We do."

"And you think it's me?" Ted asked, pointing a finger at his chest.

Liz leaned forward. "You're a person of interest."

"What did Catherine tell you about her brother?" Sawyer asked.

"Only that he died years ago. That he was killed and his murderer was never punished. I could tell the subject was painful for her, so I never pushed about details."

"Did she seem angry about it?" Sawyer wondered.

"No," Ted said flatly. "It happened a long time ago. Still upsetting, but not enough to turn her into a cold-blooded killer."

"When did you get engaged?" Liz asked.

"About three weeks ago."

"Right after you got engaged to Catherine Smith, the fires and murders started." The statement from Liz hung in the air like a bad smell when she didn't follow it up with a question, only staring at Ted.

The fire chief pulled back his shoulders. "What are you implying? That I burned down businesses and killed people as—what?—some kind of sick, twisted gift to my bride-to-be?" He made a sound of outrage. "I'm no killer, and I certainly wouldn't do it for a woman. I love Cathy. I'd do almost anything for her. *Almost*. I come up short in that area a lot. Ask my ex-wives. That's why I'm about to get married for a third time."

"Stick to answering the questions only," his

lawyer said to him. "Don't elaborate. Don't offer anything additional. Understand?"

Ted nodded.

"Let's say it's not you." Sawyer sat back in his chair. "Then it's somebody you know. Someone Catherine knows. Someone who knew her sixteen years ago. Someone who shares her pain and anger. Someone who knows fire. Compassionate Hearts was deliberately turned into an inferno. The restaurant was blown to smithereens. But the cabin was more controlled. Like the one at the Cowboy Way. Help us clear you so we can focus on the real bad guy. The real killer."

As Ted thought about it, his face became stark with tension, and he looked away, causing Sawyer to groan. There was something.

"Ted," Liz softened her voice, "share what you know."

His gaze flashed up at them, his mouth thinning. "I didn't hear a question."

"You thought of someone," Sawyer said, calm and low, hoping to get through to him. "Who?"

"You want me to give you a name and put someone in the seat I'm sitting in right now based on—what?—conjecture," Ted said through gritted teeth. "I won't do that."

Liz's cell phone buzzed. She glanced at the screen. "Would you be willing to let us fingerprint you and administer a polygraph?"

The lawyer whispered in his ear, undoubtedly explaining his options and consequences of each.

Ted nodded. "Sure, fingerprints, DNA, polygraph," he said easily, like a man who wasn't guilty. "I'm willing to do it."

Liz gestured to the hall. Sawyer stepped out with her, and Holden joined them.

She accepted the call. "Kelley." She listened for a moment. "Let me call you right back, Ernie." Liz clicked off. "Forensics are in."

In the office, Liz dialed Ernie and put him on speaker. "You've got me, Fire Marshal Sawyer Powell and Chief Deputy Holden Powell."

"Must be nice to be a Powell in Laramie," Ernie said lightly. "Let's get into the meat, starting with the car bomb. Ammonium nitrate was used. A rudimentary, fairly simple timer with a remote detonator. Small, quite compact. That's where the skill factor comes in. The cap from the gas tank was removed, and the device was inserted there. Moving on to the fires. The marshal's guess was correct. The accelerant used was indeed gasoline. The device consisted of a plastic container, housing the gas with a similar timer but modified to trigger the tool that started the fire. This is where it got intriguing for me and explains why your fires burned so hot. A flare was used each time."

Happy to have his assessment confirmed, Sawyer nodded. "Like I suspected."

"Was it a road flare?" Liz asked.

"Nope," Ernie said. "It was a short fusee that burns at nineteen hundred degrees Fahrenheit. The kind they use in the forestry division."

Liz turned to him in confusion. "They use flares to suppress wildfires?"

"As counterintuitive as it seems, yeah," Sawyer said. "The folks fighting the wildfires are also purposively setting them. Prescribed burns and backfires to starve the fire of natural fuel before it has a chance to break through a certain line. The best defense is a good offense."

"That's all I have for you," Ernie said.

"Thanks. We really appreciate it. Lunch is on me when I get back."

"Lunch for a week."

Liz smiled. "You got it." She disconnected. "We need to speak to Ted again."

Sawyer led the way to the interrogation room. Neither he nor Liz bothered sitting.

He pressed his palms on the table and bent over, staring Ted straight in the eyes. "Forensics came back. Fusees were used to start the fire. It is a firefighter. One who works for the forestry division."

Clenching his jaw, Ted looked sick.

"Give us a name," Liz demanded. "Time is running out. The mayor is missing. This guy blames Bill Schroeder for Timothy's death."

Ted squeezed his eyes shut. Lowered his head

as though the truth was unbearable. "I didn't know it was him. I swear it. Right under my nose the whole time." He cursed and pounded a fist on the table. "It's Cathy's best friend. Joshua Burfield. Sometimes I'd wonder if there was something going on between them, maybe they'd dated before, but she swore they hadn't. That they were just friends. But they have a weird bond." He sighed. "Honestly, I think he's in love with her," Ted said, and Sawyer understood why the chief had kept Burfield so close. "Josh has been a wildland firefighter with the forestry division since he was eighteen. A volunteer firefighter at twenty. One of the best—intense, yeah, but dedicated. I didn't know. I swear, I had no idea he was capable of this." Ted looked up at them, eyes filled with anger and disbelief.

"You did the right thing in telling us." Sawyer patted his shoulder and then hurried behind Liz out into the hall. "What was Burfield's alibi for the night of Mike Steward's murder?" he asked Holden.

"His brother, Caleb, confirmed they were together."

Liz shook her head. "This is exactly why I don't trust it when an alibi is a loved one. We need to find him and the brother and bring them both in."

Holden was already moving down the hall. "I'll put out an APB on them," he said over his shoulder.

"We also need search warrants for both their houses," Liz said. "Fast."

Holden gave a dark chuckle. "We'll only need one search warrant. Burfield and his brother live together. Don't worry about fast. The mayor is missing. The judge will hop to it."

Chapter Eighteen

From his usual discreet spot, he spied on Birdie as she finished her laps in the swimming pool at the rec center. The way she glided through the water was beautiful. Such long, clean strokes. Such stamina. He loved watching her do anything. Run. Eat. Sleep.

She was his favorite thing in the whole wide world.

And today, he was finally going to win her heart, take back what was his from Ted Rapke.

She climbed out of the pool, graceful as a swan, water glistening on her skin. Wrapping the towel around her lithe body, she slipped into flip-flops and went to the locker room.

He walked outside to wait for her. Wearing his sunglasses and Stetson, he leaned against his truck. His last gift for her was tucked securely away in the flatbed with the aluminum cover, keeping it a surprise. He imagined what it would be like once she found out how hard he'd worked—the effort, the planning, the sacrifice—to make her happy.

The love nest where he was taking her was prepared. Champagne on ice. After lighting some candles, he'd confess everything. She'd be so grateful, so overwhelmed with emotion that she'd realize how much she loved him. More than anyone else. More than Ted. Because only he would go to such lengths for her.

You're so cool. That's what she'd say to him. *No one loves me like you do.*

Then they'd make love. It'd be like the first time. The only time. After he burned down the Wild Horse Ranch.

This was going to be a *true romance.* One for the storybooks. They'd tell their children about it, omitting a few incriminating details.

The door to the rec center opened and Birdie breezed outside. He smiled, excitement buzzing and crackling like electricity in his veins. He waved and she caught sight of him.

Surprise flittered across her face followed by a bright grin. "Hey, Josh, what are you doing here?" she asked, coming over. "Going for a swim?"

Her inky black hair was wet, her milky white skin damp, and she smelled of chlorine and vanilla.

"I came to get you."

"Me?" She cocked her head to the side. "How did you know I was here?"

"I knew you were off today." He brushed damp strands from her brow, and she pulled away. She did that a lot lately. "Guessed you might be here."

"It's like we have a psychic connection."

No telepathy involved. He always knew where she was, what she was doing, who she was with thanks to the spyware he'd downloaded on her phone.

She was his hobby. His addiction. His love. His world.

"Yep. Psychic connection." He opened the passenger's side door of his truck. "Get in." He offered her his hand to help her up. "I've got a surprise for you."

She glanced around, as if looking for someone or something. "What kind of surprise?"

"The best kind. Trust me, you're going to love it."

"What about my car?" she hiked her thumb over her shoulder at her Jeep.

"We'll come back for it later."

Birdie hesitated, thinking about it, a flicker of something he hated flashed in her eyes. But she took his hand, stepped on the running board and slid inside. He shut the door. Grinning, he ran around, tapped the flatbed, hopped in and pulled off.

She took out her cell phone.

"Who are you calling?" he asked.

"My mom. I don't want her to worry."

No need for nosy Louise to know. He snatched the phone from her fingers and tossed it under his seat.

"Josh. What are you doing? We've talked about this. Boundaries are important."

Boundaries were for the Teds of the world. Not for him. "After the surprise, you can have it back. Come on, you love our games."

They'd played all sorts. The flirting game. The teasing game. The jealousy game, like the one they were playing with Ted, though the fire chief had lasted the longest, made it the furthest. And her favorite—the denial game, where Birdie made a wish for something bad to happen, he'd make it come true, she'd ask if he did it, and he'd deny.

Deep down, she must've known it was him. The denial gave her the luxury to enjoy it without any nasty guilt.

When Birdie didn't respond, he asked. "Trust me?"

Doubt flickered in her eyes again, but she still trusted him. If she didn't, she wouldn't have gotten in the truck. The bond they had was strong.

Unbreakable.

Sixteen years ago, she'd told him her brother, Josh's friend, was being bullied. He'd talked to his manager at the feed store and arranged to make the deliveries at the Wild Horse so he could check on Tim. Witnessed the harassment and how evil and cruel Bill could be. Even spoke to Dave

Durbin about it. The day of Timothy's murder, Josh had been there. He saw the group of them riding off. Timothy, Parrot, Unger, O'Hare, Flores, Goldberg, Tillman, Hartley, Schroeder, Steward and Kelley.

It wasn't until later, after he'd given a statement to the sheriff that had been ignored, after he'd overheard a drunk Parrot and Steward talking about the truth and the payments, that he knew what needed to be done.

He and Birdie had bonded in grief over Tim. Bonded in relishing the horrible deaths of the Durbins and the end of the Wild Horse Ranch. He'd promised Birdie he'd always take care of her, and he had.

"Yeah, I trust you," she finally said. "Where are we going?"

To the love nest. A little cabin he rented outside of town, where she'd be safe. Also, remote, just in case. "Someplace special."

"I hope this isn't anything romantic." The enticing twinkle in her eyes said otherwise. "We've talked about this."

Oh, yes. They'd talked while she flirted and teased—how she enjoyed their games. He was the only friend in the world who understood her pain. The one who made her feel safe. The one she could turn to no matter what. The one who would hold her. But not the one she wanted to have sex with. Not the one she wanted to marry.

Tonight, that would change with a new game. *The love game.* He'd show her she could only count on him, that he was the best man for her— with the greatest, grandest romantic gesture.

He put on a playlist, her current favorites. Once he got her singing, she started to relax. Twenty minutes in, her bare feet rested on the dashboard, and her sundress had slid to her hips, taunting him with the sight of her creamy pale thighs.

The cabin was right down the road, only a minute away when his cell phone rang. He took it out. His brother Caleb. "What's up? I'm almost there."

"No fair you get to use your phone," Birdie snapped, "and I don't."

"What am I supposed to do?" Caleb asked with urgency, which meant something was wrong. "The sheriff is here with two deputy cars. FBI. Fire marshal. They just pulled up. They're getting out of their vehicles. Shoot. Kelley and Powell are eyeing my motorcycle."

No, no, no.

Alarm was a gaping pit in his stomach, but he couldn't panic. Not now. "Grab the lighter fluid from under the sink. Go to my office and burn everything." He didn't want them to know about his big finale. "Then take the spare bike. Try to get here. We'll do plan B."

Caleb disconnected.

Don't lose it. Don't lose your cool in front of Birdie.

"What's happening?" Straightening, she stiffened in her seat. "What's wrong?"

He parked in front of the cabin. "Nothing. A project Caleb is helping me with."

Boom. Boom. Boom. Thudding came from the rear of the truck.

Her brown eyes flaring wide, Birdie spun around in her seat. "Is someone in the flatbed?"

This was not how he wanted things to go. How he wanted to show her proof of his love. He had it all planned out in his head: the champagne, the candles, slowly revealing what he had done. Putting an end to the denial game, because it hadn't served him winning her heart.

Boom. Boom.

Ugh!

"Who is in the flatbed?" Birdie demanded.

Rolling his eyes, he pressed the button on the remote, retracting the aluminum cover over the flatbed. "Go see for yourself."

She got out and ran to the back while he reached over, popping the lid of the glove compartment. Quickly, he opened a bottle and saturated a cloth with chloroform.

The door to the flatbed lowered with a clunk. "Josh!" Birdie screamed.

Holding the cloth behind his back, he hopped out and went to the rear of the vehicle.

"It's the mayor! Why is Bill Schroeder tied up and gagged in your truck?"

Wrists zip-tied behind his back, ankles bound, Bill tried to plead for help around the rancid gag Josh had shoved in his mouth. A big red shiny bow had been tied around his neck.

This was not the ta-da moment he had imagined. "I brought him for you," Josh said. "The one who killed Tim. I made the others pay, too, just like you wanted."

"What are you talking about? I never wanted this!"

"You inspected Chuck Parrot's restaurant, getting him on every violation possible. The rating was so bad he had to close and renovate. You told me you wished you could blow his place sky high. Get back at all the liars. All those who sold their soul to the devil named Schroeder."

"Oh my god! That was you?" The horror and fear in her eyes was real, only making his anger burn hotter. Before Ted came along, she would've been grateful. "Josh, you killed all those people?"

Of course he did. He narrowed his eyes. "Who else?"

Birdie's frantic gaze volleyed between him and Bill. "You burned down the Wild Horse, too, didn't you? I thought you had, loved you for it, even though it was wrong. But you kept denying it."

That was the game.

She wished to see the Durbins dead and the

Wild Horse Ranch in ashes. He made it happen. No guilt for Birdie.

She wished for hell to rain down on the others. He made that happen, too. Once again, no guilt for Birdie.

But also no acknowledgment, no appreciation for him.

Did she think she had a fairy godmother of doom waving a magic wand on her behalf?

"I did it because I love you." *I want you. I need you. More than anything.* "You can't marry Ted. He'd never sacrifice for you. He's selfish. There's no way he'd do anything for you the way that I have. This is proof." He gestured with his left hand at the high-and-mighty mayor, keeping his right hand behind his back.

"I love you, but not in that way. I've told you that. You're like a brother to me." She backed away. "Ted was right about you. He said you were obsessed with me."

"That twice-divorced loser wouldn't know what real love looked like if it punched him in the face. I won't let you marry him. He doesn't deserve you. I do. I've put in the work. I've lit the fires. I've shed blood for you. You're mine!"

Birdie whirled, trying to run, but he grabbed her by the hair and shoved the cloth over her mouth and nose. She fought to break free. The struggle didn't last long.

"We'll work this out in Canada," he whispered

in her ear, even though she couldn't hear him. "You, me and Caleb." Only a ten-hour drive.

There I'll make her feel right about all this. About me.

He kissed her forehead. Then he picked her up in his arms and carried her inside the cabin. Fishing in his bag, he got the zip tie and bound her wrists. He also grabbed his just-in-case rope. No gag. Nobody would hear her scream out here. He put a blanket on the floor in the bathroom, laid her down gently and, using the rope, tied her bound wrists to the pedestal of the sink. She had enough room to reach the toilet. If she got thirsty, she could get water from the sink. He'd already removed the mirror as a precaution. *Just in case.*

Wiping his brow with the back of his hand, he locked the bathroom door. He'd get rid of Bill in the big finale. Hopefully Ted as well. Every firefighter between Laramie and Bison Ridge would have to respond to the crisis, including the chief, whether on or off duty. Many would die.

With any luck, Ted would be one of them.

Chapter Nineteen

Two deputies shoved a handcuffed Caleb Burfield into the back of a sheriff's cruiser. Liz waited outside while Sawyer finished putting out the fire in the office in the house and started airing it out enough for her to come in soon and take a look. In the meantime, she glanced at the motorcycle that either Josh or Caleb had used in the drive-by when they tried to gun them down.

The radio clipped to Holden's shoulder squawked.

"Chief, you there?" dispatch said, and Liz moved closer to him out on the lawn to hear.

"Go ahead, over."

"The ME got back to us. Norris claims the old report is hogwash. He used harsher language, but you get the gist. Based on the wound, someone else hit Timothy Smith in the chest with a large powerful firecracker. Impossible that it was self-inflicted. Also, a traffic cam on US 30 picked up Joshua Burfield's car traveling north. We enhanced the photo. Burfield was driving. Catherine Smith was sitting in the passenger's seat."

Holden mouthed to Liz, *Are they in it together?*

She shrugged. Entirely possible, but Smith's involvement with Ted Rapke gave her serious doubts. The engagement seemed to be the trigger for Burfield, answering Liz's question about what prompted the murderer to act now. His jealousy and anger were the only things that explained why the fires and murders would coincide with the proposal.

Burfield was afraid of losing her. Must want Catherine for himself.

Was this some grisly romantic gesture? The thought gave Liz goose bumps.

"Does she appear to be under duress?" Holden asked.

"Uh, no. It sort of looks like she's...singing."

"They're close friends," Liz said to Holden. "Best friends. Maybe to her, this is any other day. Business as usual. But we should consider her a suspect as well until we talk to her."

"Roger that," Holden said into the radio. "Deputy Russo and I are going to head up on US 30. Have Deputy Livingston notify the state troopers of the last mile marker where he was spotted. I also want him to track the vehicle as far as he can and check Burfield's recent financial transactions."

"Let the FBI track the financials," Liz said. "We're faster and can go deeper."

"Sounds good. Got that?" Holden asked dispatch.

"Got it."

Holden headed for his sheriff's SUV. "Let Sawyer know," he said, and she nodded. He and Russo climbed in and sped off.

Liz took out her cell, dialed her boss and filled him in. "The suspect is Joshua Burfield. A wildland firefighter with the forestry division and part of the volunteer fire department." She relayed his address and last known whereabouts. "In case Catherine Smith is an accomplice, we should check her financials, too."

"We'll get right on this. Good work. How is everything else going for you?" SAC Cho asked.

"Close call with a car bomb and drive-by shooting, but I'm still standing."

He sighed. "One thing you won't have to worry about is the mayor. I spoke with Schroeder. He got the message you're insulated."

"Speaking of the mayor, he's missing. We believe he's Burfield's next target."

"You've got your hands full out there. If you need any other assistance, don't hesitate to reach out. We're here for you. And Liz, stay safe."

"I'll do my best, sir."

Sawyer came to the doorway of the house and waved her inside. "It's okay for you to come in."

Crossing the threshold, she passed him. "Hope you didn't take in too much smoke."

"I'm good. No worries." He led the way to the office. "You're not going to believe what's in there." He let her step inside first.

On the large wall facing the desk a myriad of photos and notecards had been pinned up. String had been tied to certain pushpins, linking them to others. Caleb had sprayed lighter fluid in a rush, struck a match, and ran. He made it to another motorcycle and had gotten it started, but a deputy tackled him before he took off. The haphazard arcs of fire had burned through entire notes and pictures, leaving others partially intact, a few in their entirety.

Burfield had created a detailed problem-solving flowchart.

Liz went up to a partially burned card that had YER POWELL on it, along with notes beneath Sawyer's name. Then she followed the threads to other cards. "Look at this. He anticipated you being a problem. Saw the Shooting Star Ranch as an impediment to neutralize you. That's why he went with the car bomb. And here." She directed his gaze to what Burfield had considered a subset issue. "He saw Holden as a secondary problem until you were eliminated."

"One problem he didn't anticipate was you." He put a hand on her lower back.

It was warm and comforting. Together they had gotten this far. They had to keep pushing. They were close to getting him.

She stepped back, taking in the full picture, piecing it together. The various problems with multiple solutions, or rather multiple ways, to enact his retribution.

This wasn't a flowchart at all.

"He visually brainstormed murder using a *mind map*," she said, half to Sawyer and half to herself. Fascinating and creepy, but fascinating, nonetheless. "He's a nonlinear thinker. This type of tool works best for them."

"What if he were linear?"

"For someone who thinks in terms of step-by-step progression, a flowchart works better. Partially destroyed, that's what I thought it was at first."

"What's the difference?"

"With a flowchart, the steps you take to solve a problem are easy and straightforward until you find a logical solution."

"Seeing as how a killing spree isn't logical, I can understand why he'd bypass that one."

She gave him a grim smile. "Now, with the mind map, the center is where he'd start, his main focus and branch out from there." Right in the middle was a card with the remaining letters LL SCHR. "This has always been, ultimately, about getting Bill Schroeder. Everyone else was a lesser piece on the game board to him. Bill's the one he holds responsible for Timothy's death."

"Then his punishment will be worse," Sawyer said. "Look at what's left around Bill's card. One for Ted. And a device."

"He only plans to use one, a single timer, but more complex. Sophisticated. This is different than the others he's used." A tremor of fear raced through her. "To be used where? How?"

"Car bomb isn't good enough for Schroeder. Right? Burfield has taken the more complicated route. It needs to be big for the last one."

"More painful. He didn't just want to kill the others, he wanted to make them suffer. Took away what was important to them. The charity store for Aleida. The restaurant and financial ruin for Parrot. Steward lost his son and shop."

"Schroeder is the mayor, but if he wanted to take out city hall, he wouldn't have kidnapped him. He could've shown up one night while he was working late."

"Bill's reputation and money are everything to him," she said, thinking aloud. "But how could Joshua Burfield take that away from him? And how would it solve his Ted problem?"

Turning, Sawyer looked around the office. "The brother didn't just burn the wall. He tried to burn the desk also. But he was in too much of a rush. Didn't have time to do it right." He went around the desk. Pulling on latex gloves he took from his pocket, he sat down. A cabinet drawer squeaked open. He thumbed through files. "This guy is macabre. He has a folder labeled *Finale*."

Liz came around the desk beside Sawyer as he opened the folder. They riffled through the contents. Page after page of information about the Schroeder Farm and Ranch Enterprises.

"Bill's family holdings are more than one company," she said. "It's way too big and diversified to take out with one device. They have various offshoots in different locations. Seeds, seed treatments, crop protection, financial services for the smaller farmers, precision agriculture services—"

Sawyer swore. "There might be a way. A horrible way." He fingered through pages quickly, stopping when he found what he wanted. "The fertilizer plant." He pulled out a collage of photos that had been taken of the plant the Schroeders owned.

Liz took a page and scrutinized the angles, what he had zoomed in on. "Burfield took pictures of all the weaknesses. No fenced perimeter. No guardhouse. It doesn't even look like there are cameras on the buildings. How is this possible?"

"Unfortunately, it's more common than you'd realize. This is where he stole the ammonium nitrate that he used for the car bombs."

"How bad are we talking if he sets a fire there?"

"The most recent incident at a fertilizer plant that I can think of was in North Carolina."

"Yeah, I heard about that. The entire town had to be evacuated."

"They had five hundred tons of combustible ammonium nitrate housed at that plant. That's almost more than double was present at the deadly blast in Texas, which killed many, injured hundreds, damaged homes and left a hundred-foot-wide crater. Doesn't he realize or care that most of the people who died there were first responders?"

"I think he's interested in one particular first responder dying—Ted Rapke." All this to get rid of one man and to have one woman? Sickening. "Doesn't OSHA regulate these facilities?" she asked, referring to the Occupational Safety and Health Administration.

"It's complicated." Sawyer homed in on a different page. After poring over it, he handed it to her. "Looks like OSHA didn't put the Schroeder Fertilizer plant on their national emphasis plan that has strict guidelines because it's exempt as a retail facility." He slid another page over to her. "This isn't good. Burfield pulled a copy of the Schroeder's last filing with the EPA."

She picked up the document. "This is public data?"

"Sure is. Do you see it?"

"What exactly am I looking for?"

"Any facility that has more than one ton or four hundred pounds of ammonium nitrate on hand is supposed to report it under federal law. Based on these pictures of the facility that Burfield took, there's close to a thousand tons at the Schroeder plant, but they haven't been reporting it."

"Why wouldn't they report it?"

"Tighter federal scrutiny, additional regulations. To save on expenses."

"At the cost of jeopardizing lives," she said, disgusted.

"If Burfield sets a fire and the plant explodes, it not only destroys the Schroeder reputation and could ruin them financially, but it'll be catastrophic."

"THEY'RE GOING TO do it." Liz disconnected from the Laramie Police Department, looking somewhat relieved.

Driving to the Schroeder Fertilizer Plant, Sawyer nodded and swerved around a vehicle, then hit the accelerator. They were on their way to make sure Burfield wasn't at the fertilizer plant and, if he arrived, wouldn't be able to go through with his diabolical plan.

Calling the LPD had been their best option since his brother Holden and the sheriff's office were busy tracking Joshua Burfield, questioning his brother, Caleb, and searching for the mayor.

"They're going to start evacuating the northwest part of town that would be most impacted in a worst-case scenario," Liz said, "but they think they'll have difficulty getting the residents of the Silver Springs Senior Living and Memory Care Center out. Took longer than I expected to coordinate because the chief of police is on vacation."

"With the sheriff. They're together. Didn't think to mention it."

"Holden's brother-in-law, the sheriff, is engaged to the chief of police?"

"Yeah."

"I take it my mother is aware of that also?"

"She met them both at the wedding."

Liz stiffened.

He put a hand on hers. "She wasn't being disloyal to you. We both love you."

"I guess I'm mostly mad at myself, if I'm being honest. I was in the dark because I wanted it that way." She let out a heavy breath, but her shoulders remained stiff. "Did you have any luck reaching someone at the plant?"

"They closed an hour ago. No one answered. No emergency number was left on the outgoing voicemail."

Pulling up to the Schroeder Fertilizer Plant, Liz pointed out the three-story building with a heavily slanted roof that had been the primary focus of Burfield's surveillance. "It's that one."

They entered the premises, passing several buildings. Sawyer drove across a large dirt lot where big delivery trucks were parked, heading toward the large gray building in the back of the property. Coming around the row of trucks to the front of it, he came to a halt.

A silver truck was parked near the entrance. Same license plate that authorities were looking for. "Burfield is here."

"I'll call it in." Liz whipped out her phone again

and notified the LPD. "Get SWAT out here. We have to assume he has Mayor Schroeder and Catherine Smith inside." Irritation crossed her face as she listened. "Fine. But don't send any uniformed officers here. In case this goes wrong, I don't want them getting killed in the blast. Focus on evacuation." She disconnected. "The captain told me it would take SWAT a couple of hours to get here. Why on earth would it take that long?"

"They're coming from Cheyenne. Laramie doesn't have the funding for our own special weapons and tactics team. Not that our community usually has much need for SWAT."

"This is the first time I miss Virginia."

"I'll go in through the front," Sawyer said. "You go around back."

Liz grabbed his arm, stopping him. "Move the vehicle to the side of the building where there are no windows and Burfield can't see it. Then I'll go in through the front. You through the back."

"Why?"

"Who do you think Burfield will see as the bigger threat? You or me? Of course you and Burfield would be wrong," she said, and he tried not to take offense. "Which one of us would be better at getting inside his head?"

He stifled the growl climbing up his throat.

"I'll convince him I'm here alone," she said. "You go in through the back or some other way."

"I can't put you in his crosshairs."

"Half the town is already in his crosshairs. We have to stop him. If you get a shot at him, take it. No matter what."

He didn't wait fifteen years to get her back only to lose again now. "I won't do it if you're in the line of fire."

"This is the job I signed up for. One of us might have to make a tough call in there. Trying to save me won't save the town or ultimately me. If he detonates, we're all dead anyway," she said matter-of-factly.

She was amazing, more incredible than he'd realized, and her logic irrefutable. Nonetheless, his heart protested.

He drove to the side of the building, parked and shut the engine.

Liz turned to get out, but he put a hand on her shoulder, stopping her.

He cupped her face and kissed her on the lips. Quick and hot and sure. "Marry me?" He'd never gotten to ask her, and he wasn't going to let another chance slip by.

She blinked in surprise, her lips parting before her expression turned stony. "I don't want a doomsday proposal. We get through this and you still want marry me, ask again." She jumped out of the vehicle.

Man, he loved her. He jumped out as well. They left the doors open, drew their weapons and went in opposite directions.

In the back, he darted past the large rolling bay doors where trucks would enter to be loaded up and caught sight of exterior stairs that led to the top. On one side of the staircase was a long chute that ran from the third floor to the ground. Another way to load trucks with materials. He scanned the top. A conveyor belt system ran from the chute inside the building. That was his way in.

LIZ WAS ALMOST at the front door when her cell vibrated. She looked at the text message from her boss.

Burfield rented a cabin in Wayward Bluffs. Sheriff's dept found C. Smith tied up inside.
No sign of the mayor.

She slipped the phone back in her pocket.

Taking a deep breath, Liz slowly opened the front door. A slight creak in the hinges announced her presence. Tension twisted in every muscle in her body. She wished Sawyer better luck.

She eased inside, her gun in a two-handed hold. Passing equipment and stacks of empty sacks labeled with the Schroeder name, she inched deeper into the building. She eyed seven massive bins lined up in a row against the back wall and edged around a couple of front-end tractor loaders.

There was an aluminum wall instead of a four-foot thick concrete one per OSHA regulations, with an opening large enough for two tractors to get through simultaneously. Beyond the wall, a large mound of ammonium nitrate sat in the middle of the building.

She crept forward. Her skin crawled. Wherever Burfield was, he knew she was there, and he was watching.

Her heart hammered in her chest as she glanced around. A conveyor belt ran from the top of the building near the ceiling, across its length, down to the heap of chemicals. She eased around the pile of whitish-gray granules. Braced for anything.

Then Bill Schroeder shuffled into view, ankles bound, a red bow around his neck as Burfield hauled him forward, hiding behind the mayor. Lean, with an athletic build, Josh was taller by a couple of inches and had to hunch. Schroeder's terrified eyes met hers, sweat beading his forehead, his skin sickly pale.

Liz raised her weapon, taking aim.

"I wouldn't if I were you." Burfield held up the detonator in his other hand and gestured with his head at the device he'd planted next to the ammonium nitrate. "I'll blow us all to kingdom come right now. Where's Sawyer?"

"Not here."

Burfield laughed. "You expect me to believe that he left you all alone."

This monster saw her as a helpless damsel incapable of holding her own. "We split up. Your truck was captured on cameras on US 30. He's trying to track you down," she said, not wanting him to know they'd found the cabin and Catherine. It might set him off.

His angular face tightened with worry. For a second his concentration slipped, and he let his head edge to the side enough for her to take a shot, but his focus snapped back, and he put his head behind Bill's again.

"Sawyer wanted to keep me safe, thinking you're headed north," she said, "and I didn't want to be a distraction to him. I agreed to make sure the fertilizer plant was secure and that there were no devices hidden while he went to arrest you."

The wariness in his eyes dissipated, but it didn't vanish. "Not sure I believe you, Liz. Maybe Holden is on US 30. And Sawyer is lurking around here."

"Holden is pursuing your brother. Caleb got away on a red motorcycle out back. The entire sheriff's department is after him. The tip on you, on US 30, came in later," she said, studying him. He looked like he might be swallowing her story, but she needed something stronger. "One thing my training did for me was remove the fear of dying. I can come into this facility knowing a twisted man such as yourself, might be inside, prepared to blow the place up with me along with it. Yet here I stand. But what I *am* afraid of more than anything else is something happening to Sawyer. If I know you're here with hundreds of pounds of explosive material, I'm not letting him anywhere near it."

Triumph gleamed in his eyes and a smile tugged at his lips. That did it. He believed her. Now she prayed Sawyer didn't make any noise.

"Glad to get you all to myself. Drop your weapon."

She held her hands up, gun flat against her palm and then set her Glock on the ground.

"Come closer." Doing as he said, she got within two feet of Bill. "Stop," he ordered, and she did. "Any other weapons? Knives?"

She removed the knife from around her ankle, taking it from the sheath, and dropped it on the ground. She dangled cuffs from her finger and let them fall.

"I'm sure you've got more. What else?" he asked.

"Nothing. That's it."

"Am I supposed to take your word for it? Take off your clothes. I need to be certain." His voice was arrogant, almost amused as though this were a game.

She didn't move.

"I don't have all the time in the world and neither do you. As soon as you saw my truck, you called the cops. They're on the way."

"They're all evacuating the town. You've proven how serious you are about vengeance."

"Big, bad FBI agent. You don't need backup?"

Everyone needed backup and she had more than enough. "I don't want innocent cops to die."

"Do it. Take off your clothes. Remember, I'm holding all the cards."

In a way, with the detonator in his hand, he was.

"Now," Burfield ordered.

Liz shrugged off her field jacket and it dropped to the ground. Next, she lost the scarf. She'd done this before when the bomb maker for the extremist group wanted to be sure she wasn't wearing a wire. For some reason, baring her scars to monsters in service of a mission didn't bother her. Slowly, she began to unbutton her shirt.

Sawyer was close. She knew it but didn't dare glance around. Her only concern was him taking a shot if he got an opening.

She tossed her shirt on the ground, leaving only her bra, feeling more naked without her weapon than her top.

"Turn around," he ordered.

Holding her hands up, she did. As she came almost three hundred degrees, she spotted Sawyer inching along in the conveyor belt at the top of the building. But he wasn't at the right angle yet for a good shot. He needed to worm his way another ten feet. Even then, with the height and the awkward position from the conveyor belt, he still might miss.

"You're the only person I've seen up close and

personal who's danced with the fire." His gaze raked over her and darkened with intense energy.

"A fire you set." She needed to buy Sawyer time.

"You deserved what you got. I saw you go out riding with this scumbag." He shoved Schroeder to the ground, the man landing with a muffled grunt, and Burfield stepped closer. "You witnessed what happened to Timothy and stayed silent. Did they pay you, too? Not that it matters. Either way, not coming forward makes you culpable."

She shook her head. "I went out riding with them. My horse lost a shoe. Chuck made me turn around and go back to the ranch. I never saw what happened to Tim. They told the rest of us who didn't go out that Tim broke his leg."

"Liar!" His finger slipped off the button on the detonator.

"I would never cover up a murder, much less take hush money. That's not me. I saw how Bill bullied Tim. I confronted him myself, spoke to CP and the Durbins about it." Though it had done little good. "I want to bring Bill to justice."

A wicked laugh rolled from his lips. "Yeah, right."

"I've never liked this man. He's despicable. His family's money can't influence me. We reviewed the coroner's report on Tim. The current ME says it shows the wound that killed him couldn't have been self-inflicted. He was murdered. The old coroner and sheriff were corrupt."

"He'll claim it was an accident. Same story he tried to tell me. That they were messing around with fireworks. He only wanted to scare Timothy. Didn't mean to kill him. Bill Schroeder will get off."

"Even if Bill claimed it was an accident, he could be charged with manslaughter." She doubted it would stick since Joshua Burfield had killed all the witnesses to the crime. They had no evidence that Schroeder was the one who launched the fireworks, but she needed to talk Josh down. "Evelyn Steward can testify that Neil was paid hush money. And I found the EPA filing for the fertilizer plant. The Schroeders are breaking a federal law by not reporting how much ammonium nitrate they have here. They will see the inside of a jail cell." That was true. "I promise you."

He considered it. For a heartbeat. Maybe two. "No, no." He shook his head. "Men like Bill and his father always find a way to wriggle out of trouble. This," he said, holding up the detonator, "is the only kind of justice I can count on."

A gunshot fired, hitting Burfield in the forearm, and the detonator dropped. Another shot and he staggered backward. Too far back. The pile of ammonium nitrate would block Sawyer's view.

The bullet had struck his shoulder near the collarbone. If the shot didn't put him down, it would make his adrenaline kick in. He glanced at the floor and he went for the detonator.

Liz scooped up her knife from the ground. Adrenaline pumping through her, she raised the blade, driving it up into his chest.

Burfield raised his shocked gaze to her and then fury exploded across his face. "Go to hell."

She backed away from him, Burfield's blood on her hands. "You first."

With a fierce growl, Burfield lunged for her. *Pop! Pop!* Sawyer fired a third and fourth shot.

Burfield dropped to his knees, his eyes still with the flatness of death, and fell to the ground.

Liz raced forward and secured the detonator. Kneeling beside Burfield, she checked his pulse to be certain the monster was dead.

She climbed to her feet, put her weapon in the holster and slipped on her shirt. As she went over to Bill Schroeder, she smelled how he had soiled himself. Thinking about what an awful person he was, her dislike for him intensified. She tugged the gag down from his mouth. "Can you breathe?"

"Untie me. I can't believe he was going to kill me. I've got to get out of here."

She stared down at him and considered it. "Zip ties can be tough. Let me go find something to cut through it."

He wiggled around on the ground. "Pull the knife out of that SOB's chest and cut it with that."

"Can't." She shook her head. "It's evidence."

Liz stood and headed for the exit. Bill Schroeder yelled and cursed behind her.

Outside, the sun shone brighter now that Burfield was dead and this ordeal was over.

Sawyer ran up to her, and she fell into his arms. He held her tight, and she squeezed him right back.

"Good shooting in there," she said after a couple minutes.

"Anything for you." He pulled back a little and looked at her. "Where's Bill?"

"On the floor, writhing like the snake that he is. We'll cut him loose soon."

Chuckling, he grasped her chin and tilted her face up to his. "Those were some gutsy moves you made. Risky ones, too."

"Are you going to give me a hard time?"

"Maybe." He kissed her gently. "Definitely. You better get used to it."

"Oh, really. Why is that?"

"Because we're getting married."

She laughed. "First, you have to ask me again. Then I have to say yes."

"Nope." He roped his arms around her waist. "This time I get to make a unilateral decision for both of us."

She laughed harder. Even though they'd had another close call with death, they had survived, and it was time for her to start living.

"Liz Kelley, I have loved you more than half my life. There's no one else in the world who I want to be with. Marry me."

She took a shuddery breath. This was really

happening. "My life is in Virginia. Yours is here. And what about your family? You're all so—"

He kissed her, and the reasons why they shouldn't simply evaporated.

"I can be a fire marshal anywhere. Ted and Gareth would be thrilled to get rid of me," he said, and she chuckled. "We can get married at the ranch if you want."

"I'd like that."

"We could take the kids there every summer. We'll have Thanksgiving there with your parents. Maybe Christmases, too. Our folks will spoil them rotten," he said, painting a picture of exactly the life she wanted but had been too afraid to hope for.

"Kids, huh?" she asked, playfully.

"Only if you're still interested in having them."

She'd always wanted to have Sawyer's children. "I definitely want to have a family with you. Someday."

He brushed his lips across hers and kissed her softly. "Where you go, I go from now on. Please marry me so I don't look like a stalker."

She laughed until tears of joy filled her eyes. Her heart glowed in her chest like a bulb, getting brighter and hotter with each breath. "Yes, Sawyer Powell. I'll marry you."

* * * * *

Don't miss the stories in this mini series!

COWBOY STATE LAWMEN

Wyoming Mountain Investigation
JUNO RUSHDAN
July 2024

Wyoming Ranch Justice
JUNO RUSHDAN
August 2024

MILLS & BOON

Campus Killer
R. Barri Flowers

MILLS & BOON

R. Barri Flowers is an award-winning author of crime, thriller, mystery and romance fiction featuring three-dimensional protagonists, riveting plots, unexpected twists and turns, and heart-pounding climaxes. With an expertise in true crime, serial killers and characterising dangerous offenders, he is perfectly suited for the Harlequin Intrigue line. Chemistry and conflict between the hero and heroine, attention to detail and incorporating the very latest advances in criminal investigations are the cornerstones of his romantic suspense fiction. Discover more on popular social networks and Wikipedia.

Visit the Author Profile page
at millsandboon.com.au for more titles.

DEDICATION

In memory of my beloved mother, Marjah Aljean, a
devoted lifelong fan of Harlequin romance novels,
who inspired me to excel in my personal and
professional lives. To H. Loraine, the true love of
my life and best friend, whose support has been
unwavering through the many terrific years together;
and Carole Ann Jones, who left an impact on me
with her amazing talents on the screen; as well as
the loyal fans of my romance, mystery, suspense
and thriller fiction published over the years. Lastly, a
nod goes out to my great editors, Allison Lyons and
Denise Zaza, for the wonderful opportunity to
lend my literary voice and creative spirit to
the Harlequin Intrigue line.

CAST OF CHARACTERS

Paula Lynley—A detective sergeant at Addison University's Department of Police and Public Safety, in Rendall Cove, Michigan, she is investigating a string of suffocation murders of female professors. She enlists a criminal profiler to help crack the case and finds herself drawn to the handsome ATF special agent.

Neil Ramirez—A visiting criminologist, he uses his expertise on violent offenders to assist the beautiful detective while gathering intel on a suspected local arms trafficking operation. Could the cases be connected? When Paula becomes a target of a serial killer, Neil is determined to keep her out of harm's way.

Gayle Yamasaki—An investigator for the Rendall Cove Police Department's Detective Bureau, she is working the Campus Killer case and feels the pressure to solve it before there are more victims.

Michael Davenport—A campus police detective, he is committed to tracking down the serial killer, whatever it takes.

Craig Eckart—A local arms trafficker under investigation. But could he also be doing double duty as a campus serial killer?

The Campus Killer—A cunning and determined serial murderer of attractive female professors, who deviates from the norm when going after Paula for the kill.

Prologue

Debra Newton loved being a journalism associate professor in the College of Communication Arts and Sciences at Addison University in the bustling college town of Rendall Cove, Michigan. In many ways, it was truly a dream come true for her, having graduated from the very school a decade earlier. Now she got to teach others, inspiring young minds for the formidable challenges of tomorrow. And with the summer session well underway, she was doing just that, putting her journalistic skills to the test with each and every passing day.

She only wished her love life could be nearly as thought-provoking and satisfying. Bradford Newton, her college sweetheart turned husband, had turned out to be a total jerk, with a roving eye that went after anyone wearing a skirt at his law office. After one time too many of being played for a fool, she finally kicked him to the curb five years ago, and Debra only wished she had done it sooner. Since her divorce, she had just dated occasionally, with most men seemingly less interested in her brain and sense of humor than her flaming long, wavy red hair, good looks and shapely physique. While these various sides to her were important in and of themselves, she wanted to be seen as the total package and wanted the same in a partner.

Which was why she had turned down a date with a handsome and persistent colleague who, though also single, was a little—make that a lot—too full of himself and a bit scary at times in his demeanor. Similarly, a former administrator, who on paper checked a lot of the boxes for what she was looking for in a potential mate, did not measure up in practice and real time, forcing her to reject his half-hearted advances.

As if that wasn't almost enough to turn her off of romance for good, there was the fact that one of Debra's students had become fixated on her to the point of stalking. Though she had made it abundantly clear that she would never even consider dating a student—not even one who was nearly her own age, having been a late bloomer as an undergrad—this one didn't seem to take no for an answer. She had decided that enough was enough. She would bring it up to the director of the School of Journalism, as well as report it to the campus police, for the record.

After classes were over, Debra hopped into her black Audi S3 sedan and headed home. Peeking into the rearview mirror, she could have sworn that she was being followed by a dark SUV. Was her imagination playing tricks on her? Maybe she was getting paranoid for no reason, brought on by her musings.

This apparently was the case, as the vehicle in question veered off onto another street, the driver seemingly oblivious to her imaginative thoughts. Much less, out to get her. Relaxing, Debra drove to her apartment complex just outside the college campus on Frandor Lane, parked in her assigned spot and headed across the attractively landscaped grounds. She climbed the stairs to her building's second-floor two-bedroom, two-bath unit. Inside, she put down her mini hobo bag with papers to grade, kicked off mule loafers and strode barefoot across the maple hardwood flooring to the galley kitchen. She took a bottle of red wine from the refrigerator, poured herself a glass and considered if she should eat in or go out for dinner.

While still contemplating, Debra bypassed the contemporary furnishings and took the wineglass with her to the main bedroom. *Maybe*

I'll just have a pizza delivered, she told herself, while removing the hairpin holding her bun in place, allowing her locks to fall free across her shoulders.

Then she heard the sound of a familiar voice say almost comically, "I was beginning to think you'd never get here, Deb."

The unexpected visitor's words gave Debra a start, causing her to drop the glass of wine, its contents spilling onto the brown carpeted floor. He was standing in her bedroom as if he owned the place. How did he get inside her apartment? What did he want?

"When I sensed that you might be on to me as I followed your car, I took a shortcut to beat you here, while giving you a false sense of security."

She recalled the SUV that had been following her and then seemingly wasn't. Why hadn't she remembered the type of vehicle he drove?

"Sorry about the wine," he said tonelessly, glancing at it and the glass on the floor. "At least you managed to have a sip or two. As for what's probably foremost on your mind, honestly, it wasn't all that difficult to break into your apartment. It has a relatively cheap lock that's easy to pick for someone who knows what he's doing."

Debra froze like an ice sculpture while weighing her options, then asked him tentatively, "What do you want?" Was he actually going to rape her to get what he wanted? Then what? Leave her alone to forever remember what he did? Or report it to the police and have him arrested and charged with a sex crime?

Why couldn't he have simply put the moves on someone else who may have been interested in his advances? Or did he get his kicks from power tripping by forcing the action? No matter how she sliced it, Debra didn't like the outcome. Maybe she could outrun him and escape the apartment, wherein she could whip the cell phone out of the back pocket of her chino pants and call for help. Except for the fact that he was now standing between her and the exit from the room.

"It's not good for you, I'm afraid." His voice burst into her thoughts, while taking on an ominous octave. "You need to die, and I'm here to make sure it happens."

As her heart skipped a few beats in digesting his harrowing words, this was when Debra knew she had to make her move before it was too late. What move should that be? The answer was obvious. Anything that could get her out of this alive. And, hopefully, not too badly injured.

HE ANTICIPATED THAT she would try to hit him where it hurt, easily blocking her futile efforts. He was also way ahead of her next instinct to try to somehow worm her way around his sturdy frame and escape what was to be a veritable death trap. He caught her narrow shoulders and tossed her toward the platform bed, expecting her to fall onto the comforter. But she somehow managed to stay on her feet and was about to scream her pretty head off, alerting neighbors. He couldn't let that happen.

It only took one well-placed hard blow to her jaw to send Professor Debra Newton reeling backward and flat onto the bed, where she went out like a light. Now it was time for him to finish what he started. She had no one to blame but herself for the unfortunate predicament she was now in. They were all alike when it came right down to it. Believing they could screw guys like him over and not be held accountable. Wrong.

Dead wrong.

He lifted the decorative throw pillow off the bed and, just as she began to stir, placed it over her face, pressing down firmly. Though she struggled mightily to break free, he was stronger, far more determined and, as such, took away her means to breathe air before she lost her will to resist altogether and became deathly still. When he finally removed the pillow, he saw that her blue eyes were wide open, but any life in them had gone away for good.

He sucked in a deep breath and tossed the pillow back on the bed beside her corpse, pleased with what he had done to the professor and already looking ahead for an encore. After all, she wasn't the only one who needed to be taught a lesson that only female educators could truly appreciate. He laughed at his own sick sense of humor before vacating the premises and making sure he was successful in avoiding detection while engineering his masterful escape.

IT WASN'T LONG before he picked up right where he'd left off. Again and again. Now yet another one bit the dust. Or, if not quite ashes to ashes, dust to dust, the good-looking professor was very much dead. He had seen to that, watching as the life drained out of her like soapy water in a tub. She had been expecting someone else, apparently. But got him instead. Her loss. His gain.

Like the ones that came before her, he did what he needed to do. What they forced him to do, more or less. Suffocation was such a tough way to die. Fighting for air and finding it in short supply when being cut off from the brain was challenging, to say the least. But that was their tough luck. He made no apologies for playing the villain, falling prey to his inner demons. The ones that drove him to kill and get a charge out of it when the deed was done.

He took one final look at the dead professor and imagined her looking back at him, had her eyes not been shut for good. Maybe she would meet up in the afterlife with the others and form a dead professors' society or something to that effect. He nearly burst into laughter at the devious thought but suppressed this, so as not to alert anyone of his presence.

Leaving the scene of the crime, he made his way down the back stairs, and like a thief— make that murderer—in the night, he moved briskly away from the building without looking back. Only when he was in the safety of his car and on the road did he allow himself to suck in a deep and glorious breath, knowing that he had escaped successfully and could go on with his life as though he hadn't just committed another cold-blooded murder that, like those before her, she never saw coming.

Not till it was much, much too late.

Chapter One

"Looks like the Campus Killer has taken another professor's life." The words lodged deep in Detective Sergeant Paula Lynley's throat like a jagged chicken bone stuck there, as she relayed this depressing information over speakerphone to Captain Shailene McNamara, her immediate superior in the Investigative Division of the Department of Police and Public Safety at Addison University. Paula was behind the wheel in her duty vehicle, a white Ford Mustang Mach-E, en route to the crime scene, the office of Honors College Associate Professor Odette Furillo.

Shailene made a grunting sound. "That's not what I wanted to hear to start my day."

You and me both, Paula told herself, in total agreement on a Wednesday at 9:00 a.m. Unfortunately, there was no getting around this, painful as it was for both of them to digest. "Ms. Furillo was apparently working late. Her body was discovered by a student this morning," Paula informed the captain, implying that it didn't appear to be an active crime situation to prompt a shelter-in-place order. "All signs seem to indicate that the victim was suffocated to death."

At least this was what Paula was led to believe by the first responder to the scene, Detective Michael Davenport, one of the investigators under her command in the AU DPPS. If true, this would mark the fourth suffocation-style murder of an Addison University female professor on or close to the campus in Rendall Cove over the past few months. The first came during the early part of the summer session, when a thirty-three-year-old associate professor in the School of Journalism, Debra Newton, was found asphyxiated to death in her apartment. And a month later, thirty-four-year-old Department of Horticulture Assistant Professor Harmeet Fernández was discovered dead in the Horticulture Gardens.

Near the end of the summer session, thirty-six-year-old Kathy Payne, a professor in the College of Veterinary Medicine, was fatally suffocated in her residence. Now, just a couple of weeks into the fall session, Paula had to consider the very distinct possibility that a fourth professor had been murdered in a similar manner by the so-called "Campus Killer," the moniker the unsub was given by the press. If so, that would leave little doubt that they were dealing with a bona fide and devious serial killer on and around the campus, where there had been an increase in patrols after the first professor was murdered near the university. Apart from a general belief that they were likely dealing with a male perpetrator—based on the nature of the crimes and circumstantial evidence—as of now, there had been no identifiable DNA or fingerprints to point the blame at anyone in particular. And no reliable surveillance video that could give them a clue about the unsub. Nor had any of the suspects panned out thus far. Would it be any different this time around?

The ongoing case was being jointly investigated by the Rendall Cove Police Department, considering that the first and third murders linked to the killer had occurred off campus, within the Rendall Cove city limits. Paula hoped that they would be able to soon crack the case with the latest purported homicide at the hands of the unsub. "Of course, we won't know anything for certain on this front till the autopsy is completed," she told her, as if Shailene wasn't aware of this.

The captain responded tersely, "I get that. Keep me posted on the developments in this disturbing investigation."

"I will," Paula promised as always, before disconnecting. She sighed, feeling just as disturbed that they were involved with this type of crisis in what was normally a peaceful, beautifully landscaped campus environment, split by the Cedar River, with countless imposing trees, lush green spaces, winding paths and newly renovated buildings. But someone had chosen to threaten that tranquility in the worst way possible.

While keeping her bold brown eyes on the lookout for bicyclers, who at times recklessly believed they owned the roads, Paula's thoughts slipped to her personal trials and tribulations over the past eighteen months. At thirty-five, she was a year removed from her divorce from Scott Lynley. The veteran FBI special agent had once been the love of her life. It was a love that seemed destined to last forever. But somewhere along the way, things fizzled between them and, once it became apparent that no magical elixir would fix them, they decided it would be best to go their separate ways. For Paula, an African American, an interracial marriage was never a problem to her. A clash of strong wills between her and Scott, however, proved to be a major issue.

Deciding she needed a clean break, she relocated from Kentucky to Central Michigan, where in a lateral transfer, Paula landed an opening with the Addison University PD. Equipped with a Bachelor of Science in Criminal Justice and a minor in Law, Justice and Public Policy from the University of Louisville, where she excelled and was a member of a sorority, she welcomed the opportunity to return to a campus atmosphere for police work. But now it was being put to a major test, and it was one she fully intended to pass at the end of the day.

Same was true for her love life that had been nonexistent since her divorce. Though her past failure in a relationship had made Paula extra cautious and extremely picky, she believed there was still someone out there for her. Just as she was available for the right man. For whatever reason, the new criminology professor at the university, Neil Ramirez, came to mind. Aside from being a drop-dead gorgeous Hispanic, the ATF special agent and renowned criminal profiler seemed to know his stuff in the classroom as a visiting professor, and had proven to be popular among criminology students, from what she understood. Out of curiosity, she had sat in on his lecture a couple of times, only speaking briefly to him afterward, but leaving with a favorable impression nonetheless as someone she could imagine building a rapport with.

She knew little of his backstory, other than that he had recently lost someone close to him, a fellow ATF agent, who was killed in the line of duty. As would be expected, apparently Neil Ramirez took it pretty hard, just as Paula knew would be the case were someone in the department dealt a similar fate. The special agent's reputation as a hardworking, honest and dependable agent made him a valued addition to Addison University and the School of Criminal Justice, both of whom apparently welcomed him with open arms.

Paula was indeed a bit curious about his life off the job. Or if Professor Ramirez even had a life outside of work, which she found herself short on these days. For all she knew, he was happily married and had a few kids to go back to. Paula lamented over never having started a family with her ex and wondered if that might have made a difference in her failed marriage. Or was she grasping at straws for something that had simply run out of steam, no matter how painful it was to have to reconcile herself with that?

She returned to the here and now as she pulled into the parking lot of the Gotley Building on Wakefield Road that housed the Department of Mathematics. After finding a spot, she parked and exited the vehicle. Slender, at five feet nine inches in height, she was wearing a one-button black blazer over a moss-colored satin charmeuse shirt and midrise blue ponte knit pants, along with square-toed flats. Tucked inside her jacket in a leather concealment holster was a SIG Sauer P365 semiautomatic pistol. In a force of habit, she tapped it as if to make sure it was still there, and then ran a hand through her brunette layered and medium-length haircut, parted squarely in the middle, before heading into the building.

On the third floor, where Professor Furillo's office was located, Paula found it already cordoned off by barricade tape, and members of the Crime Scene Investigation Unit were busy at work processing the site. Bypassing them, she was greeted by Detective Mike Davenport. The tall, forty-year-old married father of three girls was blue-eyed and had short dark locks in a quiff hairstyle and a chevron mustache.

"Hey," he said tonelessly.

"Hey." She gave him a friendly nod and then got down to business. "What's the latest?"

"It's not good." Davenport frowned. "Appears as though Professor Furillo was grading papers when someone took her by surprise," he remarked. "From the looks of it, she apparently fought with her attacker but, unfortunately, came up short. The seat cushion beside the body suggests it was the murder weapon used to suffocate the victim."

Paula wrinkled her dainty nose at him. "And a student discovered her?"

"Yeah. Name's Joan McCashin. Says she had a scheduled meeting with Furillo this morning, came upon the body and then immediately called 911. McCashin's prepared to give a formal statement to that effect."

"Good." Paula glanced over his shoulder. "Which office is the professor's?"

"This one," he answered, leading the way as they passed by two closed office doors to an open door.

Stepping into the small and cramped windowless office, Paula glanced at the gangly and bald-headed crime scene photographer who gave her a nod, then resumed his snapping of pictures routinely, before she spied the deceased associate professor on the floor beside an ergonomic computer desk. Odette Furillo was lying flat on her back on the beige carpeted floor. In her thirties, she was slender and about five-six, blond-haired with brown highlights in a stacked pixie, and fully dressed in a button-front light blue blouse, navy straight-leg pants and black loafers. Next to her head was a gray memory foam office chair pillow. The impressions on it seemed to contour with that of a face when pressed against it.

Cringing, Paula could only imagine the horror of knowing you were about to die and not being able to do a thing to prevent it. Still, she noted what appeared to be blood on one of the hands of the professor, suggesting that she might have scratched her attacker, collecting valuable DNA in the process. "Maybe Professor Furillo got the unsub's DNA to help us ID the killer," Paula pointed out optimistically.

"I was thinking the same thing," Davenport said, knitting his thick brows. "Hopefully the medical examiner and forensics will make that happen and we'll go from there."

"We need to find out who else may have been working in the building last night. That includes students and custodial workers. Let's see what surveillance cameras can tell us." In Paula's way of thinking, no one could be excluded as a suspect, given that more than a few people had access to the Gotley Building.

"Yeah." Davenport scratched his jutting chin. "And then cross-check it with anyone who might have been in the vicinity of the second victim of the alleged Campus Killer on school grounds."

Paula eyed the professor's laptop and wondered if her computer and online activities before, during and after the attack might provide clues about the unsub. "Let's get the Digital Forensics and Cyber Crime Unit over here pronto and see what they can find from the laptop, if anything. Along with Odette Furillo's cell phone," Paula added, noting it on the desktop.

He gave a nod. "Will do."

They heard some chatter and left the office, careful not to taint potential evidence. In the hallway, approaching them was Detective Gayle Yamasaki of the Rendall Cove PD's Detective Bureau. In her midthirties, single and slim with small brown eyes and long, curly black hair tied in a low bun, the pretty Indigenous Hawaiian was heading the investigation into the murder of Professor Debra Newton, who was strangled to death in her apartment in June.

"Came as soon as I got the word," Gayle said, wringing her thin hands. "So, what are we looking at here?"

Paula furrowed her brow. "You can see for

yourself, but by all indications, including the appearance of the victim and the killer's MO, we're looking at another homicide courtesy of the Campus Killer."

Gayle sighed and took a peek at the deceased before muttering an expletive. "Four and counting," she groaned.

"Tell me about it." Paula made a face. "We need to find out if the victims were connected in any way." *And if so, how exactly*, she thought.

"Assuming these aren't just random killings," Gayle countered.

"There is that." Paula understood that if they were in fact chasing a single killer, the unsub could just as easily be someone the victims knew as a total stranger. Whatever the case, as they were all professors, that in and of itself indicated some relationship to this institution of higher education.

"The bottom line," Davenport told them, "is that someone is on a killing rampage on this campus and in our town, and it's up to us to stop him."

"There's no other option," Paula agreed, knowing that to think otherwise would be playing right into the unsub's deadly hands. "We have to figure this out, sooner than later."

Shays County Chief Medical Examiner Eddie

Saldana arrived, and they parted the way to let him through. In his early fifties, short and of medium build, he had red hair blended with gray in a side-swept style to partially cover his pate and wore square glasses over sharp gray eyes.

"This is getting to be a bad habit," he grumbled, frowning.

"One we're all hoping to kick," Paula said humorlessly. "Whatever you can give us on the deceased would be helpful in that regard, Dr. Saldana."

"I'll see what I can do." He stepped into Odette Furillo's office and, after squeezing into nitrile gloves, methodically did a quick examination of the victim, before saying glumly, "All things considered, my initial assessment is that the professor likely died as a result of violent asphyxia. I'll be more definitive once the autopsy is completed, including an estimation of the time of death."

Even the preliminary conclusion was more than enough to convince Paula that this was not only a homicide, but one that mirrored the three other deaths attributed to a single killer with a singular modus operandi. "We'll look forward to reading the autopsy report when it's ready," she told him, which Paula assumed would be the next day. Until then, they needed to do whatever was necessary to try to gather evidence and build a case toward eventually pinning the crime on the one responsible.

THE CAMPUS KILLER relished this opportunity to catch the action, hidden very much in plain view. Endless chatter about the death of Professor Odette Furillo seemed to grip those around him, as though it was the worst possible thing that could happen. Actually, even worse for those standing around would be if they themselves suffered the same fate as the attractive Honors College associate professor. He laughed inside. As it was, they were not the targets of his murderous ways. Unfortunately, the same could not be said of the other three pretty professors who managed to find their way into his crosshairs and were given a one-way ticket to an early death.

He mused about the campus and city police trying to stop him in his deadly tracks. They were undoubtedly freaking out about his uncanny ability to run rings around them while handpicking his victims right under the authorities' collective noses. Another laugh rang in his head as he wound his way through the bystanders, speaking only when spoken to. And even then, limiting what he said and how he said it, so as not to tip his hand in the slightest as to his guilt. For all they could see, he was merely one of them, content with complaining and speculating about the homicides, but otherwise keeping the worst of it at a safe distance so as not to be contaminated like spoiled food.

He watched as the good-looking female university detective left the building, seemingly in a huff, while giving only a cursory glance his way, as one of many. Not having the slightest clue that she was looking at the Campus Killer and was within her power to take him into custody. Except that she never really saw him for who he was. Just as he anticipated when making himself visible as part of the thrill from the kill.

As Detective Paula Lynley headed down the sidewalk, he resisted the desire to follow her, deciding it was more of a risk than he was willing to take at this time. Something, though, told him that an opportunity would likely present itself for them to meet face-to-face. At which time, she would very likely regret having ever laid eyes on him in ways she would never see coming.

Till it was much too late.

OUTSIDE THE BUILDING, some professors and students milled about aimlessly, probably in somewhat of a state of shock, while likely wondering when and if they would be let back inside. Or perhaps, Paula considered, if and when it would be safe to do so. She wondered the same thing herself. Or, for that matter, when the entire campus could go back to normal, without the looming threat of a serial killer hanging in the air like an unsettling dark rain cloud.

Short of solving this case overnight, Paula suspected that her boss would soon be sending out a request to the FBI to join in on the investigation. A routine thing when it came to creating serial killer task forces and utilizing the far reach of federal law enforcement and seemingly unlimited resources of the federal government. She had seen this all too often when married to an FBI agent, who also had a brother working in the Bureau. At the very least, Paula believed that a behavioral profiler was needed to help them better size up who and what they were after in the dangerous and lethal unsub.

This brought Neil Ramirez back to the forefront of her thoughts. As a criminal profiler, who also happened to be an expert on violent serial offenders from what she learned during one of his lectures, the professor was just the person they needed to utilize his expertise in their current investigation. Would he be up to the task? Or would his professional demons stand in the way? Those notwithstanding, she was sure that Captain McNamara would welcome Neil Ramirez into the fold as a paid consultant. As would Gayle Yamasaki and her boss with the Rendall Cove PD's Detective Bureau, Criminal Investigations Sergeant Anderson Klimack.

Paula walked to Horton Hall, three buildings over on Creighten Road, where Professor Ramirez was currently giving a lecture. She was eager to speak with him and a bit nervous at the same time, though unsure if that was due to her impending request. Or the sheer presence of the good-looking man himself.

The latter was on full display as she slipped in the back of the packed room, but had no trouble sizing up the ATF special agent, filling in the blanks of her memory. Standing in front of the class, Neil Ramirez was a good six feet, three inches tall at least, and rock solid in a way that could only come from regular workouts and a healthy diet. His thick brown hair was cut in a high razor fade. He had a diamond-shaped, square-jawed face, gray-brown eyes that shone in their intensity, and sported a heavy stubble beard that looked really good on him. Wearing a red Henley shirt, black jeans and tennis shoes, he seemed to fit right in as a college professor.

When he seemed to home in on her, Paula's heart did a little leap and check. But just as quickly, as if she had suddenly become invisible to him, Professor Ramirez turned in a different direction as he talked about profiling a criminal, giving Paula time to catch her breath and put together enough of a sell to bring him on board.

VISITING CRIMINOLOGY PROFESSOR NEIL RAMIREZ would've had to be foolish not to notice the stunning African American detective sergeant with the Department of Police and Public Safety at the college, Paula Lynley. As it was, his sight was better than twenty-twenty the last time he had his eyes examined, and he had no trouble seeing what was staring him right in the face, more or less. In fact, he'd been checking her out each time she decided to pay his lecture a visit. And even once or twice when he happened to notice her elsewhere on campus from afar. Tall and well put together on a slim frame, she thoroughly captivated the detective with her caramel complexion, heart-shaped face, big and pretty brown eyes, delicate nose, wide mouth and most generous smile. She had a stylish look to the chestnut brown hair grazing her shoulders.

Though they had exchanged a few words now and then, Neil had resisted going beyond the surface in getting to know the detective better. Still dealing with some personal and professional issues, he had chosen for the time being to focus on just trying to fit in to his temporary new world of teaching college students about criminology, criminal justice and criminal profiling.

As a thirty-six-year-old Mexican American special agent with the Bureau of Alcohol, Tobacco, Firearms and Explosives, Neil had gone through the ATF National Academy, located at the Federal Law Enforcement Training Center in Glynco, Georgia, and been assigned to the Federal Bureau of Investigation's Behavioral Analysis Unit to earn his stripes. Before that, he had graduated from the University of Arizona in Tucson with a Bachelor of Science in Criminal Justice Studies and a focus on Social and Behavioral Sciences. Now, thirteen years into his career, he was primarily working out of the ATF's field office in Grand Rapids, Michigan, as a behavioral profiler and providing technical support in ATF, FBI or task force investigations.

Neil lamented as he pondered the death of his colleague, Ramone Munoz, who died during a shoot-out last year with drug traffickers as a member of the ATF Special Response Team. Between that and Neil's breakup with his girlfriend, Constance Chen, who went looking for another man and found him in a musician, Neil had decided to take a step back from his full-time duties as a special agent, giving him some time to clear his head.

With a bestselling book on criminal profiling to his credit, he accepted a position as a visiting professor with Addison University's School of Criminal Justice this past summer. The short-term contract left the door open for a longer commitment both ways, if all went well. But Neil wasn't looking beyond the current fall semester at this point. Especially since he had also been tasked by the ATF with gathering intel on a suspected arms trafficking operation in Rendall Cove that had been uncovered through chatter on the dark web. With an undercover agent on the inside working with the Rendall Cove Police Department's Firearms Investigation Unit and the Shays County Sheriff's Department, Neil was confident they would be successful in putting the brakes on this purported online trafficking in contraband firearms and ammunition operation, as well as unlawful possession of arms and ammunition.

Neil forced himself to take his eyes off the detective just long enough to snap out of the trance. He gazed at Paula Lynley again, curious as to why she was there. *Maybe she'll decide to fill me in*, he thought. It wasn't lost on him that an investigation was underway between the school's DPPS and the city's police department involving the murders of three female professors. Were they actually connected? Was there a single perp involved? It admittedly piqued the interest of the profiler in him. Up to a point.

He turned back to his students, remembering how difficult it was when he was in college to hold his attention. So far, so good. They seemed to be buying what he was selling in offering them a well-rounded look at criminality and the devious minds of hard-core criminals. But for how long?

When the class ended, Neil finished routinely with, "We'll pick it up the next time. But don't let that stop you from heading over to the library, where I've got some books on reserve, for further insight into the subject matter."

After the students, about half male and half female, began filing out of the classroom, Neil watched Paula Lynley come forward in measured steps as he was placing some papers into his faux-leather briefcase. He grinned at her and said curiously, "Detective Lynley. Nice to see you again." He met her eyes for a long moment, trying to read into them but having little luck. "So, what brings you to my class this morning?"

She held his gaze and, without preface, responded straightforwardly, "Professor Ramirez, I need your help."

Chapter Two

Paula was momentarily at a loss for follow-up words as she took in the very good-looking visiting professor. It somehow seemed easier to approach him when it was just a hello in passing than when she had to seek his assistance in an important criminal investigation. But rather than chicken out like a schoolgirl with a crush on the star quarterback, she managed to gather herself and say coolly, "I'm sure you're aware that three female professors at the university have been murdered over the past three months."

Neil nodded to that effect. "Yeah, I know about it," he said cautiously. "Sad thing."

"That's putting it mildly." Paula took a breath. "This morning, a fourth professor was found murdered in her office."

"What?" He cocked a slightly crooked brow. "I hadn't heard about that one," he confessed.

"We're just getting the word out, while trying to wrap our minds around the fact that this is happening at all."

"Has anyone been arrested?" Neil seemed to rethink the question. "I assume that would be a no?"

"Correct assumption." She lifted her chin. "Unfortunately, the unsub is still on the loose and obviously has to be considered as possibly armed and definitely dangerous," she pointed out. "But as of now, we don't believe there is an immediate threat to students and staff, per se. That could change, of course, as more info comes in on the homicide."

He regarded her with interest, then asked with a catch in his voice, "So, what exactly did you need from me?"

Paula pushed a strand of hair away from her forehead and responded frankly, "Your expertise as a profiler, Professor Ramirez. Or should I say Special Agent Ramirez?"

"Neil will be fine, Detective Lynley," he told her evenly.

"Okay, Neil. And please call me Paula," she said, feeling as though they had already broken the ice in getting what she needed from him. "Anyway, it appears as if we're dealing with a serial killer here that the press has already dubbed the Campus Killer. The Department of Police and Public Safety is working with the Rendall Cove PD to bring the perp to justice and solve the case. In the meantime, we can use all the help we can get in developing a profile on the unsub to aid in the investigation. As a visiting professor who also happens to be a criminal profiler, I thought I'd reach out to see if you'd be interested in working with us as a paid consultant on the case?"

Neil rubbed his prominent jawline. "I kind of have my hands full at the moment," he said ambivalently. "Teaching these kids can be exhausting."

Though in complete agreement from her own college years and dealing with some of the misbehaving students today, Paula locked eyes with him and responded sharply, "So can murder. I understand that you're here to teach. But keeping them safe is even more important, don't you think? I could reach out to the FBI, as long as it isn't to my ex-husband," she found herself saying candidly. "However, since you're on campus, I wanted to give it a go first." She realized she was putting him on the spot unfairly, but desperation at times called for dirty tactics.

Neil gave her an amused grin. "Since you put it that way, ex-husband and all, I'll be happy to come aboard as a profiler in your investigation."

"Thanks." Paula blushed. "I'm sure that tapping into your expertise will give us some valuable insight into the unsub, before and after apprehension."

"Why don't you email me what you have on the unsub and case," Neil said, "and I'll take a look for a preliminary assessment."

"I'll do that," she promised, excited at the prospect of getting to know him. At least on a professional basis.

He nodded and grabbed his briefcase. "I'll walk you out."

Paula smiled, leading the way into the hall. "So, how's it been teaching, compared to working out in the field as an ATF agent?" She immediately saw the question as too trivial.

Neil laughed. "Well, for one, the teaching is mostly inside and investigations for the ATF are often outside. But apart from that difference, I have to say, I love trying to influence young minds, even if only for a short while, whereas I'm not as keen on having to take down the bad guys these days. But that's a story for another time..." He frowned thoughtfully. "Anyway, it's a good living, so I suppose I shouldn't complain."

Paula considered the tragedy he'd experienced with the death of a fellow agent. She wondered if there was more that soured him on working for the ATF. Maybe there would be another time to get the scoop. "Believe me," she told him, "we all have professional complaints from time to time. Comes with the territory." Not that she had issues with her current employer, but she knew that there were always good and bad days for every job. Hers was no exception. Such as now, when she was dealing with a serial perp and needed it solved sooner than later.

"You're right, of course," he said. "Life is always about what you make of it, for better or worse."

"True." Neil brushed shoulders with her and Paula immediately felt an electrical spark surge through her. Had he experienced this as well? At the door to the outside, he flashed a sideways grin and said, "My office is on the third floor."

She smiled, understanding that he was headed there and, as such, this was where they parted. "Thanks for agreeing to work with us," she expressed.

"I'm happy to do what I can to help out." He opened the door for her and said, "By the way, no pay is necessary to consult on the case as a profiler. Consider it an extension of my work as a visiting professor that maybe my students can learn a thing or two from."

"If you say so." Paula welcomed his involvement, whatever the terms. And she did believe that his criminal justice students stood to benefit from whatever he chose to bring to the table. As she would herself, she believed.

Out of Horton Hall, Paula headed for her car, equipped with a new weapon in the ongoing investigation.

Neil Ramirez.

NEIL WATCHED FOR a moment as Paula Lynley walked away from the building. He found himself undressing her in his mind, sure he would like every bit of what he saw. How could he not? Coming back down to earth, he knew that he needed to stay on another track where it concerned the police detective sergeant. At least till he had a chance to get a read on the so-called Campus Killer. Then maybe the vibes he'd picked up when they touched shoulders—or even met each other's eyes—might be something to explore further. Or was the sour taste in his mouth from his last failed relationship still bitter enough not to want to jump back in the ring with another woman?

Inside his temporary office, Neil sat at the

L-shaped computer desk in a well-worn brown faux-leather chair and mused about the lovely detective he would be working with. So, she'd been married to an FBI agent. Any children in the marriage before they parted ways? How did Paula's ex ever let her get away? Or was it a mutual thing of simply growing apart and wanting something different in their lives?

Neil wondered if she was seeing anyone right now. Or was Paula cautious about opening her heart to another man any time soon? If so, could he really blame her? Was he any less guilty of preferring not to rush into anything these days? Then again, would it be foolish not to keep an open mind for the right person, whenever she entered his orbit?

His thoughts moved back to the consulting as a profiler job he'd just agreed to. He questioned just how advisable it was to take on another assignment with his plate already full. Since when had that ever stopped him? He always tried to do what was best in any given situation. In this instance, how could he not agree to assist in the case, with what sure looked like a serial killer lurking on and around the campus? One who threatened the lives of female professors. And could easily target female students as well, if the unsub was not stopped.

Paula drew a hard bargain, Neil told himself, sitting back. He looked forward to reviewing the particulars of the case and lending his knowledge in the hunt for the killer. Beyond that, Neil still had to deal with the fact that a suspected arms trafficker was also in their midst and needed to be brought under control before unleashing more gun violence in Rendall Cove and abroad.

PAULA PARKED IN the employee parking lot of the Addison University Police Department on Cedar Lane. She went inside the building and headed straight for the office of Captain Shailene McNamara. After being waved in, Paula stepped through the door. Shailene was at her standing desk on the phone. She studied the captain, who was fifty years old, on the slender side and had strawberry blond hair styled in a choppy bob. Her blues eyes looked bigger behind prescription eyeglasses. Shailene was on her second marriage and the mother of four children.

She ended the call and, gazing at Paula, said, "So, where are we on the case?"

Reiterating what had already been reported, Paula filled her in with more details on Associate Professor Odette Furillo's murder, which fell short of naming a suspect. Or having the official cause of her death, pending release of the autopsy report. Then, as Paula watched the captain's expression meander between frustration and resignation, she told her, "I've asked Visiting Professor Neil Ramirez to join the investigation as a criminal profiler."

Shailene perked up upon hearing this. "Really?"

"Yes. Given his expertise on killers, including serial killers, it seemed like a good idea to take advantage of the ATF special agent's presence at Addison University. To pick his brain, if you will," Paula stressed.

"A very good idea." Shailene nodded in agreement. "With the murder of four of our professors, at this point, getting Agent Ramirez on board is a smart move." She touched her glasses. "I take it he accepted the offer?"

"Yes," Paula was happy to announce. "Moreover, Neil doesn't want any compensation, believing that it's his duty as a visiting professor and profiler to lend a hand to the investigation."

Shailene's face lit with approval. "Actually, I read Agent Ramirez's book on profiling. Good stuff. You should check it out, when you get a chance."

"I will." Paula exchanged a few more thoughts

while glancing about the spacious office with its contemporary furnishings and plaques on the wall. When Shailene's cell phone rang, it was Paula's excuse to leave.

En route to her own office, she ran into Detective Mike Davenport. "Hey," she said to him.

"Hey." His broad shoulders squared. "Got some info for you."

"Okay." She met his eyes with curiosity. "Why don't we step into my office?"

"All right."

He followed her into the corner office, which Davenport had once thought would be his, until Paula got it instead, after being promoted to detective sergeant. Though things had been a little tense between them for a while, he had seemingly gotten past the disappointment and they were in a good place right now, as far as Paula was concerned. She believed Davenport was a good detective and valued having him on her squad.

Rather than essentially pulling rank by taking a seat at her three-drawer desk and inviting him to sit on one of the two vinyl black stacking chairs on the other side, Paula remained standing. Eyeing the detective, she asked, "So, what do you have?"

Davenport ran a hand through his hair and

replied matter-of-factly, "Well, I was able to pull up security camera footage from inside and outside the Gotley Building, where Professor Odette Furillo was killed. Seems as though a number of people, mostly students by the look of it, were out and about, along with vehicles, between last night and this morning. Once we get the official time of death, we can better sort through them and see if we can narrow down potential suspects."

"Good." Paula nodded, expecting to get this information from the autopsy report in the morning. "Anything else?"

"Yeah," he said. "As expected, we'll be checking out any cell phones that pinged around the time Furillo was murdered. And, of course, we're waiting to see if there's DNA to work with in unmasking the unsub."

Paula smiled thinly, knowing they were going about this the right way. "I have some news too," she told him.

"What's that?"

She told him about Neil Ramirez agreeing to work with them. "As a criminal profiler, Professor Ramirez should give us some crucial insight into the killer," she finished.

"I agree." Davenport bobbed his head. "Heard about Ramirez's successes in helping to nab some perps. If he's willing to step away from teaching long enough to profile our unsub, more power to him. It's all about solving the case and making the campus and surroundings a safe environment again, right?"

"Absolutely." Paula showed her teeth, glad to see that he didn't believe Neil was somehow using his fed credentials as an ATF special agent to take over the case. On the contrary, she believed that the visiting professor was an asset, lending his skills in teaming up with the DPPS's Investigative Division and the Rendall Cove PD's Detective Bureau in their pursuit of justice.

After Davenport left the office, Paula sat in her ergonomic mid-back leather desk chair and phoned Gayle Yamasaki to let her know that Neil Ramirez would be assisting them.

"That's wonderful," Gayle expressed. "Seems that Agent Ramirez's reputation as a profiler precedes him."

Paula chuckled. "Appears that way."

"What have you gotten out of him so far?"

"Not much. I'm sending him the info we have on the unsub shortly."

"Can't wait to get his take on the perp," Gayle said.

"Same here," Paula had to admit, as if Neil's assessment alone could nab the unsub. If only it were that simple. As it was, cracking this case had been anything but simple, thus far. Only diligence in their collective efforts would lead to favorable results.

Later, Paula copied some digital files, emailed them to Neil and did some paperwork. Her thoughts drifted here and there between her former married life and the present, where she was divorced but still wanting to be in a stable relationship with respect that was mutual and not one-sided. She couldn't help but wonder if this was something that Neil was looking for too in a partner. Had he left someone behind during his current stint on campus? Or was he seeing someone locally these days?

Better not allow my imagination to run wild, Paula scolded herself, no matter how tempting to do so.

After work, she headed over to the campus bookstore on Blaire Street and picked up a copy of Neil's book, entitled appropriately, *Profiling the Killers*. From there, Paula stopped off at Burger King and ordered a fish sandwich and onion rings for takeout, not in the mood for making dinner.

She drove home, which was an upscale penthouse condominium in Northwest Rendall Cove on Sadler Lane, a block from Rendall Creek

Park. Exiting her car in covered parking, Paula bypassed the elevator and scaled the flights of stairs to her two-bedroom, two-bath fourth-story unit. The two-level unit had an open concept, with a nice great room and engineered eucalyptus hardwood flooring. Floor-to-ceiling windows and a covered deck overlooked a creek, where Canada geese loved to hang out, and paw-paw trees. She had picked out some great rustic furnishings and accent pieces for downstairs. The gourmet kitchen came with granite countertops and stainless steel appliances.

Sitting in a corner of the kitchen, as though waiting for Paula to come home, was her cat. She'd had the female Devon rex for a year now, named it Chloe, and thought she was adorable. Setting her Burger King bag on the counter, Paula scooped up the medium-sized cat and said, "Bet you're hungry too, huh?"

Chloe purred lovingly. Paula set her down on the floor, put some shredded chicken cat food in a bowl and watched as Chloe went for it hungrily. After heading up the quarter-turn staircase to the second floor, Paula stepped into the spacious bedroom with its large windows and farmhouse-style furniture, where she removed her sidearm and holster, before freshening up in the en suite.

Back downstairs, she poured herself a glass

of white wine and ate her meal standing up, while watching Chloe scamper off as if having something better to do than hang out with her, now that she had been fed. Paula finished eating and took the wineglass with her to the great room, where she sat on a barrel club chair and started to read Neil's book with interest.

NEIL HAD RENTED the custom and newly built, two-story home in a subdivision on Leary Way in Rendall Cove at the start of the summer session. It was right across the street from Rendall Creek Park. He still maintained his colonial-style house on a few acres of land in Grand Rapids. But for the time being, he was living in this college town and making the most of his surroundings, which included a woodland behind the house with a running trail. Inside, it had crown molding and a symmetrical layout with wide open spaces and interesting angles, a high ceiling, large windows, vinyl plank flooring, a traditional kitchen with an island and an informal dining room. It came fully furnished with modern chairs and tables.

Basically, the place had everything he needed and more, Neil believed. If he didn't count living there alone when, deep down inside, he would have preferred sharing his space with someone who actually wanted to be there. Maybe that day would come again. Or maybe he was asking for too much, after what turned out to be a debacle in his last relationship.

With a bottle of beer in hand, Neil sat on a solid wood leisure chair in the living room and opened up his laptop. He accessed the files Paula had sent him on the Campus Killer case. Since June, there had been one, two, three and now four murders to occur on and off the college grounds, with all the victims female professors. Each victim had been suffocated by the unsub, who somehow managed to get away, with little to tie the perp to the murders.

"Hmm," Neil muttered out loud. He was sensing a distinct pattern among the homicides. One that was hard to ignore for a profiler. The actions by what appeared to be a serial killer were deliberate and methodical. In Neil's mind, the perp—most likely a male by serial murder standards—had to have been stalking the victims, targeting them one by one.

Tasting the beer, Neil took a sharp breath, knowing that the unsub would almost certainly not call it quits. Being successful in the killings thus far was only inviting the perpetrator to strike again when the opportunity presented itself.

That thought was perhaps scariest of all.

Chapter Three

The following afternoon, the Campus Killer Task Force assembled in a Department of Police and Public Safety conference room at the university for the latest information on the investigation. Paula, who got little sleep last night after reading Neil Ramirez's entire book on profiling, was happy that he showed up today with her invitation. She was mindful that even with his participation in the case, he still had his duties as a visiting professor that had to be respected.

As much as I might like to, I can't hog up all of the special agent's time, Paula thought, as she gave him a friendly nod before she took to the podium. She glanced at Mike Davenport and Gayle Yamasaki, both of whom would have something to say in the scheme of things, and then Paula got down to business. Grabbing a stylus pen, she turned to the large touch-screen monitor and brought up an image of the first victim.

"In June, Debra Newton, a thirty-three-year-old associate professor in the School of Journalism, was smothered to death in her apartment on Frandor Lane in Rendall Cove." Paula was glad that, for the purpose of identifying them today, they had photos of the victims when they were alive and healthy, rather than their melancholy images after death. She regarded the attractive, white, blue-eyed professor with long wavy crimson locks and feathered bangs. "Professor Newton was divorced and had no known enemies, but obviously ended up with a real target on her back."

Paula switched to another image of a striking Latina, with pretty brown eyes and long, straight brunette hair, and said, "In July, thirty-four-year-old Harmeet Fernández, an assistant professor in the Department of Horticulture, was found dead in the Horticulture Gardens on Moxlyn Place, due to suffocation. She had just broken off what was described as a contentious relationship with a fellow professor, Clayton Ricamara. His alibi of being at an economics conference in London when she was killed held up."

After taking a breath, Paula brought up on

the screen a picture of an attractive African American woman with blondish boho braids and big sable eyes, before saying, "In August, Kathy Payne, a thirty-six-year-old professor in the College of Veterinary Medicine, was murdered in the same fashion in her Rendall Cove residence on Belle Street. Dr. Payne was a widow and not known to be seeing anyone at the time of her death."

The last image Paula put on the monitor was of a gorgeous white woman with long blond hair with brown highlights in a stacked pixie and green eyes. "In September, just yesterday morning, Odette Furillo, a thirty-four-year-old recently separated associate professor in the Department of Mathematics, was discovered on the floor of her office in the Gotley Building on Wakefield Road. According to the autopsy report from the county chief medical examiner, Professor Furillo's death was ruled a homicide, with the cause being asphyxia. Estimated time of death was somewhere between eight p.m. and eleven p.m."

Paula sighed and furrowed her brow. "All four homicide victims were suffocated to death by whom we believe to be the same unknown assailant. There is no evidence that any of the women were victims of a sexual assault. While we are still gathering and processing information, as of now, this unsub remains at large and can be considered extremely dangerous for female professors specifically, and all women who spend time on campus or who reside in the local community—so long as the perp is able to dodge being identified and taken into custody." Paula gazed at Neil, who seemed attentive in gazing back at her. "To that end, we've brought on board ATF Special Agent and criminal profiler, Neil Ramirez, who's currently doing double duty as a visiting professor of criminal justice. Agent Ramirez will give us his take on our unsub. But first, Detectives Mike Davenport and Gayle Yamasaki will provide updates on the investigation."

Paula gave both a brief smile and waited for them to come up and take her place. Davenport put a friendly hand on her shoulder and said in earnest, "This isn't easy for any of us, but we'll get through it and solve the case, one way or the other."

Paula nodded. "I know," she agreed, while feeling that day couldn't come soon enough for all concerned.

Gayle said to her, "You nailed it in setting things up, Paula, especially for our newcomer, Neil Ramirez. Hope I can add a bit more clarity on my end of the investigation."

"I'm sure you will," she told her with confidence, as Paula squeezed her hand and walked off to the side. She glanced at Neil, eager to hear what he had to say, especially after reading his excellent book last night.

Gayle went through the backstories on Debra Newton and Kathy Payne, the two professors killed off campus. Gayle was operating as the lead investigator with the Rendall Cove PD in trying to piece together some of the similarities in the homicides beyond the surface, which included relatively easy points of entry into the residences and lack of security systems. In an annoyed tone of voice, she concluded, "It's pretty clear that our unsub is deliberately choosing to rotate the kills off and on campus, perhaps to throw us off the trail, or otherwise play a deadly game of cat and mouse. We have to find a way to turn the tables and stop this before it gets much worse for both our police departments."

She stepped away from the podium and Davenport took her place. He wasted little time in getting to the heart of the evidence in the latest murder at Addison University, as Davenport said evenly, "As you all know, we have surveillance cameras covering most locations on campus. Kind of makes it tough to do something bad and slip away quietly, even in the dark of night. At least not so we can't eventually track you down. I've had a chance to take a look at video recorded on campus the night that Professor Odette Furillo was murdered."

Lifting the stylus pen, he brought security camera footage to the large screen. "What you see is surveillance video taken outside the Gotley Building, where Furillo's office is located, around the estimated time of her death. Here, on the south side of the building, you can see what appears to be a white man moving away quickly on foot, as if he'd just seen a ghost. But more likely, it was because he had just committed a heinous crime and was making his getaway."

Paula homed in on the monitor. Though the video was grainy, it was clear enough to see that the unsub did seem to be an adult male who was tall, solid in build and wearing dark clothing and a hoodie, obviously intended as a deliberate means to camouflage his appearance. He was certainly making haste in vacating the building and surroundings. Was this their Campus Killer?

The man's making a good case for being guilty of something, Paula told herself.

"We're still studying other surveillance camera video, with different angles and distance from the Gotley Building, to see if the unsub got into a vehicle and where else he might have gone," Davenport pointed out. "As well as to see if any other serious suspects might emerge, given the timeline. But as of now, I'd have to say that the man you see is definitely a person of interest we need to track down."

Paula couldn't agree more, and she glanced at Neil to see him nod his head in concurrence. She turned back to Davenport, who was saying, "DNA was collected from beneath the fingernails of Furillo. As this doesn't belong to the professor, the forensic unknown profile was sent to CODIS, in hopes of getting a hit in the database of convicted offender or arrestee DNA profiles, or forensic indexes from crime scenes." He frowned. "Unfortunately, there was no match. Looks like the unsub isn't in the system. But we have this DNA sample and we have a person of interest on our radar. We just need to find him, interrogate him, compare his DNA with the unidentified DNA profile and see what happens."

With any luck, we'll be able to do just that, Paula mused, optimistic that they could and would track down the suspect.

When Davenport was through, she reintroduced Neil to those in attendance as he stood and approached her.

NEIL TOOK IN everything that was said as he shook the hands of Paula, noting how soft her skin was, Gayle Yamasaki and lastly Mike Davenport, who said to him, "Great to have you as part of the team, Agent Ramirez."

"Thanks." Neil noted that he had a firm grip in the handshake, matching his own. "Happy to help in any way I can." As the detectives walked away, he regarded the members of the task force, having already been acquainted with some from the Rendall Cove PD, doing double duty, like him, with the Firearms Investigation Unit. "First, let me say thanks to everyone here for bringing me up to speed on what I didn't know when looking at it from a small distance as a visiting professor. Hopefully, the surveillance video and DNA evidence will lead to an arrest soon. As a criminal profiler and ATF special agent, I doubt that it would surprise many of you in my belief that, based on the modus operandi in the murders, it's a safe bet that we are looking at a serial killer in our midst." In his mind, Neil considered that these days the FBI defined even two such homicides fitting the criteria as serial murders. Double that number and it left little doubt that they were dealing with a serial killer.

"On the other hand, you may or may not

know that serial killers operating on university campuses and in college towns is far from unusual," Neil had to say. "Quite the contrary, with the warm and fuzzy welcoming environment and relatively easy and multiple escape routes. In many ways, this is the perfect setting for serial killers to prey upon victims. Think of Ted Bundy, John Norman Collins and Donald Miller, to name a few, all of whom went after female college students—any of which among the predators could just as easily have turned their deadly attention to female professors."

Neil allowed that to sink in for a moment and then continued, "As for this so-called Campus Killer, my early read is that the unsub is obviously someone who has knowledge of the campus and its surroundings—such as a professor, student or university employee—and uses it to his advantage to target those whom he has likely stalked surreptitiously and gone after when most advantageous to him. I see the unsub as a narcissistic, opportunistic vulture, who likely has a giant chip on his shoulder and has chosen to use this to go after the women whom he may deem as beneath him or think they are better than him. He could have been rejected by one or more of the victims," Neil reasoned. "Or simply used rejection of his advances or desires in general to target these victims who, through one means or another, came into his crosshairs."

Davenport, who was standing off to the side, asked him curiously, "What are your thoughts on the racial and ethnic mixture of the victims? Is this the unsub's way of saying he hates all women? Or at least those who are involved in higher education as educators?"

"Good question," Neil acknowledged. As it was, the differences between the four victims in terms of being white, African American and Hispanic were not lost on him. He contemplated this for a moment or two, then responded coolly, "I don't see this as hating all women, per se. Or racist. Or even the unsub fancying himself as an equal opportunity serial killer. More likely, it's a ruse or smoke screen, meant more to throw the investigation off by questioning the nature of the attacks, rather than the real reason behind them. My guess is that the perp may have homed in on one victim, in particular—whether acquainted with or a complete stranger, and not necessarily the first— then cleverly mixed up the other murders, by race or ethnicity, to make it more difficult to identify the culprit and bring him to justice."

"So, Agent Ramirez, is there any chance

the unsub will save us the trouble of capturing him by turning himself in, with the guilt eating away at him like an insidious cancer inside his body?" Gayle threw out seriously.

"Afraid there's little chance of that," he responded honestly. "In my experience of profiling serial killers, in particular, and observations of the lot, in general, very few have a case of conscience where it concerns owning up to what they have done. Certainly not where it concerns walking into a police station and giving up. Unfortunately, most such killers have no wish to be captured and held accountable for their crimes. And few will actually stop killing, as long as the fever for continuing to victimize persists and the risk for detection remains low, in their minds."

"Figured as much." She made a face. "Had to ask."

"Of course." Neil flashed a small smile. "That's why we're here."

Paula, who had taken a seat, leaned forward and asked directly, "What else can you tell us about the unsub's psyche that might be helpful in understanding who we're up against, in terms of what to look for in our pursuit? As well as when we have him in custody...or have eliminated the threat."

Neil knew that in that last point, she was referring to the reality that the unsub might choose not to surrender when given the opportunity, leaving them no choice but to take him out. As far as he was concerned, Neil preferred that the Campus Killer, if convicted, spent the rest of his life behind bars. But that would be up to him, by and large. Gazing at Paula, Neil responded to her question. "With respect to the psyche of the killer, we're definitely talking about ASPD here—antisocial personality disorder," he stressed, lifting his shoulders. "The unsub's not delusional, based on his actions and skillful ability to have avoided capture thus far. But his penchant for such antisocial behavior with little regard for the human lives he's taking makes him a serious threat to the public, for as long as he's on the loose. I see the unsub as both control-driven and hedonistic in his killings," Neil told her. "That is to say, he gets off on having the power to decide when they live and die."

Paula wrinkled her nose. "What a creep."

"And some other choice words might apply too," Neil said thoughtfully.

"How about the off campus, then on it again killing pattern of the unsub?" she wondered.

"Is there some method to this? Or is he merely toying with us in this regard?"

Taking a moment to consider what was an inevitable question, Neil answered evenly, "My guess is that it's largely an attempt by the unsub to keep us guessing by targeting professors on campus and off. But he could also be more haphazard and opportunistic in his MO, whereby he picks his prey and location to murder based upon whatever he deems the most effective and least vulnerable to himself for exposure."

"Hmm..." Paula smoothed an eyebrow. "What about some of the other dynamics, like character traits and background of the unsub, that may be a factor in his homicidal behavior?"

"In this regard, the unsub is just as likely to have come from a stable family as to have been a victim of child abuse and/or broken home," Neil made clear. "And be in a current relationship as much as a loner, and vice versa. He probably supplements his murderous appetite by using alcohol, illegal drugs or both, as an added means to drive him to kill. Whether or not the unsub has been motivated by other serial killers who have made news over the years, such as Bundy, Jeffrey Dahmer, John Wayne Gacy or even Jack the Ripper—or, for that matter, the plethora of true crime documentaries on cable and streaming television or the internet—could go either way."

"Got it," Paula told him, with an amused catch to her voice.

She offered him a weak smile to imply TMI, but Neil took it as more of an indication of satisfaction that he had laid out a solid foundation about the unsub to work with. He suspected that she may have wanted him to go even further in profiling the perpetrator. He was happy to oblige, but didn't want to overdo it by getting too academic or technical in advancing his remarks, at the risk of losing his audience and, in the process, any usefulness in applying this to the investigation.

If the case went on much longer, Neil could see himself adjusting his characterization of the unsub accordingly. But for now, he needed to see how this played out and hope they could get the bead on the Campus Killer sooner than later.

AFTER THE TASK force meeting ended, Paula approached Neil, who was chatting with Davenport, and invited them both to join her and some others for a drink at Blanes Tavern, a local hangout for cops. It had been Gayle who prodded her to ask him. Not that she needed much prodding concerning Neil, as Paula welcomed being able to spend more time with him. Between reading his book and listening to his characterization of the Campus Killer unsub, she was even more fascinated with the man, professionally and personally.

Davenport responded first, saying, "Wish I could. Unfortunately, I have to get home to the missus, who keeps me on a short leash, and my girls, adorable as they are."

"I understand." Paula smiled, envious of him as a family man. She turned her attention to Neil, wondering if this was a path he too was interested in going down, if given the chance. "What about you?"

His jaw clenched as Neil responded musingly, "Sorry, I'll have to pass too. Already have plans."

"I see. No problem," she assured him, even while wondering just what those plans might be. Perhaps to get together with someone he was dating? Would it be so surprising that he had a love life, even if she didn't at the moment?

"Rain check?" he threw out, as if a lifeline.

"Yes, that works for me," she told him, not wanting to put either of them on the spot for making any plans beyond that.

"Great." He favored her with a sideways grin.

Paula smiled back and walked away from the two men, while wondering if they were comparing notes on the investigation. Or her.

"Will they be joining us?" Gayle asked, approaching her.

"Afraid not," Paula almost hated to say. "Both have other things on their plates this evening."

"Too bad." Gayle frowned. "Oh, well. I think we can survive with whomever shows up."

"Agreed." Paula glanced over her shoulder and caught Neil spying on her, alone, as Davenport had already left the room. This eye contact seemed to be the trigger for Neil to follow suit, while avoiding her.

Chapter Four

Damn, Neil muttered to himself as he left the Department of Police and Public Safety. He regretted missing out on the opportunity to hang with Paula in a more relaxed setting than a task force meeting. Or even a classroom, for that matter. He expected other opportunities would present themselves, as he definitely wanted the chance to get to know the detective sergeant better.

Unfortunately, in this instance, duty called. He had a prescheduled meeting with the ATF undercover surveillance agent, Vinny Ortiz, working on the inside in their arms trafficking investigation. Neil couldn't afford to jeopardize the mission, even if Paula Lynley had managed to occupy a portion of his thoughts.

He climbed into his dark gray Chevrolet Suburban High Country and texted Ortiz to say he would be there in ten minutes. Neil drove off while running through his mind the ultimate goal of getting illegal weapons off the streets, both at home and in other countries when coming from the United States.

Turning onto Prairie Street, his thoughts switched to the Campus Killer investigation. The task force seemed well suited to solve the case. Even if he could feel the frustrations from the meeting that were so thick you could almost cut through them with a knife, Neil was sure that the unsub would not get away with this. Most serial killers either got sloppy, unlucky, ran out of steam or were upended through strong police work. He was always betting on the latter when push came to shove, as there was no stronger motivation for those in law enforcement than putting an end to a serial killer or mass crimes of violence. Whatever it took. There would be no difference here.

The fact that Paula was spearheading the investigation, along with Gayle, gave Neil the confidence that, with his help, and the advances in forensics and digital technology, it was only a matter of time before the unsub was apprehended.

And it couldn't come soon enough for female professors.

On Tenth Street in a low-income part of town, Neil pulled his car up behind a red Jeep Wagoneer. He could see a man behind the wheel but couldn't identify him. Reaching for the ATF-issued Glock 47 Gen5 MOS 9x19mm pistol in his duty holster, Neil wondered if he would need to use it. Those tensions lessened when he watched a husky man with messy brown shoulder-length hair, parted on the left side, and a beardstache, emerge from the Jeep, and Neil recognized him as Agent Vinny Ortiz. The thirty-five-year-old Hispanic divorced dad had worked in undercover assignments for the past four years, successfully meandering between risky operations involving arson, explosives and illegal firearms. It had played havoc with his love life, though Neil knew that Ortiz was currently romantically involved with an international flight attendant.

Putting his gun away, Neil waited for Ortiz to get into the passenger seat. Once he did, Neil said cautiously, "Hey. Everything okay?"

"Yeah, I'm fine," Ortiz said, running a hand across his mouth. "Took me a minute to get away without being noticed, if you know what I mean."

"I do." Neil understood fully just how risky the covert work was, having gone undercover himself a time or two during his career with the ATF. He certainly didn't want to jeopardize the operation. But Ortiz's safety was even more important. "What do you have for me?" Neil asked him.

"The arms trafficking operation is on," Ortiz replied in no uncertain terms. "The gunrunner, Craig Eckart, is setting up shop in Rendall Cove, using the dark web as a back door to collect and traffic in contraband firearms and ammunition, as well as gun trafficking in our own neck of the woods. Berettas, Glocks, Hi-Point, Uzis, Walthers, you name it."

"Yeah, I gathered as much." Neil considered the intel he had picked up on Craig Eckart, a forty-five-year-old who'd presented himself as a legal gun dealer and internet businessman, while operating on the fringes in his criminal enterprises. Though his legitimate interests had proven to be a good cover, selling guns and ammo on the black market had proven to be far more profitable. But if this didn't go south, they would soon be putting Eckart out of business, once and for all.

"I've set myself up as a buyer," Ortiz said, "promising to bring in loads of cash and a distribution system to kill for, figuratively speaking, both domestically and abroad."

"Good." Neil grinned at his ability to remain poised and use humor in the face of danger.

He knew that the ATF was willing to front the money needed with a bigger payout in return, in breaking up the arms-dealing network. "When is this going to go down?"

"Soon," the agent promised. "I need a bit more time to ingratiate myself with Eckart, ever wary, and his goons, then we should be all set to blow this thing wide open."

"Okay." Neil regarded him. "If you ever get the sense that they're on to you, get out of there in a hurry and we'll do what we need to."

"I will." Ortiz jutted his chin. "You know me. I try to stay two steps ahead, at least, while watching my back at every turn."

"I get that." Neil nodded. "I also believe you can never be too careful. If you're ever in trouble, you know where to reach me."

"Back at you," Ortiz said, meeting his gaze. "Heard from one of the guys in the FIU with the Rendall Cove PD that you were getting involved in the Campus Killer investigation."

"I was asked to come on as a profiler," Neil acknowledged, "in hopes of nailing the unsub before anyone else gets killed."

"Good luck with that. A serial killer on the loose is bad for everyone, including Craig Eckart, who's been living with a professor, Laurelyn Wong, when he's not dirty dealing."

"Hmm... Interesting." Neil reacted to the irony. "Does she know about him as a gun-runner?"

"I don't think so," Ortiz indicated. "Eckart seems to have her totally fooled as Mr. Nice Guy."

"Could Eckart be responsible for the serial killings?" Neil wondered seriously. "Perhaps as a deadly diversion to his arms trafficking?"

"I doubt it. In my opinion, we're talking about two lanes here. I've been watching Eckart like a hawk for weeks now and, though he's deadly in his own right in pushing contraband small arms and ammo, leading to gun deaths around the world, I don't see him masquerading on the side as a serial killer. Wouldn't be very good for business with law enforcement on the case stepping into his space, with Eckart's full knowledge that he's in the hot seat. As opposed to what he's not privy to," Ortiz added in reference to his undercover assignment.

"Maybe you're right." Neil gave the gun-runner the benefit of the doubt, knowing that they were angling at the moment for the unsub picked up on surveillance video that likely wasn't Craig Eckart. Particularly with Ortiz shadowing his every move.

"Anyway, hope you nail the son of a bitch," the undercover agent said. "Soon."

"Yeah," Neil muttered. "Back at you."

"That's the plan, right?" Ortiz ran a hand through his hair. "I better go."

"Okay." Neil certainly didn't want his cover to be blown. Or his life endangered any more than it already was. "Talk to you soon."

Ortiz nodded and left the car. Neil watched as he got back in the Jeep and drove off. He followed suit, detouring in a different direction as Neil headed home, his mind on the dual investigations he was now part of.

BLANES TAVERN WAS on Mack Road and already pretty busy by the time Paula arrived with Gayle in separate cars. They sat together, separate from colleagues, and ordered organic beer. For her part, Paula wished Neil could have joined them. But he was otherwise engaged. Maybe next time. She wasn't about to allow herself to get too attached to the visiting professor—who may or may not have been single—even if she felt comfortable conversing with him.

Gayle broke into her thoughts by asking, while holding a mug, "So, what do you make of Professor Ramirez's observations about our Campus Killer unsub?"

"He nailed it," Paula decided, based on what she already knew about serial killers, thanks in part to her former husband and his siblings in law enforcement. "Or at least he certainly seems to know what he's talking about in characterizing the unsub and what we need to look for in our search."

"I agree. His perspective can certainly aide the cause in knowing what we're likely up against."

"Yes, it can." Paula tasted the beer.

"Doesn't hurt matters any that the man's hot," Gayle remarked.

"True." It was something Paula could not deny one bit. She regarded the detective, who had recently ended a long relationship and almost immediately jumped back in the ring. Was she angling for Neil?

"Unfortunately, he's not my type," Gayle said, as if reading her mind. "Seems more like yours."

"You think?" Paula blushed.

"Based on what you've told me you look for in a man, definitely." Gayle sipped her beer. "Whether or not he's available is another matter. If you're interested, maybe you should find out."

"We'll see." Paula was noncommittal as to whether or not to go down that road. "My divorce is still relatively recent, so I have to tread carefully in putting myself out there again."

"I understand. But a year is an awfully long time to do without. I'm just saying, if you know what I mean," Gayle said with an amused grin.

"I think I do." Paula laughed at her brazen nature. "Still, I can wait till the right guy comes along, whoever that might be."

"Okay." Gayle tasted more beer. "Speaking of Agent Ramirez, I learned from the guys in the department's Firearms Investigation Unit that he and the ATF are working on a major illegal weapons probe."

Paula cocked a brow. "Really?"

"Yep. From what I understand, it's international in scope." She grabbed a handful of peanuts from a bowl on the table. "Not too surprising that the visiting professor can walk and chew gum at the same time, to coin a phrase."

"That he can, and then some," Paula concurred, while curious about the arms investigation and even more so about other aspects of his life. "We'll take whatever Agent Ramirez can send our way in the Campus Killer investigation."

"Amen to that." Gayle laughed and popped a couple of peanuts in her mouth. "So, how's your friend doing on her vacation on Maui?"

"Having a ball." Paula was mindful that Gayle grew up on the Hawaiian island and lived on Oahu as well, in Honolulu, before she relocated to the mainland and Michigan a decade ago. "She can't seem to get enough of working on her tan and sipping piña coladas."

Gayle gave a chuckle. "Sounds like she has the Hawaii fever."

"I think so." Paula grinned and grabbed some peanuts, while wondering when a fever for stepping out of her comfort zone would overtake her.

When she got home an hour later, Paula watched as Chloe jumped off a chair and rubbed against her leg. She giggled. "Show the love," she teased her.

After feeding the cat, Paula phoned her sorority sister and former college roommate, Josie Woods, knowing that while on vacation with her latest boyfriend, Rob, Josie was on Hawaii time, which was six hours behind Michigan time.

Josie accepted the video chat request, appearing on the small cell phone screen as Paula stood by the window in the great room. The thirty-five-year-old senior analyst for a Wall Street firm was attractive and green-eyed, with long, straight brown hair and curtain bangs. She broke into a big smile. "Aloha!"

"Aloha." Paula grinned. "Hope I didn't catch you at a bad time?"

"You didn't. Rob's out for a game of golf on a Ka'anapali course, leaving me all by my lonesome to soak up the afternoon sun."

Paula laughed. "I can see that." She could tell that Josie was lounging on a beach chair beneath an umbrella on the West Maui coastline, while wearing a red tankini.

"Wish you were here," Josie told her.

"Me too." Paula was envious, having never been to Hawaii. Between Josie and Gayle singing its praises, this was something she hoped to rectify. "Maybe someday I'll hop on a plane and check out Maui and the other Hawaiian Islands for myself."

"You should. It's like no other place on Earth."

"Hmm…" Paula didn't doubt that. But visiting it alone might not be half as enjoyable as being in the company of a romantic partner. She wondered if Neil had ever been to Hawaii. The thought that he might well have taken another woman to paradise somehow ruined the fantasy, which Paula felt she had no right to have at this stage, if ever.

"Imagine what trouble we could get into if we went together." Josie broke into her reverie.

"That's what I'm afraid of." Paula giggled

and watched as Chloe came over to her, as if jealous that she was being ignored.

"I'm sure you'd keep us on the straight and narrow at the end of the day, Detective Lynley," Josie quipped.

"Absolutely," Paula concurred, as her mind turned to the current serial killer case and where it might be headed with Neil on board as part of the task force.

WITH HER LEGS folded beneath her, Gayle Yamasaki sat on a faux-leather love seat in the living room of her Pine Street town house, watching cable television. Or trying to anyway. Her mind was elsewhere. Weighing heavily on it was her latest case. Having a serial killer in their midst, terrorizing females who happened to be teaching at Addison University, wasn't exactly what she'd signed up for when joining the Rendall Cove Police Department ten years ago. Or even, for that matter, when she'd been promoted to the Detective Bureau six years later. Both had followed her time as a detective with the Honolulu Police Department, once she'd graduated from the University of Hawai'i Maui College with an Associate in Applied Sciences Degree in Administration of Justice.

But, then again, no one she currently worked

with wanted to be going after the so-called Campus Killer. Not that they had much choice. The unsub was still at large and needed to be stopped. As the lead detective in the investigation—at least for the two murders that occurred within the city limits outside the college—she felt the pressure to solve this case. With time being of the essence.

Gayle knew that the same was true for Paula Lynley, her detective sergeant friend who headed the university's Department of Police and Public Safety probe into the murders, with two occurring on campus. Together, along with their task force, Gayle hoped one thing led to another in putting the brakes on the unsub's homicidal tendencies before they got totally out of hand.

Having Professor Neil Ramirez on board as a criminal profiler might be just what they needed to unmask the perpetrator. The handsome ATF special agent was equally important to the Rendall Cove PD's Firearms Investigation Unit for his role in the joint investigation into the sale and distribution of illegal arms. Based on what she'd heard about him, she felt that Agent Ramirez was up to the challenge of juggling his multiple assignments without missing a beat.

Gayle's thoughts shifted back to the Campus Killer investigation. Or more specifically, one of the detectives working the case for the DPPS, Michael Davenport. Honestly, she had the biggest crush on him. Definitely her type. Too bad he was a happily married family man. Or was that only a facade?

Not that she wanted to test the waters, even if tempting. Yes, she was single again after her last serious relationship fell apart. And she'd started dating again. But she knew where to draw the line. Davenport was nice to be around, but that was it. She would turn her attention elsewhere as it related to romance.

Gayle grabbed the remote to turn off the big-screen television. She unfolded her legs and stood up, her bare feet feeling the cold of the hardwood flooring, and headed upstairs for bed.

ON FRIDAY MORNING, Paula tied her hair in a short ponytail and threw on a black tank top, pink high-rise leggings and black-and-white running sneakers for a quick jog in Rendall Creek Park before work. Though Paula had found it to be a safe place to run, or otherwise spend time in the forested setting with plenty of trails and great scenery, mindful of the serial killer at large, she had begun bringing along her SIG Sauer pistol. She kept it in an ankle holster, but she'd have no trouble grabbing it quickly, if needed, to defend herself. Beyond that, she had taken some classes in Krav Maga, a method of self-defense comprising a combo of such techniques as boxing, karate, judo and even wrestling.

I've never had to put it in practice, knock on wood, Paula told herself, as she started her jaunt though the eastern white pines and maple trees and thick shrubbery in the park. She spotted a squirrel or two, along with some robins and sparrows, none of which seemed to pay her much mind.

She had just begun to get into a comfortable groove when Paula heard footsteps behind her. They seemed to be growing closer, even as she sought to put some distance between her and the runner. With her heart pounding, as much due to the rise in her heart rate from jogging as an overactive imagination in being brazenly attacked by the Campus Killer, Paula was determined not to go down without a fight. Instincts kicked in, and she mentally prepared to grab her firearm and whip around to face her assailant, even while continuing to move forward. Though she had no reason to believe that she had suddenly gone from a detective hunting the unsub to becoming a target of the killer, Paula was taking no chances in having her life cut short.

Just as she slowed her movement, bent down and removed the SIG Sauer pistol, Paula heard a familiar voice say in an ill at ease tone, "Paula...?"

Having already been in the process of turning and pointing the barrel of her gun at him, she gazed into the intense gray-brown eyes of Neil Ramirez. He came to a screeching halt, close enough to kiss her, before taking an involuntary step backward, with the SIG Sauer separating them.

Raising his hands in mock surrender, Neil said, wide-eyed, "Whoa! Don't shoot. You've got me, Detective Lynley."

I do, at that, Paula mused, still gripping the pistol firmly, but lowering it ever so cautiously. "Neil. You startled me!"

"My apologies," he asserted. "Didn't mean to come up on you like that. Guess I was caught up in my own thoughts."

Or was that a convenient excuse? Paula asked herself. She held his gaze. "Are you following me?" Her first thought was that perhaps he was doing so as another secret assignment, in protecting her from a serial killer, while part of the joint task force. But, if so, wouldn't her boss, Shailene McNamara, have told her?

"Wish I could say that were true, in the nicest way, of course," he answered, an amused grin playing on his lips. "As it is, I just happened to be out for a run, like you. Believe me, I'm just as surprised to see you as you clearly are to see me. I assure you that our nearly running into one another was purely happenstance. Nothing more."

"Oh, really?" Paula was still a little suspicious but knew it was totally unwarranted. Even if unexpected. She gave him a once-over and could see that, like her, he was dressed for a run, wearing a black workout jersey, gray jogger pants and black running sneakers. His muscular long arms had her imagining being wrapped in them. "So, you live around here?" she asked curiously.

"Right across the street from the park," he explained. "I'm renting a nice little house while I'm in town." He paused. "Where are you?"

"I live a block away," she told him, knowing he could easily have found out for himself, had he been interested.

"I see. So we're neighbors?"

"I suppose." The idea of having him so proximate did admittedly have its appeal.

He brought his arms down and peered at her gun, still halfway raised. "You want to put that thing away?"

"Yes, sorry." Embarrassed that she had held on to it as long as she had, Paula stuffed the pistol back into its holster. "Guess I'm just a bit spooked these days, with a serial killer on the loose."

"Perfectly understandable." Neil's voice was soothing. "Better safe than sorry, right?"

"Right." She flashed her teeth and said, "Better get back to it."

"Care for some company?"

"Yes, I'm up for a running partner who can keep up with me," Paula expressed boldly.

"Sounds like a challenge." Neil laughed. "I'll try my best not to disappoint."

Something told her there was little chance of that. She put him to the test anyway, breaking away speedily, only to see him catch up with little to no effort at all. "Do you run at the park often?" she wondered, while acknowledging that it was entirely possible that they had simply missed each other previously.

"Not so often," he told her. "I usually try to get in a short run on campus between classes, given all the inviting paths with lots of scenery for distractions. How about you?"

"I run in the park maybe three times a week and go to the gym once a week," Paula added, as if she needed to prove her fitness.

"Good for you. Haven't gotten to the gym yet since I've been in town, but I try to work out whenever I can."

"Could've fooled me," Paula teased him, needing only to get one look at the man as a physical specimen to know that he was in tip-top shape. "I'm sure that comes often enough."

Neil chuckled. "Ditto. You obviously know what it takes to maintain an amazing physique, from what I can see."

She blushed. "Back at you."

He grinned. "So, how was the outing after the task force meeting?"

"Good," she said. "Just drinks and conversation, before everyone went home for the night." Paula eyed him. "How did you make out with your plans for the evening?" Did she truly want to know if he was with another woman?

"Good," he answered vaguely. "Just had something I needed to tend to."

So, he doesn't want to elaborate, she thought. Maybe that was a good thing. "I bought a copy of your book."

"Really?" He lifted a brow.

"Yes, and read the entire thing in one sitting," Paula admitted, at the risk of giving him a big head. "It was quite interesting in giving a deeper perspective on criminal profiling."

"Glad you were able to pick up something from it," Neil said, wiping perspiration from his brow with the back of his hand. "You never know how much will register and how much won't."

"It registered," she assured him. "As did what you had to say during the task force meeting."

"Good." He grinned sideways. "I really do want to help in any way I can to bring this unsub to justice. Or at least give you more to work with in delving into his psyche as a serial killer."

She nodded. "You're succeeding on both fronts."

Abruptly, Paula raced him to the clearing, beating him by a fraction, though suspecting he had let her win this time. As they caught their breaths, laughing like being in on a good joke, she suddenly decided to kiss him. Cupping Neil's chiseled cheeks, she just laid a big one on his mouth, which he returned in kind till Paula unlocked their lips, feeling embarrassed at her unusual boldness. Yet she wasn't at all sorry she did it.

"Sorry about that," she apologized nevertheless. "It was just something I wanted to do and went for it."

"Nothing to be sorry about." Neil grinned out of one corner of his mouth. "Happens to the best of us. And it was a nice kiss at that."

Though she didn't disagree in the slightest, Paula felt this probably wasn't the best moment to go down this road. So, she told him awkwardly, "Uh, this is where I head home. I have to go get ready for work."

"Okay." He met her eyes, but his own were unreadable. Was that good or bad?

"I'll see you later." She turned away and started to jog down the sidewalk, almost expecting Neil to follow, as if he had nothing better to do.

It never happened, leaving Paula to ponder the kiss and the man himself alone.

Chapter Five

Neil welcomed a hot shower after his run, but felt his temperature rise while thinking about the unanticipated kiss from Paula. Her full lips were as soft as cotton and contoured perfectly with his own. He'd be lying if he said the thought of kissing her hadn't crossed his mind once or twice. Hell, even more than that. But she had beaten him to the punch, indicating they were on the same wavelength.

Then Paula had hastily left him hanging, even if understandable that she, like him, still had another workday to prepare for. Neil could only wonder where they went from here. Or had her divorce made Paula more squeamish when it came to anything more than a quick kiss before a goodbye?

After dressing and having a quick bowl of cereal to go with a strong cup of coffee, Neil dropped by his office at the college, picked up the exams for his first class and went to it.

Waiting for him there, before the undergraduate students began to pour in, was Desmond Isaac, a twenty-five-year-old graduate teaching assistant.

Working on a Master of Arts in Criminal Justice, Desmond was about his height and more on the slender side, with dark blond hair in a layered men's bob and a chin puff goatee. Behind retro glasses were blue eyes. "Hey," he said casually.

"Hey." Neil sat his briefcase on the desk and opened it. "Brought something for you." He handed him the exams, which Desmond would soon be handing out and collecting from the students.

"Think they're up to the challenge?" Desmond joked.

"If not, then I haven't been doing my job very well."

"We both know that's not true. Seems like you have them eating out of your hands."

Neil laughed. "Don't know if I'd go quite that far. But I am here to teach what I can."

"Speaking of which, I heard that you're working with the Department of Police and Public Safety in trying to identify and flush out the Campus Killer."

"Word travels fast," Neil quipped, though

not at all surprised, as the school newspaper had picked it up. "I'm offering my thoughts on what—and whom—the authorities investigating the case are up against," he said, downplaying his credentials as a criminal profiler.

"Well, it's smart of them to take advantage of your presence on campus," Desmond told him. "We'll all be a lot better off when this serial killer nightmare is over."

"I hear you." Neil spotted students beginning to file in. "Right now, let's see if we can get the next generation of law enforcement personnel to pass my class and graduate."

"Yeah. There is that hurdle they need to climb." Desmond dangled the multiple-choice tests in his hand.

Neil greeted students, while also collecting their cell phones to be returned after the exam. "Good morning," he said routinely, often getting in return, "Morning, Professor Ramirez." He was still trying to get used to being seen as a visiting professor instead of an ATF special agent. Could the former replace the latter as a more permanent thing?

He honed in on one student, in particular, named Roger Woodward. The twenty-two-year-old senior and honors student stood out because of his rainbow-colored gelled Mohawk hairstyle, lanky frame and dark eyes. Neil saw him as one of his smartest students, who had indicated a strong interest in working for the Bureau of Alcohol, Tobacco, Firearms and Explosives. He grinned at Roger and said, "Good luck with the exam."

"Thanks," Roger said, a crooked smile on his lips.

Not that Neil thought he needed any luck acing the test. This common, but useful for some, phrase was passed along to other students that Neil engaged, with Desmond following suit.

THE KISS THAT landed on Neil Ramirez's firm lips was admittedly still on Paula's mind as she pulled up to the two-story Tudor home on Winsome Road in Rendall Cove that Odette Furillo had owned with her estranged husband, Allen Furillo. Paula had been trying to speak with him since his wife was murdered, but the man had seemingly kept them running around in circles. Till now. Furillo had requested the meeting, while making it clear that he didn't need to have a lawyer present. That by no means made Paula believe he had nothing to do with the murder, but at the very least suggested that he wanted to give that appearance.

Exiting her car, she noted the blue Dodge Charger parked in the driveway. Paula knew that a white Honda Insight belonging to Odette Furillo that she'd driven to the campus was still being processed for possible evidence in a homicide. Paula's sidearm was tucked away in her gun holster but could be quickly accessed, if needed. The thought of pointing it at Neil this morning crossed her mind, causing her to blush as the potential threat had turned out to be the ATF agent turned visiting professor, whom she wound up kissing instead of killing.

I need to not be so jumpy in the future, Paula mused. At least where it pertained to Neil. But when it came to the Campus Killer, all bets were off.

Before she could ring the doorbell, the door swung open. Standing there was a medium-sized, short man in his midthirties with dark hair in an undercut fade and blue eyes. Paula showed her badge and said, "Detective Lynley. Are you Allen Furillo?"

"Yeah, that's me," he muttered. "Come in."

She followed him inside and took a sweeping glance around at the traditional furnishings and gray carpeting.

"Would you like something to drink?" Furillo asked her.

Glancing at some empty beer cans on the kitchen counter, Paula wasn't sure if he was referring to alcoholic beverages or not. Either way, she passed. But she did agree to sit on an accent chair, while he sat across from her on a sofa, so she could keep her eye on him. "We've been wanting to talk to you about your wife's death…"

"I know. I just needed some time to clear my head before speaking with anyone," he said, lowering his eyes. "The way Odette died really shook me."

"I understand that you and your wife were separated," Paula pointed out, not yet willing to give him the benefit of any doubt. "What was that all about?"

"That was her choice, not mine." Furillo pursed his lips. "I wanted to try and make the marriage work, even if we had trouble seeing eye to eye of late. But she wasn't interested in that and asked me to leave. I did, but still hoped she might come to her senses, before it was too late."

Paula peered at him and asked bluntly, "Did you kill your wife, Mr. Furillo?"

"No, I could never have done such a horrible thing," he asserted. "I loved Odette."

Isn't that what most say before and after kill-

ing their spouses? Paula thought. "I need to know where you were the night your wife was murdered," she demanded, supplying him with the estimated time frame.

Squaring his shoulders, Furillo responded straightforwardly, "I was at work as a warehouse picker on the afternoon shift at a distribution center on Hackett Road. Didn't leave till after midnight. Plenty of other workers saw me. You can check."

If true, Paula knew this would mean he couldn't have been at his wife's office on campus during the time of her death. "I'll do that," she promised. She regarded him directly. "Do you know of anyone who may have wanted to harm your wife?" Paula didn't discount that the unsub could have targeted a specific victim and added the others for effect, and to throw them off his trail.

Furillo's brow furrowed. "Maybe the man Odette decided to give her affections to."

Paula narrowed her eyes. "Are you saying your wife was having an affair?"

"Yeah, she was." His voice thickened. "Hard as it is for me to come to terms with, even if she believed our marriage was over."

"Do you know the name of this other man?" Paula asked interestedly.

"Yeah. His name is Joseph Upton. He worked with her as a professor in the mathematics department at the university," Furillo muttered glumly. "He could've killed her if Odette had a change of heart and wanted to come back to me."

"I'll have a chat with Professor Upton," Paula promised, while wondering if Odette Furillo might have done a reverse course. Or had her relationship with her husband been doomed either way? Paula understood all too well that was inevitable in some marriages.

She asked Furillo a few questions about the other victims attributed to the Campus Killer and decided that it was unlikely that he had anything to do with their deaths.

"HE CAME IN VOLUNTARILY," Mike Davenport told Paula an hour later, as they looked at the video monitor of Professor of Mathematics Joseph Upton sitting in an interview room in the Department of Police and Public Safety.

"Smart move on his part," she uttered, after an attempt to reach Upton had come up short. Paula studied the professor, who was white, blue-eyed, fit and in his late thirties, with jet-black hair worn in a short pompadour cut.

"There's more," Davenport indicated. "Upton

says he's the man in the surveillance video from outside the Gotley Building that we released to the media."

"Really?" Paula eyed the professor again and wondered if he was there to confess to killing his lover. "I'd better get in there and see what he has to say."

"Let me know if you need backup on this one."

"Okay." She headed into the room, where the suspect sat in a metal chair at a square wooden table. "Joseph Upton, I'm Detective Lynley. Mind telling me what you're doing here?" She decided to be coy about it.

Fidgeting, he responded, "To talk about Odette Furillo."

Paula sat across from him and advised that the conversation was being video recorded, having hit the switch to activate it on the way in. "What about her?"

"Odette and I were having an affair," he said thoughtfully.

"For how long?" Paula wondered.

"A few months." He paused. "But it wasn't just about sex. We were in love, and she was preparing to file for divorce."

Paula peered across the table. "But that never happened..."

Upton lowered his head. "I know she was murdered...and that security video showed someone fleeing the building where Odette and I had our offices." He drew a breath. "That was me," he repeated what had already been told to Davenport.

"Are you saying you murdered Professor Furillo?" Paula asked point-blank.

He lifted his eyes and met hers unblinkingly and said firmly, "No, I didn't kill her. But I saw Odette in her office, where we were supposed to meet." He sighed. "She was dead. Someone had killed her."

"Did you call 911?" Paula asked skeptically.

"No."

"Why not?"

"I don't know," he claimed. "Guess I panicked, not knowing if the killer was still on the floor. Or if I would be blamed for what happened. Not thinking clearly, I just took off, knowing there was nothing I could do to save Odette. It was too late for that."

Paula didn't disagree, per se, based on the autopsy report. But who knew for certain, had he acted promptly? "Did you see anyone else coming or leaving the building?" she pressed him.

"No." Upton's brows knitted. "There were other people outside, going about their business and whatnot, but I was in too much of a hurry to get away, so I never really focused on anyone else. Sorry."

"How did you get to the Gotley Building in the first place?" Paula asked, knowing it was centrally located on campus, but not usually walkable.

"I drove," he admitted. "But I didn't want to go to my car, fearing it would be seen on surveillance video, so I ran off and came back for it in the morning. As I said, I panicked. I know it was an unwise thing to do. When I saw the video footage on my tablet, I recognized myself and knew it was only a matter of time before someone else did. So…here I am—"

She glanced at the camera and wondered what Davenport thought. For her part, Paula felt the professor's story was credible, if not suspicious and sad at the same time. "Would you be willing to submit a DNA sample?" she asked him.

Upton hedged, but then responded as if having an epiphany, "Yes, since I have nothing to hide insofar as what happened to Odette."

That remains to be seen, Paula thought, but welcomed the opportunity to collect his DNA to see if there was a match with the unidentified DNA profile scraped from underneath

Odette Furillo's fingernails. There would be more questions for Joseph Upton down the line, but this was certainly a good step forward in seeing whether he was a killer. Or a misguided former lover to a dead woman.

Twenty minutes later in her office, Paula made the same observation to Davenport, while they awaited the DNA results. "My gut tells me that Upton did not kill Professor Furillo. Much less the other professors."

"You're probably right," the detective concurred, frowning. "The unsub likely wouldn't have been as sloppy in his comings and goings, based on the trajectory of the other killings attributed to the Campus Killer."

"Upton almost certainly contaminated the crime scene," she complained.

"As did Joan McCashin, the student and presumably first to arrive at the scene that morning," he observed. "That notwithstanding, and even if it turns out that Upton isn't our unsub, we still have enough to work with in moving ahead."

Paula did not disagree. "If Upton's on the level, his own life might have been spared," she contended, "had the unsub stuck around long enough to make sure there were no living witnesses to the perp's criminality."

"You're right." Davenport twisted his lips. "In this case, timing does seem to be everything. The killer is using it to his advantage. But that won't last forever."

"It had better not." She frowned at the thought, with a serial monster undoubtedly still hungry for more victims.

As THE NOON hour approached and turned into 1:00 p.m., Neil wondered if Paula was free for lunch. If she was like him, she probably passed this up often when in the heat of an investigation. On the other hand, a person had to eat sometime. He hoped this would be a chance to get to know one another better.

He was in his office when he phoned her. "Hey," he said when she answered, the thought of that kiss immediately entering his head.

"Hey." She left it at that.

"If you're not busy and haven't eaten yet, I was wondering if you'd like to join me for lunch?" Neil didn't want to spook her by calling it a date, in case that wasn't something she was open to right now. "We can talk shop and—"

"Yes, I'd be happy to meet you for lunch," Paula broke in enthusiastically. "Where?"

"I thought we could eat at the Union Building food court," he suggested, as a neutral spot.

"Sounds perfect. I can be there in five minutes."

"See you then." Neil disconnected and found himself excited at the prospect of seeing the lovely detective in mere minutes. He conferred briefly with his TA, Desmond Isaac, who would be grading the exams and either putting smiles or frowns on the faces of students, before heading out of the building.

In his Chevy Suburban SUV, Neil drove across campus to the Union Building on Bogle Lane. He parked in the lot and went inside to the food court, where he was surprised to see that Paula was already there.

He grinned. "Hope I didn't keep you waiting too long," he kidded.

"Maybe just a bit," she tossed back at him lightheartedly. "But I'll live."

Neil laughed. "That's good to know."

They found a table, and he went with the mac and cheese, while Paula settled for street-style nachos. Both had coffee.

Rather than get back to the kiss and what it could potentially mean, Neil asked casually, "Any news on the investigation?"

Paula, who had been deep in thought while eating, looked at him and said, "As a matter of fact, there has been some…"

"Oh?" He met her eyes curiously.

"The man seen in the surveillance video at the Gotley Building has been identified as Joseph Upton, a mathematics professor," she informed him. "Who also happened to be the lover of Odette Furillo."

"Really?" Neil knew she was estranged from her husband. But still.

"Yep. Upton came in voluntarily and admitted to coming upon Professor Furillo's body, after making plans to meet in her office." Paula dabbed a napkin to her mouth. "He says he panicked and fled the scene without calling 911."

"Did you believe him?" Neil asked.

"Honestly, I was on the fence there, but he agreed to supply a sample of his DNA."

"And...?"

"Upton's DNA didn't match the unidentified sample collected from beneath Odette's nails." Paula furrowed her brow. "Apart from leaving the scene of a crime, there was no reason to believe he's the unsub."

"Makes sense." Neil scooped up some macaroni and cheese on a fork. "What about the husband?"

She poked at her nachos. "Allen Furillo has a solid alibi for the time frame in which his wife was murdered. He couldn't have done it."

"Can't say I'm too surprised in either instance," Neil remarked thoughtfully. "As victim number four of the so-called Campus Killer, Odette Furillo most likely wasn't intimately connected to her murderer as much as the unsub could have been to the first or second victim—then moved beyond that, were it the case, in the subsequent killings."

"Sounds logical, coming from a profiler," Paula agreed. "Of course, as a crime investigator, we can't afford to leave any stones unturned."

"Wouldn't expect you to." Neil sat back in the chair and lifted his coffee cup. "Until you get the guy, no one's above suspicion. Nor should anyone be."

She smiled. "I figured we'd see eye to eye on this."

And even more, he thought, tasting the coffee and grinning at her. "Absolutely."

Paula lifted her own cup in thought. "As for going after bad elements, I hear that you're working with the Rendall Cove PD on an arms investigation."

Neil wasn't at all surprised that information flowed back and forth between the DPPS's Investigative Division and the city police department's Firearms Investigation Unit, given that they typically worked hand in hand on cases with common ground. Consequently, he didn't try to dance his way around this. Even if, technically speaking, he needed to keep a low profile on the case while it was at a near tipping point.

"Yes," he confessed without elaborating.

"I see." She met his eyes musingly. "Is that the real reason you're in Rendall Cove?"

Neil thought about his friend and late fellow ATF agent, Ramone Munoz. And then his ex-girlfriend, Constance Chen, who turned Neil's life upside down. Locking his eyes with Paula's steady gaze, he told her straightforwardly, "Not exactly."

Chapter Six

It occurred to Paula that perhaps Neil was on a mission that she was not supposed to pry about. Even if they were on the same team in her serial killer investigation. Or was there something more to his taking a position at the university as a visiting professor?

"Sorry if I've overstepped," she put out, after nibbling on more of her nachos.

"You didn't," he insisted, flashing her a small grin. "You're entitled." He paused. "I can't really talk about the ongoing arms investigation, other than to say it's what the ATF does, and sometimes with help from its partners in law enforcement."

So, there's obviously a big operation going down, Paula told herself. One she was not entitled to be privy to, in spite of working with him as a profiler in a separate case. "I understand," she said tactfully.

Neil rubbed his jawline. "Apart from that,

I took the position as a visiting professor as a needed getaway from the life I had..." He pressed his hands together. "Last year, a good friend of mine, ATF Special Agent Ramone Munoz, was ambushed during an ATF Special Response Team raid on a drug trafficking compound. He was killed in the process, leaving behind a wife and two little girls. The entire thing shook me up like I'd never been before."

Paula was almost speechless in hearing the shocking details of Agent Munoz's death and its aftermath, having already learned the basics about the mission gone awry. "I'm so sorry," she managed.

"Me too." Neil stared at the remnants of his macaroni and cheese. "Ramone deserved a hell of a lot better than he got as a dedicated ATF agent. But it is what it is and I have to accept that, no matter how difficult."

"These things can take time..." Paula resisted the desire to reach across the table and touch his hand. "And there's no hurry." She sensed there was more to his story.

He nodded and met her eyes musingly. "A few months back, I was in a relationship with an anthropologist named Constance Chen. She dumped me for another guy, without giving me a good reason, and I needed to come to terms

with this as well. Putting some distance between me and Constance seemed like a good
idea. Along with taking a break when it came
to romance."

"I'm sorry that happened to you." Paula
meant every word of it. Even if in the process,
it told her that he was, apparently, not seeing
anyone. She felt like jumping for joy that he was
available, but wondered if this was true. Perhaps in guarding his heart, he wasn't looking
to jump back into a relationship any time soon.

"It was probably a good thing," Neil told her
in earnest. "If I'm honest about it, things had
been treading in the wrong direction between
us for a while. But I chose not to see it for what
it was."

"I know what you mean," Paula couldn't help
but say.

"What happened with your marriage?" He
regarded her intently, taking the opening she
had given him.

Holding his gaze, she admitted straightforwardly, "We simply ran out of steam." She
tasted her coffee, which had started to get cold,
knowing he wanted more from her than that.
"Scott was a good man. His parents and siblings were either in law or law enforcement. In
some ways, this seemed to put extra pressure

on our relationship, in addition to us both being in law enforcement ourselves. Eventually, it, along with personality clashes, took its toll on the marriage and we decided to end things."

Neil tilted his head. "Any regrets?"

"There are always regrets whenever a relationship fails and you play the blame game and wonder what you might have done differently," she answered, "which I'm sure you would attest to. But if you're asking me if I still love Scott and want to get back together with him, the answer is no on both fronts. He'll always be a part of my history," Paula did not deny. "Not my future." She looked at Neil. "Does that answer your question?"

"Yes, it does." He grinned sheepishly. "And you're absolutely right. We all have regrets on past failures. But they can—and should be—a bridge to getting things right the next time. Or the time after that."

"Agreed." She smiled back at him, believing they had climbed one hurdle in getting to know one another better. Would there be more to follow?

"Do you have family?" Neil asked, sitting back while taking a sip of water.

Paula bobbed her head. "My mom lives in

Georgetown, Kentucky. I lost my dad to a heart attack when I was a teenager."

"Sorry to hear that."

"It came without warning, but was quick," she told him sentimentally. "I have no siblings. What about you?"

"Just an older sister," Neil said, resting an arm on the table. "Yancy works these days as a freelance translator in Brazil. I lost my parents in different years to cancer and an accidental fall."

It was Paula's turn to tell him she was sorry, knowing how devastating it could be without one's parents. She recalled that Scott and his siblings lost their parents in a car accident and, fortunately, had each other to lean on. "Are you and your sister close?" she asked Neil.

"Yes," he replied with a smile. "Yancy's four years older, but the difference never seemed that great when we were kids. In any event, we've always had each other's back."

"That's nice to hear." Paula wished she'd had siblings to always be able to lean on. She would have to settle for her best friend, Josie, along with her ex-sister-in-law, Madison, whom Paula had remained close with since her divorce. Even better was the notion of forming a bond with someone she could share her life with.

After they left the Union Building, Neil walked Paula to her car. "Thanks for lunch," she told him, after he'd insisted on paying for it.

He nodded, grinning. "Anytime."

She waited a beat then, looking into his eyes, said, "Guess I'll catch you later."

"All right." Neil flashed her a serious look. "About that kiss…"

"What about it?" She was almost afraid to ask, her heart pounding.

He suddenly cupped her cheeks and kissed Paula on the mouth. The kiss was powerful enough to make her go weak in the knees. Something told Paula that Neil would catch her were her legs to go out from under her.

After his lips parted from hers, his voice dropped an octave when Neil uttered soulfully, "I just wanted to let you know that the feeling of something between us is mutual."

As she caught her breath, Paula realized that he had just given them permission to try and unwrap those feelings over the course of time.

BACK AT HIS office that afternoon, Neil reflected on what he saw as a breakthrough on the connection he was starting to feel with Paula. He had no idea if it would go anywhere. Or if both of them were merely spinning their wheels in seeking to get beyond broken relationships. He, for one, was willing to put one foot in front of the other and see what happened. From the way Paula's lips contoured perfectly with his, it indicated to Neil that she was up for meeting him halfway. That was all he could ask for at this point, given that they both were in the midst of criminal investigations, occupying their time.

On his laptop, Neil contacted his sister for a video chat. He noted the minor time difference between Rendall Cove and São Paulo, Brazil, where Yancy lived with her bank manager boyfriend, Griffin Oliviera. She accepted the call and Neil watched his sister's face light up. At forty, she looked ten years younger, with dark blond hair in a medium-length A-line cut. Like him, Yancy had their father's deep gray-brown eyes.

"Hey," he said.

"Hey back, Neil."

"You busy?" Like him, he knew she worked long hours, often at the expense of quality time, in spite of being in a long-term relationship with Griffin.

"I think I can spare a few minutes for my brother," she teased him.

"Okay. Just wanted to check in with you."

"And I thank you for that." Yancy went on to

bring him up to date on her current comings and goings, before he talked a bit about himself.

"So, being a professor agrees with you these days?" she asked curiously.

"Yeah, you could say that," he told her. "Still keeping my day job, though, just in case teaching blows up in my face."

"I doubt that will happen." Yancy laughed. "But at least you'll have two directions you can go in."

"That's true." *Make it three directions*, Neil considered, when it came to Paula.

As if on the same wavelength, Yancy eyed him carefully and asked, "So, how's your love life these days? Or shouldn't I ask?"

"You can ask." He grinned wryly.

"Then I'm asking. And please don't tell me you're still pining for the one who let you get away?"

"I'm not," Neil made clear. Not by a long shot. "There is someone in the picture," he told her.

"Really?" Yancy's eyes brightened. "Tell me more…"

He did, while being clear that things were still in the early stages with Paula, with neither of them knowing if, like birds, they had the wings to make this fly. But at least she was giving him something to shoot for, and vice versa.

His sister concurred and wished them both luck, while even being presumptuous in inviting them to come for a visit to Brazil. Neil laughed, while taking that under advisement as something he could imagine happening down the line, should things progress accordingly with the nice-looking detective.

When Neil noticed that his TA had poked his head in the office, the call to Yancy was ended, with the promise to speak again soon.

"Sorry, didn't mean to interrupt," Desmond said.

"It's all right." Neil looked at him. "What's up?"

"Finished grading the exams." He stepped inside the office.

"How did they do?" Neil wondered.

"Better than expected," Desmond said. "At least for some, who aced it. Others still need to study harder to get up to snuff."

Neil nodded. "I'll have to do better to motivate them in that regard."

"You're doing a great job," the TA contended. "The onus is on them to get with the program, if they hope to graduate and move on to bigger and better things."

"Can't argue with that." Neil smiled. He was glad to see that Desmond was able and willing to keep the pressure on students to try and be the best they could be, instead of being handed life on a silver platter. Just how many students would buy into this argument remained to be seen.

"I'll send out the exam scores and wait to see how they respond," Desmond said.

"Good. I'll go over the results and see where to put greater focus," he told the TA and watched him leave. Neil then got on the phone with Doris Frankenberg, the resident agent in charge of the ATF's Grand Rapids field office, to update her on the illegal arms joint operation.

On Monday morning, Paula was at her desk, comparing information on the four homicides credited to the Campus Killer. There appeared to be little commonality among the murder victims, per se, apart from being victimized female professors. Though this, in and of itself, showed an undeniable pattern of targeting that needed to be taken into account, there was no indication that the victims were connected otherwise in a meaningful way. This lent credence, to some degree, to the random or opportunistic theory on the crimes. But what were they missing in this equation?

There must be something, she told herself, sipping coffee, while poring over the individual case files. Her mind wandered briefly to the passionate kiss she shared with Neil the other day. The man could kiss, she established. Made her believe he could be just as great a lover. If not better. As a flicker of desire coursed through her, Paula allowed it to dissipate, filing it away for another time and place, as she put her eye back on the ball.

She went back through the cases and searched for anything that could link them together insofar as a pattern that might lead to a serial killer. Something suddenly caught her eye— or someone—as Paula honed in on the name Roger Woodward. The twenty-two-year-old senior had been questioned this summer about the murder of Debra Newton, because the associate professor had mentioned to at least one other professor that a student in her journalism class had been stalking her.

That student was identified as Roger Woodward. He had produced an alibi and been let off the hook as a suspect in her death. Now Paula saw that Woodward, an honors student who had a dual major in journalism and criminology, had been taking a class in mathematics as an elective this semester, with Professor Odette

Furillo. *Hmm, coincidence?* Paula had to ask herself. Or not?

She looked up his current class schedule and saw that Roger Woodward also happened to be taking a criminology course with Visiting Professor Neil Ramirez. One that was in session right now.

Think I'd better have a little chat with Woodward, Paula told herself. If he had something to hide, such as a pattern of serial homicides, perhaps with Neil on hand they could flush it out of the honors student together.

AFTER GOING OVER Friday's exam results without mentioning any names or grades specifically, Neil put on a good face and tried to make all the students feel as if they could talk to him if they had any trouble grasping the lectures and reading assignments. In the meantime, he would continue to do his job in the classroom as a visiting professor of criminology and hope that it was resonating to the point of motivating those in attendance to do their best in getting a good education and doing something with it.

It was about five minutes before class ended when Neil got a text message from Paula. He glanced at his cell phone, reading with interest.

One of your students, Roger Woodward, is a suspect in the Campus Killer investigation. On my way. Keep him there till I arrive.

Neil couldn't help but cock a brow with shock that someone in his class was considered a possible serial killer. He gazed at Roger Woodward, who was sandwiched in the middle row between Adriana Tilly and Fiona Liebert. Roger, not too surprisingly, had aced the exam. *He clearly got it*, Neil thought. And seemed to enjoy playing the role of amateur sleuth. Could this have evolved into becoming a real-life serial killer? He didn't seem to fit the profile. But then, profiles didn't always tell the tale where it concerned the capabilities and modus operandi of killers.

Neil turned away from him, not wanting to tip his hand that something was up. But he couldn't allow Roger to leave either. Not till Paula had questioned him and determined he was not the unsub.

Dismissing the class a little early, Neil gave them a new assignment, then casually asked Roger Woodward if he could stick around for a moment to talk about his test results.

"Yeah, sure," he responded, wide-eyed at being singled out.

After the others had left, Neil eyed him intently and said, "You did great on the exam, Roger."

"Thanks."

Neil paused. "I was asked to hold you over."

Roger looked at him warily. "By who?"

"A police detective who would like to ask you a few questions pertaining to a homicide investigation..." Neil gauged his reaction, while trying to picture one of his prized students doubling as a serial killer. Before he could respond to the question, Paula walked into the room.

"Professor Ramirez," she spoke formally. "I can take it from here..."

"Okay." Neil ceded to her authority in the matter as the lead investigator on the case, but was more than an interested observer.

Paula walked up to the student and said equably, "Roger Woodward, I'm Detective Lynley. We spoke before, during the investigation into the death of Professor Debra Newton."

"Yeah, I remember." He ran a hand nervously through his hair. "I had an alibi," he reminded her.

"You did," she conceded, "which checked out. Now I'd like to ask you about another one of your professors, Odette Furillo, who was found murdered in her office last Wednesday."

"I heard about that. Like everyone else on

campus." Roger put his weight awkwardly on one foot. "What does that have to do with me?"

Paula glanced at Neil and back. "Maybe nothing. Or maybe everything."

"I don't follow," Roger said, furrowing his brow. "Are you accusing me of something?"

"Not yet." Her tone deepened. "I do find it odd though that you happened to be taking classes with two dead professors—at least one of whom you had a fixation on."

"I admit that I was attracted to Professor Newton, okay? I thought the feeling was mutual. Guess I was mistaken. But I didn't kill her and I didn't kill Professor Furillo." His nostrils flared. "Or, for that matter, the other murdered professors. I'm not this Campus Killer."

Though Neil wanted to give him the benefit of the doubt, that didn't work on the face of it when on the hunt for a serial killer. He gazed at the student and decided to get in on the questioning. "Relax, Roger. Detective Lynley is simply doing her job," Neil told him, playing the good cop, bad cop game as he regarded Paula and got her approval through an expression. "I assume you have an alibi for when Professor Furillo was murdered?" He gave him the date and time of death.

"Yeah, I do." Roger set his jaw. "I was with my girlfriend. Spent the night in her dorm room."

Paula peered at him. "Does this girlfriend have a name?"

"Last I checked," he quipped. Then Neil flashed him a stern look and Roger said, "Her name's Adriana... Adriana Tilly—"

"Adriana?" Neil said, reacting to the name of another student in his class. Like Roger, she tended to stand out with her mermaid hairstyle, featuring a blend of orange, green and red long locks with a round face. "I didn't realize you two were an item, and not just classmates."

"Yeah, we've been hanging out for a few weeks now," Roger stated coolly. "Been pretty much inseparable of late at night, if you know what I mean."

Neil took him at his word. "What you do and who you choose to do it with outside the classroom is your business." *So long as it doesn't involve criminal behavior*, he thought.

"I'll need to talk with Adriana," Paula made clear.

"Be my guest." He shifted his weight to the other foot. "She just left. If you hurry, you can probably catch her..."

Before Paula could respond, all three of them received a text message on their cell phones.

Neil regarded his and frowned as he favored Paula with a look of concern.

A bomb threat had been made at Addison University. More specifically, someone had claimed that pipe bombs had been planted at Horton Hall, the building they were currently standing in, set to detonate at any moment.

Chapter Seven

With an active bomb threat at Addison University's Horton Hall, the building was ordered evacuated immediately. A lockdown went into effect at other buildings across campus as a safety measure. Paula had been through this before. More than once. Most times, it turned out to be a false alarm. A prank that was anything but funny. This did little to quell the tension in the air, thick as fog. In the post-9/11 era, nothing could ever be taken for granted when it came to potential terroristic activities.

Not knowing if a hidden bomb could explode at any time, Paula was admittedly on pins and needles as she, along with Neil and Roger Woodward, headed hastily toward the nearest exit, followed by others. A Regional Special Response Team, which included highly trained members from the DPPS, Rendall Cove PD, Shays County Sheriff's Department, and the Bureau of Alcohol, Tobacco, Firearms and

Explosives, stormed past them and entered Horton Hall tactically. They were prepared for anything they might find in trying to defuse the situation.

"Let them do their job," Neil told her firmly, as Paula had fought her instincts to want to go back inside to be in on the action in confronting the threat on campus. She knew he was right in leaving this to the RSRT.

"I will," she promised smartly, as they moved away from the building and behind barricades that had been set up. Paula took note that Roger Woodward and other students were being escorted by law enforcement to a location that had been cleared. "So, what's your take on Woodward?" she asked Neil, though having already sensed that he believed she was barking up the wrong tree with him as a suspect.

"Well, he's one of my best students. But that doesn't make him incapable of being a serial killer." Neil brushed up against her and Paula felt it down to her toes. "I don't see that here, honestly. Especially if his alibi for the first suffocation murder held up."

She considered this. "Woodward said he was at the school library at the time. A number of other students who were there verified this, more or less, though surveillance video from the library was unable to substantiate this conclusively," Paula pointed out.

"I don't see other students covering for him intentionally," Neil said doubtfully. "That includes his alibi for the latest campus killing, Adriana Tilly."

"The girlfriend student of yours," she stated knowingly.

"Afraid so." He gave her a plain look.

"I'll see if she will corroborate his story."

"If not, we'll go from there…"

Paula nodded. She liked the *we* in his words, knowing that beyond being a visiting professor, his loyalties lay with helping them get to the bottom of their serial killer investigation. Wherever it took them, on campus or off.

She lifted her eyes to his face. "Do you think this bomb threat could have anything to do with the Campus Killer case?"

Neil turned to her. "Doesn't seem likely. What would the unsub gain by diverting attention from the serial killer probe only temporarily, especially since this would be under a different set of investigators. Unless the connections put us all under the same tent in terms of a serial killer bomber."

"I was thinking the same thing," Paula told him. "We certainly wouldn't be scared off in pursuing our mission till completed, even if there were a bomber on campus. Still, it's odd that the latest threat should manifest itself at this moment in time."

"Can't argue with you there," Neil said. "But it happens. Let's just see what the RSRT comes up with, if anything."

As the situation remained tense for the next hour, they were approached by RSRT Lieutenant Corey Chamberlain. In full uniform, the tall, brawny, fortysomething man had gray hair in a military undercut. His blue eyes were narrowed as he uttered, "We located two crude homemade pipe bombs hidden on the lower level. Both have been successfully deactivated and removed from the building."

"Wow." Paula's mouth hung open for a moment at the thought of someone being killed had the bombs exploded in their presence. Herself and Neil included. "Could there be more bombs inside?"

"I don't think so," Chamberlain said. "We've done a sweep twice and come up empty, insofar as any more pipe bombs."

"What do you know, if anything, about the bomber?" Neil asked him, brows knitted.

"Still working on that. The threat was posted online to two social media sites—as if to ensure we didn't miss it." Chamberlain jutted his chin. "These were traced back to a computer in the university's main library. We have investigators and technicians at the scene examining surveillance video and collecting forensic evidence, even as we speak."

"That's good," Paula commended him. "The unsub or unsubs cannot be allowed to get away with this."

"They won't," the lieutenant assured her. "Not on my watch."

"Be sure to keep us in the loop," Neil advised Chamberlain.

"Will do." He eyed them and said thoughtfully, "If you need to go back into Horton Hall, the evacuation order has been lifted."

Paula felt relieved to know that. She imagined this was even more true for Neil, given that it housed his classroom and office. As she watched Lieutenant Chamberlain move away from them to confer with his colleagues, Neil got on his cell phone, explaining, "I need to check in with the field office on this bomb incident."

"I understand," she told him, offering a tiny smile as he put a little distance between them. She wondered just how long it would be before he had vacated the visiting professorship and moved on to other ATF duties. The idea that whatever this was between them would be short-lived disturbed her. But she had no right to expect anything lasting. Did she?

When Paula's cell phone rang, she pulled it from the back pocket of her pants and saw that the caller was Mike Davenport. "Hey," she answered.

"Are you okay?"

"I'm fine. The situation has been neutralized."

"Glad to see that the all clear has been issued on campus," he remarked tentatively.

"Me too." Even so, Paula still felt unsettled for some reason, as if the proverbial shoe had yet to drop. "And no one got hurt, thankfully."

"Yeah. Unfortunately, we have another problem to deal with..." Davenport sighed. "Another female professor has been found dead—"

Paula's heart skipped a beat. "On campus?"

"Off," he replied tersely. "According to an officer on the scene, it looks like the same MO as the other victims of the Campus Killer."

She winced and got more info before disconnecting, only to find Neil standing right beside her. "What is it?" he asked perceptively.

Swallowing thickly, Paula told him soberly, "We have a new murder on our hands that is believed to be the work of the unsub serial killer."

THE CAMPUS KILLER celebrated his latest kill, while knowing full well that others would find it unsettling, if not downright horrific. He laughed to himself as he drove down the street, making sure he didn't go over the speed limit, drive erratically or otherwise give the cops a reason to pull him over. Were that the case, they just might be suspicious enough that he could be brought in and his carefully constructed life and living could well come tumbling down like dominoes.

Never mind the fact that he'd suffocated the good-looking professor hours ago. More than enough time to have put some distance between himself and the scene of the crime. She had been taken by surprise. Or he made it seem that way when accosting her and allowing a very false sense of security. Could he help it if she should have known not to trust anyone? Especially right now with a serial killer on the prowl.

But, like the others, she had played right into his hands like putty. And he had been more than willing to act accordingly in seeing it through. Right up until her breathing had ceased entirely and her days of teaching pesky students had come to an end. Then, like clockwork, he had left his magnificent handiwork behind for others to discover.

The Campus Killer turned left at the light, heading back onto the campus grounds—where he felt just as much at home as off campus. It made for an interesting mix while he plied his murderous trade and got away with it like this had been his destiny all along. Made him almost drool for more pretty professors to come into his grasp, before discovering there was no escape but death itself. And who knew who else might capture his fancy while he was in the mood for killing?

DETECTIVE GAYLE YAMASAKI drove her blue Ford Escape down the tree-lined Pickford Road, fretting over both the pipe bomb incident on campus and the more disturbing news that a woman had been found dead. All initial signs pointed toward this being a homicide—with the indicators sounding the Campus Killer alarm, as the victim was identified as another Addison University professor.

This can't be happening, Gayle told herself, even in the face of knowing otherwise. She had contacted Paula and Mike Davenport to this effect, warning them of the situation and agreeing to meet at the scene. Gayle pulled into the strip mall on the corner of Fulmore Street. It included a convenience store, dentist's office, shoe store and hair salon. She spotted two patrol cars, lights flashing, parked haphazardly. A male and female officer were talking to a young woman. Eyeing a corner of the small parking lot, Gayle saw that beneath an oak tree was a red Nissan Altima. A lone occupant was inside, behind the steering wheel.

After parking, Gayle checked the Smith and Wesson M&P 5.7 pistol in her custom Kydex holster and got out, approaching the officers. She flashed her identification and said, "Detective Yamasaki. What do we have?"

The twentysomething biracial female officer, who was around Gayle's height of five-five, with a black Afro puff hairstyle and brown eyes, responded glumly, "A female is deceased inside a vehicle. It appears as if she was the victim of foul play."

Gayle nodded perceptively. "We have a name?"

The male officer, who towered over them both, was in his thirties and had raven hair in a crew cut fade style and blue eyes. He answered, "Ran a make on the license plate of the Nissan Altima. It's registered to a Laurelyn Wong."

Gayle nodded and walked over to the car. The driver's side door was open. Sitting there, with the seat belt strapped across her body and wearing a floral-print midi dress, was a slender and attractive Asian female with highlighted brunette hair in a digital perm. She looked to be in her early thirties. Her head was tilted slightly to the right, eyes closed in death. A trickle of blood came down from one nostril onto her face. There was a white cotton towel with bloodstains on it, lying messily atop presumably the victim's satchel bag on the passenger seat, to suggest it was the weapon used to suffocate the victim.

A chill ran through Gayle in that moment as she stared at the woman who could very well have been an Indigenous Polynesian person like herself—telling Gayle that her own number could have come up, under other dire circumstances. She turned bleakly toward the male officer, who glanced at the other woman standing by the female officer, and said, "According to the one who discovered the body, Ms. Wong is a music professor at the university."

Gayle approached the woman, who was older than she had first thought—perhaps midthirties—and petite, with long and multilayered ombré hair, and again identified herself, "Detective Yamasaki. And you are?"

"Jeanne Roth," she told her. "I own the Roth Salon—" she pointed toward the strip mall "—

over there. Professor Wong had her hair done yesterday."

"At what time?" Gayle wondered.

"Around seven p.m." Jeanne's voice shook. "She left the salon just before we closed at eight."

"Did you see Professor Wong go to her car?" Gayle cast her eyes back at the vehicle. "And was she accompanied or followed by anyone?"

"She came and left the salon alone," Jeanne responded. "I never saw anyone following her…" She took a breath. "I closed up shop and didn't notice her car till I came in this afternoon. That's when I saw Professor Wong inside, not moving, and called 911."

Gayle looked up at a nearby surveillance camera, believing it could be key to ID'ing a suspect. But the female officer threw cold water on that when she told her, "Apparently, for whatever reason, that camera isn't operational right now."

"Figures." Gayle wrinkled her nose. She could only hope that there were security cameras in the shops on the streets that might provide useful information. As she pondered this, Gayle watched Mike Davenport drive up in his white Mustang Mach-E duty vehicle. He had arrived before Paula. "Hey," Gayle said calmly as she met him halfway, while ignoring the charge she got out of being in his presence.

"Hey." He met her eyes, then glanced at the victim's vehicle. "Where are we on this?" he asked tonelessly.

As she told him and got his initial thoughts, Gayle saw that Paula, accompanied by Neil, who was driving, had pulled up. Both were undoubtedly as disturbed as she was at this latest turn of events, coming after the pipe bomb scare at the college. Though she didn't believe the two were in any way connected, Gayle kept all possibilities on the table, so long as no one had been taken into custody for either criminal act.

THE VICTIM'S NAME, Laurelyn Wong, rang a bell in Neil's head. He'd heard it before. It took a moment or two before suddenly registering. According to ATF undercover agent Vinny Ortiz, the gunrunner they were investigating, Craig Eckart, had been living with Professor Laurelyn Wong. Now she was dead—in what was all but certain a homicide and fitting the MO of the Campus Killer—and Eckart had to be considered a suspect, all things being equal involving victims acquainted with their offenders. This definitely complicated the arms trafficking case being built against the suspect.

Neil didn't shy away from that when coming clean with Paula—once he had pulled her off to the side and away from the other detectives, crime scene technicians and the chief medical examiner, all who had a part to play in the investigation. "Professor Wong may have been killed by the gun trafficker who's currently under investigation by the ATF," he told her candidly.

"Seriously?" Paula frowned. "What am I missing?"

"Just that the suspect in our arms case, Craig Eckart, was romantically involved with the professor, which was told to me recently by an undercover agent." Neil dipped his chin. "Laurelyn Wong's name stuck in my memory."

"You think she may have been involved in gun trafficking?"

"I doubt it," he contended. "The romance was likely unassociated with the illegal weapons network. But with this latest twist, Eckart could also be moonlighting as a serial killer." Though Neil had strong doubts about that, especially since Ortiz was tracking the gunrunner's movements, they had to consider all possibilities in the serial killer probe. That included those closest to the victim being involved in her death.

Paula regarded him dubiously. "Please don't tell me you want us to look the other way, with your federal case taking priority over our local investigation?"

"Actually, it's just the opposite." Neil held her gaze without blinking. "I'd like you to stay the course in your investigation, while determining one way or the other, sooner than later, if Eckart is in fact the unsub. If not, you need to take him off the suspect list, so as not to impede our ongoing arms trafficking case."

She nodded. "Understood."

"In the meantime, the fewer people who know about Craig Eckart being the subject of a federal probe, the better," Neil thought to warn her. Not that he believed for one instant that Paula would do anything reckless to jeopardize their investigation. But the same might not be true for everyone working the Campus Killer case.

"I get it." Paula touched his arm and Neil felt the warmth radiate through the sleeve of his shirt. "I, for one, will do my best not to step on your toes, Agent Ramirez, where it concerns questioning Craig Eckart about the murder of his girlfriend."

"Okay." He flashed her a grin and got one back in return, giving Neil a good feeling inside and confidence that there was something between them that needed to be explored more thoroughly.

THE VISUAL OF the latest presumed victim of an unsub serial slayer gnawed at Paula like a hideous replay of a movie she wished would just go away, as she went with Gayle to the address on Vernon Drive, where Laurelyn Wong reportedly lived with her boyfriend, Craig Eckart. In respecting Neil's wishes that Eckart be treated as only a suspect in the Campus Killer case, while not revealing that he was also the primary person of interest under federal investigation for trafficking in contraband arms and ammunition, along with other firearms-related offenses, she kept this information to herself. Once the story broke, Gayle would learn about it from her department's Firearms Investigation Unit.

If Eckart did murder Professor Wong and the other women, he would be held fully accountable, irrespective of the federal çase against him, Paula told herself determinedly, as they left the car. Passing by a silver Lincoln Navigator Reserve parked in the driveway, they headed up the walkway to the two-story American foursquare home to notify the next of kin or significant other about the professor's death.

"I hate these moments," Gayle remarked softly.

"Don't we all," Paula said, knowing that it came with the territory, no matter how painful it was having to upend the lives of the dead's loved ones. Only, in this instance, the victim's boyfriend could have more than one thing to hide in his grieving.

Gayle rang the bell, and there was the instant sound of a large dog barking inside, before it was told in a commanding voice to be quiet. A moment later, the door opened. Standing there was a tall and muscular man in his mid to late forties, with dark hair in a disheveled cut and a salt-and-pepper corporate beard.

He trained gray eyes on Paula and asked cautiously, "How can I help you?"

She showed him her ID while saying, "Detective Lynley, Investigative Division of the Department of Police and Public Safety at Addison University."

Gayle flashed her badge and said, "Detective Yamasaki, Rendall Cove PD. And you are…?"

He hesitated, then answered, "Craig Eckart. You want to tell me what this is about?"

"Maybe we should go inside," Paula suggested, while wondering if this was where he was storing the illegal weapons. As he contemplated this, she added, "It's about Laurelyn Wong... She does live here?"

"Yeah." His mouth pursed, ill at ease.

"And what is your relationship with Ms. Wong?" Paula asked for the record.

"I'm her partner," he said matter-of-factly.

Gayle peered at him. "Can we come in?"

He nodded. The moment they stepped through the door, Paula picked up the pungent odor of marijuana. She also noted the Staffordshire bull terrier, growling threateningly, standing on all fours on bamboo flooring beside a leather sectional in the great room. Before she or Gayle needed to react, both armed, Eckart claimed, "She's harmless."

"All the same, would you mind putting your dog in another room while we talk?" Paula demanded.

"If you say so." He snickered. "C'mon, girl."

As he led the dog away, Paula glanced around at the contemporary furnishings, which may have been a facade for a criminal enterprise being investigated by the ATF. Then there was the question of multiple murders that could lead right to Craig Eckart.

When he came back into the room, Eckart

eyed them back and forth and spoke bluntly, "Laurelyn's dead, isn't she?"

Gayle glanced at Paula and responded straightforwardly, "Yes. She was found in her car in a strip mall parking lot early this afternoon." Gayle paused. "She was murdered..."

Eckart's broad shoulders slumped and an expletive escaped his lips. "By that Campus Killer?"

"The investigation into Ms. Wong's death is still ongoing," Paula responded simply. After a beat, she asked directly, "When did you last see her?"

He ran a hand roughly across his mouth. "Yesterday, around noon."

"That's more than twenty-four hours ago," Gayle pointed out. "Why didn't you report her missing?"

Paula knew that one could file a missing person report at any time, even if the authorities might take longer to act upon it, depending on the circumstances.

"Didn't think she was," he replied matter-of-factly. "We both have busy schedules and came and went as we pleased. It wasn't unusual for us to miss one another during the course of our days—or nights."

Paula regarded him skeptically. "Do you mind

telling us where you were last night between eight and nine?" she asked, knowing that Laurelyn was likely killed shortly after leaving the hair salon.

Eckart looked Paula directly in the eye while answering without preface, "I was at Rennie's Bar on Twenty-Second Street, having drinks with my buddy J. H. Santoro. We met there at seven and didn't leave till after midnight."

"Where can we reach this J. H. Santoro?" Gayle asked him.

"He's staying at an apartment complex on Yackley Road past Diamond Street. I have his number."

As Gayle added it to her cell phone, Paula considered digging deeper but, mindful of the arms case against him, thought better. Instead, she said evenly, "While we check out your alibi, we'll need you to come to the morgue to identify the body of Laurelyn Wong."

Chapter Eight

"J. H. Santoro is the moniker of ATF under-cover agent Vinny Ortiz," Neil informed Paula after he'd invited her over to his rented house for a nightcap and she'd brazenly accepted.

"Really?" She eyed Neil as they stood in the kitchen, both holding wineglasses half-filled with red wine. Its open concept provided a nice view of the downstairs and, from the pristine looks of it, it was clear that he spent little time there socializing. She wondered if the same were true in his permanent residence. Or was it more a matter of merely having the right reason to socialize—and the right person to do so with?

"Yeah," Neil told her. "And Ortiz confirmed that he did drink the night away with Craig Eckart at Rennie's Bar—pumping the arms trafficker for information to use to take him down."

"Well, apart from that, it looks like Eckart's

off the hook, insofar as the murder of Laure-lyn Wong," Paula said, tasting her drink. "And ostensibly this would extend as well to all the murders perpetrated by the unsub we're refer-ring to as the Campus Killer."

"That's a solid deduction. It feeds into the theory that, though the victims are likely being targeted by the unsub, the targeting, per se, may be more opportunity driven in a random way than the work of someone intimately acquainted with the victims." Neil sipped the wine. "This, in and of itself, would've put Eckart lower on the totem pole as the serial killer, with his girl-friend apparently the fifth victim of the unsub."

"I suppose, when you put it that way." Paula gave a little smile as Neil seemed totally in his element as an ATF special agent profiler. It made her wonder if he could ever give it up. Perhaps to become a full-time professor?

Neil grinned and said, "And what if I were to put it this way…" He lifted her chin and then kissed her solidly on the mouth. After she felt like she was floating on air, he pulled away. "What do you think?"

Paula touched her inflamed mouth and knew precisely what she was thinking. No reason to deny what she sensed they both wanted, over and beyond solving their criminal investigations. Gazing into his eyes, she responded honestly, "I'm thinking that I'd love to pick this up somewhere more comfortable."

"Such as?" he challenged her.

"Such as your bedroom." She took the bait. Why not?

"I was thinking the same thing," he uttered desirously. "Shall I lead the way?"

She took another sip of the wine, set it on the quartz island countertop and said bluntly, "Yes, please."

Neil smiled and kissed her again. "It would be my pleasure." He set down his drink and took her hand.

They headed up a central staircase to the second floor, passing by a couple of rooms down the hallway, before arriving at the primary suite. Stepping inside the spacious bedroom, they engaged in some more passionate kissing that left Paula breathless and wanting so much more. She backed away from Neil and scanned the room, taking in the midcentury modern furnishings and sash windows with Roman blinds. Her gaze landed squarely on the king-size platform bed with its fluffy pillows and navy patchwork quilt.

The thought of making love to Neil excited Paula beyond words, if the hot kisses between them were any indication. But that moment was also a realistic reawakening. Always responsible in her sexual practices, there was no reason to turn away from that now, no matter how strong the desire to have him. "Do you have protection?" she asked equably.

"Absolutely," Neil responded, as if anticipating the question. "I believe in better safe than sorry with sex too," he assured her with a straight face.

"Cool." She offered him a smile and watched as he disappeared into the bathroom and returned with the condom packet.

"Do I do this now?" Neil held it up. "Or later?"

Paula chuckled. "Uh, I think you can take your clothes off first."

He laughed. "Yeah, there is that."

She watched him set the packet atop a walnut nightstand and start to disrobe, as she did the same, feeling slightly self-conscious in the process. That went away for the most part as Paula reveled in checking out Neil's six-pack abs and the rest of his taut frame.

She hardly realized he was just as riveted on her till Neil commented, while giving Paula the once-over, "Has anyone ever told you just how gorgeous you are?"

Blushing, Paula admitted, "Not lately."

"Then I'm saying it," he declared. "You are stunning…and perfect, all of you."

"Back at you," she assured him, gazing at him from head to toe and in between.

They bridged the gap and resumed kissing, before making their way to the bed, where more intimacy followed with sizzling foreplay. When she could stand it no more, Paula cooed, "Make love to me, Neil…"

"Are you sure you're ready?"

"Oh, yes, I'm definitely ready for you," she declared.

"Then why wait a second longer," he uttered in a raspy voice, kissing her passionately again.

After Neil put on the condom, Paula waited with bated breath as he made his way between her legs, and she took him in whole, meeting him two-thirds of the way with each deep thrust into her. Their bodies pressed together and heartbeats were in sync as Paula felt the orgasm course through her in rapid fashion, moaning as she quivered with delight. She clung to Neil while he followed suit shortly thereafter, his body quaking as his own powerful release manifested itself wildly.

When it was over, their sexual appetites satiated through their actions and the invigorating scent of intimacy left behind, Paula rested her head on Neil's chest. She gushed, "Wow. That was amazing!"

He laughed. "It was, wasn't it?"

She blushed. "Yeah, truly."

"Some things in life have a predictable outcome," he suggested. "This was definitely one of them."

Paula giggled at his confidence. "Oh, you think so, do you?"

"I saw the sparks between us early on," Neil maintained. "It was just a matter of letting the flames erupt, sizzle, or whatever."

"How poetic," she said with a chuckle but couldn't disagree, having felt the connection too practically from the moment they first laid eyes on one another. But now that the spell had been broken, where did they go from here? If anywhere?

He laughed. "You bring the poet out in me, Paula, what can I say?"

She could think of a few things, but perhaps it was best not to delve too deeply in what this could mean potentially. Realizing the time, she separated from him and said, "I have to go."

"So soon?" Neil frowned. "I was hoping we might make a night of it—continuing this carnal exploration."

"Hmm… I'd love to," she admitted, climbing off the bed, "but I need to go feed my cat."

Neil sat up. "You have a cat?"

"Yep, her name's Chloe. She gets pretty ornery when she's hungry."

"I know the feeling. Need some help?" He eyed her body devilishly.

Paula got past the self-consciousness, knowing full well he liked what he saw, and then some. "Feeding the cat?"

"Sure." He grinned sideways. "I'm pretty good with my hands."

"That you are." She laughed thoughtfully. "You're welcome to come and help feed Chloe. Or whatever," she added, leaving the door open for whatever might come next.

NEIL FOLLOWED PAULA to her penthouse condo, eager to check out her place and extend the time they got to spend together. He was admittedly still caught up in the afterglow of the mind-blowing sex they had earlier. Though confident they would click in that department, the proof was very much in the pudding, as both had measured up beyond his expectations. It made him wonder where this thing was headed. Could she see a future with him? Could he see one with her?

What Neil knew for certain was that he wanted more than one quick romp where Paula was concerned. Beyond that, he was certainly willing to keep a very open mind as to what may lay in store for them once his time as a visiting professor had run its course.

Once they reached the condominium and went inside, Paula said, waving her arms around, "Well, here we are."

"I love it," Neil told her, sizing up the condo and the furnishings that seemed a perfect fit.

"Thanks." She smiled. "Make yourself at home while I give Chloe something to eat."

"Allow me," he insisted, figuring this was a good way to score points with Paula by warming up to her cat. He spotted Chloe wandering along the baseboard as though lost. Neil enticed the cat to come his way and scooped her into his arms. He gently rubbed her head and ears. "I'm Neil," he said lightheartedly. "Let's get you fed and content for the night."

"Looks like she's warming up to you in a hurry," Paula said with amusement.

Neil grinned. "I have that effect on—" he was about to say people, or her, in particular, but changed course midsentence "—cute, furry felines."

She laughed. "I can see that."

After feeding the cat, Neil turned his attention to Paula, and vice versa, as they made their way upstairs to her bedroom and upholstered farmhouse bed for another round of sexual relations. Only this time, without the sense of urgency, Neil was able to more slowly explore Paula's beautiful face and every inch of her body, giving her the same courtesy with him, as they made love into the wee hours of the night, before sleep and sheer exhaustion overtook them.

In the morning, Neil awakened from a bad dream about a killer running amok using illegal firearms. He didn't get a look at the unsub's face, but he was certain that the nightmare was a confluence of the Campus Killer meets the gunrunner, Craig Eckart. Only the two weren't one and the same in real life, Neil knew. Meaning that both cases were still open and needed to be successfully brought to a close, with the perps taken into custody.

When turning over and expecting to find Paula, naked, hot and still bothered, instead Neil saw that her spot beneath the covers was empty. He got up, slipping on his pants that had made their way onto the wood flooring, and looked for her.

He found her downstairs in the kitchen,

where his nostrils picked up the scent of cooked sausage, before Neil saw Paula fully dressed and making breakfast.

"Hey," she said, offering a smile. "Hope you like blueberry pancakes and sausage, to go with coffee?"

"Absolutely to all." He smiled back, walked up to her in his bare feet and kissed her. "But most of all, I like you." He made no bones about it.

"I like you too." She beamed. "So, let's eat and we can talk about our plans for today."

"Okay. Let me go put on the rest of my clothes and I'm all yours."

Her lashes fluttered while standing over the griddle. "We'll see about that."

Though his words may have been a metaphor, Neil felt they had a good ring to them nevertheless and he was beginning to take them quite literally. In spite of not knowing if they both had what it took to see it through, for better or worse.

IN HER OFFICE, Paula pushed past thoughts of last night's red-hot sex with Neil or whether or not she was falling in love with the ATF special agent—and instead focused on the autopsy report on her laptop on Laurelyn Wong's death.

As expected, the Shays County Chief Medical Examiner Eddie Saldana ruled this as a homicide. Similar to the other homicides thought to be perpetrated by the Campus Killer, the cause of the associate professor of music education's death was asphyxia. The time of death was believed to be between 8:00 p.m. and 10:00 p.m. A towel left at the crime scene was thought to be the murder weapon.

I'm sorry you had to die this way, Paula thought, knowing that Laurelyn Wong, like the other victims, had plans for her life. Now these had been squelched permanently by a cold-blooded killer who decided their lives were not worth living.

But who was the unsub? With Laurelyn's lover, Craig Eckart, ruled out, it brought Paula back to Neil's student, Roger Woodward. He had alibis for the murders of two of his professors, Debra Newton and Odette Furillo. But Paula had yet to check out his alibi for Professor Wong's murder. Was he enrolled in Laurelyn Wong's music class?

Pulling up Woodward's class schedule, Paula did not see him as a student of Laurelyn's. She checked the last semester and got the same result. Similarly, there was no information that directly linked the honors student to professors

Harmeet Fernández or Kathy Payne. But did that mean he was innocent? Or a clever serial killer, above and beyond an obviously bright senior?

AT THE SCHOOL OF CRIMINAL JUSTICE, Neil sat in the conference room with the other faculty and two teaching assistants, Desmond Isaac and Rachelle Kenui. Director Stafford Geeson, the former police chief of Mackinac Island, Michigan, had convened the hastily arranged meeting to talk about the pipe bombs discovered in the building yesterday.

Geeson, who was fifty-five and thickly built, with slicked-back gray hair and a receding hairline, stood in front of the room and shifted his blue eyes as he said earnestly, "I'm sure everyone here knows about the bomb incident that took place on the ground floor of Horton Hall. Though the Regional Special Response Team was able to locate the pipe bombs and deactivate them before they could explode, it's still troubling that this happened on campus—and in this building, in particular." His chin sagged. "As of now, the perpetrator or perpetrators remain at large. Till apprehended, I'm asking everyone who works for the School of Criminal Justice to be extra diligent in looking out for anyone acting suspicious. The directors of the other departments in this building are telling staff the same thing. And if you know anyone who might have a beef against someone in Horton Hall or the university itself, don't hesitate to bring this to my attention or the authorities."

Geeson took a breath and, eyeing Neil, said, "As our resident criminal profiler, Professor Ramirez, I'm hoping you can maybe shed some light on the pipe bomber and what's behind this terroristic attack on the campus."

Neil said evenly, "Sure, I can shed a bit of light on the subject." He had anticipated he might be called upon in this manner. Standing, he walked to the front of the room, got a pat on the shoulder from the director, and then Neil got right to it, saying thoughtfully, "Well, without being privy to the specifics about the current case, my general view on bomber unsubs is that they tend to be narcissists who choose to use fear tactics such as a bomb threat to get attention and/or cause death and destruction as a matter of retaliation for perceived wrongs against them. Or to make a statement of one type or another.

"Though they are often loners," he explained, "and obviously antisocial, some are paranoid schizophrenics, while others are mentally sound but still willing to involve themselves in abnormal behavior for reasons aforementioned. We'll have to see which way the pendulum swings in this instance."

Desmond asked, "So, are we talking about a student or ex-student bomber with a grudge against the school or a professor?"

Neil peered at him. "Is there something you want to confess to us, Isaac?" he asked the TA lightheartedly.

"Not that I can think of," Desmond said with a chuckle.

"Just checking." Neil flashed a crooked grin. "As for whether or not the unsub is a current or former student, that's a distinct possibility. But—" he felt it needed to be emphasized "—the perp could also be an employee or ex-worker at the university. As well as someone who has no connection at all, but found the campus location attractive and had the means to both use the library to announce the bomb threat and deliver the pipe bombs, while managing to get away."

"Sounds very much like the Campus Killer," Rachelle Kenui remarked. The twentysomething TA was thin, green-eyed and had short wheat-blond hair in a mullet cut. "Could they be one and the same?"

"Anything's possible," Neil stated. "Generally speaking, though, unless we're talking about a serial bomber, heaven forbid, the profiles of a single incident bomber and serial killer do not usually measure up. As for the school bomber, hopefully we'll get a better idea of who—and what—we're looking for once forensics has examined the pipe bombs for DNA, prints, etc."

After a little more insight into the bombing incident, the meeting broke up and Neil headed to his office to prepare for his next class. Even with the current uneasiness on campus, given the unusual criminal activity of late, he wanted to keep the classes as normal as possible for his students, in spite of Neil knowing that this would be next to impossible. As long as a serial killer and pipe bomber remained on the loose.

Chapter Nine

Paula walked down the fifth-floor corridor in the Acklin Residence Hall on Wells Lane. Along the way, she passed a group of giggling female students, before reaching Room 557. The door was open, and Paula could see a slender young woman with multicolored long hair, standing while looking at her cell phone. A knock got her attention. "Are you Adriana Tilly?"

"Yes, I'm Adriana." She put the phone in the back pocket of her jeans.

Paula stepped inside the cluttered two-person room and showed her identification. "Detective Lynley. I'm investigating the murder of Honors College Associate Professor Odette Furillo. Mind if I ask you a few questions…?"

Adriana arched a thin brow worriedly. "You think I had something to do with that?"

"I'm sure you didn't," Paula responded, giving her the benefit of the doubt. "A name that's come up in the investigation is of one of Professor Furillo's students—Roger Woodward. Do you know him?" she asked for effect.

Her blue eyes grew wide. "Yes. Roger's my boyfriend."

"He says that he was with you the night Professor Furillo was killed," Paula said, giving her the date and time frame. "I need you to verify his alibi."

Adriana wasted little time doing just that. "Yes, Roger was with me the entire night," she confirmed unabashedly.

Paula gave her a direct look. "You're sure about that?"

"Yes." She paused before adding, "Roger would never kill anyone. Certainly not one of his professors."

Maybe you don't know your boyfriend as well as you think, Paula thought, aware that denial was often the order of the day when someone you were close to was suspected of murder. "Had to ask as part of my job," she told her. While at it, for the record, Paula thought to ask if Woodward was with her when Professor Laurelyn Wong was killed. Adriana claimed calmly that he was.

With no real reason to dispute this, Paula went with that and saw herself out. It appeared as if Neil's student, Roger Woodward, was not their Campus Killer. Which meant that the hunt to unmask and apprehend the unsub was still on.

AT 4:00 P.M., Neil pulled his car up behind Agent Vinny Ortiz's Jeep Wagoneer on Quail Lane in Rendall Creek Park. Ortiz, aka J. H. Santoro as his undercover handle, had requested the meeting to discuss the latest developments in the arms trafficking investigation. For his part, Neil was curious as to whether the murder of suspected gunrunner Craig Eckart's girlfriend, Laurelyn Wong, had changed the dynamics of the case any.

Ortiz exited the Jeep and made his way to the passenger side of Neil's Chevy Suburban, where Ortiz muttered, "Thanks for meeting with me on short notice."

Neil regarded him. "What's up?"

"Not sure," the undercover agent said flatly. "With the death of Eckart's girlfriend, Laurelyn, at the hands purportedly of a serial killer, it's kind of freaking the man out."

"How so?" Neil hesitated to ask.

"Well, apparently Eckart feels it's bad karma that someone he had a thing for has been murdered. He's wondering if it's trying to tell him something."

"Such as?"

"If he has an X on his own back," Ortiz said bluntly. "Though Eckart was glad we happened to be hanging out at a bar together the night she was killed, he believes Laurelyn's death is a sign that he needs to put his plans for arms trafficking into a higher gear—so that he can get rich and maybe get out of the business."

"That so?" Neil didn't see that happening of his own free will, karma or not. For most traders of contraband small arms and ammo—especially when operating on the dark web—the money they could make and perceived lower risk of detection made the illicit activities almost addictive. He doubted it was something Craig Eckart could easily walk away from, even though someone had murdered his girlfriend. Neil gazed at the ATF agent. "What do you think?"

Ortiz shrugged. "I don't see him calling it quits. He's got too nice of an operation going. Or so he thinks. But I do believe that Eckart is even more suspicious that he's being set up. Meaning, I have to go even deeper undercover to protect myself, without stepping over the line."

"Do what you need to do," Neil advised him. "Be smart about it. We can get you help whenever you need it."

"I'll keep that in mind." Ortiz scratched his

beardstache. "I think things are about to go down. When it happens, I'll be sure to get the word out so we can nail this bastard. Hopefully, before any more illegal weapons can change hands, in this country or abroad."

"The team will be ready to pounce," Neil assured, wanting this to be over almost as much as Ortiz did.

Ortiz tilted his face with curiosity. "So, with Laurelyn yet another victim, are you any closer to getting the jump on the Campus Killer?"

Neil furrowed his forehead. "I'd like to think we're closing in on the unsub with each and every hour," he responded, his voice steady and thoughtful. "But that's not exactly the same as knowing who we're dealing with and having him locked up behind bars, is it?"

"No, it isn't." Ortiz sighed. "You'll get the perp. He can't go on killing professors forever and not have to face the music for his crimes."

"I'm thinking the same thing." Neil squirmed. "Not much consolation, though, for those who fall prey to the unsub." This told him that the task force needed to step up even more than they already were, if this meant sparing the lives of other professors that could come within the unsub's viewfinder.

"Talk to you soon," Ortiz said succinctly.

Neil nodded. "Yeah."

After Ortiz drove off, Neil followed suit and once again found himself weighing his options on what to do with the rest of his life beyond his current caseload. Was he truly cut out for being a full-time educator? Or was being an ATF special agent and behavioral profiler too much in his blood to ever truly want to walk away from?

Then there was Paula. She had come into his life practically out of the blue. And just at a time when he wasn't sure he would ever again click with a woman who could earn his trust. She had already passed both tests with flying colors. But would he be enough to check all the boxes she had for a workable relationship, after falling short in her marriage to another man who made his living in federal law enforcement?

Neil knew that whatever decisions he made could well rest on how he fared on Paula's litmus test or desire to carry on with what they had started.

ON WEDNESDAY AFTERNOON, the latest task force briefing took place at the Rendall Cove Police Department. Gayle stood alongside Paula at the podium in the conference room, knowing that all eyes were on them as they had to give the highlights and lowlights of the investigation now that yet another victim had been added to the list of those targeted by the Campus Killer. This was starting to get old in a hurry, Gayle felt, sure that Paula concurred. But this was where they were and they had to put on their best faces in meeting the challenge head-on.

Holding the stylus pen, Gayle turned to the large monitor and brought up the image of the latest victim to die at the hands of an unsub. "Two nights ago, Laurelyn Wong, a thirty-two-year-old music professor, was murdered in her vehicle, after having her hair done at a salon on Fulmore Street," Gayle reported. "According to the autopsy report, Professor Wong's death was due to asphyxia, with the murder weapon being a cotton towel. It was the same cause of death attributed to four other female professors at Addison University. Though the investigation is well underway and we're looking at each and every angle here, as of now, the killer remains at large..."

Gayle swallowed as she looked at the man in charge of the Detective Bureau, Criminal Investigations Sergeant Anderson Klimack. At fifty-five and solid in build beneath his uniform, with short, tapered brown-gray hair parted to the side and blue eyes, he was bucking to become lieutenant. She was sure that putting this case behind the bureau would help him make his case for the promotion.

Averting his stare, while feeling the pressure, Gayle made a few more comments, before turning it over to Paula, who gave her a supportive little smile and then said in a serious tone, "Losing another professor to a senseless murder is something none of us wanted to hear. Much less have to investigate. But a cold and calculating serial killer has reared his ugly head again in targeting the popular music professor Laurelyn Wong. In the process, the unsub has put us on notice that he has no intention of ending the killing of professors off and on campus—not till we stop him."

After going over the victims again, locations of the murders and efforts to gather forensic evidence and surveillance video on the latest homicide as with the earlier deaths, Gayle and Paula took turns laying out the investigative efforts. Neither sought to sugarcoat the frustrations within the task force in its inability to solve the case as yet. But both insisted that this made them even more determined to do just that—whatever it took.

Davenport and another investigator from the Detective Bureau, Larry Coolidge, a tall and bald-headed five-year veteran of the PD, provided additional updates; then Neil pitched in with observations, while doing his best to try and put the Campus Killer case into proper perspective by stating coolly, "Undoubtedly, losing five women in the prime of their lives to a serial killer is almost too much to bear for all of us. But, just to be clear, the number of victims thus far pales to those killed by such serial monsters as Samuel Little, who murdered at least sixty women over several decades, Gary Ridgway, convicted of forty-nine murders, Juan Corona, found guilty of killing twenty-five. Even the infamous female serial killer, Belle Gunness, claimed at least fourteen victims. Or, in other words, we have time to stop the perp long before he can reach these goals as a serial killer."

To Gayle—and she read as much in Paula's expression—this was something to keep in mind as further motivation to prevent the unsub from joining the ranks of these killers in their bloodthirsty appetite for murder.

THAT NIGHT, Paula slept in Neil's bed, where the two recreated the first time they made love. Only this occasion was more thorough, demanding, fervent and, yes, all-consuming. Neither seemed to want it to end. At least this was how Paula read the passion. Could she have mistaken Neil's body language for anything other than being just as intoxicated by the experience?

When they were totally spent and gratified, she laid in his arms, with neither saying a word. For her part, Paula hesitated sharing her thoughts for fear of having her heart broken. Telling someone you were starting to fall in love with them could backfire, she believed. Especially if it was not reciprocated by a person who likely wouldn't be around much longer. She wondered if there was any wiggle room in the special agent's future plans. Or were they set in stone, and he had no desire to start a relationship he couldn't finish?

IN THE MORNING, they got up early for a run in the park. Had it been up to Neil, he would have let Paula get more sleep and gone it alone. Between the passionate lovemaking and restlessness from the stresses associated with tracking a serial killer, neither had gotten much shuteye. But she had been insistent upon joining him, having kept jogging clothes in her car for that purpose.

If the truth be told, Neil welcomed her company, as Paula was growing on him in ways that he could never have anticipated fully upon coming to Rendall Cove. Last night only reinforced that. Having someone to open his heart to again excited him. He could tell that the feeling was mutual. But there was still the matter of what it all meant for the future. And if their relationship had what it took to survive the criminal investigations that brought them together.

The run was mostly silent, aside from the chirping sounds of black-capped chickadees in the woods. After taking turns racing ahead of the other, Neil broke the ice by asking perceptively, "What's on your mind?"

Paula faced him and said point-blank, "You... and wondering where this—" she pointed her finger at him and then herself "—is going. Or do you even know?"

He took a breath. "I'm wondering the same thing," he admitted, following with, "Honestly, I haven't a clue."

"That's helpful," she said sarcastically.

"Not sure what you expect me to say." He stiffened. "I care for you, Paula. I'm sure you know that. I think that we have something here." Another pause came. "I'm just not sure how things will play out once my time at the university is up. Are you?" If she had a concrete plan for them, he was certainly ready to listen.

Paula sucked in a deep breath. "No, not really," she confessed.

"So why don't we just go with the flow and see how things turn out?" Neil put forth. He hoped he wasn't backing her into a corner so she wanted to end things between them prematurely.

"All right." She favored him with a convivial smile. "We'll do that."

"Good." *That tells me she wants this to work as much as I do,* he told himself. This gave Neil hope that they were truly on the same wavelength. Even if the future was still very much up in the air. But at least it had given them a sense of direction that neither could turn away from.

WHEN THEY ARRIVED back at his house, Paula was still pondering the prospects for making a life with Neil. Or not. With much dependent upon who would be willing to sacrifice the most in making this work between them. Selfishly, she would love to see him stay in Rendall Cove as a professor. But was that even feasible? Could she handle giving up her job, if it came right down to it, in the name of love? Or would she be falling into an old pattern with predictable results?

Her reverie was broken while they were in the kitchen making breakfast—French toast, orange juice and coffee—when both their cell phones rang at the same time. Paula grabbed hers first and saw that the caller was Mike Davenport. "Hey," she answered.

"If you're by the television, you might want to put on the news to see what's about to break."

As she was hanging up with Davenport, she saw that Neil had been told the same thing, as he had already stepped inside the living room and was holding the TV remote, turning the set on. Joining him, Paula watched the flat-screen LCD television as an attractive red-haired female news anchor was saying animatedly, "An arrest has been made in connection with the pipe bombs found two days ago at Horton Hall on the campus of Addison University." An image of a dark-haired, grim-faced young man appeared on the screen. "According to sources, taken into custody was Harold Fujisawa—a twenty-two-year-old former student at the university. The global history major, who was reportedly expelled from school last year because of unspecified threats made, was arrested without incident outside a café on Long Street in Shays County."

Neil cut the TV off and, with his brow furrowed, uttered, "Looks like we've nipped one headache in the bud."

"Hope so." Paula wrinkled her nose thoughtfully. The arrest of the pipe bomb suspect was certainly a relief. "The university doesn't need a disgruntled ex-student resorting to terrorism to settle a score."

"Tell me about it." Neil met her eyes. "Nor does it need a serial killer run amok. But that will be dealt with too."

She nodded agreeably. "Not soon enough."

"I'm with you." He put his hands on her shoulders, pulling them closer. "In more ways than one."

"Same here," she promised him, resolving not to look too far ahead while still trying to sort out feelings and happenings between them in present terms.

When Neil dipped his head and kissed her, Paula returned the kiss in full, enjoying the firmness of his mouth upon hers and the over-all way it made her feel.

Minutes later, they returned to the kitchen and the French toast, ate the breakfast and talked about the crimes being investigated, while avoiding discussing things best left off the table for the time being.

Chapter Ten

That morning, Neil attended a Regional Special Response Team briefing in a Shays County Sheriff's Department conference room. The subject matter was the pipe bomb terrorist attack on the Addison University campus. Neil was all ears in wanting to know just how they identified and took down the suspect. Just as important was whether or not the perp could have been involved in the suffocation murders of female professors.

RSRT Lieutenant Corey Chamberlain was at the podium, giving the update. "As you know by now, at approximately seven twenty-nine a.m. today, we made an arrest in relation to the pipe bombs planted at the university. The suspect is Harold Fujisawa, who was kicked out of the school at the junior level last fall, due to making threats against faculty in the College of Social Science, where he was enrolled, after he was caught cheating on exams. Though there were no formal charges filed, Fujisawa, twenty-two, had been on our radar ever since.

"We were able to link him to the computer used at the school library to post bomb threats on social media through forensic analysis and surveillance video," Chamberlain said. "Once identified, we located the suspect—who was apparently living on the streets these days—at the Creekside Café. We waited for him to emerge before placing Harold Fujisawa under arrest. He made a full confession, blaming his actions on an addiction to the so-called zombie drug, Xylazine. Mr. Fujisawa is being charged with a number of federal offenses related to the manufacturing and possession of an explosive device, planting two pipe bombs on university property and more..." The lieutenant took a breath. "As of now, we believe the suspect acted alone."

Neil was confident that Harold Fujisawa would no longer pose a threat to Addison University or the city at large. But it still begged another important question that needed to be answered. "What can you tell us about the suspect's DNA and prints in relation to any other crimes?" Neil asked interestedly.

Chamberlain ran a hand across his face and responded, "We collected a sample of Fujisawa's DNA, along with fingerprinting him. The

DNA was put into CODIS to check for a match. Unfortunately, it came back negative."

Or, in other words, Fujisawa's DNA was not a match for the unknown DNA profile taken from beneath the nails of a victim of the Campus Killer, Neil told himself, which corresponded with his feelings that the serial killer and pipe bomber were likely two different perpetrators. "And the prints?"

Chamberlain frowned perceptively. "The suspect doesn't have a criminal history to work with. So, no fingerprints on file and verified as such through the Michigan Automated Fingerprint Identification System."

Which, Neil knew, corresponded with the FBI and Homeland Security AFIS. Meaning that Harold Fujisawa almost certainly wasn't at the crime scenes of the murdered professors, with no match to any of the finger and palm prints collected and entered into the databases.

As such, his attention as a profiler had to be refocused on an unsub in the search for the Campus Killer. Neil thought about Paula, who had left his rented house shortly after breakfast. He believed they had turned the corner somewhat in their relationship, even if neither of them knew precisely what road they were headed down. Or how long it might take to get there. But at this point, he would take any positive development in terms of building something together, which he felt ready for at this point. He could only hope she would not let her own past romance drama stand in the way of what they could potentially have.

PAULA STOOD ON the deck, observing Canada geese huddled together by the creek, as she called her former sister-in-law, Madison. They had stayed in touch as real friends, in spite of Paula's divorce from her brother, Scott.

When Madison came onto the small screen, her bold turquoise eyes lit up, surrounded by an attractive face and long blond hair worn in a shaggy wolf cut with curly bangs. "Hey, there," she said sweetly.

"Hey." Paula grinned, noting that Madison was in uniform as a full-time law enforcement ranger in the Blue Ridge Mountains of North Carolina. She had recently gotten married to a National Park Service Investigative Services Branch special agent. "How's life treating you these days in the ranger's world?"

"Good. Rarely a dull moment on and off the Blue Ridge Parkway," Madison told her, referencing the 469-mile National Scenic Byway that meandered through North Carolina and Virginia. "Keeps me on my toes. What's up with you?"

"Well, besides investigating a serial killer on campus and surviving a bomb threat in one piece—" Paula pretended like they were merely run-of-the-mill occurrences "—I've met someone," she ventured forth. She felt comfortable sharing this with her, knowing Madison had encouraged her to move on past Scott.

"As if a serial killer and bomber aren't enough to deal with, right?" Madison made a face. "We'll get back to that. So, who have you met and it's about time…?"

"His name is Neil Ramirez," Paula told her. "Neil's an ATF special agent who's currently a visiting professor at the university."

"Hmm…" Madison widened her eyes with curiosity. "Interesting. Tell me more."

Paula did just that, while not getting carried away in her fondness for the man. Or what may or may not be in store for them. Only that they got along well and liked one another. "We'll see how it goes," she finished with, resisting the urge to admit she hoped it could go as far as possible between two people attracted to one another.

"I'm definitely pulling for you," Madison promised. "You deserve to be happy. We all do."

"Thanks, Madison." Paula knew she was referring to her ex as well and had no problem with that, wishing him the happiness that had eluded them over the long term. She told Madison a bit more about her current investigation before hanging up.

After setting out food for Chloe, Paula headed off to work.

IN THE AFTERNOON, Neil had the pleasure of having not one, but two teaching assistants in Desmond Isaac and Rachelle Kenui on hand to pass out the essay exams in the Auditorium on Slane Drive, where Neil taught a class in criminology to a captive audience of students. He was optimistic that they would be able to keep their eyes on the ball, as it were, even in the midst of some of the unsettling events happening on campus of late.

Handing Desmond and Rachelle a batch of the exams, Neil joked, "Think you two can handle this very tough assignment and earn your stripes?"

Rachelle giggled. "Can't speak for Desmond here, but I believe I'm more than up to the task."

Desmond gave a little laugh. "It's going to be challenging, I admit," he quipped, "but I'll just have to push myself harder and not quit before I get started."

Neil chuckled. "Figured I could count on you both." He grabbed more of the exams from his briefcase. "So, let's do this before my class thinks they'll get lucky and get a free pass here, or a delayed exam. Not happening."

"Not on our watch," Rachelle agreed, flashing her teeth.

Desmond looked at her and said, "As Prof Ramirez said, let's get this over with, and we can have fun watching them sweat it out while seeing if they've learned anything."

"They better have," she voiced in earnest.

Neil eyed the two TAs as they headed toward the students seated throughout the lecture hall. He suspected that Rachelle and Desmond may have started dating. Whether this meant they had a future together was anyone's guess. Neil was more concerned about his own relationship with Paula and if the love he was feeling for her was the real deal. If so, he didn't want to blow it with her. But he did have his career to think about too. As did she as a campus detective sergeant. Was there enough room in their lives for each other when all was said and done?

PAULA WAS IN her office going over notes on the Campus Killer case when the Addison University alert came in, reporting a suspected armed robbery near the Communication Arts and Sciences Building on Rafton Street. The suspect was described by the female victim as a tall, slender and blue-eyed female in her early twenties, wearing dark clothes and a hoodie that was still able to expose curly crimson hair beneath. Patrol officers had been dispatched to the location, with the unsub having fled the scene and still at large.

Hmm, that's not too far from here, Paula thought, getting up from her chair. Maybe she could help nail the culprit, even if it was a distraction from her current investigation. She checked the SIG Sauer P365 semiautomatic pistol tucked in her concealment holster and then was out the door.

No sooner had she left the building and was about to hop into her car, when Paula spotted someone who resembled the unsub running north down the sidewalk. Trailing her, Paula narrowed the distance, while noting that the suspect appeared to be holding a pocketknife. *No match for a loaded gun*, Paula told herself.

Removing the semiautomatic pistol, she wasted no time barking orders to the suspect. "Stop! Drop the weapon!"

The young woman stopped on a dime and rounded on her. "This isn't what you think," she expressed, with the hood still covering her head.

"I've heard that line too many times," Paula said sardonically. "I'm Detective Lynley, campus police department. Drop the weapon—please—so I don't have to shoot you."

"Okay, I give up." She placed the knife on the sidewalk and pulled the hood down, revealing a cropped red pixie around a pretty heart-shaped face, and then raised her hands.

"Keep them raised!" While keeping the gun aimed, Paula approached her carefully and ordered, "Turn around." The suspect obeyed and Paula removed chained handcuffs from a nylon handcuff holster attached to her waistband on the back side and, twisting the suspect's arms around, quickly cuffed her. "So, what's your name?"

"Nikki Simone."

Paula faced her. "Are you a student here?"

"Yeah. I'm a senior."

And you want to destroy your life this close to graduating, Paula mused sadly. "Nikki, you're under arrest for a suspected armed robbery," she told her flatly.

"I never robbed her," Nikki snapped. "I only took what was rightly mine—the engagement ring she got from my ex-boyfriend, Lester Siegel. He gave it to me, then stole it from me, once I ended things after I caught him cheating on me with her."

Paula lifted a brow to the tale that seemed

too incredible to be untrue. "You have the ring on you?"

"Yeah, in my pocket." Her eyes watered. "I just wanted it to remember him from when things were good, you know?"

"I sympathize with you," Paula had to admit. "Unfortunately, you went about getting back your property the wrong way and will now need to sort it out through the criminal justice system. If you're lucky, your ex won't press charges and you can chalk this—and him—up to a bad experience."

As a squad car approached, Paula reluctantly turned the suspect over to the two fresh-faced officers, while explaining the situation as the suspect told it to her, leaving it for them to decide if they wanted to let her go.

She texted Neil to see if he wanted to grab a coffee. He quickly responded, asking her to meet him at the Auditorium, where he had a class. Agreeing, Paula headed for her car, still wondering how they might make things work once Neil's stint as a visiting professor was over. Did any long-distance, relatively speaking, relationships ever work over the long term? Or might they find an acceptable way to bridge the gap?

After parking, Paula went inside the Auditorium and had just arrived at the lecture hall as the students were filing out. She went inside and saw Neil conversing near the front with a twentysomething male and female.

Neil looked up and grinned when he saw Paula and said, "Hey."

"Hi," she responded.

"These are my teaching assistants, Desmond Isaac and Rachelle Kenui." Neil introduced them. "Detective Paula Lynley."

"Hey," the two TAs said in unison, smiling.

"Hey." Paula smiled back at them.

"They make my job a whole lot easier," Neil claimed.

"I'm sure they do." Paula went along with this.

"I think it's more the other way around," Desmond said. "Prof Ramirez is easy to work with."

"True." Rachelle beamed and regarded Desmond. "We should go."

"Yeah." He placed a hand on the small of her back. "Let's get out of here." He eyed Neil. "We'll have the graded essays to you tomorrow afternoon."

Neil nodded. "Good."

"Later," he told Neil and glanced smilingly at Paula and back to Rachelle.

After they left, Paula asked Neil, "Are you ready?"

"Yeah. Let me just get my briefcase."

They walked in silence the short distance to the Union Building food court, where both ordered lattes and took a seat.

"Got a briefing on the bombing at Horton Hall," Neil remarked, sipping the coffee. "Looks as though the suspect, Harold Fujisawa, had a beef against the College of Social Science faculty after being expelled. This was his misguided attempt at payback, using the excuse of being high on Xylazine to justify his actions."

"Excuses, excuses." Paula rolled her eyes and shook her head. "When will they ever learn?"

"Not soon enough for too many." Neil sat back. "Though Fujisawa's going down for various terrorism charges, he's not the Campus Killer unsub. His DNA and prints didn't match those found at any of the crime scenes of the serial murders."

Paula tasted the latte and said, "Not too surprised to hear that." She noted that Neil had already, more or less, believed that the unsub bomber didn't fit the profile of the Campus Killer and vice versa. "Would've been nice though if the two perps were one and the same and we could have wrapped up our case in one fell swoop." She shrugged. "Oh, well…"

"That's the way it goes," Neil said, taking it in stride. "There are many dangerous individuals out there waiting to do bad things that we have to clean up, one way or the other."

"You're right. Can't exactly read their minds ahead of time, can we?"

He tilted his head to the left side. "If only."

Paula thought about her latest crime incident. "I just caught an armed robbery suspect," she told him.

"Really?" Neil gazed at her. "I saw the campus alert through the emergency notification system on my cell phone."

"Yeah. Only it wasn't exactly what I expected." She drank the coffee, then recounted the unbelievable circumstances that apparently led up to the armed robbery.

Neil laughed. "Talk about getting on one's bad side, not once, but twice..."

Paula thought of the irony, knowing that Neil had been the victim of a cheating girlfriend. Only he had handled it much differently—thank goodness. "I guess when it comes to having one's heart broken, and having the audacity to take back the ring for good measure, people can lose their minds."

"Unfortunately, that's true," he concurred thoughtfully. "For some of us, we simply move on from infidelity and try not to look back."

She favored him with a thin, pensive smile. "I think that's the best way to go."

"Me too." He grinned at her, and Paula felt a tingle from its effect on her and the firm belief that he was better off having gotten past a failed relationship. As had she. While positioning themselves to learn from it in forging new paths toward happiness.

When her cell phone rang, Paula paused those thoughts and lifted it off the table. She saw that the caller was Davenport and answered, "Hey." She listened to the detective and said tersely in response, "All right."

Neil fixed her intuitively. "What?"

Paula's chin jutted as she responded bleakly, "A female professor has been reported missing."

Chapter Eleven

Charlotte Guthrie, a forty-one-year-old associate professor of fisheries management in the Department of Fisheries and Wildlife at the College of Agriculture and Natural Resources, was last seen late yesterday afternoon. The avid runner and widow loved to jog on campus and had apparently gone for a run after finishing her last class of the day at 4:00 p.m. With her blue Tesla Model 3 located in the employee parking lot, and no signs of a break-in or other criminal activity, a search for the missing professor had begun on the campus grounds.

"I don't like the looks of this," Paula voiced as a gut feeling told her that the professor's disappearance would not end well. From all accounts, Charlotte Guthrie was a responsible and careful person and not prone to disappearing like a magician in a staged performance without explanation. No, Paula sensed that her mysterious absence was far more sinister in light of the murdered female professors at the university, two of which occurred on campus. Charlotte's faculty photograph—she was white, attractive and hazel-eyed with shoulder-length blond hair, parted to the side—had been posted on the school newspaper site and popular social media sites for Addison University students online.

"Neither do I," Neil said, as they joined in the search, walking through dense shrubbery near the Pencock Building, where the college was located and the professor had completed her last class. "There is the possibility that she was kidnapped by someone and could still be alive."

"Yes, that's a possibility," Paula allowed. Realistically, she wasn't very enthusiastic that this was an abduction that Professor Guthrie would be able to walk away from. The more likely scenario was that she had run into harm's way from which there would be no escape for her. Still, why put the cart ahead of the horse? Stranger things had happened. Maybe, just maybe, the professor hadn't been targeted by the Campus Killer. Or even someone else.

As a runner herself, who had occasionally run off course and could have potentially gotten hurt with a stumble here or there, Paula didn't discount altogether the possibility that

Charlotte had injured herself during the run and, against the odds, been unable to call for help. Or hadn't been discovered by someone.

If that's the case, hopefully, we can find you in time, Paula told herself, as she moved alongside Neil, with Davenport, Gayle and others ahead and behind them, in what had quickly become a desperate search for the missing associate professor—with her very life possibly hanging in the balance. If she was alive at all.

As they moved along the banks of the Cedar River, Paula heard Davenport yell, with a disturbing catch to his voice, "I think we may have found her—"

Paula raced ahead with Neil, until they came upon an area with a large group of mallard ducks congregating by the river. Thick fauna lined the winding riverbank. In it, Paula spotted what was undeniably a thin and pale arm. She cringed when, upon closer inspection, it became clear that it was the arm of an adult female, who lay face down in the dirt.

"IT'S PROFESSOR GUTHRIE!" A petite female student, with a face-framing layered brunette bob and wearing pink square glasses, shrieked from outside the perimeter of the cordoned-off crime scene as the Shays County Chief Medical Examiner Eddie Saldana turned the decedent's body over.

Neil had already reached that conclusion, along with Paula, Gayle and Davenport, based on the physical description of the missing professor, along with her attire of an orange striped V-neck T-shirt, black track pants and white running sneakers. Beyond that, he could see that her blond hair was matted around a dirt-smudged face. Though there was no murder weapon or signs of trauma, with the generally good shape that the professor appeared to be in as a runner, there was little doubt in Neil's mind that she was the victim of foul play. He guessed that, based upon the initial positioning of the body, she had likely been caught from behind and forced down to the dirt before being able to adequately react.

Saldana was of the same mind and said, his brow furrowed, "The decedent appears to have been suffocated by someone pressing her face down into the soft dirt till she could breathe no more. I would estimate the time of death to be somewhere between four p.m. and six p.m. the prior day."

"So, we're looking at a homicide, to be sure?" Paula threw out, her expression exaggerated.

"That would be my preliminary conclusion,"

the chief medical examiner responded levelly, flexing the nitrile gloves he wore.

Gayle pursed her lips. "She was obviously targeted by our serial killer—"

Saldana's chin sagged. "I would assume this to be the work of the so-called Campus Killer, based on the similarities to the recent murders of Addison University female professors. But that will need further investigation from us all, I think."

"It's pretty clear to me that this is the work of our serial killer," Davenport said bluntly. "The MO is there, along with the calling card, if you will. In this case, it's the victim herself, whose death was by asphyxia, I'm sure you'll confirm, Dr. Saldana."

"Can't argue with you there, Detective," he concurred. Then, almost as an afterthought, Saldana lifted one of Charlotte Guthrie's discolored hands, studying it like an archeologist might a rare artifact. "Looks like there might be blood beneath at least two of the fingernails."

"Which likely belongs to her attacker," Neil ascertained.

"Seems a reasonable conclusion, unless proven otherwise," Saldana said, standing and removing his gloves. "We'll get her to the morgue and have the autopsy completed by ten a.m. tomorrow."

Paula angled her face and said with a sigh, "I look forward to your report, even if the results are predictable, more or less."

Davenport added humorlessly, "Hate to say it, Doc, but she's right. The autopsy reports are beginning to sound all too familiar these days—not too surprisingly."

Saldana refused to take the bait. "Let's just wait and see," he said in a toneless voice.

Neil considered the probability that the DNA would be a match for the forensic unknown profile collected from beneath the nails of Professor Odette Furillo. Which would therefore tie the two homicides to one unsub, plausibly connecting them to the other murders attributed to a single killer.

After the victim's body was removed, crime scene technicians went about their duties searching for evidence, and investigators were dispatched to interview witnesses and persons who knew Charlotte Guthrie, as well as access surveillance videos on campus that might reveal the unsub's identity or other useful information. Neil watched as Paula directed things like a maestro. He knew that she was in her element as a university detective sergeant and seemed as though her feet were planted firmly on the ground insofar as having made a solid career on the college campus.

Unlike him, who was there on a short-term contract. Would she ever be comfortable relocating to Grand Rapids—hours away—where they could be closer? Or would it be unfair to ask her to upend her life again, after having moved from Kentucky to Rendall Cove? Could they give it a go even if they were living their lives hundreds of miles apart?

Or would one or the other need to be totally unselfish in breaking from comfort level and any necessary sacrifices in the name of finding love and all the happiness that came with it?

THE CAMPUS KILLER watched gleefully as bystanders and law enforcement wandered around in seemingly a state of shock near the banks of the Cedar River, where the latest body had been found as intended. Professor Charlotte Guthrie had made it painfully easy for him to pick up her routine, play nice and then, once she let her guard down, strike with total efficiency and satisfaction.

As she staggered from the blow he'd landed to her head from behind, it didn't take much to assist her into falling flat on her face onto the dirt. He pounced upon her like a leopard and held her head down, ignoring the indecipherable sounds that somehow managed to escape her mouth. They didn't last long before there was total silence, save for the quacking mallards hanging out lazily along the river's outer banks and a flock of cedar waxwings occupying sprawling eastern red cedar trees that bordered it.

His work was done, as he'd added the good-looking associate professor to his list of killings and had once again gotten away with it. But even he didn't believe that would be a given every time. The authorities weren't that naive. Sooner or later, they might figure things out. Or maybe they never would and this might never end. Either way, he needed to hedge his bets, so he didn't wind up going down—and never getting up again.

He regarded Detectives Paula Lynley and Gayle Yamasaki. They were conversing almost conspiratorially. He could only imagine what they were talking about. Most likely him. Wouldn't they love to get their hands on him. If the detectives played their cards right, he just might give them their wish.

Only it would be on his terms. Not theirs. And with him having the advantage of being invisible in clear view, he was totally in the driver's seat and would have no problem running them down, metaphorically speaking. In reality, should this come to pass, he'd rather they met the same fate as the other victims of the Campus Killer.

Only time would tell.

He looked grim-faced while playing his part to mourn the loss of the professor as another educator fell victim to a murderer on the loose who no one could seem to lay a finger on.

AFTER WORK, Paula met up with Gayle at the Rendall Cove Gym on Newberry Drive. Paula loved going to the gym as a way to decompress and stay fit at the same time. She had a like mind in her fellow police detective and wasn't afraid to take advantage of that. They both had on their workout clothes as they moved their arms and legs on the side-by-side elliptical exercise machines.

"It's so annoying," Gayle complained, "having this jerk picking off professors like flies and right under our noses."

"I know, right?" Paula didn't disagree with her in the slightest. How could she when they were singing out of the same book of hymns. Only there was nothing lyrical about a serial killer targeting women working in higher education. Nor was there any reason to believe he planned to stop the killing any time soon. Not as long as he stayed seemingly a few steps ahead of their efforts to capture him. "The fact that the unsub appears to have no qualms about going after professors in broad daylight—on a campus filled with students coming and going—tells me that the perp is either extremely confident that he's untouchable or is overconfident and getting reckless. Which is it?"

"That's the million-dollar question," Gayle said, taking a swig from her water bottle. "I wish I had the answer, believe me. If so, maybe I could use that info to help nail him to the wall. As it is, we're still trying to play catch-up with him. We're not exactly losing the battle, but we're not winning it either. At least not soon enough to have prevented yet another poor professor from losing her life at the hands of this monster."

"That's not our fault," Paula defended their actions. "We're police detectives, not magicians or mind readers. Like you, I feel absolutely terrible at the precious loss of life here. Just as everyone working in our departments does, I'm sure. But we can only work our butts off in investigating the murders and seeing where it takes us. I'm confident this will not turn into a cold case that is never solved. We won't let that happen, right?"

"Right." Gayle grinned. "Okay, so you've convinced me to not let it become too personal.

The fact that we're both under pressure to crack the case doesn't mean it has to crack us. Not if we don't allow that to happen."

"We won't." Paula lifted her hand and they did a high five. "We're two strong women and more than capable of leading this investigation," she stressed. "I'm more determined than ever to finish what we've started, even if there are a few road bumps along the way that we just need to deal with."

"Me too." Gayle picked up the pace. "So, does that mean finishing whatever you've started with Neil Ramirez?"

Paula blushed. Was it that obvious? "Of course," she admitted freely. "Wherever things are meant to go between us, they will."

Gayle took a breath and, gazing at her, asked thoughtfully, "Does that include going down the aisle again, should it ever come to that?"

Paula laughed. "We're nowhere near that point in our relationship," she had to say. At least she didn't think so. "But, generally speaking, yes, I think I would be willing to marry again, if the right person came along."

"Maybe that right person already has," she said brashly.

Or not, Paula told herself as she grabbed her water bottle. Far be it for her to try and read Neil's mind as to how far he wanted to take things. Maybe he didn't consider marriage in the cards for him. She would just have to wait and see which way the arrow pointed as they both weighed the future.

Paula imagined the same was true for Gayle. She knew the detective had a crush on Mike Davenport. Wisely, she didn't go after the happily married man. No reason to rock the boat and risk it sinking for all parties concerned. Besides, she was sure that Gayle would have no trouble attracting someone who was single and available. As long as it wasn't Neil, whom she had already said wasn't her type, but was very much Paula's.

THAT EVENING, Neil watched through his rear-view mirror as Vinny Ortiz's Jeep Wagoneer came up behind him. The undercover agent emerged from the vehicle and headed toward Neil's Suburban. He glanced around to make sure neither had been followed—or was otherwise in danger of being exposed as they rendezvoused.

When Ortiz climbed into the passenger seat, he said with an edge to his tone of voice, "Heard that another professor has been murdered on campus."

"Yeah." Neil took a ragged breath. "Wish it weren't true. Unfortunately, the Campus Killer seems to have struck again—seemingly becoming more and more emboldened to take down his prey."

"Too bad. This dude's definitely creating a stir around town, even in the gunrunning business. Craig Eckart is still lamenting over the murder of his girlfriend, Laurelyn Wong, by this serial killer."

"Nice to know that a man who sells and distributes illegal guns and ammo that kill people would be torn up when someone he's close to becomes a victim of violence." Neil made a sardonic face. "Cry me a river."

"I get where you're coming from, trust me," Ortiz said and ran a hand through his hair. "Eckart's definitely not one of the good guys. But you and I don't have the luxury of picking and choosing between creeps."

"Very true." Neil leaned back musingly. He needed Eckart to go down as much as the serial killer unsub. With Ortiz's work, they were about to make that happen. One victory at a time. "So, where do things stand?" he asked him anxiously.

"Everything's falling into place," Ortiz responded intently. "Eckart's got his dark web operation in full gear, with a variety of guns and ammo he's ready to make available to anyone who wants them. At the same time, he's built up a stash of firearms locally that he's prepared to distribute across the country to gang members, drug traffickers and others who want to purchase guns on the black market."

"Sounds like Eckart is ripe for the taking," Neil remarked knowingly.

"Yeah. It's definitely going to blow up in his face."

"What do you need from me?" Neil fixed his eyes on the undercover agent, aware that he had the most at stake in the dangerous operation.

"You need to let all the relevant parties know that it's crunch time," Ortiz told him tensely. "I'll text you just before, so everyone's in place to do what's needed to put the gunrunner out of commission."

"I'll take care of it," Neil promised, more than ready to do his part in harnessing the combined power of the ATF, Rendall Cove PD's Firearms Investigation Unit, with assistance from the Shays County Sheriff's Department, to put an end to this major arms trafficking enterprise.

"Okay." Ortiz gave him a solid nod and exited the vehicle.

As Neil started the ignition and then drove off, he only hoped this thing went down without a hitch. Beyond that, there was still the issue of trying to help Paula and company to put a perilous serial killer behind bars before the unsub could add to the string of victims he'd left behind.

Half an hour later, Neil showed up at Paula's front door. When she opened it, he said sheepishly, "Thought you could use some company."

Her lashes fluttered interestedly. "Oh, did you?"

He grinned, raising an arm to show what he was holding. "I brought white wine."

"Hmm…" She licked her lips and took the bottle. "Come in."

The moment Neil did, her cat, Chloe, pedaled across the floor and affectionately rubbed herself on the leg of his pants. He laughed. "Looks like someone missed me."

Paula smiled nicely. "Guess you're starting to grow on her."

"Must be catching," Neil tossed back at her, feeling that she was growing on him in ways that cut deep into his heart and soul.

"Must be," she agreed without hesitation.

Chapter Twelve

On Friday morning, Paula was at her desk, going over the autopsy report on Charlotte Guthrie. As expected, the chief medical examiner determined that the associate professor of fisheries management's death was due to forceful asphyxia and ruled a homicide. Paula winced at the thought, hating the notion that doing something Charlotte obviously loved—running for fitness—should end this way.

Under other circumstances, I could have run into harm's way myself, Paula considered, while reading more of the mundane details of Eddie Saldana's official report on the decedent. The DNA removed from beneath Charlotte's fingernails was sent to the forensic lab for analysis, while the unsub remained at large.

Paula pulled up the surveillance video on her laptop of that section of campus, near the Cedar River. A male was seen running away from the area. Though the image was less than sharp, she could see that he was white, with short dark hair, tall and of average build, wearing a red jersey, blue jeans and black tennis shoes. It was enough to shake her foundation as a potential breakthrough.

Who are you? Paula asked suspiciously, believing his identification could be crucial as a viable suspect in the investigation.

She headed over to the Department of Police and Public Safety's Forensic Science Lab, where Paula met with Forensic Scientist Irene Atai, who was in her thirties and petite, with brown hair in a braided bun and sable eyes behind oval glasses.

"Hey," Irene said from her workstation. "I think I know why you're here, Detective Lynley."

Paula gave a little smile. "So, what do you have for me on the DNA removed from beneath the nails of our latest homicide victim, Charlotte Guthrie?"

"Well, when the DNA sample was compared with the forensic unknown profile analyzed from below the nails of Professor Odette Furillo, it was a match." Irene's face lit up. "The two DNA samples belong to the same unsub," she asserted.

"Meaning the professors managed to scratch a single assailant who was present at both murders," Paula uttered, having anticipated this finding.

"Exactly," Irene said succinctly. "Though the unsub was able to avoid being clawed by the other victims, this certainly links two of the murders in building your case against the Campus Killer."

"You're right, it does." Paula knew they still needed more to really put the squeeze on the culprit. A confession would be nice. But since she doubted that would come voluntarily, the next best thing was to stitch together the hard evidence to make the unsub's guilt all but certain. "Did you come up with anything from the Crime Scene Investigation Unit's work at the site of Charlotte Guthrie's murder?"

"Yes," Irene responded with a lilt to her voice. "There was a partial footprint discovered in the dirt near the body that did not match the shoes worn by Professor Guthrie. Our analysis indicated that the print came from a male tennis shoe that was likely a size eleven. It may or may not have come from the killer," she cautioned, "given that, from what I understand, it's a popular area for runners on campus."

"That's true," Paula allowed. "But where there's even a little smoke, there could be fire ready to light up." She thought about the suspect on the surveillance footage who was wearing tennis shoes. Coincidence? Or a further indication of guilt?

IN HIS OFFICE, Neil touched base by video chat with the Grand Rapids field office's resident agent in charge, Doris Frankenberg, wanting to keep her up to speed on the arms trafficking investigation. In her early forties, with blond hair and highlights worn in a shaggy lob and green eyes behind contacts, she had made no secret of her desire to be promoted to the International Affairs Division. For his part, Neil was pulling for her to succeed. Even as he was thinking more and more about his own future with the organization, and whether or not it was truly where he belonged when looking down the line. Still pained by the death of his friend, Agent Ramone Munoz, Neil was well aware of how one's entire life could change in a flash. He didn't want to shortchange himself when it came to prioritizing the things he felt were most important in life. Such as finding love with someone he could grow old and have a family of his own with.

"Busting this international arms ring wide open would be another coup for the ATF," Doris voiced with eagerness.

"Yeah, it would be great for the organization." Neil offered her a smile. "Even better would be to take the guns and ammo out of the hands of human traffickers, gang members, domestic assaulters, unstable lone shooters, etc."

"That too," she concurred. "Whenever Agent Ortiz gives the signal, we'll be ready to go in with everything we've got to take down Craig Eckart and his associates."

Neil nodded to that and talked a bit about the recent bomb threat at the university and the ongoing Campus Killer investigation.

Doris shot him a supportive look. "It's how we roll, Agent Ramirez," she said matter-of-factly. "Whatever the bad guys do, we—along with our law enforcement partners—are even better at stopping them. Even if the path can be downright bumpy at times."

"That's a good way to look at it," Neil told her, knowing that winning the war was what it was all about in the final analysis, in spite of losing a few battles along the way sometimes.

"It's the only way," she told him keenly. "Agent Munoz lost his life with that very philosophy in mind."

"I know." Neil thought about Ramone making the ultimate sacrifice, with his wife, Jillian, being left to raise his two girls alone. "I have to go," he told the resident agent in charge.

"All right." She flashed him a smile. "I'll see you soon back in the office."

"Yeah." He grinned weakly at her and ended the chat, while again contemplating his life as he looked ahead and behind at the same time. In each instance, what stood out was meeting Paula and not wanting to lose her, whichever direction he chose to take in his life.

PAULA WAS STANDING in Captain Shailene Mc-Namara's office, briefing her on the latest in the investigation, when Mike Davenport interrupted. His expression was indecipherable before he said intently, "We just received a tip that the unidentified male in the surveillance video is Connor Vanasse, an undergrad at the university. I looked him up and saw that he's twenty-two years old and a junior, majoring in biochemistry and molecular biology in the College of Natural Science."

"Does he live on campus?" Paula asked curiously.

"Actually, he's living off campus in a nearby apartment building," Davenport said. "But he should be at school right now. I have his class schedule."

Shailene leaned forward from her wooden desk, practically rising out of her high-backed leather chair. "Find him," she ordered, moving her gaze between them. "If this Connor Vanasse is our Campus Killer, we don't want him to target any more professors before we can get him off the streets."

"I couldn't agree more," Paula said, peering at Davenport. "Do we know who the caller is?"

"No, it was anonymous," he replied.

She didn't put too much stock in that at the moment, as Paula understood that people knowledgeable about persons suspected of crimes were often reluctant to identify themselves for fear of reprisal from the suspect. Not wanting to get involved officially. Or, in some instances, preferring to keep a low profile from the often intrusive media that lived for stories on real-life serial killers.

"Let's go bring Connor Vanasse in," Paula told Davenport, adding, "I'll give Gayle and the Rendall Cove PD a heads-up on the suspect as a serious person of interest in our investigation." And Paula intended to do the same in keeping Neil in the loop on what seemed to be a major breakthrough in the case.

WHEN GAYLE RECEIVED the news alert that a credible suspect named Connor Vanasse was wanted for questioning, she wasted little time in heading for the Moonclear Apartments on Drake Drive where he lived. Was this actually their killer? A student? How had he managed to stay one step ahead of them—till now?

She pulled up to the complex and drove around the parking lot, looking for the white Toyota Camry registered to Vanasse. It was nowhere in sight. As Gayle had been told that the suspect was likely on campus at this hour, she assumed he wasn't in his apartment. But she was not taking any chances that Vanasse could somehow slip through the cracks.

With Paula and Davenport searching for the suspect at the university, Gayle left her car and rendezvoused with other detectives and officers from the Rendall Cove PD. A knock and then another on Vanasse's second-floor door produced no response. There were no sounds coming from within and no reason to believe he had been tipped off that they were looking for him, as Gayle preferred the element of surprise.

She left the officers there, in case Vanasse showed up, and to secure the scene, should they need to go in with a search warrant later. In the meantime, Gayle hopped back in her vehicle and headed to Addison University, eager to be in on a takedown of the suspect who was now at the top of the list as the possible Campus Killer terrorizing professors since June.

NEIL JUST HAPPENED to be in Horton Hall for a lecture, when he was informed by Paula via text that they had identified a suspect in the serial killer investigation, a third-year student named Connor Vanasse, who was thought to be in a different class in Horton Hall presently. Having been sent a student ID photograph of the suspect—he was white and square jawed with blue eyes and black hair in an Edgar haircut—and given a general description of being around six feet, two inches in height and of medium build, Neil sprang into action. Wanting to do his part to assist in detaining the person of interest till the school authorities could bring him in, he headed straight for the second-floor classroom where a lecture on the pharmacology of drug addiction was underway.

Entering the room up front, Neil gazed at the forty or so students seated, looking for anyone who resembled Connor Vanasse. No one stood out at first glance. He caught the attention of the slender, white-haired male professor in his sixties, who stopped lecturing on a dime as Neil approached him.

"Can I help you?" the professor asked curiously.

Flashing his ATF special agent ID away from the view of students, Neil whispered, "As part of an investigation, I'm looking for Connor Vanasse. I understand that he's one of your students, taking this class—"

The professor cocked a thickish white brow. "That's correct. Only I don't believe that Mr. Vanasse is attending class today, for whatever reason. You're free to check for yourself, though," he offered.

Though he had no reason to doubt the professor, Neil knew that, as a visiting professor, he was able to establish in his smaller classes who was in attendance and who was not. Still, given the stakes, he had to be on the safe side, so he peered again into the classroom, looking more carefully at each face. Finally, convinced that the person of interest was not present, Neil said levelly to the students, "I'm looking for Connor Vanasse. Does anyone know where I can find him?"

"Yeah, I think so," said a husky male student with dark hair in a two block cut and a Balbo beard. "At least later. Connor can be found most Friday nights hanging out at the Dillingers Club on Young Street."

"Thanks." Neil made a note.

"What's he done this time?" the student asked humorously, getting a laugh from other students. "Or should I ask?"

"Probably better that you don't," Neil said expressionless, believing it was best not to tip his hand. "Just need some information from him regarding a class I'm teaching." He wasn't sure they were buying that, but hoped it was enough to keep them from giving Connor Vanasse a warning that someone was looking for him.

Neil left the classroom just as Paula was walking toward him, along with Mike Davenport. He caught up to them and said, "Hey."

"Hey." Paula met his eyes. "Is Connor Vanasse in there?"

"Afraid not," Neil replied. "But short of finding him in his next class for today, I have a lead on where we can find Vanasse tonight."

"Where's that?" Davenport asked with interest.

"According to a student, Vanasse spends his Friday nights at Dillingers, a nightclub on Young Street."

"I know the place," Davenport said. "It's known for being pretty rowdy."

"Not too surprised to hear that," Neil said, knowing that the college town had a reputation for partying, drinking and recreational marijuana usage.

Paula sighed and said, "It could also be the

location where a serial killer has chosen to hide out."

Neil nodded and responded accordingly, "If so, we'll be there to flush him out."

AT 9:00 P.M., Paula showed her badge to the burly and bald-headed man at the door to the Dillingers Club to be let through without explanation. Neil, Gayle and Davenport followed suit and all went inside. As expected on a Friday night, it was packed with students and twenty-somethings, milling about or standing in place with drinks in hand, chattering as loud music was piped through loudspeakers overhead.

"Why don't we fan out," Paula suggested to the others, knowing they were all carrying concealed weapons, with armed officers and sheriff's deputies waiting outside the club as backup. "If anyone spots Connor Vanasse, keep an eye on him and text the location."

"Will do," Gayle said tensely.

"If he's here, he might make a run for it if we're made," Davenport told them.

"We have to consider that he's armed and dangerous, assuming Vanasse is our killer," Neil pointed out.

Paula didn't discount that in the slightest and responded, "True, which is why we can't spook him. But we also can't allow him to leave this building and endanger others."

Neil met her eyes. "If it's all the same to you, I think I'll just tag along—as an added measure of precaution."

Holding his gaze, she understood that this was his way of wanting to protect her as someone he cared about beyond their jobs in law enforcement. As she felt the same way toward him, Paula nodded with approval, wanting them both to get through this in one piece. "Let's head out," she ordered and started moving through the crowd.

"Maybe we should have waited till Vanasse came out," Neil said, trailing her close enough that Paula could feel his warm breath on the back of her neck. "He'd be easier to spot."

Though he made a good argument, she countered with, "Given the situation we're facing with six victims, there's nothing easy about this. We need to catch the perp wherever he happens to be—before someone else gets hurt."

"Point taken. I'll follow your lead, Detective."

"Good." A tiny smile of satisfaction that they understood each other played on Paula's lips. As they moved about, she peered through the throng of bar goers, looking for the suspect.

She wondered if the intel on him was faulty. Perhaps Vanasse had never shown up at the club. Had yet to arrive. Or had already given them the slip. Then Paula homed in on a man who was putting the moves on an apparently interested attractive, curvaceous blonde female. "That's him," Paula told Neil as she recognized the suspect from his picture.

"Yeah, I can see that," he agreed. Neil moved alongside her. "Why don't we see if Vanasse will come in peacefully...?"

Just as she agreed, Paula got an answer from the suspect, who spotted them and intuitively saw them as cops and abruptly shoved the young blonde woman at them and took off running.

Instinctively, Paula took off after him, with Neil hot on her heels. Along the way, they had to dodge others, clueless as to what was going on, as Paula felt her heart pounding rapidly. She saw that Gayle and Davenport were now also in pursuit of the suspect.

When Vanasse appeared to be reaching for something in the pocket of his jeans, Paula was about to remove her SIG Sauer pistol from its holster, when Neil stepped in front of her and leaped onto the suspect. Both fell to the ground, with Neil on top. In the blink of an eye, he had twisted Vanasse's arms behind his back and was joined by Davenport, who handcuffed him and declared toughly, "Connor Vanasse, we're taking you in on suspicion of murder—"

Paula reminded the suspect of his rights as he was lifted to his feet and the four of them led him off as quite possibly the Campus Killer.

Chapter Thirteen

Early Saturday morning, Paula sat beside Gayle in the interrogation room at the Department of Police and Public Safety. On the opposite side of the table, Connor Vanasse was seated, with a dour expression on his face. His hair was a bit longer than on the student ID but was still in the same style. She noted a small cut on his neck and wondered if that had come from Charlotte Guthrie, before he killed her. If so, the DNA sample collected upon his arrest last night would link him to both her death and that of Odette Furillo.

Admittedly, chomping at the bit to get the suspect to confess, Paula got right to the questioning, having already made it clear that he could stop this and request legal representation at any time. "Mr. Vanasse, as was indicated, we brought you here to see what you know about a murder that occurred on the Addison University campus on Wednesday—the victim being

Associate Professor of Fisheries Management Charlotte Guthrie."

Vanasse's nostrils flared and he snorted, "I had nothing to do with what happened to that professor!"

"Is that so?" Gayle's tone was cynical. She narrowed her eyes at the suspect. "We have you on surveillance video near the scene of the crime. You care to explain that…?"

Vanasse flinched. "There's nothing to explain," he argued. "Yeah, I hung out a bit by the river like I always do. But I never saw Professor Guthrie. And I sure as hell didn't kill her."

"Why don't I believe you?" Gayle rolled her eyes. "I think you took note of her jogging pattern, and when an opportunity came, you attacked her."

"That's not true!" His voice snapped, and he gazed at Paula as if to help him out.

She wasn't inclined to do so, but did want to keep him talking. "Would you mind telling me how you got that cut on your neck?"

He shrugged. "Cut myself shaving."

"Is that so?" Her eyes narrowed with skepticism. "Does that happen often?" She thought again about the unidentified DNA found beneath the fingernails of not one, but two victims of the Campus Killer.

The suspect rubbed his nose. "Not so much," he claimed.

"What size shoe do you wear, Mr. Vanasse?" she asked politely.

"Eleven." His response was without hesitation, and he eyed her with misgiving. "Why do you need to know that?"

Paula gave him a direct gaze and answered bluntly, "A size eleven tennis shoe footprint was found near Professor Guthrie's body—" she glanced under the table at his tennis shoes "—much like the ones you're wearing."

Vanasse's expression grew ill at ease. "Hey, you can't plant this on me! I was never near her body, I swear."

Paula wasn't necessarily buying this. Far from it. "So, if you're innocent, why did you run when you saw us at the nightclub?" she challenged him.

He hesitated, running a hand nervously across his mouth and glancing from one detective to the other. Then, in a shaky voice, he said, "I panicked, okay. I've been dealing drugs on campus. Mostly prescription pills, weed and ketamine. I thought that's what this was all about and freaked."

As Paula weighed his response, Gayle dismissed it. She scowled and said to Vanasse,

"That's not very convincing, in light of the circumstances. Why don't we go over this again. Why did you run away from the crime scene, in effect, if you had nothing to hide as it related to murdering a professor…?"

Vanasse stiffened but maintained his story. "I never knew it was a crime scene. All I did was walk alongside the river, smoking a joint, and left. That's it."

Glancing at Gayle and aware that Neil and Davenport were watching this in another room on a video monitor, Paula chewed on the suspect's claims and decided to shift gears a bit. "Let's talk about Mathematics Professor Odette Furillo—"

Vanasse lowered his brows. "What about her?"

"Did you know the professor?" Paula had gone over his classes for the entire school year and gotten no indication that he had taken classes with Professor Furillo. Or, for that matter, any of the deceased professors. But this didn't mean he hadn't become fixated from afar, or had otherwise targeted them.

"Not personally," he said wryly.

"You think this is amusing?" Gayle snapped at him.

"Of course not." Vanasse wiped the grin off

his face. "No, I didn't know the professor—personally or otherwise—and I didn't kill her. If that's what you're thinking."

The thought has crossed my mind, and with good reason, Paula told herself, but said to him, "We're only here investigating a series of homicides, on and off campus, including the aforementioned professors. Getting back to Professor Furillo, do you have an alibi for the time of her death?"

Paula provided this information. The suspect was unable to account surely for his whereabouts, claiming that he had probably been on a drug high somewhere. The same pathetic story was used when asked where he was when professors Debra Newton, Harmeet Fernández, Kathy Payne and Laurelyn Wong were murdered by suffocation.

When Paula received a text message on her cell phone, she looked at it and whispered to Gayle, "We have the results of the DNA testing." As she reacted to this, Paula stood and, fixing her eyes on Vanasse, told him comically, "Don't go anywhere."

Outside the room, Paula called Irene Atai in the Forensic Science Lab for a video chat. "Hey, what did you find out?" Paula asked her attentively when she appeared on the screen.

Irene flashed her a look of excitement. "The DNA sample collected from the suspect, Connor Vanasse, was a direct match with the two DNA unknown profiles obtained from beneath the nails of professors Odette Furillo and Charlotte Guthrie."

"You're sure?" Paula asked this more out of habit than questioning the validity of the DNA testing by the forensic analyst.

"Absolutely." Irene's voice lifted an octave. "Vanasse's DNA was definitely taken off him somewhere by both decedents. He's your unsub—"

"Thanks, Irene." Paula gave her a smile. "Good work."

After ending the chat, Paula considered this for a moment, before heading back inside the interrogation room, where she conveyed the information in Gayle's ear, who said gleefully, "We needed that."

It proved to be more than enough solid evidence to make their case for the suspect being the Campus Killer. Paula cast her eyes upon him and said doggedly, "Your DNA was found below the fingernails of Charlotte Guthrie and Odette Furillo, leading me to believe that you murdered the professors."

"No way!" Vanasse yelled an expletive, then

said in fear, "I think this is where I ask for a lawyer—"

"I understand," she told him, knowing this was a wise move on his part. "You probably should lawyer up, at this point."

Upon ordering him to stand, Gayle cuffed him and said inflexibly, "Connor Vanasse, you're under arrest for the murders of Charlotte Guthrie and Odette Furillo, with other charges sure to follow."

NEIL WATCHED THE whole thing unfold in the monitoring room, along with Davenport, who remarked with confidence in his tone, "Looks like we've got him!"

"Seems that way." Neil couldn't knock the unmistakable DNA evidence that linked Vanasse to two of the serial murders. The MO of the killer and similarities of the homicides made it all but a certainty that they were perpetrated by the same person.

Connor Vanasse.

"Let's see if forensics can match the pattern from Vanasse's tennis shoe with the print found at the crime scene of Guthrie's murder," Davenport said.

"That would help," Neil admitted, in making the case for Vanasse as the Campus Killer.

"Yeah, definitely." The detective sighed. "This college town was certainly under siege as long as he remained on the loose," he uttered.

"I couldn't agree more." Having worked there these past few months, Rendall Cove had almost begun to seem like home to Neil. That was made more so by the presence of Paula in his life. The thought of ever losing that was something he suddenly found hard to even comprehend. Much less see put into practice.

When she and Gayle joined them in the hall, Neil could see the relief in Paula's face as she said with a catch to her voice, "Making an arrest in this case was imperative on so many levels."

"You're telling me," Gayle said and gave her a friendly little hug. "It was obvious that, when faced with the hard evidence of his guilt, Vanasse was completely tongue-tied."

Neil agreed somewhat, telling them, "Deny, deny, deny—or unwillingness to face up to one's own actions, even when they hardly have a leg to stand on to the contrary—is usually the case whenever a suspect is cornered like a rat and doesn't have anywhere else to turn, short of fessing up. Clearly, this was where Connor Vanasse found himself."

"Up a creek without a paddle," Davenport quipped, grinning.

Gayle laughed. "Hope the man's a good swimmer."

"Before we get too comfortable about Vanasse being put away for good," Paula stressed, "let's make sure that the Shays County prosecutor, Natalie Eleniak, plays ball in throwing the book at Vanasse."

"Give it time," Neil said prudently. "If Vanasse is the Campus Killer, he's not about to be let off the hook by the prosecutor or anyone else with a vested interest in seeing that justice is served."

"You're right." Paula showed her white teeth, which he loved seeing. "That process has only just begun, and I'll be around to see it through as long as it takes."

"Same here," Gayle pitched in. She eyed Neil curiously. "How about you, Agent Ramirez? Or will you have moved on to bigger and better things?"

He met Paula's gaze uncomfortably, knowing she was even more keen to hear his response. Though he didn't particularly like being put on the spot—with Gayle obviously knowledgeable about his romantic involvement with Paula—Neil didn't shrink away from the question. He couldn't do that. "You can be sure that whenever a verdict is reached in this case, I'll be on hand to watch the guilty party hauled off to prison." He knew that this wasn't necessarily what Paula wanted to hear but, for now, it was the most he could commit to while putting a few more important things in order in his life.

Neil sensed that Paula was all right with that for the time being.

WITH MORE THAN enough probable cause to believe that Connor Vanasse was responsible for multiple murders, a judge signed off on search warrants of the suspect's Toyota Camry and apartment—looking for any physical, forensic, demonstrative, digital and other evidence against Vanasse as it pertained to the Campus Killer investigation.

Paula and Gayle, along with other armed detectives and crime scene investigators, entered the suspect's apartment. It was only sparsely furnished and included two bedrooms and an open concept, stained brown carpeting and evidence throughout of illicit drugs and drug paraphernalia.

"A dealer and a druggie by his own admission," Gayle pointed out straightforwardly.

Paula concurred, but had to say, "That's the least of Vanasse's problems."

"True, even if they're all likely linked to one degree or another."

"Let's see if he can use the substance abuse and drug trafficking defense for murdering six professors," Paula said humorlessly. Once the all-clear signal was made, she put her gun back in its holster and continued surveying the premises.

By the time the team was through, having confiscated Vanasse's laptop, along with other potential evidence, taken photographs and headed out, Paula was satisfied that they had done their job as part of the overall investigation that figured to ultimately put Connor Vanasse away for the rest of his life.

ON SUNDAY, Paula went jogging with Neil at Rendall Creek Park. Though they spent the night together, with neither seeming to be able to get quite enough of the other, there was little talk about building bridges and crossing over them together, which she had agreed to. Instead, both settled into enjoying what they had and neither made any waves. That didn't prevent Paula from hoping there was a serious path forward that could give her the type of lasting love and committed relationship that had evaded her with Scott.

Neil, who had worked up a good sweat, broke her reverie when he said contemplatively, "I was thinking... What if Connor Vanasse didn't kill those professors?"

Paula arched a brow. "The evidence suggests otherwise."

"Evidence can sometimes be misleading. Distorted. Or even planted."

"What are you saying?" All she could think of was that he was implying that the police had set up Vanasse. Did Neil truly believe them capable of this?

"Whoa..." Neil made an expression as if reading her mind, as they continued to meander side by side through the groves of maple and eastern white pine trees. "I wasn't suggesting that the case against Vanasse was manufactured by the DPPS or PD," he made clear. "Nothing of the sort. I was only putting out there the notion that this all somehow seems just a little too cut-and-dried for me."

She narrowed her eyes at him. "We have Vanasse's DNA on two of the victims, a matching shoe print at one crime scene, security camera footage showing him fleeing the area and circumstantial evidence tying him to the murders. What more do you need, short of an outright confession?"

Neil sucked in a deep breath. "So, maybe I'm way off base here." He paused. "There's still the motive to nail down. It's just something to think about."

Seriously, Paula mused. What was there to think about? Did he know something she didn't? "If Vanasse is innocent, who do you think is the Campus Killer?"

Neil took a long moment before favoring her with a determined look and replying candidly, "I have no idea. Just call it a gut instinct by a criminal profiler."

Though she respected his expertise, Paula wondered if he was searching for something that wasn't there. Or were his instincts spot on? Was it possible that Connor Vanasse, against all odds, was being railroaded? With the guilty party still on the loose? If so, why? And by whom?

Chapter Fourteen

On Monday morning, Neil followed his instincts that told him something felt off about the case against Connor Vanasse. The last thing he wanted to do was poke holes into the investigation and presumed guilt of the suspect. Or overstep his bounds as a criminal profiler and not one of the actual investigators, such as Paula—certainly not wanting to get on her bad side—who did all the dirty work in reaching the consensus on Vanasse.

But Neil went with his gut on this one. No harm. No foul. Right? Simply having a little chat with Vanasse would in no way hinder the progress of the case, which the Shays County prosecutor had yet to sign off on. *If Vanasse, who has maintained his innocence thus far, tries to play me, it won't work*, Neil told himself, from a metal chair as he watched the serial killer suspect enter the interview room at the Rendall Cove City Jail on Flagstone Avenue.

Wearing a horizontal black-and-white-striped jumpsuit while handcuffed, Connor Vanasse peered at him curiously and barked, "Who the hell are you?"

"Special Agent Ramirez," Neil told him. "Have a seat." He proffered his long arm toward the metal chair across the square wooden table.

Vanasse did as told, while Neil asked the tough-looking, bald headed, husky guard who accompanied him into the room to leave them alone. Though seemingly reluctant to do so, the guard left.

Vanasse cocked a brow. "So, why am I here?" he asked tentatively.

"I'd like to discuss the case against you." Neil got right to the point.

The suspect stared for a long moment and shrugged. "What's there to discuss?"

"Why did you do it?" Neil asked straightforwardly, peering across the table.

"I didn't do anything!" Vanasse stuck to his story. "Like I told the other detectives, and my lawyer, I had nothing to do with those murders."

Neil snickered. "If I had a dollar for every time a suspect claimed innocence when the evidence clearly suggested otherwise, I'd be a very rich man and probably living the good life in the Caribbean or Hawaii."

"It's the truth!" Vanasse snapped. "Whether you choose to believe it or not."

Not—at least not necessarily, Neil told himself. He asked point-blank, "Mind telling me how your DNA ended up beneath the fingernails of two professors who were suffocated to death?"

"I have no idea." Vanasse pursed his lips thoughtfully. "Must have been a mistake or something."

"Highly unlikely." Neil knew that while cross contamination was always possible with people coming and going across crime scenes, any notion that the DNA was not his would not fly. "Forensic testing puts you at the crime scenes and, by extension, that makes you the prime suspect in several other homicides. Do you have any thoughts of how it might have gotten there, since you allege you weren't there?"

Vanasse's shoulders slumped. "Maybe it was planted."

"Try again." Neil dismissed this at a glance. He regarded the small cut on the suspect's neck. "You said you cut yourself shaving. Is that true? And, if so, who had access to the blood other than yourself?"

Vanasse leaned back contemplatively and, after a moment or two, responded evenly, "Someone else cut me."

"Who?"

"Just a friend who was goofing around while we were getting high. It was no big deal."

"What's the friend's name?" Neil asked.

"Desmond Isaac," Vanasse answered matter-of-factly.

Neil's eyes widened at the name of his teaching assistant. "Desmond Isaac?" He repeated this as though having misunderstood.

"Yeah," Vanasse confirmed. "We were smoking weed and whatever…and when he was playing around with a switchblade, it accidentally nicked me."

How the hell did my TA wind up in the middle of this? Neil wondered, disturbed at the thought. "Where did this take place—and when…?"

"At my apartment—the same day that Professor Guthrie was killed."

"Who cleaned up the cut?" Neil asked curiously, in wanting to give Desmond the benefit of the doubt that his role was purely innocuous.

"We both did," Vanasse claimed. Then he changed this to say, "Actually, Desmond had a handkerchief that he used to wipe away the blood, then I grabbed a paper towel to finish it up." He frowned. "Wait a sec… You're not suggesting that Desmond—a friend—would use my blood…my DNA to set me up, are you?"

"I'm not suggesting anything of the sort," Neil argued, even if the possibility suddenly was weighing heavily on his mind. "Just looking for other ways that your DNA might have been beneath the nails of two victims, if you weren't scratched by them."

"I wasn't." Vanasse hunched his shoulders. "As I said, it must have been some kind of mix-up in the lab or something."

The *something* was what intrigued Neil more. "It's not possible that this would be the case in two different homicides that occurred days apart. Let's talk about Professor Odette Furillo," he said. "Since your DNA was also found underneath her nails, did you or someone else happen to cut you that day too?" He provided the day and time of death for Vanasse to ponder, aware that he had no solid alibi for any of the Campus Killer murders.

"Truthfully, I can't remember," he claimed. "I think I may've had a nosebleed that day."

"Did your buddy Desmond Isaac happen to be around at the time?" Neil asked intently.

"Yeah, probably. We've been hanging out a lot lately—doing drugs…and just kicking back between classes." Vanasse furrowed his brow. "Me and Desmond are cool. He wouldn't betray me like that. Or, for that matter, kill professors. To believe otherwise is just plain ridiculous!"

Neil's jaw clenched. "Would it be any more ridiculous to think that your good friend Desmond could plant your DNA at crime scenes rather than be arrested and charged with multiple murders that you claim you didn't commit?"

Vanasse snorted on a breath. "No, I guess not."

Admittedly, Neil still had his own doubts about pointing the finger at his TA as the Campus Killer. But as an ATF criminal profiler and visiting professor who needed to have an open mind, even when he was looking at the presumed serial killer, Neil was not about to give Desmond Isaac a free pass as a possible killer.

"What do you have to say about the fact that your size eleven tennis shoe, including dirt on the bottom, was a match for a print left at the crime scene of Charlotte Guthrie's murder?" Neil asked pointedly, narrowing his eyes at Vanasse.

"Can't explain it," he argued, "other than to say that half the dudes I know on campus are size eleven and wear the same brand of tennis shoes. Some of them even like to hang out on the banks of the Cedar River, like me. Does that make them guilty?"

"Does that include Desmond Isaac?" Neil couldn't help but wonder, even as he pictured the TA routinely wearing black tennis shoes that could have been a size eleven.

Vanasse wrinkled his nose. "You'll have to ask him that."

"Okay." Neil sighed thoughtfully and stood. "I'll be in touch."

"Does that mean you believe me?" Vanasse made a face. "That I'm being railroaded?"

"Let's just say I'm not as convinced as some that you killed those professors," Neil told him honestly. "Of course, if the evidence continues to prove me wrong, then you'll have your day in court."

Neil called the guard to come in and left the detainee there to ponder this.

"So, you're back!" Paula smiled while sitting at her desk as she took the video call from her friend, Josie Woods, recognizing the floor-to-ceiling windows overlooking New York City in Josie's Wall Street office.

"Wish it weren't true but, unfortunately, all good things must eventually come to an end." Josie pouted. "It was fun while it lasted though."

"I'll bet." Paula still dreamed of going to Hawaii herself someday—perhaps with Neil, if things worked out between them as she hoped would be the case. "So, what's happening in the Big Apple?"

She listened for a few minutes as Josie droned on about business meetings and her millionaire boyfriend Rob's latest obsession with rare collectibles. Paula had just skimmed the surface on her latest investigation and begun to touch on her relationship with Neil, when her cell phone buzzed and she saw that he was the caller. "I need to take this," she told Josie, who smiled with understanding before they disconnected.

Paula hoped to get out to New York to visit soon as she answered the phone. "Hey, there. What's up?"

"As out there as this sounds, I think my teaching assistant Desmond Isaac may have set up Connor Vanasse to take the rap as the Campus Killer," Neil said tonelessly.

"What?" Paula's lower lip hung down as she pressed the phone to her ear with disbelief.

"I went to see Vanasse," he confessed.

"You did?"

"Yes. I wanted to clear up some things that, as a profiler, rubbed me the wrong way during his interrogation." Neil breathed into the phone.

"According to Vanasse, he and Desmond did drugs together."

Paula jutted her chin. "And that proves what?"

"Vanasse says that on the same day that Charlotte Guthrie was killed, Desmond accidentally cut Vanasse's neck with a switchblade when toying around—and used a handkerchief to wipe the blood. Desmond could have technically rubbed Vanasse's DNA beneath Guthrie's nails after he suffocated her to death," Neil argued.

"You really believe that's possible?" Paula asked doubtfully.

"It's not impossible to think that someone clever enough—a criminology student, for example, with knowledge of crime scene techniques, DNA evidence, planting evidence and such—could have found an unsuspecting scapegoat to take the fall for a string of murders and allow the true culprit to go unpunished."

"But what about the DNA found beneath Odette Furillo's nails?" Paula questioned. "Are you saying this was a setup as well?"

"Why not?" Neil answered tersely. "Vanasse claims that he can't remember for certain if he had a nosebleed or how he ended up losing blood the day Furillo was murdered. But he does think that he may have been hanging out with

Desmond at the time. This might all be nothing more than happenstance," Neil indicated, "but my instincts are telling me otherwise."

"Meaning what exactly?" she asked him keenly, knowing that reopening the investigation—and coming away with a different conclusion—would still need more than just a hunch and questionable circumstances.

"For starters, I think you need to go through the surveillance videos—before and after the murders," he told her. "Some serial killers like to come back to the scene of their crimes. If that's true here, we might expect to see Desmond lurking about here or there, knowing he wasn't on our radar. Basically, revisiting everything you have in the case against Connor Vanasse that may open up the possibility that he's not the Campus Killer. If there are no loose ends or discrepancies to that effect, then Vanasse is your killer."

And if he's not, I can't let an innocent man go down, she told herself, wanting to keep an open mind against the present trajectory of the investigation. "All right," Paula agreed. "And what will you do next to check out your TA?"

"Whatever is necessary to see if he's been playing us all and is truly a stone-cold killer," Neil said with an edge to his voice.

WHEN TEACHING ASSISTANT Rachelle Kenui walked into his office, Neil was sure she believed this was a routine visit pertaining to her duties for one of his classes. He only wished it was that simple. As was the case, this was anything but simple, if his fears about Desmond held water.

"Have a seat," Neil offered, as he leaned against a corner of his desk. Once she was on the black accent chair, he asked her knowingly, "I'm sure you heard that there has been an arrest made in the Campus Killer investigation?"

"Yes. The news spread like wildfire across campus." Rachelle pushed up her gold retro horn-rimmed glasses. "It was a real relief to know that the killer's behind bars."

Neil regarded her. "Do you know Connor Vanasse?"

"Not directly," she replied. "I've seen him around campus, but that's as far as it went."

"Do you know if Desmond knows him?"

"I couldn't say." Rachelle shrugged. "If so, he never shared it with me."

Neil paused musingly. "I need to know the nature of your relationship with Desmond. Are you two just colleagues or…?"

"We're friends," she responded quickly. "We've been spending time together lately, but it's nothing serious." She hesitated. "Why are you asking about this? Did you hear something…?"

"To be clear, what you and Desmond do outside the department is your business," Neil needed to say. "This has nothing to do with that, per se... As part of the Campus Killer Task Force, I have some concerns involving Desmond."

Rachelle's lashes fluttered. "What type of concerns?"

Gazing at her, Neil said sharply, "I have reason to believe that Desmond not only hung out with Connor Vanasse, but may have set him up for the murders..."

"Seriously?" She pushed her glasses up again. "How's that even possible?"

"You'd be surprised," he told her forthrightly. "People can be capable of almost anything, if given the right tools, cunning and motivation." Neil gazed at her. "Did Desmond ever talk to you about the Campus Killer murders or any of the professors as victims?"

Rachelle thought about it and said, "Well, yeah, he—or we—talked about the murders as they happened. I figured his interest was that of a criminology grad student, wanting to pick my brain and vice versa on the dynamics of the murders. I don't know if I can say he had a particular fixation on the Campus Killer's crimes."

"Did Desmond ever ask you to be his alibi?" Neil wondered.

"No, not that I can recall."

That doesn't mean he wouldn't have, were such an alibi needed, Neil thought. He angled his face and asked if she was with Desmond at the times the victims were believed to have been killed—giving these to her one by one. In each case, Rachelle asserted that they were not together, taking away any potential line of defense for the TA, which now had Neil believing there could be a far darker side to him than ever imagined.

"Do you really think that Desmond could be capable of such heinous actions—including pinning this on someone else?" she questioned with incredulity.

"That's what we need to find out," he replied, a catch to his tone. "Was there anything at all that stood out to you with Desmond where it concerned the Campus Killer investigation?"

She sucked in a deep breath, and her voice shook while saying, "Actually, there was one thing I found kind of weird... After we were introduced to Detective Lynley, Desmond did comment that he had the hots for her—saying that she reminded him of someone he once dated and wished he could have another shot at. I had the strange feeling that he would have welcomed the opportunity to go out with the detective, if he had the chance."

Neil cringed at the thought of someone like Desmond trying to put the moves on Paula. Had he tried to romance any of the Campus Killer victims? Was he the guilty party? Instead of the one languishing in jail?

I have a bad feeling that Desmond is guilty as hell, Neil told himself. And just might decide to go after Paula to fulfill some dark and deadly fantasies. He wasn't about to let that happen.

After Rachelle left the office, Neil called Mike Davenport and said gravely, "Hey, I need you to get me everything you have on the anonymous tip that pointed the finger at Connor Vanasse as the purported killer of Charlotte Guthrie and, by virtue, the Campus Killer."

"Uh, okay," Davenport hummed. "You wanna clue me in on what this is all about…?"

"I'd be happy to. I have strong reason to believe that one of my teaching assistants may have set up Vanasse to take the rap," Neil told him sadly. "Now I just need to prove it…"

And make sure that justice didn't take the wrong turn in bringing the hammer down on the Campus Killer.

Chapter Fifteen

Paula studied the surveillance video taken outside the Gotley Building the morning after Odette Furillo was murdered. She zoomed in on one of the bystanders. *It's him*, she told herself, recognizing the face.

Desmond Isaac.

He appeared calm and collected, while fitting in, almost unnoticeable. His gaze was constantly shifting—as though on guard, even as he presented himself as an innocent onlooker in the wake of a homicide.

Was this a serial killer returning to the scene of one of his crimes?

Paula considered that, according to Neil, this was part of the MO of some killers, who liked hiding in plain view at crime scenes as part of some vicarious thrill of pulling one over on their pursuers. *Is that the sick game you're playing here, Desmond?* she mused absorbedly.

Was Connor Vanasse the perfect mark for him to set up?

Going through more security camera footage, Paula saw in at least two other instances at or near crime scenes of other victims of the Campus Killer, Desmond Isaac's face showed up. How had they missed this? Was he merely a true crime addict?

Or a lethal killer, who got his kicks out of pushing the limits of exposure and apprehension?

As she contemplated this, Davenport came into her office, his expression unreadable. "What is it?" Paula asked perceptively.

"Looks like we have a problem…"

"Would that problem have anything to do with Desmond Isaac?"

Davenport nodded, his brow creased. "Neil phoned me an hour ago, asking for info about the anonymous call we received that identified Connor Vanasse as the unsub on video seen running from the area where Charlotte Guthrie was killed."

Paula shifted in her chair. "What did you learn?"

"Well, for starters, the caller used a burner phone," Davenport told her. "Given the obvious implications pertaining to our case against Vanasse, I obtained a search warrant to track the location of the phone. It pinged from inside the Quinten Graduate Center. According to Neil, his graduate student TA Desmond Isaac lives in this dormitory—and was believed to have been there at the time the call was placed."

Though this wasn't necessarily an indictment of guilt in being a serial killer in and of itself, Paula felt that this only added to the case that was quickly starting to build against the teaching assistant. And move away from Connor Vanasse.

"Ramirez made a compelling case for Isaac setting up his drug buddy, Vanasse, by planting his DNA to take the fall as the Campus Killer," Davenport remarked, leaning against the wall. "Seems like Rachelle Kenui, his other TA, has some interesting things to say about Isaac that lends credence to him being our killer."

"There's more," Paula told him. "Come take a look at the surveillance videos I pulled up that show Desmond lurking about at more than one of the murdered professors' crime scenes."

After digesting this, Davenport muttered strongly, "We need to bring Desmond Isaac in for questioning."

"I agree. The sooner, the better." The last thing Paula wanted was to let the latest—

and perhaps most cunning—person of interest somehow worm his way out of the weeds as a killer, without being held accountable for his crimes. If, as she was beginning to believe, Desmond Isaac proved to be the Campus Killer. Still very much at large. And perilous.

Once they took this to the captain, she didn't hesitate to come on board in the fight for justice. And against an injustice. In Paula's mind, these were one and the same. Desmond had a lot to answer for. But would he play ball? Or try to climb out of a hole that seemed to be getting deeper and deeper for the TA?

WHEN NEIL GOT the word that the anonymous tip came from the Quinten Graduate Center on campus, his focus on Desmond Isaac grew more intense. As it was, the timing of the call, using a burner phone, corresponded within minutes to a call Neil made to his TA's cell phone number. He recalled Desmond telling him that he was at the dorm when the call was made. Coincidence?

I don't think so, Neil told himself, as he left his office. Not when combined with other damning evidence against his TA.

He headed to Jamison Hall where, according to Associate Professor George Tyler, Desmond was currently in Tyler's Criminal Justice Behavior and Ethics class. Given his strong suspicions toward him, Neil found it almost laughable in a humorless way that Desmond would be enrolled in the class, contrary to his own suspected behavior as a purported serial killer.

After driving to the building, Neil went inside and, though armed, hoped Desmond would allow himself to be taken into custody peacefully. But he had to be prepared that the killer suspect could resist. And even potentially use the professor or other students as shields to hide behind.

All of that proved to be a moot point when Professor Tyler sent Neil a text, just before he entered the classroom, to report that Desmond Isaac had abruptly left the class moments earlier. After verifying this, Neil searched for his TA, believing that he must have used the back stairwell to escape. Had he been tipped off? Or had the alleged Campus Killer developed a sixth sense as part of his cold and calculating psyche, warning him of danger?

While heading back to his office, Neil notified Paula and other members of the team that Desmond had managed to evade him.

WITH NEWS THAT Desmond Isaac was still on the loose, Paula drove with Davenport to the

Quinten Graduate Center, equipped with arrest and search warrants for the individual now suspected of being a suffocation-style serial killer.

"This case keeps getting weirder and weirder," Davenport commented from behind the wheel with a frown on his face.

"I know." Paula pursed her lips. "The pieces did seem to fit where it concerned Connor Vanasse," she noted. "Which made him the perfect patsy for the criminology graduate student, Desmond Isaac."

"Yeah," the detective concurred. "Except his master plan has started to unravel."

"Which makes him all the more dangerous, with his back suddenly against the wall," Paula said thoughtfully, as they drove into the Quinten Graduate Center parking lot.

After checking the lobby and cafeteria for any signs of the suspect and finding none, they headed for his fifth-floor room in the east wing and knocked, to no avail.

Davenport sighed with annoyance. "Doesn't look like he's come back here."

"Unless he wants us to believe that's the case," Paula said suspiciously. "Why don't you stand guard here and keep an eye out for him. I'll go get someone to let us in…"

"All right."

Down at the front desk of the dorm, Paula flashed her identification at the hazel-eyed slender young female attendant, with thick hair in a platinum blonde balayage style, and told her, "I'm Detective Lynley. I have a search warrant to get inside the room of Desmond Isaac."

The young woman glanced at the search warrant and sighed with indifference. "What's he done?"

"Maybe nothing," Paula answered dispassionately, though strongly suspecting it was just the opposite.

She rolled her eyes. "Whatever," she said dryly, phoning someone from management to meet Paula at the room.

Moments later, they were inside the single occupant room and found it empty. Judging by the untidiness, it appeared as though Desmond had come and gone in a hurry. Missing was his laptop and any cell phones. Donning a pair of nitrile gloves, Paula searched the suspect's desk and chest of drawers for anything that might be visibly incriminating in the case. All she found was drug paraphernalia, a bag of marijuana and a small amount of illicit opioids.

"You may want to take a look at what's in the closet." Davenport got her attention.

When Paula walked to the closet, the sliding

door was open all the way and hanging clothes were pushed to one side. On the back wall were photographs of all the victims of the Campus Killer, printed out from a computer. It gave her a chill. "Who keeps pictures of a serial killer's victims hidden inside the closet?"

"Someone who gets his kicks out of collecting and looking at them whenever the mood suits him," Davenport answered matter-of-factly, wearing gloves. "Such as the Campus Killer."

She wrinkled her brow. "I was afraid you'd say that," she moaned.

"There's something else." His voice dipped uneasily.

Her eyes turned to his. "What…?"

"This." Davenport moved the clothes to the other side of the closet to reveal a school newspaper clipping on the wall of Paula and Gayle during the investigation. "Looks like the creep has a fascination for female detectives too…"

Paula gulped as another chill ran through her at the thought of her or Gayle being suffocated to death by Desmond. She voiced firmly what surely went without saying, "We have to find him—"

"I know." Davenport favored her with a supportive look.

A BOLO was put out for Desmond Isaac and the black Mazda CX-30 the murder suspect was believed to be driving.

GAYLE WAS IN disbelief that they apparently had the wrong person in jail in Connor Vanasse. The persuasive evidence—if you could call it that—while compelling, to say the least, had been an attempt by the real Campus Killer to point them in the wrong direction. Hard as it was to believe that Desmond Isaac had nearly pulled this off, she trusted Paula, Mike and Neil in the investigating they'd done that led them to conclude Neil's teaching assistant was actually the true culprit. He'd used his grad student studies in criminology and evidence manipulation to make Vanasse the fall guy.

Equally disturbing to Gayle, as she drove on Ellington Street at Addison University in search of the suspect's vehicle, was the thought that Isaac had evidently had her and Paula on his target list, along with the professors. Would the so-called Campus Killer have really come after them, while trying to finger Vanasse as the serial killer? Or had Isaac fully intended to kill her and Paula beforehand, but never had the right opportunity to do so?

Whatever the case, Gayle was on guard for

as long as the suspect was on the loose. She had no wish to die before her time and by his hand, any more than Paula, as both had too much to live for. In Paula's case, she needed the longevity to move things along with Neil in the proper direction. And for herself, Gayle was sure there was someone out there for her. She only needed to stay alive to find him.

Her reverie ended when she spotted the black Mazda CX-30 parked crookedly across the street, next to the Intramural Sports Building. Knowing it matched the description of the suspect's vehicle, Gayle did a U-turn and pulled her Ford Escape up behind the Mazda. It appeared to be empty. She ran the license plate and saw that the car was indeed registered to a Desmond K. Isaac.

Gayle called it in and requested backup. She got out of her car and drew her weapon, in case the suspect was hiding inside the Mazda. Approaching carefully, she determined that there was no one inside. Scanning the area, she decided that Isaac had ditched the vehicle and was on the run. But where to, as a desperate man who may be even more dangerous if he believed he had nothing to lose?

NEIL LEARNED THAT Rachelle Kenui had texted Desmond Isaac, asking that he turn himself in.

Rachelle believed she was helping facilitate a peaceful surrender of her fellow teaching assistant. For that, Neil did not fault her. Unfortunately, giving Desmond a heads-up seemed to have backfired as, by all accounts, he was making a conscious effort to avoid capture.

Of even more concern to Neil was the clear indication that Paula, along with Gayle, was in the serial killer suspect's crosshairs. When combining Rachelle's intuition about Desmond with the proof Paula and Davenport had found in Desmond's dorm room of his fixation on Paula—in spite of the attempt to lay blame for the Campus Killer murders on Connor Vanasse—Neil was even more fearful that Desmond might go after Paula.

I can't allow him to hurt her, Neil told himself, as he headed out of Horton Hall, having just received word that the suspect's vehicle had been found abandoned nearby. Paula was on her way over to his office, where Neil had hoped to strategize more with her in putting the finishing touches on this case, once and for all. With Desmond on the loose and in the area, Neil didn't want to take any chances that he might actually show up at the building, for whatever reason.

Desperate people could do desperate things,

Neil knew. Desmond Isaac certainly fit into that category. Along with being a cold and calculating serial killer, as it now appeared was all but certain.

All Neil could think of at the moment was that he loved Paula too much to let Desmond take what they could have away from them. But when Paula was not responding to calls or texts on her cell phone, Neil feared that he may already be too late to stop his soon-to-be former TA.

Chapter Sixteen

Paula wondered how Desmond Isaac had managed to slip through the cracks earlier in their investigation, as she headed over to see Neil to compare their notes and coordinate their efforts toward bringing his teaching assistant in for questioning. With the signs all pointing toward his guilt and Connor Vanasse being set up to take the fall as the Campus Killer, it was imperative that they put an end to this. Before Desmond Isaac could do more damage.

In Paula's mind, that included going after her or Gayle, as the hidden newspaper clipping inside his closet seemed to imply. The fact that Desmond had ditched his car on campus meant that he was likely on foot. Though she couldn't rule out that he had grabbed a bicycle or moped in a desperate means to evade capture. With the BOLO alert, there were few places he could hide on campus, or in Rendall

Cove, for that matter. This meant that his arrest was imminent.

But until such time, Paula knew neither she nor Gayle could or should rest easy. *I'm sure Neil feels the same way*, Paula told herself, pulling into the parking lot of Horton Hall. With the connection between Desmond as his TA and the School of Criminal Justice, Neil had added incentive to want him off the streets and the investigation into the Campus Killer finally brought to a close the correct way.

Beyond that, Paula found herself wondering where that would leave her and Neil on a personal level. She wanted so much more with and from him—the man she had fallen hopelessly in love with—and couldn't imagine their momentum hitting a brick wall once his work as a visiting professor had come to an end. But that would have to wait, with other matters more pressing at the moment.

When she emerged from her car, Paula realized that her cell phone was buzzing. She pulled it from the pocket of her high-rise flare pants and saw that it was Neil, bringing a smile to her face. *Can't wait to see you, too*, she thought.

Only before she could answer the call, Paula heard a low but steady male's voice say intently, "I wouldn't answer that if I were you, Detective Lynley."

Paula looked into the icy eyes of Desmond Isaac and then down at the Beretta 3032 Tomcat Kale Slushy pistol in his hand, pointed at her, recognizing the .32 ACP gun from a previous case she had worked on. She resisted the urge to respond to the call and tell Neil she was in danger, and instead furrowed her brow at the suspected serial killer and said sharply, "Just what do you think you're doing, Desmond?"

"I'm sure you're well aware what's going on, Detective Lynley." His brows twitched. "You and your colleagues, thanks to Prof Ramirez, are looking for me... Well, it's my lucky day— you've found me. I'll take that phone from you now."

How had he managed to remain on the loose? Paula peered at him. "You're making a big mistake, Desmond."

"You'll be making a bigger one, if you don't do as I asked!" he countered menacingly. "The phone, please..." She did as he requested, handing it over, then watched as Desmond tossed it into a clump of common witch hazel shrubs. "Now I need your gun, Detective!"

As Paula weighed whether or not she should comply, or even attempt to take out the firearm and use it in self-defense, Desmond had taken it upon himself to remove the SIG Sauer P365 semiautomatic pistol from the holster that was tucked just inside her beige one-button blazer. He placed it in the pocket of his black fleece shirt jacket and said, "Next, I need you to help me get off this campus—in your car," he snorted.

"If you want the car, take it," she spat, ready to hand him the key fob.

"I don't think so." His expression hardened. "You're driving."

Paula hesitated, knowing that getting into any car with him—even her duty vehicle—was not in her best interests. She wrinkled her nose defiantly at Desmond. "Seriously? Are you really going to add to your troubles by kidnapping a police detective?" Even in asking this, Paula knew that it was not likely going to move the needle in her favor for someone who had nothing to lose at this point of desperation. She was even more concerned about what he might have in mind for her, given what she had seen in the closet of his dormitory room.

Desmond gave a derisive chuckle. "I'm way past wondering if it's a smart move or not, don't you think? As it is, Detective Lynley, you've really left me with no other choice, given the rather precarious predicament you and the other cops hunting me have put me in." He aimed the gun at her face and said forcefully, "Let's go…"

Knowing he had her at a disadvantage, Paula

didn't make any waves just yet, if only to buy time without being shot. She began heading toward her Mustang Mach-E, hoping that someone—if not Neil—would spot Desmond as a passenger in her car and prevent them from getting too far. Short of that, she needed to be prepared to do anything necessary to come out of this alive.

Or die trying.

NEIL HAD JUST come out of the building when he spotted Paula's white Mustang leaving the parking lot, with her in it. At first glance, he found this odd. Where was she going? Why hadn't she responded to his calls or texts?

Then he saw that she wasn't alone in the car. As it turned onto Creighten Road, it became apparent to Neil that the occupant in the passenger seat was Desmond Isaac.

His heart skipping a beat, Neil knew instinctively that his former teaching assistant had taken Paula against her will. Most likely at gunpoint. Desmond was hoping to dodge the dragnet for his capture by using her as an escape mechanism.

Then what?

Neil had good reason to fear that Desmond would like to add Paula to his victim count before this was through, given his track record and knowledge that they were on to him. *Not if I have any say in it*, he told himself determinedly, as Neil raced toward his own car. He was well aware that allowing them to leave the campus would place Paula in even greater danger. The alternative of stopping this from happening at risk to her life would undoubtedly get under Desmond's skin too, should he fail. It was a chance Neil was willing to take, with stakes that couldn't be higher for the woman he loved.

Along with everything they dreamed of that was within their grasp. So long as a serial killer didn't destroy it, as he had so many other dreams.

Getting on his cell phone, Neil told Davenport, "Desmond Isaac's got Paula."

"What?"

"He abducted her in broad daylight from outside Horton Hall and forced her to drive him in her vehicle." Neil was certain. "They're headed down Creighten Road."

Davenport muttered an expletive, then said solidly, "I'll notify patrols to set up roadblocks at Grand Avenue, Rockfield Road, and Notter Street. They won't get very far."

I'll believe it when I see it, Neil thought, not taking anything for granted where it concerned the cunning killer grad student. He got into the car, started the ignition and said, "We need to bring in a SWAT team, K-9 unit—and even a hostage negotiator in case that's necessary."

"I'll get right on it," Davenport promised, seemingly masking his own concern for Paula's safety. "I'll let Gayle and the Rendall Cove PD know what's going on," he added, and Neil was certain this was for his benefit, so as to present a united front in tackling this latest turn in the investigation.

"Yeah," he told the detective simply and drove onto the street. "I'm going after them."

"You really think that's a good idea?" Davenport questioned. "If you're made by Isaac, there's no telling how he might react..."

Though this consideration was surely on his mind, Neil responded straightforwardly, "And if I do nothing and something bad happens to Paula, apart from being nabbed by a man we think has already murdered six females, I'd never be able to live with myself."

As if he understood that Neil was speaking from the heart in his words, Davenport told him, "Do what you need to." He paused. "We'll get through this."

Neil disconnected. He sure as hell was not leaving that to chance. Something told him that Paula felt exactly the same way, as he sped down the street until he caught sight of her vehicle.

PAULA SPOTTED IN the rearview mirror a car that had seemed to be moving fast, but then slowed down. As if to give them some room.

Neil.

How did he know? Did he somehow find her phone?

It meant Neil had notified others and, as such, help was on the way. But not necessarily soon enough to keep her gun-toting passenger from becoming suicidal and taking her with him.

I have to distract him, Paula thought as she glanced at Desmond. He was holding the gun on her and definitely jittery, as she rounded the traffic circle and headed onto Aspen Lane. She sucked in a deep breath and said, "So, what was this all about, Desmond? Why did you kill those professors? What did they ever do to you?"

He gave an amused chuckle, glancing out the side window and back. "What did they do to me?" he asked mockingly. "Well, other than Debra Newton—who decided I wasn't good enough for her, too young, too weird or whatever, and had to pay the ultimate price—the other professors had to die because they thought the world revolved around them. At least that was how I took it while observing them from afar. Someone needed to knock them off their pedestals. I volunteered for the job," Desmond boasted and laughed.

So full of yourself, Paula thought as she drove. "Why kill them off and on campus?" she asked curiously. "Or was this all just a big game to you, sadistic as it was?"

He jutted his chin. "Yeah, I suppose you could say it was a game of sorts," he admitted. "I definitely got my kicks out of suffocating some of them to death on campus and others elsewhere. But, truthfully, I also wanted to keep you guys off balance by mixing things up a bit. Beyond that, the laws of average told me that killing them all on campus, which was my natural inclination, was only asking for trouble, with surveillance cameras, too many people out and about, and so forth."

Paula shook her head in disgust. "Did you really think you would get away with this," she decided to challenge him, "by setting up Connor Vanasse to take the fall for what you did?"

"Uh, yeah, I thought it was a good possibility," he admitted. "I laid out my game plan to near perfection. Taking out one victim after another, using what I'd learned as an Addison U criminology graduate student and basic common sense to put this into motion." Desmond laughed with satisfaction. "It was also admittedly good research for my thesis on homicides in society and its impact on local communities." He chuckled again. "As for poor Connor, it wasn't all that difficult to take advantage of his distractions with taking and dealing drugs to collect his DNA and plant it on a couple of the victims. The nosebleed Connor had gave me the perfect excuse to relieve him of some of the blood to smear beneath the nails of Professor Odette Furillo. Later, I pretended to cut Connor accidentally and insisted upon cleaning up the blood. Unbeknownst to him, I kept enough to rub below the nails of Professor Charlotte Guthrie."

"That's sick," Paula hissed at him, trying to fathom the lengths he was willing to go to as a serial killer. "Too bad it's all fallen apart now."

Desmond sneered. "Honestly, I wondered how long it would take you and the others to figure out who was truly behind the killings—if ever. Then Prof Ramirez had to interject himself into the case, thanks to you, and used his skill set as a profiler to piece everything together."

Paula glanced at the rearview mirror and saw that Neil was still lying back, undoubtedly not wanting to rock the boat prematurely. "Don't blame him for what you did," she said snippily. "That's all on you—"

"And I own up to it." He chuckled nastily.

"At least now I do. With the cat out of the bag, I might as well enjoy the glory of being the Campus Killer—who's not quite through yet..."

He kept the gun on her, as if to prove his point. This told Paula what she already sensed. She would not come out of this alive. Not if Desmond had his way. She prayed that wouldn't be the case.

NEIL WATCHED AS Paula approached the road-block on Grand Avenue, then took a sharp turn onto Beasley Road, headed toward Rockfield Road. It too would be cut off, preventing Desmond Isaac's escape with his captive. With no-where to go, what might the suspected serial killer do next?

The thought made Neil cringe as he continued to trail them from a safe distance, though he seriously doubted that anyone with Desmond's cunning and awareness would be kept from knowing they were being followed for long. When backed into a corner, he might go on the attack at any time. With Paula being left to fend for herself.

I trust that she's capable of doing whatever it takes to survive, Neil told himself. He just wasn't nearly as certain it would be enough against the likes of a heartless serial killer, seemingly wanting to win at any and all costs.

Putting on his criminal profiler hat, Neil found himself sizing up more of the negative character traits of his ex-teaching assistant. He saw Desmond as the classic narcissist, somehow believing himself to be smarter than everyone else—and certainly more bloodthirsty in his thought patterns. From what he knew about him, as seen in a new light, Neil was sure that Desmond also suffered from borderline personality disorder and antisocial personality disorder.

It went without saying that his former TA had proven himself to be a sadist, Neil concluded. Meaning that Desmond would have no sympathy for Paula, no matter how Neil sliced it. He had to find a way to save her, as well as put a stop to Desmond's unnatural thirst for murder.

"Looks like we've got company," Desmond said with a sneer as he looked behind them. "Professor Neil Ramirez. Or should I say ATF Special Agent Ramirez? Why am I not surprised? He seems to have a real knack for continuing to stick his nose in my business."

Paula saw no reason to deny the obvious. "All of the law enforcement personnel involved in this case are on to you, Desmond," she pointed out matter-of-factly. "Why do you think the roads leading off campus are being blocked?"

Desmond grumbled as he looked ahead and saw patrol cars forming a barrier in front of Rockfield Road. He muttered an expletive, then barked defiantly, "If you want me—come and get me!"

"It's over, Desmond." Paula hoped to convince him to quit while he was ahead. And while both of them were still alive. "There's no way out of this for you. Why don't you let me pull over. Just give yourself up and no one else has to get hurt."

"By *no one*, you mean yourself?" he snickered.

She eyed him keenly. "I mean either one of us," she offered succinctly. "Killing me means killing yourself. You don't want that. Think of all you could offer from your experiences. Let's end this now!"

He cackled, the gun still firmly aimed in her direction. "I don't think so. I have a better idea. Why don't we bypass the patrol cars up there and take a little drive around the circle to the Campus Arboretum…and wait for Prof Ramirez to join us."

Paula recoiled at the thought of leading Neil into a deadly trap. But given that Desmond was unstable enough to shoot her right then and there, she didn't see where she had much choice. Other than to go along with the Campus Killer, knowing that Neil and the rest of the team were converging on them to end the threat.

One way or the other.

NEIL WAS SURPRISED to see that Paula had circumvented the roadblock by turning onto Leland Road, the last street before Rockfield Road. They were headed toward the Campus Arboretum. He notified Gayle and Davenport of this development, and the SWAT unit was already getting into place for a shot at the kidnapper and alleged serial killer.

What is Desmond up to? Neil asked himself. He had to put himself in the shoes of his former teaching assistant turned villain. All things considered, Desmond had probably come to realize that this was likely the end of the line. But it was unlikely that he intended to go down without a fight. Or at least without ending things on his own terms.

To Neil, this meant positioning himself away from easy targeting by SWAT members or other authorities. Desmond most likely wanted him as payback for ruining his best-laid plans with Connor Vanasse. And taking Paula's life too would give Desmond the ultimate satisfaction to take with him to the grave.

Neil sucked in a deep breath as he headed for

the Campus Arboretum, while hoping to avert a catastrophe that could cost him and Paula their lives.

Not to mention a future together.

PAULA PARKED IN an area that was off Mumbly Drive, the main road to the Campus Arboretum. She was quickly forced out of the car by Desmond at gunpoint and made to move through the woodlands—featuring a plethora of silver maple, black ash and beech trees, various herbaceous plants and a migrant bird sanctuary.

"This is pointless, Desmond," she protested, trying to buy more time. "Give it up. I can protect you from harm, if you hand me your gun and mine. You'll get a fair trial—"

"Yeah, right." He gave a sardonic chuckle. "There's not much defense for suffocating six pretty professors. And, very soon, you can add to that killing a visiting professor with ATF credentials. Oh, and did I forget—a good-looking campus police detective too. Thanks, but I think I'll see what awaits me on the other side after a bit of unfinished business…"

They heard the rustling of trees and crunching of dirt, causing Desmond to instinctively grab Paula from behind and place the gun to her temple. "Come out," he demanded. "Or I'll put a bullet in Detective Lynley's pretty head before you can even think about dropping me."

"All right, all right," said the deep and most familiar voice. Out of the trees came Neil, who had his Glock 47 pistol out and aimed directly at Desmond. "I'm out. You've got me, Desmond. I assume this is what you wanted...?"

"Yeah, sure." Desmond laughed. "I have to admit, Professor Ramirez, you gave me a bit of a start. Thought I had more time to work with in getting my captive here to a more secluded location, while waiting for you."

"You thought wrong." Neil's voice raised an octave. "I'm a profiler, remember? I was able to anticipate your latest moves before you could make them. Now let her go and we can settle this man to man."

Desmond growled like an animal. "You'd like that, wouldn't you?" He tightened his grip on Paula. "She stays right where she is. I suggest you drop your gun, Special Agent Ramirez. Or I'll simply blow the detective's brains out, right here and now. Then you can shoot me to death before the cavalry arrives and take all the credit for downing the Campus Killer. Your call."

It was clear to Paula that Neil had no intention of giving in to Desmond's demands, no matter how tempting, knowing full well that to do so would be signing both their death warrants. On the other hand, she could feel the tension in the killer's body, pressed up against hers. He was a powder keg that was ready to explode at any time. She couldn't let that happen. She wouldn't allow Desmond to call the shots any longer. Not when it literally meant the difference between life and death for all three of them.

For two, at least, she had a better plan of action and survival.

Paula lulled Desmond into a false sense of security by saying meekly, "You win, Desmond. I'm done with this. Go ahead and get it over with and I'll die knowing that Neil took a serial monster off the streets of Rendall Cove..."

As the Campus Killer seemed momentarily confused, using her skills in Krav Maga, Paula caught him off guard by swiftly slamming the back of her head into his face as hard as she could. At the same time that she heard his facial bones fracturing, she pushed the gun away from her head as it fired off one round up into the trees.

Desmond howled like a seriously wounded animal, and his firearm fell harmlessly onto the ground while he put both hands to his face. Whipping around, Paula was taking no chances for a quick recovery by the serial killer—using a self-defense technique to knee him hard in the groin.

While he bowled over in pain, her adrenaline rush was still high, but Paula felt herself being pushed aside. She watched as Neil took over, landing two solid blows to Desmond's head, before the kidnapper and killer fell flat on his bloodied face, knocked out cold. Neil quickly put Desmond's arms behind his back and Paula cuffed him.

"Are you all right?" Neil asked her gingerly, taking her into his protective arms.

She nodded, glancing at Desmond. "I'm a lot better than him," she answered unsympathetically.

"Did he hurt you?"

"Not really." She made a silly face. "Only the pain of knowing he'd managed to get away with it for so long."

"Well, that's over now. Thanks to you." Neil pulled back, so she could see the little grin playing on his mouth as he looked at the still unconscious serial killer. "I didn't realize you had that fighting combo in you. Wow!"

She laughed. "Guess there are still things you need to learn about me."

"I suppose. Where did that come from?"

"A very wise self-defense instructor in Krav Maga," she told him, separating from him as she went over to the fallen foe and reclaimed her SIG Sauer pistol. She put it back into its holster. "Figured the martial arts would come in handy someday. Guess today is that day."

"And very timely, if I say so myself," he said with a laugh.

Paula met his eyes. "Can't argue with you there." She paused. "Desmond fessed up about everything, including setting up Connor and hoping to get away with it."

"I expected as much." Neil gave a knowing nod. "Guess Desmond was glad, in his own way, to get this off his chest."

She tilted her face and glanced at his former TA. "That he did, though you'd know better than I would about how the psyche of a serial killer works."

Neil regarded her in earnest, and his voice cracked when he uttered, "If I had lost you—"

Paula put a finger to his lips, knowing she felt the same way about losing him. "You didn't," she told him. "And I didn't lose you either, thank goodness."

"True." He took a breath. "But with the thought of that, and before the team comes and takes over, I don't want to wait a moment longer to tell you just how much I love you, Paula."

"Then don't," she teased him.

Neil laughed. "Yeah, I love you, Detective Lynley."

"That works both ways, Agent Ramirez. Very much so." She cupped his cheeks and laid a hearty kiss on Neil's lips, so as to leave no doubt.

Paula only wished that the same could be true for where things went from here, as the criminal investigation that brought them together wound down with the capture of the real Campus Killer, at last.

Epilogue

Members of the Bureau of Alcohol, Tobacco, Firearms and Explosives, Rendall Cove Police Department's Firearms Investigation Unit and the Shays County Sheriff's Department converged on the American foursquare home on Vernon Drive. Parked in the driveway was the silver Lincoln Navigator Reserve registered to alleged gunrunner Craig Eckart, and a blue BMW 228i Gran Coupe registered to known Eckart associate Salvador Alonso, and a red Jeep Wagoneer belonging to ATF agent Vinny Ortiz. The undercover operative had just sent out a text, signaling that the time had come to break up the firearms trafficking network, once and for all. They hoped the raid would send a message that would resonate globally.

Wearing a ballistic vest and armed with his Glock 47 Gen5 MOS 9x19mm pistol, Neil joined his heavily armed law enforcement partners, equipped with arrest and search warrants for the takedown. That included bringing in an officer from Animal Control to handle the potentially aggressive Staffordshire bull terrier that Eckart was known to own. Waiting in the backdrop were crime scene investigators and an ambulance, if needed.

Using fierce determination, overwhelming power and a battering ram, the front door was forced open and the house inundated with the team, able and ready to handle any resistance. The dog was quickly subdued and removed from the premises. Fanning out to each and every room, arrests were made of three men and two women. The former included Craig Eckart and J. H. Santoro—Ortiz's alias. Ortiz, who put up a good act of appropriate belligerence and outrage over the arrest, was handcuffed along with the other suspects.

"Tell it to the judge," Neil snapped at him believably, while handing him over to an FIU detective.

"I will," Ortiz muttered convincingly, as he was led away without further incident.

Neil watched as Craig Eckart looked shell-shocked at the prospect of his gunrunning business going up in smoke, while facing potentially decades behind bars for his trouble.

When the dust finally settled, along with a

treasure trove of detailed information on contraband firearms and ammunition seized with five cell phones and three laptops, the raid uncovered a cache of unlicensed firearms and rounds of ammunition, huge quantities of fentanyl and quantities of methamphetamine and further evidence of criminal activity that Eckhart and his colleagues were engaged in.

FRESH OFF THE successful raid of Craig Eckart's illegal weapons enterprise, Neil was back at Horton Hall, having already mapped out his future where it concerned Paula and a life together, when he was summoned to the office of School of Criminal Justice Director Stafford Geeson.

He walked in to find Geeson standing by a picture window, seemingly deep in thought. Neil imagined that he was wondering how he could have missed the signs of the evil that lurked within his teaching assistant, Desmond Isaac. *Believe me, I'm asking myself the same thing,* Neil thought, but he took solace in knowing that he had figured out Desmond's true character before he was able to successfully pin the murder rap on Connor Vanasse. Not to mention add Paula as another notch on his belt of victims.

"Stafford—" Neil got his attention.

Geeson faced him and forced a grin. "Neil—thanks for coming."

"No problem." He met the director's eyes curiously. "Everything okay?"

"Yeah, I'm fine. The School of Criminal Justice will continue to do its thing in educating and preparing the next generation of people in law enforcement to fight the good fight, in spite of our one giant setback and disappointment in Desmond Isaac."

Neil frowned. "We're all disappointed in him and the horrible choices he made."

"He'll have a lot of time to digest it behind bars," Geeson pointed out with satisfaction in his voice. "Anyway, I didn't ask you to drop by to talk about him." He paused. "Have a seat."

"All right." Neil sat on a blue task chair by the window and watched as Geeson sat nearby. *So, is this where he cans me with my contract nearing an end?* Neil mused. Or the opposite?

After a moment or two, Geeson eyed him squarely and said, "I'm not sure what your plans are, insofar as returning to full-time work as an ATF special agent or another avenue, but during your short tenure here at Addison University, you've become one of the most liked and respected professors in the School of Criminal Justice. Using your expertise to help flush out the Campus Killer—especially when it was one of our own—only enhanced your stature around here." He paused. "What I'm trying to say is that I'd like to offer you a full-time position as an associate professor of criminology—if you're interested…?"

"I'm definitely interested." Neil didn't have to think very long about the offer. Particularly since it was an avenue he would have pursued, had the director not beaten him to it.

"I'm happy to hear that." Geeson's face lit up. "So, are you in…?"

"Yeah." Neil grinned. "I'm in."

"Welcome aboard for the long term, Professor Ramirez." They stood up and shook hands firmly.

Back in his own office, Neil rang his boss at the Grand Rapids ATF field office, Doris Frankenberg, and said in earnest, "We need to talk."

A few minutes later, he was in his car, where Neil got Paula on speakerphone and asked coolly, "Where are you?"

"On my way home," she told him, and he could hear some background noise. "Where are you?"

"Headed to your house," he responded simply. "See you shortly."

"I'll be waiting..."

After disconnecting, Neil couldn't wait to be face-to-face with her. But first, he had a stop to make.

PAULA WAS HAPPY to chill at home, following a workday that included clearing up a few loose ends in the Campus Killer case. There would still be more to come, even with Desmond Isaac's capture and confession. Such as piecing together how he had been able to succeed in his depravity for as long as he had and what could be learned from this for future serial killer investigations by the Department of Police and Public Safety.

But at the moment, Paula admitted that she had butterflies in her stomach knowing Neil was on his way over. She suspected he wanted to talk about their future. Or perhaps his waning time as a visiting professor. For her part, she had decided that as much as she loved her job, it paled in comparison to the love she felt for Neil. She would gladly relocate to his work place if that was what it took for them to be together.

When he knocked on the door, Chloe meowed, as if she'd been anticipating his arrival and welcomed his presence as much as Paula. The cat ran to the door, and Paula followed the

Devon rex in her bare feet and opened it, only to see a grinning Neil standing there, holding a dozen long-stemmed red roses.

"What's this?" She batted her eyes demurely.

"For you," he said with a lilt in his voice. "Just a little something I picked up along the way."

Neil handed them to her, and Paula put the roses up to her nose and took in the delightful floral scent. She flashed her teeth at him. "They're lovely," she gushed as they made their way into the great room.

"Not half as lovely as you," he asserted while allowing Chloe to rub against one of his brown Chelsea boots.

"Thank you." She blushed and went into the kitchen to put the roses in water.

When Paula returned to the great room, she could tell that something was on Neil's mind. *Me, I hope*, she told herself, but asked evenly, "So, what's up?" She'd heard that the ATF-led operation against suspected arms trafficker Craig Eckart had been successful. It was a big win for the task force and city of Rendall Cove in curbing the proliferation of illegal weapons across the globe.

After he commented keenly on this, Neil took her hands and looked Paula directly in the eyes and asked casually, "Feel like getting married again?"

Her eyes ballooned at his face. "Is that a proposal?"

"Yeah, it is," he made clear. "I'm in love with you, Paula. You already know how I feel. I think the same is true from your end. So, why not make it official? Be my wife and we can have a great marriage and all that comes with it."

Paula felt the beat of her heart, erratic as it was. This was something she had dreamed of—a second opportunity to find true love. Neil checked every box in that department and then some. There was one other thing to address though, even if it had no bearing on her decision, per se, but was important nevertheless.

"What did you have in mind for us once your visiting professorship stint ends?" She angled her eyes at his curiously. "To be sure, I'm more than ready and willing to relocate to Grand Rapids—or elsewhere, if necessary, to be with you…"

A smile played on Neil's lips as he said nonchalantly, "Actually, about that… I was just offered a full-time position by the director of the SCJ, which I happily accepted. So, I'm not going anywhere. Not unless you want to leave Rendall Cove. If that's the case, count me in on wherever you want to set up shop. It doesn't matter, as long as we're together."

Paula beamed. "Congrats on the wonderful news in becoming a faculty member and no longer just a visiting professor. I'd love to stay put in this college town in my current position with the Investigative Division of the DPPS—and build a family with you, Neil."

"Are you saying what I think you're saying?" His voice cracked.

Her teeth shone. "Yes, I'm madly in love with you, Professor Neil Ramirez, and would be delighted to become your bride and mother to any children you'd like to have."

"As many kids as we're comfortable with, while being able to balance that with our work lives and quality time as a couple," he told her, his tone genuine.

"Well, all right, then." She chuckled, excited at what was to come for them. "It looks like we're now engaged to be married." Paula knew the engagement ring would come soon enough. Right now, she was more than content simply to have his heart.

"I couldn't be happier," Neil promised, wrapping his arms around her protectively. "But I think it's imperative that we seal the deal with a…"

He pulled them apart just enough for Neil

to give her a hearty kiss that left Paula light on her feet and feeling that, in this instance, a single action truly did speak louder than hearing the word.

EIGHT MONTHS LATER on their honeymoon, Neil and Paula Ramirez lounged on beach chairs at the Ka'anapali Beach Resort on the island of Maui, Hawaii. Wearing sunglasses and floral-print swim trunks while sipping on a lava flow, Neil checked out his wife as she talked on her cell phone with her friend, Josie, the two comparing notes on their Hawaiian experiences.

Paula had on a hot red halter bikini top and matching bottoms, showing off her shapely legs. *She's so hot*, Neil told himself admiringly, as Paula took a sip of her blue curaçao before resuming the conversation. She was even more beautiful as the blushing bride when they tied the knot a month ago, showing off her princess-cut diamond wedding band to everyone she saw. Attendees included Paula's mother, Francine, and Neil's sister, Yancy, along with Gayle Yamasaki, Mike Davenport and Vinny Ortiz, among others.

Neil shifted his gaze to the seemingly endless Pacific Ocean. There were a few gentle waves brushing against the shore and a couple of boats out for some leisure time. Neil thought about the happenings since he and Paula took Desmond Isaac out of commission. They had located Desmond's laptop and cell phone, each of which contained important evidence attesting to his guilt as the Campus Killer.

His full, official confession to six murders, one attempted murder and kidnapping and a few other charges thrown in for good measure landed Desmond Isaac in the Ionia Correctional Facility, or I-Max, in Ionia County, Michigan. There, the maximum-security state prisoner would spend the rest of his life. Thanks in part to Connor Vanasse, whose cooperation in the case against Desmond allowed Vanasse to cop a plea for drug-related offenses, rather than multiple murders, resulting in a few years behind bars.

With Desmond's reign of terror at Addison University over, the campus had returned to being a great place to study. Not to mention a perfect setting for Neil to teach criminology full-time as an associate professor. He had been retained by the Bureau of Alcohol, Tobacco, Firearms and Explosives as a consultant on high-profile cases. Such as the one that brought down arms trafficker Craig Eckart, who, it turned out in an ironic twist, had sold

Desmond the Beretta 3032 Tomcat Kale Slushy pistol he used to abduct and try to kill Paula.

Eckart had been convicted on a slew of federal charges and would be spending decades rotting away in the Federal Correctional Institution, Milan, in York Township in Washtenaw County, Michigan. Joining him in FCI Milan was pipe bomber Harold Fujisawa, who would also be incarcerated for a very long time as a convicted domestic terrorist.

But, most of all, Neil was delighted to be a husband to Paula, the gorgeous detective sergeant who continued to make her mark in the school's Investigative Division, in helping to keep it a safe environment for professors and students alike. He was just about to have another sip of his cocktail, when instead Neil felt the softness of Paula's lips on his.

"Just wanted to make sure you were awake," she teased him after the long kiss had ended.

"I am now," he joked, tasting her blue curaçao on his lips.

She laughed. "What do you say we jump into the water for a swim?"

Tempting as that sounded, Neil responded desirously, "I have a much better idea. How about we head back to our room and flex our limbs in a different way?"

"Hmm…" Paula pretended to think about it while flashing her teeth. "Why, that sounds like a fabulous idea, Mr. Ramirez. Works for me."

"I was hoping you'd say that, Mrs. Ramirez." His eyes lit up lovingly as Neil got to his feet, bringing Paula up with him. He kissed her again, allowing it to linger a bit, enjoying this. Then a bit more and a little more after that, before he stopped for now and said definitively, "Let's go."

* * * * *

Don't miss the stories in this mini series!

THE LYNLEYS OF LAW ENFORCEMENT

MILLS & BOON

INTRIGUE

Seek thrills. Solve crimes. Justice served.

Available Next Month

Renegade Wife B.J. Daniels
Mile High Mystery Cindi Myers

....

Bounty Hunted Barb Han
Captured At The Cove Carol Ericson

....

Wyoming Ranch Justice Juno Rushdan
Mississippi Manhunt R. Barri Flowers

Larger Print